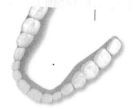

"AIN'T DEAD YET"

"THE GEEZERS HAVE GONE ROGUE."

ADVENTURES OF THE OLD BLUES

SENILE SQUAD

CHRIS LEGROW

Omaha, Nebraska

SENILE SQUAD: ADVENTURES OF THE OLD BLUES

CL1557 Publishing, LLC books may be ordered
from your favorite bookseller.

www.SenileSquad.com

CL1557 Publishing, LLC
13518 L. Street
Omaha, NE 68137

ISBN: 978-0-9977036-1-0
ISBN: 978-0-9977036-2-7 (Mobi)
ISBN: 978-0-9977036-3-4 (EPUB)

Library of Congress Cataloging Number: 2016944368
Library of Congress Cataloging-in-Publication data on file with the publisher.

PRODUCTION, DISTRIBUTION AND MARKETING:
Concierge Marketing Inc. www.ConciergeMarketing.com

Printed in the USA

10 9 8 7 6 5 4 3 2

To my friend Pam, who upon hearing my idea about this novel looked at me and simply said, "Start writing."

Of course, to my wife Kara, my family, and my friends, who read and helped so much with the early drafts.

My sincere apologies to all my childhood English teachers who, out of disbelief, are now striking their heads in their caskets.

THE STREET

"I HEAR YOU LIKE TO TALK ABOUT ME." A TOWERING Sudanese man holding a wooden bat in his hands spoke loudly, as he paced back and forth in front of the kneeling, terrified woman. Her mouth had been gagged and her hands bound behind her back with silver duct tape. To the people of Omaha, she was another nameless Sudanese immigrant, who never seemed to walk far from the public housing she had been given as a residence.

Even now, at the time of her impending death, she was on display in the small field across from that same depleted public housing building. The apartments were filled to capacity with Sudanese immigrants. Each apartment had windows facing that small field, ideal for this "education" to be visible to the other residents. There, she knelt in front of four Sudanese "soldiers," each anxiously waiting for an order given by the tall, pacing man. The residents could all be seen staring out of those windows, viewing the scene in horror. Not one of them spoke English, but all of them clearly understood the warning that they were being given. Don't talk about the man with the bat—the mistake this young, nameless woman had made, being overheard while talking to other immigrants.

The man with the bat looked to the east, "Good," he said to himself. The sun was just starting to rise, and everyone peering from behind the curtains would get a good view of the message to be delivered. The woman's eyes were wide and pleading, silently begging for mercy, just as he liked it. The bat was resting on his right shoulder, his back to the people watching. He slowly glanced to the building, noticing the horrified people stepping away from the windows, hiding like cowards in the shadows. The man slowly turned back to the helpless woman and gave her a satisfied grin. The setting was just as he had planned.

"Since you talk too much, that is where I'll start." He spoke, in Sudanese, loud enough for the immigrants to hear. Then he reached up with his left hand and, holding the bat like a baseball player swinging at a pitch, smashed the woman's mouth. There was a short, muffled cry of pain, and blood splattered onto the extra-long white T-shirts always worn by his soldiers. The woman's head snapped back and her body dropped to the ground.

The executioner smiled as he slowly circled the convulsing body until he stopped by the woman's head. The sound of the wooden bat striking a human skull echoed into every immigrant's ear. His soldiers all stepped back. Three deadly blows completed the task, and he knew the warning was complete.

The man and his blood-splattered soldiers looked up to the building. "You talk, you die!" was chanted in Sudanese, as they slowly left the bloodied warning alone in the field.

∽

Officer Bill Taylor finally finished his field training. At the Police Acadamy Taylor had finished near the top of his class, and he felt ready for whatever the streets would dish out. He could not have been more wrong. The gangbangers in his patrol district knew more about the law than he did. They even knew the names of the other officers, the days and times they worked this precinct. Taylor was no exception. That is why someone chose to commit a murder when the new cop was on patrol.

Officer Taylor took his usual route by some public housing on Fourth Street. Taylor looked at the Sudanese who were standing on the sidewalk and said to himself, "They always seem afraid of me, just look away when I wave to them." It didn't take Officer Taylor long to notice that this time was undoubtedly different. As he drove by, he noticed that many of the immigrants just stared wide-eyed at him, then looked across the street to a small, litter-filled field. Taylor unintentionally followed their gaze and immediately spotted what they were staring at. On the ground was a contorted woman's body covered in blood.

Taylor ran to the body and upon seeing the demolished remains of the woman's head, he vomited. He felt dizzy and dropped to one knee, giving himself a few minutes before calling in the Homicide Unit.

The radio buzz for the Homicide Unit in an area of town known for gang activity caught the attention of officers in the gang unit. Gang Detectives Zach Reeves and Steve Turley showed up at the scene and immediately overheard the homicide detectives speaking to a rookie cop named Taylor.

"You puked next to the body!" The homicide investigator grilled Officer Taylor. "That could have ruined evidence. I know it was your first homicide, but next time puke somewhere you won't mess up the scene. Did anything else happen that may have screwed up my scene?"

Taylor knew not to lie, but was hesitant to say what else had happened. Sensing the new officer's reluctance to talk, the detective put his hand on Taylor's shoulder to assure him. "Officer Taylor, I need to know what else happened here."

Taylor stuttered, "Well, when I was trying to secure the scene, there was this old guy in the crowd. I didn't pay much attention to him, until I looked over and he was next to the body, looking at and around her. Like he was looking for evidence. I yelled at him to get away from the scene, and, umm—"

Taylor struggled to continue, which earned him another stern look from the detective who said, "And what?"

"He told me to tape off a bigger perimeter. Then he said to canvass the area before the hoods arrive and dummy up the witnesses. I didn't know what he meant by hoods, but I did realize I needed to expand the perimeter. I finished taping off the scene and tried to find him to ask what he had seen, but he was gone."

The detective looked up and said, "Yes, you did need a big area sectioned off to protect the scene from getting contaminated by onlookers. I'd like to know what that guy was doing though."

Gang Detective Turley told Reeves, "Hoods," he scratched his chin, "that's what they used to call gang members in the old days, and dummy up, that means to silence people." Both Turley and Reeves looked at each other and, as if on cue, scanned the crowd, and sure enough, they recognized gangbangers from two different gangs standing conspicuously around the rapidly growing crowd.

"Those are 3rd Street," Turley said, as he recognized about five young black male gangbangers standing about fifteen yards just east of the crowd of onlookers.

Reeves pointed at another group of six white guys and said, "Hatfields, over there, those are Hatfields. Those two gangs are beefin' right now." Both Reeves and Turley were ready to respond to an immediate outbreak of violence, but instead, and to their shock, members of both gangs started yelling, "Snitches get stitches! Snitches get stitches!"

Turley said, "Look, they seem to be working together to protect the guy that did this. I've never seen this before, and it doesn't make sense. These guys hate each other. We've got to make sure gang intel knows about this."

❦

Ben Mitchell, CEO and COO of Mitel Communications, sat in a wooden chair in the community room of Everville, a retirement home. The awful smell of mothballs filled the air. To his right, at the opposite side of the room were two women who apparently had difficulty hearing, shouting a pointless conversation about flowers. He found himself uncomfortable with the more elderly senior citizens just sitting in wheelchairs staring past him.

"They're just waiting to die," Ben said to himself.

Ben sat awkwardly at a small, round card table and looked about the multipurpose room. Straightening his tie, he reflected how he didn't ever like waiting, but this place seemed torturous. Ben eventually became aware of a man standing in a doorway, observing him as if sizing him up. Once identified, the imposing silver-haired, retired police officer entered the room and gave a questioning look at Ben.

After a brief introduction, Ben motioned at the chair across from him for the old cop to sit down. "I have a proposition."

Suspecting something more private than a chat about the weather, the old man said, "Then let's go to my apartment."

Ben explained the purpose of his visit and how he had selected this particular retired cop because of his reputation during his years of service for getting the tough jobs done.

The old cop listened to the proposition, sat back in his chair with eyes wide and not believing what he just heard. "You," George Martinez, the cop, said around a well-chewed, unlit cigar, "are out of your freaking mind!"

He stared at Ben Mitchell, the leader of a very low-key group of extremely successful entrepreneurs. Ben bit the inside of his cheek in an effort not to smile at the reaction. The concept he'd proposed was huge in scope and innovative in police work—maybe even ingenious. Never one to take no for a first—or tenth—answer, Ben tried again. At forty-seven, *Time* magazine had declared him the youngest multibillionaire in the United States, and he hadn't built his business by pussyfooting around or listening to naysayers. "No, sir. I'm not."

"Where—how?" the older man sputtered, his bushy salt-and-pepper eyebrows furrowing together. He lifted a weary gaze to meet Ben's. "Why?"

Ben folded his hands on the small table in the older man's postage-stamp–sized apartment. "Well, Mr.—"

"Sarge. Just call me Sarge. That's what I was for so long even my family calls me that—the Sarge."

"Okay…Sarge, let me explain. I have friends in the Omaha Police Department—in command."

The Sarge's eyebrows inched higher. "Well, la-ti-freak'en-da."

Unable to help himself, Ben chuckled at the gruff veteran of thirty years in law enforcement. "I only tell you that to explain my connection with police work. I'm concerned about the growing street crime in the city—"

"Aren't we all?" the Sarge growled.

"I overheard a conversation a couple years ago that showed me how much your experience and years on the job could help the current situation. I've never been able to shake that memory," Ben told the Sarge. "Now I'm in a place where I can do something about it."

"How?" The Sarge's voice almost cracked.

"I represent a group with more than sufficient means to finance this entire operation."

The Sarge grabbed the stogy between his middle finger and thumb, pointing it at Ben. "I know who you are, Mitchell. Billionaire only begins to describe you. And you're telling me that there's a bunch more just like you who want to finance this craziness?"

Ben gave the older man his most confident smile; he knew victory when he heard it. Ben folded his hands on the shiny laminate surface in front of him and leaned forward to make sure the Sarge heard every word. "That and more! But I need a linchpin to make both operations run smoothly and silently."

"Both?"

"Overt and covert," Ben said. "You pick the men you want for each."

The Sarge immediately said, "Tiny Thomas, one of the best cops I ever knew."

Ben held up his hands, "You know the guys for this job, not me. I'll leave all the recruiting to you." Ben settled back in the hard-backed chair and outstretched his arms. "Or you can stay here and do whatever it is you do all day. Choice is yours. But I need an answer."

The Sarge stuck the cigar back in his mouth and thought a moment. He slapped his beefy hand on the table. "When do we start?"

$\sim$

William "Tiny" Thomas resided in a studio apartment, one of many nondescript dwellings in downtown Omaha. No spectacular views of the skyline for him though. Retirement wasn't all it was cracked up to be. The meager pension he lived on didn't go as far as he'd thought. College tuition for kids, alimony to ex-wives and his own medical expenses ate every bit the state didn't take for taxes. Tiny shined a flashlight on the back of his television. "Now where does this dang coaxial thing go?" He twisted it repeatedly only to have it fall out yet again. "Ah nuts." He'd probably have to Google the instructions, and he wasn't up to another hassle at the moment.

He turned the TV off and gazed out his small living room window overlooking Heartland of America Park. He gazed through the floor fan he'd placed in the window that leaned against the screen. It wasn't much, but it kept fresh air circulating in the place. It also provided a more important tactical role. When the fan was on, he could observe the activities across the street through the rotating blades. Those in the park didn't know he was monitoring them.

With over thirty-five years on Omaha streets as a uniformed cop and as a plainclothes detective, old habits were hard to kick. In Tiny's mind, he wasn't simply watching folks in the park, he conducted surveillance.

"There you are again," Tiny mumbled to himself. A tall, dark Sudanese man stood in the middle of the park. He'd caught Tiny's attention weeks earlier. He didn't walk around and talk to people; they approached him. He'd listen and say a few words as though giving instructions. There was something suspicious about those he spoke with. They left in a way that told Tiny they were intent on carrying out information given. The area around the park housed many Sudanese refugees and immigrants. Not a problem in and of itself in Tiny's book, but this guy was special. There was definitely more to him than met the eye. Tiny watched another interaction.

"You're definitely the man in charge," Tiny said aloud.

The drama across the street was about all that brought Tiny out of bed in the mornings. All those years as a cop gave him a constant sense of curiosity that never went away. Anytime he found something suspicious, he had to check it out. He hated that in the blink of an eye, he'd gotten old. His body betrayed him at every turn especially recently. There was, however, one advantage that came with advancing age. It gave him an edge he had never possessed before.

Tiny turned away from the window and grabbed his gray sweater. Stuffing one arm and then another into the sleeves, he straightened the front and checked his reflection in the mirror. "Nobody ever sees a little old man."

Tiny locked his front door and set off across the street to check things out. He strolled leisurely around the young man and his companions. Sitting on a bench a few feet away, he stared at the pigeons waddling at his feet and tossed them breadcrumbs he kept in his pockets. He learned loads by simply being an old man in the park. "This tall Sudanese man is definitely the leader," Tiny said to himself as he worked his way back to his apartment.

Tiny returned home and hung up his cardigan. Catching a glimpse of his mirrored image, he shook his head. "If I was back on the street, I'd ride that guy's butt straight out of town."

Tiny knew trouble when he saw it. This guy had it written all over him. Every time he tried to express his concerns to a police officer, the officer listened politely for a few minutes then found an excuse to leave.

Helplessness overwhelmed him. He despised the sensation of worthlessness that weighed on his shoulders daily. Old, tired, and sick, there wasn't much use for him anymore. Tiny turned to the doppelganger in the mirror. "Why bother?"

Pulling open the dresser drawer, he stared at his .38-caliber revolver. He could end it right now. He doubted anyone would even notice his absence. "Maybe I should…"

A knock drew his attention. With a long look at his weapon, Tiny closed the drawer and strode to the door. He expected some neighborhood kid selling cupcakes for his school band, but when he opened the door, he froze. For the first time in many years, he was genuinely surprised. "Sarge?" Tiny said to the man he'd known when he was a cop and his life had meaning. The Sarge smiled, took his chewed cigar out of his mouth and said, "How'd you like a job?"

The Sarge explained what was going to be a special retirement home for old police officers, and when he told Tiny that the officers were actually going to be fighting crime without anyone knowing about it, Tiny grinned, stood up and walked to the window of his apartment.

Tiny pointed to a Sudanese man in the park that he had determined was some sort of kingpin and said, "I want to start with him."

CHAPTER 1

TO PEOPLE ON ALL COASTS OF THE UNITED STATES, THE quiet city of Omaha, Nebraska, nestled up against the mighty Missouri River, is out in the middle of nowhere. But looks can be deceiving. The city popped up repeatedly in newspaper and television articles because it consistently ranked eighth among the fifty largest cities in the country for per-capita billionaires and *Fortune* 500 companies. San Francisco might be the leader in billionaires per million people and Atlanta led the way in *Fortune* 500 companies, but no city—including the major coastal giants—could claim a ranking as high as Omaha on both lists.

In a specially remodeled top floor, downtown apartment at Eleventh and Douglas, Ben Mitchell tapped a spoon against his water glass. Ten of Omaha's wealthiest business owners, CFOs, CEOs, and COOs turned to him.

"Welcome everyone," he said. "I'd like to veer a little off our usual course of business," he said referring to their periodic meetings to discuss world conditions and political happenings.

Though varied in ages, they remained friends outside the group sharing similar core values: none of them liked attention, media or otherwise, and they knew how to get things done. They all respected integrity and dedication, and each cherished a solid work ethic. No dot-com Silicon Valley types here, no East or West Coast big money types. They were strictly Midwestern, proud of the "fly-over" designation derogatorily attached to their state on more than one occasion. They all loved the term *The Heartland*. The words encapsulated everything about the area they held dear. They'd built their empires on the principles embodied in the indomitable history of the plains and respected others who did the same. They called themselves The Bureau.

"What's up?" Steve DeGoff, president and CEO of two multibillion-dollar military defense corporations, reached for the packet Ben handed him. "This is quite the place," Steve said with an admiring glance around the room. "You acquire a new company?"

Ben glanced at the modern art decorating the walls that wasn't quite his taste. "Nah. I had the place soundproofed, which meant a new paint job. It's called surf and sand."

"Surf and sand?" Steve asked. "Beige is beige. I don't know where they come up with that stuff."

Ben laughed and finished handing out his proposal. "You sound like you're seventy—not fifty-one."

"Sounds like somebody else I know," Frieda Williams said and shot her husband, Bud, a knowing glance.

"What?" Bud asked. "I haven't done anything yet." The Williamses were pioneers of the insurance industry in Omaha. From their home city, they'd branched out not only nationally but internationally. Bud took early—very early—retirement at age fifty, and although they'd turned the day-to-day operations over to their children, they still kept their fingers in the pie and wielded considerable influence in the community and state politics.

Ben handed a spiral-bound report to Dan Roberts seated on his right. "I'm going to need your support every step of the way," Ben whispered.

Dan, who started from a home office and built the largest architectural firm west of the Missouri River, nodded. "Let me know what you need."

"What about the Platts?" Frieda asked. "Aren't they coming today?"

The door opened and two women entered. Ben handed each the same portfolio he'd prepared. The two younger women hurried to take a seat. "Sorry we're late," Pamela Platt said.

"You know how parking is around here." Bonnie Platt rolled her eyes. "There's never enough."

"Oh, please," Pamela said. "She's a lot like Dad—refuses to plug the meter and ends up driving around waiting for a free spot to open up."

Bonnie stuck her tongue out at her sister who shook her head and laughed.

"You two certainly liven the place up," Al Long said. "Tyler and I balance you out, I think." He nodded at his brother, Tyler. Al and Tyler owned and operated the largest heavy machinery construction company in the region.

Tyler shrugged and gave a small smile.

"You always monopolize the conversation?" Pamela asked the quiet brother, earning her a bit wider smile.

"Ladies, shall we begin?" Ben asked.

"Sorry," Bonnie said.

"If you'll direct your attention to the most current homicide report I handed out," Ben said, trying to maintain some semblance of control.

"Omaha made the list." DeGoff tossed his copy of the Violence Policy Center's article in front of him.

"Yes, it did unfortunately." Ben nodded solemnly. "Proportionally more people of color died at someone else's hand in Nebraska than anywhere in the country."

"The report only points out those killed. If you add to it the number wounded," Frieda said, "and the homes that were shot up, vehicles hit, I can't imagine how high the number would be."

Ben steepled his fingers in front of his lips in contemplation. "I've been talking to some friends in OPD command. The department is doing everything they can to rein it in, but they're in a lousy position. When they respond, community leaders say they aren't doing enough; if they send in a large response, they're excoriated for excessive force and racism. Command is ready to throw up their hands and say, 'Damned if we do; damned if we don't.'"

Murmurs of assent waffled through the assemblage.

"Also," Ben continued, "when cops are called to the scene of a shooting, they know gang members are mingling in the crowd, looking for people who cooperate."

"The public is terrified," Steve said.

"Who wouldn't be?" Pamela asked. "You talk to the cops, your house gets shot up and somebody dies."

"The collateral damage is getting out of hand," Dan said. "No one can live like that."

"No one should have to," Pam said.

"And it's the rookies that get assigned to those areas," Ben said. "Have you seen some of them?" he asked. "They look like they're seventeen."

"Something wrong with being young?" Bonnie asked with a wink.

"No," Ben said, "not at all. Just an observation."

"So what's this all got to do with us?" DeGoff asked.

"We've got a lot of experienced officers in some stage of retirement," Ben said. "The young ones coming in think they know everything about police work, when the reality is that they watch too much TV."

"Wait a minute," Frieda said. "Why are we discussing this?" She speared Ben with a direct gaze. "Why is this our issue?" All of the members of The Bureau looked to Ben for an answer.

Ben paused until he was sure all eyes were on him. He was confident that what he was about to say would convince the others of the value of his plan.

Two years ago, I met up with a college roommate of mine, Captain Christopher Ross. We have a monthly lunch date. He was in a meeting, so I waited for him in the Criminal Investigations Bureau.

While I was waiting, the outer doors burst open drawing my attention while two uniformed officers burst through. Caught up in an intense conversation, they didn't spare me a second glance. I could tell the younger man was a rookie still on probationary status. His demeanor gave him away, and I figured he couldn't have been on the job too long. The second, more arrogant one had to be his FTO—field training officer—even though he too looked to be under thirty.

"A felony domestic violence incident," the FTO was explaining to the rookie, "goes to CIB—the Criminal Investigations Bureau. Most of them on this shift are the freaking Ol' Blues."

"Ol' Blues?" The rookie shook his head like he was confused, and I certainly was.

"Yeah," his trainer said. "Guys so old they're practically worthless. They can't back us up on the streets cuz they can't run worth beans. They carry the old .38 revolvers with six shots—a lot of good that'll do in a firefight," he told the rookie.

"Better than nothing," the rookie had said.

"Not by much. They're old school, can't work our computers and always want us to do it for them. One has reading glasses hanging on his raid jacket next to his badge. Can't read the freaking ID of suspects without 'em," the trainer had said.

"Raid jacket?" the rookie asked.

"Oh yeah—you haven't used those yet. When you work plainclothes, raid jackets are the black vests with *POLICE* written between the shoulders."

So the trainer says, "Anyway, I saw an Ol' Blue put his readers on to Mirandize a suspect. Looked like a grandpa trying to read a children's book to a bunch of kids. Made us all look stupid."

An office door opened, and an older, balding, senior officer entered the room similar to the old guy the FTO had just described. This Ol' Blue walks up to the pair of uniforms and says, "All right. Wha'dya got, kid?" as he loudly slapped the FTO on the back.

The trainer shot the rookie a what-did-I-tell-you look, and the rookie smiled back.

"We had a domestic violence call—felony assault," the FTO explained.

The Ol' Blue picked up the report and glanced over it. "Well yes it's a felony, son, or you wouldn't be talking to the likes of me." Before either uniform could say another word, the older detective winced. "The lady found out her husband was having an affair, flew off the handle, and stabbed her husband in the throat with a fork. Ouch."

The rookie perked up and added, "And she hit him with his cell phone." The trainer shot him a dark look that I thought meant don't make this any longer than it has to be.

So the Ol' Blue's eyes narrowed. He asked, "What kind of fork?"

"What do you mean what kind of fork?" the trainer asked. "It was a freaking fork, all right?"

The Ol' Blue ignored the remark and rubbed his nose. "Sterling silver or stainless steel?" he wanted to know.

I saw the trainer give a long sigh and a shrug. The rookie rifled through the report.

So then the trainer growls at the Ol' Blue. "Look, she got pissed, she yelled at him, grabbed a fork, and jabbed it in his neck. Just your run-of-the-mill emotional, heat of passion reaction to their argument. She just snapped."

Ben looked at his fellow members of The Bureau. All eyes were on him.

He paused. "Sterling silver," the rookie crowed, glancing at the Ol' Blue over the report. The discovery earned him another withering glance from his FTO.

"First of all," the Ol' Blue had said and turned toward the trainer as though he'd had enough, "this was no emotional reaction; she didn't just snap. Today is Monday, and from my observation of the facts, this lady has suspected her man of seeing another woman for a while now. This weekend she decided to let him do whatever he wanted without question. This morning she decided to check his phone, and my guess is there was another woman's number or text there—hence smacking him with it—women are like cops sometimes." He winked at the rookie, "They always want evidence."

"So she gave him the weekend, knowing what he was going to do, collected the evidence, and confronted him with it. Then," he had said not waiting for either uniform to speak, "not satisfied that her stinging words and accusations had hurt him enough, she cracked him over the head with the phone. Then having prepared herself for this the entire weekend, she didn't grab just any fork from the kitchen. Noo-noo! She grabbed the good stuff—the sterling silver from their wedding. *That* fork held special meaning, so that's the one she stabbed him with. She didn't go off the deep end; she planned this all weekend long!"

"That makes perfect sense," the rookie had muttered.

I was astounded. The analysis was incredible, but without the years of service, dealing with people and understanding them, it couldn't have happened.

Finally, the trainer wiped the *whatever* look off his face and his entire demeanor morphed into begrudging respect.

"Is the guy at the hospital having it removed?" the Ol' Blue had asked.

Both uniforms nodded.

"If he dies from that wound, we'll have a homicide investigation, won't we?"

Again both officers nodded.

"And the choice of fork gives us premeditation." The Ol' Blue had looked directly at the rookie. "And that means the little lady goes to prison for a long time." This time he looked at wonder boy the trainer and said, "It becomes murder one versus your measly voluntary manslaughter, heat of passion crap. My aggravating circumstance versus your mitigating one. You'd get her a lighter sentence, which is exactly what she wants. Probably how she planned it except she just couldn't resist the hidden dig. So the type of fork plays an important role here." The Ol' Blue slowly turned so that his entire body faced the trainer and stared directly into his eyes. "Don't you agree?"

The FTO gave the Ol' Blue a reluctant nod.

So having drilled his point home, the Ol' Blue slapped both officers on the shoulders. "Good job. The information in your reports really helped me get a clearer picture on this. Those initial reports can be really helpful if they're done well."

Still seated in the corner chair, I marveled at the scene I'd just witnessed.

Ben slowly looked at those around his conference table and said, "Those Ol' Blues are amazing. An idea started then, and now with your help, I think we can bring it to fruition."

Ben let the silence drag out in a long pause. With everyone's attention focused on him, he leaned back in his chair. "I think we can use some of those retired officers to shore up police services."

"What?" Frieda asked.

"How?" Bud asked at the same time.

"Glad you both asked." Ben smiled and pointed to the binder everyone held. "Inside you'll find fifty names of retired officers with anywhere from twenty-five to thirty-five years of experience. They didn't want to retire, but due to their age, illness, or injury, they were forced to. These guys loved their work; they knew the streets and the criminals like nobody else. I've been researching them over the past six months and selected several for this project I'm proposing. Most of these officers are living on pensions. Some are in independent living or the basements of family members who still love them but don't understand them. These guys need to be needed."

"Why are there so many in need?" Bud asked. "Aren't their pensions enough?"

"Or families?" Frieda chimed in.

"Lots of officers are doing fine," Ben said, "but it's such a stressful occupation that too many end up with family issues—children not speaking to them, savings accounts decimated by child support and alimony payments. Law enforcement rates of divorce, alcoholism, and drug use are triple that of the rest of us. Some of these guys are in bad shape. If they don't have a hobby and a little money—well, let's just say they have a much higher suicide rate as well."

"So where do we come in?" Al asked.

"Imagine," Ben said and leaned forward, warming to his topic, "if we could harness that knowledge and experience to provide them the camaraderie they're missing—"

Looking at the back of his handout, Steve interrupted, "These are blueprints."

"Exactly," Ben said. "I haven't been this excited in years. We can create a living center strictly for older, retired cops. A place built for their needs, designed around the only thing they knew all their adult lives: police work. I envision private rooms for those who need skilled care, complete with doctors and nursing staff, social workers if required. Everything that any other retirement home offers but specifically designed to look like the precincts of the late sixties and early seventies. All the familiar sights and sounds. These cops will feel like they did when they were young officers again."

"Wait a minute," Bud said and turned to his wife. "Remember that news story last week where they went to retirement homes and everybody—even Alzheimer's patients—who were exposed to the music of their teenage years came to life?"

Frieda's blue eyes widened with excitement, and she laid her hand on her husband's arm. "Yes. Just the sound of the music started them dancing. Their families cried when they saw their grandparent's reaction. They thought it was a miracle!"

Bud turned back to face Ben. "It was like the old folks went back to a time when life was sweet and their zest for living came back."

"I love it!" Pam said. "What a great service to these men who served the community for all those years! They've been beat up, spat on, and every other disgusting thing you can think of. They did the job that regular people wouldn't."

"Or couldn't," Tyler said softly.

"The public will love it too," Bonnie said, excitement laced her words. "Imagine. All that experience in one place. They could even provide some sort of advisory board. A think tank for community crime prevention."

The room was abuzz with possibilities. Ben smiled. This was what made everything worthwhile: the synchronicity of this group and the possibilities they created.

"They could hold weekly briefings with the police or neighborhood organizations and provide advice on addressing their concerns," Pam said. "Who knows, maybe some real solutions to some of the city's problems could be addressed. I love this idea!"

"Where were you thinking we'd build this?" Steve asked.

"Turn to page twenty-eight," Ben said. "I think we've got the perfect site out west."

Pages rustled and the room went silent.

"The old veterans' retirement home?" Frieda asked. "The one on Maple, just outside the city limits?"

"That old place?" Bud said. "That was built—what—eighty years ago?"

"Exactly—but think about it. The structure is solid and well-built, the grounds are huge, and it would serve our purpose perfectly," Ben said. "We'll retrofit the entire thing with the latest medical equipment and staff. There are so many offices out there, we can offer a branch to the state's Health and Human Services for no cost plus a wing for medical staff. We'll open it to the local universities, medical schools, and their student internships."

"That ought to get the government on board," Steve said with more than a little sarcasm.

"Exactly," Ben said. "Turn to page fifty-five. The final phase will be to implement our real project."

"I thought the retirement center was the real project," Steve said and flipped through the pages of his handout. "What did I miss?"

"Nothing," Ben said. He planted his hands on the table in front of him and leaned forward glancing from person to person. "Below this retirement home is the real purpose: helping the police fight crime."

Bud gave a low whistle. "Holy cow."

"I can think of a few more colorful words," Al said leafing through the last of the blueprints.

Ben unfolded the potential of the Ol' Blues to the rest of The Bureau. "These old cops can do things the current officers can't. They can conduct surveillance, obtain evidence, and walk right up to gang members, criminals, and not even be noticed."

There were some questioning looks about the last statement. Ben read the questions on their faces and simply said, "Nobody notices the little old men in the parks or walking on the street. These Ol' Blues, as we call them, simply collect evidence and send it to the Omaha Police anonymously via their tip line. The officers just follow up on the information and then—what do they call it? Oh yes, cuff 'em and stuff 'em."

The Bureau members looked wide-eyed at each other. One by one, their faces went from shock to agreement. Some even nodded their heads.

"Platts," Ben said addressing the two real estate magnates in the group. "Can you get the state to sell us the property?"

Pam exhaled a long breath. "Wow—"

"Mom and Dad will be back from Palm Springs in a couple weeks," Bonnie said. "I'm sure they'll be glad to help. If anyone can convince the state, they should be happy to get rid of the old facility, it's Mom."

"That woman could get Eskimos to invest in ice," Tyler said.

"Good," Ben said.

"I love this idea, Ben," Pam said.

Nods of agreement started coming from every member around the table.

"This will take a lot of financial and political capital," Steve said. "Is everyone willing to do what it takes to see this through? Something of this magnitude will take everything each one of us has: workers, money, connections. You all willing to give it?"

Before anyone could answer, Steve DeGoff held up his hand for attention and said, "Last week I was parking my car by the farmers' market downtown, and I had forgotten to bring quarters for the parking meter."

Bud laughed and said, "All your money and you didn't have any quarters." This drew snickers from The Bureau members.

"I know, I know, it's what happened next that has caused me to be in complete support of this endeavor. I was patting myself down trying to find some coins I could put in the meter. I must have really looked pathetic. Then a gentle tap on my right elbow got my attention. I turned and there was this humble Sudanese woman with a kind smile. She obviously couldn't speak English, but she reached into a beaten-up purse, which had an old rope for straps, and pulled out three quarters. She looked at me, then made a gesture with the quarters in her hand to my parking meter. I was humbled that a woman of such meager means took the time to help someone like me. I could tell she was very poor; however, she was willing to share what she had with me. I tried to tell her no, but she persisted, and then when I wouldn't take the money, she put the coins in the meter for me, looked at me with a lovely smile, and walked away.

"Her sweet face burned into my memory. I haven't seen her since, until this morning when I opened the paper."

Steve held up the newspaper he carried into the meeting, and on the front page was a photo of that same Sudanese woman who had showed him such kindness. Under the photo in bold print was the headline: *Blunt Force Homicide Victim: No Suspects Arrested.*

Murmurs all around. "The article said she was found this morning. That makes a total of five identical murders over the last two months. Police have no suspects at this time." Steve looked at Ben with a tear in his eye and with a determined sound to his voice and said, "Ben, I'm completely behind this project."

"Service is the rent you pay for living in a free country. Isn't that the saying?" Frieda asked. "This is our rent."

A long pause passed while each person considered the conversation.

Bud and Frieda exchanged a pointed glance as did the Platt sisters and the Long brothers.

"You got me—" Pamela began.

"Us too," Bud said with a nod at Frieda.

"Us," Bonnie said. "All of us. We'll start working on the governor's backing."

"I'll take the county commissioners," Steve offered.

"Like there's a downside for any politician," Dan said. "Nothing will be required of them and they'll get full PR in the media. What's not to like?"

"I'm sure they can't wait to get their pictures taken at the ribbon cutting," Pamela said.

"Politics aside, Ben," DeGoff said, "what do you need from me?"

"Access to the same micro-electronic technology you give the military," Ben said. "All of it constructed, delivered, and set up on the down low. No one—and I mean no one—can know about the real purpose of this place."

Steve gave a low whistle. "You got it."

"What I visualized is the same type of system to locate, track, and destroy targets—only we won't be using drones," Ben said.

"Bud and Frieda," he said, turning to the couple. "Can you guys get the building codes, especially for the covert renovations? If your company is willing to insure the facility, the building regulators will be happy to oblige everything else."

The Williamses exchanged a pointed glance to each other, nodded, and spoke together. "Will do."

"This is great," DeGoff said. "A win-win proposition all the way around. At the least we've got a fantastic retirement home. At the best, we have a milestone in local law enforcement."

"How soon can we get started?" Bud asked.

"How's today sound?" Ben shrugged out of his navy suit coat and rolled up his sleeves.

"Apparently," Steve said, "you've thought of everything. Does that include a name?"

"You bet." A smile tickled the corners of Ben's mouth. "The Ol' Blues."

⸮

Frieda, Bud, and Ben, the senior member and driving force behind The Bureau, stepped out of their cars and into the summer sunshine in front of the old veterans' home in northwest Omaha. "I cannot believe," Frieda said, "how easily we were able to sneak those specialized renovations into the reconstruction of this place."

"Shh," her husband said and elbowed her playfully. "Covert means we don't talk about it outside the conference room."

"Yeah, yeah," she said with a bright smile.

They approached the front door slowly to allow a CNN reporter to finish her taping.

"CNN?" Bud asked.

Ben smiled and slipped his sunglasses on. "Good media attention is always a plus."

"...this facility, though not completed yet, will be outfitted with the latest technology and innovations," the CNN reporter said. "Medical staff will meet the needs of the occupants and provide the officers with the best care available. The increased space will be available for the medical schools, nursing, social work, and psychological programs. Here—" she pointed at the south wing, "are the separate wings for each program including one for the Nebraska Health and Human Services office. You name it; they've thought of it," she said into the camera with a bright smile.

"Those offices required extensive electrical retrofitting, and don't even get me started on the steam, air conditioning vents, and all the other conduits," Bud said quietly.

Ben led the group around the reporter and her photographer.

"We were lucky this place was built with a Cold War mentality and its nearness to what was then the Strategic Air Command's nuclear command post south of Omaha," he continued, referencing the old days before new tech warfare.

"Those walls are so thick, they'd stop an atomic bomb. Justifying all the changes was easy. Those old things gave us the opening we needed for any extra work," Frieda said. "The state didn't question a thing."

"The state and city inspectors seemed impressed with what they called 'above and beyond code' improvements," Ben said. "Remember when the EPA gave Omaha an unfunded mandate for sewer and wastewater separation?"

"Yeah," Bud said. "Hundreds of miles of sewer pipes had to be fixed."

"Well," Ben said, "Dan's spearheading the specially designed sewer network—not one but four that have an amazing resemblance to tunnels, so wide a couple of golf carts could easily drive the length of each. When the improvement to the city system finally reaches us out here, the plumbing will be ready to immediately link up to the city."

"And, of course, the city planners and inspectors were ecstatic," Bud drawled.

Ben smiled at the memory. "Absolutely. No charge to the taxpayers," he murmured to his companions. "Always the magic words."

❧

Downstairs, far below the public face of the project was the main supply room. Solid steel doors declared: Restricted—No Admittance. Washing machines lined one wall; janitorial and indoor maintenance supplies sat in adjacent cabinets.

"'Bout time you three got down here."

Delighted that he'd managed to induce the Sarge to head up the operation, Ben smiled and strode over to shake his hand. With a nod of approval at the tall, white-haired man, Ben turned to introduce him to his associates.

"Sarge," he said, "our compatriots in this venture: Bud and Frieda Williams. Bud and Frieda, Sarge."

The Sarge, tall and imposing in retirement, grasped each person's hand in turn to shake it. Ben remembered his introduction and the firm grip of a man who still worked out and kept in shape.

The Sarge pulled his well-chewed but still unlit cigar from his mouth, his brows knitting. "You mean the insurance gods?"

Ben, Bud, and Frieda laughed. "I wouldn't go that far," she said.

"No wonder this place is so James Bond," the Sarge said. His frown disappeared and a smile lit his lined face. "This plan is genius. It's gonna be great!"

"So who have you chosen to run this particular area?" Ben asked. "The Sarge says the supply room is the key to everything: secrecy, uniformity, and general success."

The Sarge scratched behind his ear and cocked his head. "Paps and Jerry are my pick. They were responsible for the supply room at headquarters and ran the weapons room for riot teams when we were on the job."

"That's fine for paperclips and smoke grenades," Bud said, "but this is going to be much bigger. It'll be the heart of your command center."

"Yes," Frieda added. "What we have in mind isn't only equipment, but research and development of surveillance, intelligence, light weaponry, and an entire staff of dedicated research and development personnel to tap into the local corporations for funding."

"We want the best and brightest lab technicians in the surveillance industry," Bud said. "There's an entire network of bomb shelters and tunnels under this facility, and it'll have the latest equipment, labs, testing ranges, and—"

"A supply room maybe?" Sarge asked. Stuffing the stogy back between his lips, he strode to a desk and lowered himself in what looked to be a custom-made recliner.

He pointed a long index finger at a startled Ben who knew from the first moment that this grizzled veteran of the streets was needed for his power and command. Even so, Ben wasn't used to being pointed at and ordered around.

"Look," the Sarge said. "Paps and Jerry ran that program tighter than anyone I worked with in twenty-five years. You have no idea what it takes to keep an updated inventory of every piece of equipment from paperclips to smoke grenades. Paps and Jerry do."

Ben stared at the tough, blunt ex-cop and reminded himself why he'd courted the Sarge for exactly this job. Sarge was the linchpin. Ben knew nothing about police work, surveillance, or catching the bad guys. Sarge could bring their plans to fruition. The Bureau could put all the bells and whistles they wanted into this structure, but without the right people, it would end up a money pit. Ben let out a breath he didn't know he was holding and pressed his lips together. "They sound like the perfect duo," he said.

The Sarge smiled and pointed at Ben once more. "Good. Now unclench your butt cheeks; you're crushing your checkbook," he said around the wad in his mouth.

Bud exchanged a disbelieving look with Ben and Frieda. "The Sarge knows his stuff," Ben said in a low voice. "That's why I chose him—begged him—to head up our operation."

"Guess he never heard that discretion is the better form of valor," Bud said.

"Or the one about flies and honey," Frieda said.

"Listen and learn," Ben said. "I know nothing about this stuff, do you?"

The threesome took seats across from the Sarge. "Go ahead, Sarge," Ben said. "Enlighten us."

A smile split Sarge's face. "Right. How are those butt cheeks?"

Ben couldn't help it; he laughed out loud. The Sarge might be a gruff old bird, but he was also honest and forthright to the point of bluntness. Exactly what they needed for success.

Bud and Frieda each fought back smiles, and the tension disappeared.

"Okay," the Sarge said, leaning forward. "These guys had to not only keep an up-to-date inventory, they organized and ran the entire police supply room. It was huge and they were unbelievable. They knew the expiration dates of all types of equipment—when it had to be replaced and where to get it. They regulated which personnel could go into their supply room and who could walk more than two feet inside. They went eight to ten hours in a windowless room forty hours a week, and they were as sharp at the end of shift as they were at the beginning."

The Sarge tapped his fingers on his desk and leaned closer to Ben. "You have any idea how hard it is to find one guy like that, let alone two? And it didn't matter your rank; you didn't have proper authorization, you didn't get in. Sergeant, lieutenant, captain…even the chief himself…they didn't care—believe me on this. Guys like that are always the backbone of any police facility with any type of equipment or weapon. Everything needs to be secure, and with what we're gonna have behind these walls." He thrust a wide thumb over his shoulder. "I wouldn't trust to anyone except Paps and Jerry. Whatever we have— security, organization, and the sheer know-how to keep this operation functioning smoothly—needs to be in their very capable hands."

"Wait a minute," Bud said. "Are you asking us to relinquish full control to you? You can't be serious. This will be hundreds of millions of dollars worth in—"

Ben exchanged a glance with him and shrugged. "We'll give you a year of control," he told the Sarge. "If we like the results, we'll turn everything over to you; if we don't like the results…" Ben let the threat hang in the air a long moment. "Then we've built an excellent retirement center and everything else goes away. Deal?"

The Sarge gnawed on the still-to-be-lit smoke. After a long moment, he gave them a curt nod. "Deal."

Relieved, Ben settled into the leather chair. If the Sarge and his men knew what they were talking about—and it looked like they did— they'd achieve the outcome they wanted for the city.

Ben stood to leave; Bud and Frieda followed suit. "One year," he said. "Got an address on those two?"

The Sarge scratched the names and addresses for Paps and Jerry and handed it to Bud. "Give 'em the same sales pitch you gave me."

Ben smiled and gave the older man a quick salute. "Will do."

᷍

A month later, there were Ol' Blues manning the renovated Ol' Blue Precinct. It was still in the initial phases of development. Ben Mitchell had persuaded Paps and Jerry to come out and tour the special retirement home for police officers. Paps and Jerry walked into the former vets' home and exchanged a puzzled look with each other and their escort, Ben Mitchell. "You sure this is the right place, young man?" Paps asked.

"Yes sir," Ben said. "Just walk inside. I think you'll like what you see."

Paps and Jerry did so. There was a large reception area with a beautiful white-tiled floor. There was a dark wooden information desk with a young lady talking on the telephone. From the reception area there were four different brass double-door exits that obviously went to different branches of the facility. Above each was a plaque that had writing.

Ben sensing that the men were trying to figure out the exact layout of the building pointed to the door on the left. "That corridor leads to the medical and educational wing," Ben said with a nod in that direction. "The large one in the middle leads to the precinct and the other two on the right...well, that one—" he indicated the closest to them, "goes to the state offices, and that one goes to the supply area."

"Supply area?" they asked in unison.

"Yep," Ben said with a smile. "Let's get you settled in."

Paps and Jerry were briefly shown around the wings and then taken down the hallway that said *The Precinct*.

"Strange name for a retirement wing, don'cha think?" Paps said in a stage whisper to Jerry out of the corner of his mouth.

"Can't wait to see the rooms," Jerry muttered back. "They probably have steel bars."

The two friends chuckled. Approaching two large wooden doors, Ben hopped two steps in front of them, glanced over his shoulder, and pulled the door open with a wide smile. Sounds they hadn't heard in years greeted them. A soft click-click-click tapped through the air. In a nod to safety, once the doors completely opened, they stayed open until physically pulled close or someone inside the precinct pushed a button to do so.

Paps and Jerry froze and stared in open-mouthed amazement. "That almost sounds like—"

"Typewriters!" Jerry interrupted.

Ben stepped back and gestured with his arm for the friends to enter. "Please, gentlemen, after you."

Paps and Jerry walked through the doors. Retro typewriters, old electric fans, and men involved in indiscernible conversations enveloped the room. Two steps inside Paps and Jerry stopped and stared from one side to the other and back again.

Ben watched their lined faces light up as though they'd stepped into a fog of youthful memories. Paps cast his gaze from the north wall to his left where a series of black metal file cabinets rested. On top of those an antique electric fan turned just fast enough to create a light breeze. One blade clipped the outer protective cage in a rhythmic squeak. A large chalkboard specified the local neighborhoods and announced the names of officers assigned to each. BOLOs—Be On the Look Out—clamped to clipboards hung down. Black-and-white mug shots of tough-looking criminals with small chalkboards sporting names, descriptions, and assigned inmate numbers stared out.

Sunlight flooded the room from wide windows. With no fluorescent lighting, bulbs from hooded fixtures hanging from the ceiling bathed the room in a golden glow. "How long has it been since you've seen a typewriter?" Paps asked Jerry.

"A million years—give or take," his friend replied.

White-haired officers were perched behind wooden desks scattered throughout the room. "How many do you think are working here?" Jerry asked Paps.

"Twenty max," his friend said.

"The uniforms..." Paps said. "Wow."

Each officer sported the blue hat and Omaha Police uniform. No one bothered looking up. The typing continued. "Are they writing up reports?" Jerry asked.

"And forms," Paps added.

"Look," Jerry pointed at a vintage rotary telephone. "Dials."

Paps gave a long, low whistle. "Wow."

Seated at a large desk higher than the others Paps and Jerry spotted an elderly officer with a wizened face and understanding smile. Reaching down he pressed a button and glanced back at the two guests.

"Looks kinda like the old precinct on Tenth Street before they tore it down," Jerry said.

"Kinda?" Paps asked. "Looks exactly like it!"

"Paps," Jerry said in a bad stage whisper. "They're not wearing pants."

Paps spun around to the working officers. "What?"

"They've got the hats and shirts but no slacks," Jerry said.

Instead of regulation-issued pants, the men wore hospital gowns. Their shirts covered the top but trousers were nonexistent. It was abundantly clear to anyone standing behind that some displayed adult diapers and others exhibited boxer underwear.

"Oh, jeeze," Paps said. "Their shoes!"

Black patent leather gleamed up at them. Suspenders wrapped around the lower leg holding up each man's socks.

"What the—"

Large smoked windows separated the main precinct from another office. The door swung open. The Sarge waved at them. "Yo, look what the K-9 dragged in. How'd you two like a job?"

"Sarge?" they asked in unison.

"If you're finished reminiscing?" His bushy gray eyebrows raised in query. He stuffed his cigar back into his mouth and headed to his office with a motion for them to follow.

Paps and Jerry exchanged a look, shrugged their shoulders, and followed.

"Like it?" Sarge asked around his ever-present cigar stub.

"Like it?" Paps responded. "I love it."

"I—I can't believe it," Jerry said. "It's like we went back in time."

"Back in time and then some," responded the Sarge. "You two sure didn't though. You both look old!"

"Hello, pot," Paps said.

Jerry shared a laugh with the Sarge who indicated two chairs to sit in.

After a minute or two Paps glanced around and held his hands out. "How did you get all this?"

"Well," the Sarge said. "Let's say there are some very important people in this town who want us to enjoy our 'golden years' in an extremely comfortable environment."

"I love it," Jerry said.

Paps nodded.

"Makes you feel young again, doesn't it?" Sarge asked.

Each man nodded and smiled.

"Well." The Sarge paused, his countenance growing serious. "How would you like to not only feel young again, but be needed—and I mean needed like on a professional level again?"

Paps and Jerry exchanged a quizzical look and turned to the Sarge.

"Sure," Paps said.

"But how?" Jerry asked.

"All you need to know is that there are some very rich people in this city called The Bureau. They think there's real value in a bunch of old coppers together in a retirement home, in an environment where they fought crime for years and," he pointed the cigar at Paps and Jerry, "in a specially designed facility where our decades of experience can be put to use—again." Sarge emphasized the last word and leaned back in his chair to watch Paps's and Jerry's reactions.

"What do you mean 'again'?" asked Jerry.

"The Bureau is renovating this place and not just for all the old coots who were sitting around doing nothing except wasting their old school experience. No, The Bureau thought us old guys could provide a community service as ah...ah...what did they call it? Oh! A think tank. We'd have old cops talk to neighborhood watch groups or advise current investigators on crimes they were having trouble solving.

Anyway, The Bureau loved the idea so—" he gestured around him—
"here we go."

"Wow," Jerry said. "This place really brings back a lot of good times.
I could provide advice on what we've done for decades. No problem."

"Glad you agree," the Sarge said and leaned forward. "That's phase
one—at least for the public."

"What else is there?" Paps asked.

"Sounds like there's another shoe waiting to drop," Jerry said.

"Is there ever," the Sarge leaned toward the two men. "A few of them
recognized that we could do more than advise and talk about crime.
We could actually do something about it and from right here in this
specially designed precinct." The Sarge waved his chewed cigar around
his office. "These guys included some special additions like what you
saw when you came in the front doors: the medical and student areas.
State offices are all provided at no cost. Needless to say, it made getting
special permits pretty easy to come by."

Warming to his subject, the Sarge grew more animated. "By far the
most interesting addition is the precinct itself. You saw it as you walked
in, a reconstruction of the old downtown station. That was by design.
What you didn't see was an actual functioning cop shop. The guys you
walked by at the desks and on the phones are actually working cases."
Sarge glanced excitedly from Paps to Jerry. "What do you think?"

As if both Paps and Jerry comprehended at the same time, they
slid their hands down the arm rests of their chairs, then both of them
leaned back and cocked their heads.

"You mean," Paps said as he twirled his hand around the office,
"those guys are investigating current crimes? Stuff happening
right now?"

"Uh-huh." The Sarge plopped back in his chair and simultaneously
popped the chewed cigar back into his mouth. "You got it," he said and
started rocking back and forth.

He let that thought sink in.

"But…but how can that be?" asked Paps.

The Sarge yanked the cigar out of his mouth. "We're retired from
the force but still have police know-how…well sort of, anyway. We

don't go running down the hoods, but we gather intelligence and evidence that we report anonymously to the proper investigation units at headquarters by using the Crime Stoppers phone line. How brilliant is that?"

"The what?" asked Jerry.

"Crime Stoppers," Paps said. "It's on TV all the time."

"Right," the Sarge said. "It was around before we retired but it's big right now. People can call the hotline and report crime without giving their names. A huge success all over the country. Anyway, we give the information, and the appropriate unit, like robbery, auto theft, or the gang unit gets it. Our information should be so good that they don't even have to follow up. They just mop up, cuff 'em and stuff 'em." The Sarge said with a satisfied grin. "Course sometimes we have to help them out by providing surveillance of the hood's activities and then it's just a matter of them putting the case together for the prosecutor and bingo. The punks land in jail. We've been doing this on a small scale for a couple of months, but now we're ready to move into phase two."

Paps shook his head. "And that is?"

A full-bellied laugh shook the Sarge and he leaned forward. "Full-scale operations from the precinct. Surveillance and evidence gathering from all the problem spots in the city. We go under cover as innocent old men, but we're equipped with state-of-the-art cameras, microphones, and light weapons."

"Weapons!" Jerry all but whooped.

"Shoots pepper spray twenty-five feet!" an old copper crowed outside the Sarge's office and held up his cane. He pointed the bottom of the cane at Paps and Jerry and made a *squish-h-h-h* sound.

"Put that thing down, Benson," the Sarge growled. "Last time you accidentally shot that stuff in the office, we had to vacate the premises." The Sarge looked back at Paps and Jerry. "Had to drop a piss pack on the floor where it landed so the medical staff would be none the wiser."

"You mean nobody else knows?" asked Paps.

"Nope. It's all 'spy-versus-spy' around here. We're all undercover now. Cops playing cops that people think aren't really cops anymore." The Sarge reclined in his chair. "It's awesome."

"It's freaking brilliant!" Jerry said.

"Under cover and under everybody's noses!" Paps said. "So, where's all this special equipment?" he asked. "I don't see any surveillance cameras. And who gets the equipment for you? Does someone sneak it in from the outside?"

"Well, actually someone sends it." Another mischievous smile from the Sarge. "Not in from outside, but, up from below. That's why I asked for you two to be transferred here." The Sarge pointed down at the floor. "Below this main building are old bomb shelters. Each one has been renovated. When you enter one of them through the front door, it looks like a typical supply room. One is linen and janitorial; one is medical; another is office supply."

Jerry shrugged. "That's normal."

The Sarge clapped his palms together. "Exactly what we want people to think. What the legitimate supply rooms provide, besides supplies, are a cover for our armory, computer, research lab, and our tunnels."

"What tunnels?" Paps asked.

"How do ya think we get all of the equipment and support personnel in and out of the labs?" The Sarge asked. "Or for that matter, how we sneak out of here for covert missions? The tunnels were built to help with some government sewer water separation program, so we just made them bigger than they needed to be," the Sarge replied nonchalantly.

"The real purpose of the whole supply room system is to be a façade for the precinct. Whoever runs the supply rooms are the actual guards and gatekeepers of the precinct armory, labs, and tunnels. That's why I wanted you two," the Sarge said, and pointed at each man with his cigar. "I watched you two in the supply room at headquarters. You're the best ever. Know this, if you accept this responsibility, you will be the backbone of the entire program. You'll be the ones who ensure the secrecy of our underground network and the undercover supply supervisors of the entire facility. You guys are more than needed; you'll be all that stands between what we are able to accomplish to fight crime and the exposure and subsequent folding of the entire operation."

The Sarge paused and looked point-blank first at Paps and then Jerry. "So what do you say? Will you do it?"

In a heartbeat, Paps shot Jerry a knowing look and turned to the Sarge. "When do we start?"

⁊

"It's almost time," Ben Mitchell told The Bureau at their monthly meeting. "Things are going well to say the least. The Ol' Blues have moved in, and there are only a few more projects being worked on with the rest of the facility."

"How close to completion?" Dan Stevens asked.

"Couple weeks I think," Steve DeGoff said.

"Dan," Ben said, "that sewer retrofit was quite a trial."

"Yeah," Dan said and swept his hand through his thick, brown hair, "but it finally all came together. My pipefitters and crew were incredible."

"No kidding," Pam said. "Awesome job."

"Yes," Bonnie said. "Glad we had your mad design skills on our side."

"Not to mention the manpower he provided," Bud said.

The door swung open behind him and Ben turned around. "Al, Tyler," he said in recognition of the Long bothers. "Just in time. We're all going over to the opening together."

"Great," Al said. "The local media outlets think this is the best thing since bottled water."

"True, but without you guys pulling your supervisors and construction workers from India and Malaysia, we would've lost the secrecy we needed."

"I love it when things come together like this," Frieda said.

"Yeah. This idea was gold, Ben," Tyler said. "Solid."

"The politicians love it," Bud said.

"And the preservationists are thrilled to finally get a historic building the mayor won't raze," Frieda said. "I was at their meeting last week. They think we walk on water."

"Not to mention the state snarfing up our free office space and training facilities," Bud said in reference to the Department of Health and Human Services.

"The universities and medical centers—"

Ben held up his hands. "Okay, okay," he said. "We're definitely the topic du jour and we're getting great press, but the tech center at the precinct is almost finished. Once we get that nailed down, we'll be ready for the real stuff. Steve, are we close?"

DeGoff nodded, his well-gelled hair stayed securely in place. "Couple of weeks max and we're there."

"Awesome," Ben said. "Need anything from us?"

"Another million," Steve said.

No one in the room blinked at the sum. "You'll have it by tomorrow morning," Ben said.

Nods of agreement from all members brought a smile to DeGoff's face.

"Shall we see how it all looks on TV?" Ben asked. Without waiting for a response, he turned on his favorite local television channel. "We've gotten a lot of these feel-good media videos featuring retired officers who've served the community for years."

Tyler said, "I liked the one that showed the old gents moving out of a ratty old apartment."

His brother interrupted. "Nah, the one in his kid's basement. That was great!"

"The families are really the ones selling it," Frieda said. "They love the idea that Grandpa will be in a facility that reminds him of a time when he was young. Oh." She pointed at the screen. "Turn it up."

Ben complied. A family member spoke directly to the camera and audience. "These are men who were wasting away, like my grandpa. He was just sitting around and doing nothing. Nothing really interested him and now look." The camera panned in the direction the family member pointed and zoomed in on a group of old men in a reunion of sorts. They were laughing and slapping each other on the back. Whether they leaned on canes or sat in wheelchairs, their infectious grins made compelling television.

"It's like their memories have come back to life," the reporter commented, "along with their purpose in life."

The next story quashed the euphoria of moments earlier. A body had been found in an abandoned lot just off the interstate in North Omaha. The skull had been bashed in and every bone broken in multiple spots. The police had no leads. The neighborhood wasn't talking.

"Maybe that's where we should start," Frieda said.

"As good a place as any," Ben agreed.

Nobody in The Bureau knew it, but Clubba was building his empire as they were building the Ol' Blues precinct. Making sure anyone who spoke or acted out of turn paid the price, as evidenced by another blunt force trauma victim.

CHAPTER 2

SHANESE WHITTIER STROLLED THROUGH MILLER PARK enjoying the quiet beauty of spring in Nebraska. The brutal winter wind chill evaporated into still crisp air and sixty-five degree sunshine, a welcome relief from previous months. People sat on their porches watching children on their bikes or, like her, simply meandered through the public grounds or neighborhood sidewalks.

She stopped and turned back to her thirteen-year-old sister Melia, or "Lele," bringing up the rear four steps behind. A hot pink cell phone in her hand held Melia transfixed.

"You always on that thing," Shanese said.

"Cuz I got lots of friends to talk to," Melia said without lifting her gaze off the electronic device.

"Well, come on then, slowpoke," Shanese said with a playful tug on Melia's braids. "We best head back." Melia nodded but Shanese doubted the girl had any idea of where they were.

Shanese turned and took her sister's shoulder in her hand and escorted her across an empty parking lot. "You're gonna get yourself killed if you don't look up once in a while," she told Melia.

"And you're gonna get yourself killed by that bully, Clubba," Melia said. She speared her sister with a direct gaze from her dark eyes. "You need to dump him."

Shanese turned away and began walking away. "I can't. You know that."

"He's no man. He's nothin' but trouble."

"Stop it," Shanese said quietly.

Melia shrugged and turned back to her phone.

Shanese walked along the sidewalk lost in her own thoughts. At twenty-five, she'd seen more than her share of strife—much of it brought on herself. She now found herself on a long list of girls that Te'quan Yates Koak, aka Clubba, claimed as his own. Just the thought of him was like a kick in the gut. She didn't know how to handle the continual horror he instilled in everyone…not just her. The entire neighborhood—city blocks of folks—lived in fear of him. Hardly anyone would look him in the eyes; he might take offense and call it an act of disrespect. Disrespect meant punishment and punishment…

Tires screeched behind her. In broad daylight and with his usual arrogance, Clubba skidded to a stop and shouldered open the door of his dark blue Yukon. He placed one foot outside and reached back for something. A sickening dread snaked along Shanese's spine. *Kingpin* didn't begin to describe him. He feared nothing and no one, or he wouldn't be here in broad daylight. The air of authority he wore said he never gave a thought that anyone would call the cops. His six feet two inches cast a long shadow on the cloudless day. He planted one leg on the road but left the other on the running board. He pulled his well-muscled arm out, a wooden baseball bat in his hand. That tool had sent more than one enemy—real or imagined—to intensive care or the grave. He pointed it straight at her.

Shanese froze. She couldn't swallow, speak, or convince her body to move. Tension radiated around him and through the air. He pointed the bludgeon directly at her, silently telegraphing how he'd obtained his nickname and his savage nature.

"You," he said through gritted teeth, "been seeing another man." He bit off each word.

Shanese's heart skipped a beat; her breath caught in her throat. She glanced over her shoulder to make sure Melia was safe behind her. "N-no, Clubba," she said knowing he'd never believe her. A rival had fed him a tidbit of gossip and that was enough to convict her. "I haven't."

He shrugged like it didn't matter if she did or didn't. "I'll crush every bone in those pretty legs of yours and smash every perfect tooth out of your mouth."

Clubba stopped and glared at the neighbors one by one. Conversations ceased; activities terminated. All focus centered on Clubba and Shanese and the unfolding drama before them. Each person Clubba locked onto quickly disappeared into their house, closing the doors—and any hope of aid for Shanese—behind them.

"I'm recording," Melia whispered behind her.

"You'll just make things worse," Shanese whispered back.

"Worse than broken bones and teeth? No way."

Clubba tossed the bat in the Yukon's backseat and walked toward Shanese. Outrage radiated with every step. "He's coming," Shanese whispered frantically. "Shut it off."

She willed herself to be a barrier between Clubba and Melia. It might be a vain effort to keep Melia safe, but Shanese had to at least try. If something happened, maybe Melia had a shot to run away...or so Shanese hoped. Clubba's threat was real. Though he could—and did at one time—turn on the charm, she now knew him as a vicious thug she wished she'd never met. Bad enough that she was involved with him; the last thing she wanted was her sister involved.

Fearing any movement on her part would make matters worse, she kept as still as possible and forced herself to breathe. The dread coursing through her body would thrill Clubba. He'd turned the generic beating into an art form. He loved nothing more than watching terror fill his victims' eyes when they realized what was coming and there was nothing they could do to stop it. His method was highly effective at keeping his women, his soldiers, and his enemies in check.

His promised bashing would take place at the time and place of his choosing. After all, everything in his world went according to his wishes. Clubba would personally deliver the beating, Shanese knew. He lived for that stuff.

He strode to where she stood and searched her face with an intense gaze. Shanese swallowed hard. "It's not true," she said.

His hand shot out and caught her around her throat cutting off all oxygen. She gasped and struggled, but his hand covered the front and sides of her neck. Slowly and surely he squeezed. She couldn't speak for lack of air. Her hands flailed through the air but he held her away. On her tiptoes, as darkness nibbled at the corners of her vision, Shanese stopped fighting. Suddenly Clubba's grip was broken by the scream of Melia, which startled him and caused him to let go of Shanese's throat. Shanese fell back and lay on the ground sucking in huge gulps of blessed air and coughing with each inhalation. Towering over her, Clubba pointed at Melia. "Mind your own business."

Melia just stared at him.

Without so much as a glance at Shanese, Clubba stalked back to his car and slowly drove off. Shanese watched him adjust his rearview mirror and look back at her. She was sure a smile was on his lips. Terror was his sidekick. Clubba loved the control he could impose on anyone who dared cross him. Shanese shuddered.

Her sister ran over to her and knelt by her side. "I got it."

"Y-you got what?"

"Video of Clubba," Melia said.

"All of it?" Shanese asked.

"Yes."

"You better erase it."

Her sister gave a disgusted sound. "No way." She stood and held her hand down to help Shanese up. "Come on."

Shanese rubbed her throat and asked, "Where?"

Melia's eyes narrowed and her face tightened with conviction. With one determined gesture, she pointed her phone in the direction of the local police precinct. "To the cops. If you're gonna take a beating, you're gonna get a little vengeance on him too." Melia's eyebrows furrowed and she stopped on the sidewalk. "Oh, man." She tilted her head and held up her camera.

Confused, Shanese stopped and shook her head. "What?"

"That pig left his handprint all over your neck, and I wanna get a good picture of it."

Shanese turned away. "Don't...you'll just make things worse."

"How much worse can it be than for Grandma to see you in the hospital after he gets done with you?"

"I can't." Shanese covered her face with her hands. "There's no way out with him."

"Well, we ain't sittin' around waiting for it," Melia said. "We got nothin' to lose. Now come on."

Within hours of handing the video over to the police, an arrest warrant was issued for Te'quan Yates Koak aka Clubba. It wouldn't take long to figure out who the snitch was. Clubba's informants dotted the neighborhood; one was bound to find out who dared to turn against him.

After making the police report, Shanese needed to find a safe place to hide out—and fast. She could only imagine the torture awaiting them both after this. Looking at the road ahead, she saw two of Clubba's soldiers in large white T-shirts standing on a corner about a block away. She grabbed her sister's forearm. "Come on. We got to get out of here. Now!"

⁓

Clubba's intelligence on police matters had been possible because for years he'd built his small criminal empire by forming bonds with each of the major Omaha gangs and some of their officers. They always seemed to know when the police had information on them and often found ways to avoid capture.

Zaifra Koak, Clubba's refugee mother, taught him well. Traveling through war-torn Sudan, she'd survived by establishing alliances with the Dinka, Newir, Skeluk, and other Southern tribes. Not aligning herself with any particular group gave her the freedom to move among them all and eventually escape. During the nineties, over ten thousand Sudanese refugees migrated to the Omaha and Lincoln, Nebraska, areas.

Zaifra adopted the Christian name of Grace when she landed in England from her home. After two years there, a family in Omaha sponsored her trip to the United States. Blessed with a linguistic ear, she picked up the language quickly and ended up with a delightful mix of Sudanese and the Queen's English. Once in America, she mastered the slang of the street as well as formal business jargon.

Clubba inherited his mother's ear and following suit developed the ability to sound like a native of either nation. The accents gave him an air of intelligence and expertise. When necessary, he easily switched from the vilest street talk to fluent Sudanese to an articulate Wall Street CEO. Words were his to do with as he pleased—like the rest of his life. His mother's native tongue, however, was his best recruitment tool. With it he could utilize the young immigrants and their parents.

Those more recently arrived in the community often called on him to translate letters, government papers, or employment applications. The ability to straddle both worlds gave Clubba his legitimate social standing and made him a leader in his community. The Sudanese not only looked up to him, they respected and then feared him.

To survive in Omaha's urban gang war zones, though, Clubba needed to follow his mother's example. Starting with the emerging Sudanese gangs, he moved on to the basic African-American gangs like the Bloods and Crips. Not stupid enough to sell or use drugs, Clubba quickly realized there was nothing to be gained by fighting over turf and dope. To freely associate with all gangs, he had to provide something they all wanted.

At first, it was guns. He directed his young men to burglarize homes, and then Clubba sold stolen guns to the crews. By forming contacts with individual gangs, he established himself as a partner to each without membership in any.

By chance he stumbled on something they all wanted even more, a substance that took the marijuana buzz to a volcanic level. Embalming fluid. Not just for the dead anymore; the living enjoyed it even more.

PCP had been used in the past, but it was more expensive and difficult to get. It also carried a hefty prison term. Embalming fluid was cheap, easy to come by if you burglarized funeral homes, and the high it produced was extraordinary. Dipping a joint in it made it *wet*.

The effects of smoking wet varied. Some people became so angry with people they hadn't seen since the second grade that they wanted to find them and kill them. Others became anesthetized and felt no pain at all—good if you got shot or stabbed. Others felt invincible. All reactions were ideal combinations for *bang'n* activities. They all became the perfect pawns.

With so many families from a war-torn country, Clubba had his pick of young Sudanese men who liked to fight, liked the money, and liked the adrenaline rush that came from stealing, fighting, running, or doing drugs. Within months, Clubba had his network of people he could send into dangerous situations. If they died, there were always new replacements coming up through the ranks.

Life was good, but Clubba had bigger plans. Much bigger. His plans, however, were about to be put on hold, because of a little girl and her cell phone.

෬

The door burst open. Pieces of wood shot into the living room of the apartment. Before he could react, Clubba had a couple of officers standing over him. "Te'quan Koak, we have a warrant for your arrest," announced a voice from behind a blinding flashlight. Officer Charlie Walker said, "The Domestic Violence Unit put the warrant out for you today."

"This is all you got?" Te'quan Yates Koak threw a bored glance at the two Omaha Police officers in the apartment he was using for the night. Clubba had a string of places where he would stay for a day or two. That made it hard for the cops to know exactly where to find him. This particular apartment was located in a small complex infested with drugs, crime, and the sorts of people that hated the police. Nobody took care of the grounds and nobody cared. A cynical smile perked up Clubba's lips. "I'll be back in six months."

Walker smiled and tugged the cuffs tighter. Three additional officers flanked Walker; two stood in the living room of the door they'd kicked in, and the third was stationed outside to watch for any trouble. The arrest of someone held in high esteem in this neighborhood could get ugly.

"Pretty proud of this, aren't you?" Clubba asked.

"You're just a run-of-the-mill punk in my book," Walker said.

"Nah," Clubba said. "I'm a prize collar. Or so my people tell me."

"Don't believe everything you hear." Walker turned Clubba around and grasped his upper arm. The officer outside, gang unit detective Zach Reeves knew the neighborhood well.

"Word's out," he called to the officers inside. "Let's go!" he said as much in warning as an order.

On the front stoop, Charlie stopped short behind Zach. A crowd, one appearing distinctly unfriendly to the police, gathered in the street.

"What's wrong?" Clubba glanced at the officers and with a mocking smirk. "Scared?"

Reeves didn't take his gaze off the roadway and sidewalks. "Hardly."

Clubba smiled and surveyed a mass of about thirty people. "You ought'ta be," he said softly. "Watch this." Clubba threw back his head and called out to the crowd. "Anotha' brotha' bein' arrested fo' being black!"

Charlie blinked at the abrupt switch in Clubba's speech. He'd gone from perfect American English to urban street talk. Clubba's claim had the appropriate effect.

"Let him go!" A young man wearing a black sweat shirt hollered. He tugged the hood over his forehead as far as possible to avoid recognition by the police.

"He didn't do nothin'!" A middle-aged woman with a sneer rose to the challenge Clubba's word incited. "He was wit' me da' whole time!"

Clubba's presence energized the whole block; tension arced in the air. From the back of the congregating group, a nameless, faceless bystander in the back threw down the gauntlet. "Kill the po-leece."

The threat caught every officer's attention. The antagonistic crowd warmed to the invitation. More anonymous yells, curses, and threats emanated from every face in the growing throng. Hoodies were tugged over their heads to conceal their identities.

Clubba chuckled. "Not too popular up here, are you?"

Officer Walker ignored the remark and shook his head. "This show isn't for me," he said. "Everybody out there is performing for you, currying your favor."

"Run, Clubba!" a lone voice cried out from the middle of the throng. Insults, taunts, and curses flew through the air, trying to egg the police into a fight.

"Break loose, Clubba!"

"We got yo' back!"

"No," gang detective Steve Turley, a ten-year veteran of OPD said to Walker. "I've got your back. Let's move."

Reeves led the way to the cruiser with Walker and Clubba in the middle and Turley bringing up the rear. The threats amplified, those assembled growing more daring. The officers started pushing their way through the angry crowd. Turley scanned the contorted faces surrounding him and determined the situation could get ugly and out of control with more than a few injuries in a nanosecond. No longer onlookers in a nameless crowd, they'd morphed into a mob.

As the mob edged closer, the yells, screams, and taunts were issued within spitting range of the officers. Turley figured a brick or other projectile would launch through the air any moment. Sensing a direct and real threat to their safety left only one thing to do. Turley pushed the shoulder mike. "Help an officer!" he barked out along with their location.

The call went out to every cop on duty—and a few who weren't. Within seconds, sirens shrieked; blue and red lights flashed. Half a dozen cruisers swerved to a stop wherever they could: in the streets, on front yards, sidewalks, anywhere and everywhere. Car doors opened and a stream of officers spilled out in a blue invasion.

Clubba's smile widened. "It's on now!" he said.

Half of the crowd scattered at the sound of sirens, bellowing a string of obscenities over their shoulders. Once home, they opened their windows and doors and walked onto their creaking balconies. The familiar profanity-filled tirades flowed from the relative safety of each home. Only the younger—or the really stupid—ones got up in the cops' faces. They, in turn, ended up tackled and face-planted on the ground. The derision continued.

Clubba thoroughly enjoyed himself, satisfied that it was all for his benefit. That was the point. What good was power if you couldn't make people do things just for you? Jutting his chin toward the melee, he laughed out loud.

"Look at that," he said. "Takes your army to handle my people. The next time you come to get me, though, you'll bring more officers...and that'll tip me off. I'll spot you from seven blocks away. That'll teach you to bust me on some bogus charges."

"Yeah, yeah, big man," Charlie said and lifted Clubba's upper arm higher. He stumbled forward and quickened his pace. "Move it."

The mass of people dissipated, which allowed Walker to lead Clubba down the sidewalk and to his patrol car. Clubba spotted two white-haired men across the street. One was extremely short—couldn't have been over five feet four—and the other stood about six inches taller. Both appeared unaffected by the massive police presence around and the commotion that had preceded it. Standing by the curb twenty feet away, they wore matching ear-to-ear grins. A ring of familiarity tingled in the back of Clubba's head. He'd seen them around the neighborhood but where? The park? The street corner? The grocery store? Where? Seemed like there were always old men in the hood these days.

Officer Walker's hand gripped Clubba's head, and he got one last glance at the elderly men over the top of the cruiser. They stared at him. The short one nudged the other then pointed and laughed—at him. Clubba!

White-hot rage shot through him. The officer tried to nudge him into the cruiser, but Clubba stiffened and jerked to the side, clipping his forehead as he was maneuvered into the backseat. "Ow. Watch it, you blue-eyed devil!"

"Mind your head, Mr. Koak," Officer Turley, the rear security guy, said with a fake smile, "and welcome to the cage."

One glance and Clubba knew where the name came from. The back windows were down but no one could escape. Bars covered all open areas so anyone placed in there wouldn't get out, so having the windows down was no big deal. Clubba twisted, trying to find a more comfortable position. Soft cloth seats had been removed and a slick plastic bench inserted, which made it easier to clean and much more difficult to hide drugs in the cushions. Almost impossible actually.

Clubba squirmed around and silently cursed the criminal justice game. Nothing here was for comfort; it was all about making things easy for the police.

A dull pain throbbed where he'd banged his head. Blood trickled from the cut above his left eyebrow, and sweat stung his eyes. He shook his head and caught another shot of the two old guys. What was it that fixated him?

Officer Walker slammed the caged door shut. Clubba scooted across the plastic seat to get a closer look through the bars. They stood in the same spot, mouths open wide with waves of laughter. The short one jerked his head in an odd way and Clubba watched as his dentures flopped out of his mouth. He fumbled around trying to grab them, but they slid through his fingers and all but bounced off the street, an incisor breaking off.

Clubba grabbed his turn to laugh. "That's what you get!" he bellowed at them. "Wait till I get back," he muttered. "Just wait."

With a shrug, the little guy snatched up his choppers and slid them back into his mouth. His buddy stopped yucking it up for a moment and turned toward his friend as though checking to see if everything was okay.

The smaller man waved and said something to his buddy. Clubba couldn't make out the words but a loud whistle came from the hole where the front tooth used to be. The men exchanged a wide-eyed look of surprise only to start howling once again.

Once they settled down, they fixed their attention back on Clubba. The pointing, whistling, and laughing started again. Fury enveloped Clubba. He refused to tolerate the ridicule a second longer.

"Who are you?" he called out to the duo. "I want dey names!" He screamed loud enough so his followers could hear. Jerking his head from the right side of backseat to the opposite window, he continued his tirade. "Hear me? Those two old dudes. I—want—dey—names!"

Over on the sidewalk the short one made a funny sound similar to what a person would hear at a football game during a long pass. "Wooooo-ah!"

Clubba glared at them through the black iron when he saw something fly through the air…a large tubular thing. Full of an amber-colored substance. "Beer?" Clubba asked out loud. Time slowed to a crawl as he tracked the projectile though the air. "What the—"

The bag headed straight for the barred window. The old men leaned on one another, pointed directly at Clubba without any fear. They mocked him with the smiles on their faces. They, too, followed the path of their airborne gift with almost childlike anticipation. They couldn't seem to stop laughing.

Seeing their antics enraged Clubba. He pressed his face against the bars, opened his mouth to scream more contempt on them, just as the bag hit the bars. *Ka-thwap!* The impact split the rubbery container open. Clubba caught the brunt of the liquid directly in the face. Wide-eyed, enraged, sweaty, and bleeding, he couldn't breathe, think, or swallow.

"Whaa-haaa-Haa. Wooooo-haaa-haa!" The sound filtered through the air from the crazy old guys nearby.

The mysterious liquid was a mystery no longer. A heavy concentrated, disgusting odor mixed with a slimy thick liquid doused Clubba's head, his body, and the entire backseat. He jerked away, gasping for air. Big mistake. The move slid him across the drenched plastic-covered seat; he banged the back of his head on the opposite window bars.

Surprise, pain, and rage shot through him. The sack contained the foulest, slimiest body fluid ever: urine. By the smell it had to be at least a week old. Clubba opened his mouth to yell and draw attention to his disgusting situation, but nothing came out. His stinging eyes, cut eyebrow, and gash on the back of his head combined with the putrid taste in his mouth and throat brought a lurch in his stomach. He gagged, fought the urge to vomit, and swallowed hard…repeatedly. But the impulse wouldn't be denied. On his back, he coughed up the contents of his stomach straight onto the cruiser's ceiling. "Guaaagh-ahh!"

Officer Walker settled himself into the front seat of his patrol car. "What a freakin' day." He was grateful for the help-an-officer call response. Every cop had either been in a life-threatening situation or knew they would be. Every cop who ever had to radio for help would say the same thing: the sound of answering sirens was one of the greatest on earth.

His brothers and sisters in blue had helped him control the situation. With the area secured, the melee of twenty clamoring officers dwindled to a calm mop up. Three cruisers still had their red and blue rotator lights on. Charlie's pulse slowed to a normal beat. The perp in the backseat yelled something out of the back window. Walker brushed it off and reached for his microphone. "2 Adam 22."

"2 Adam 22, go ahead, 2 Adam 22," the dispatcher responded.

"Transporting one male suspect to Central Headquarters for—" The back of his vehicle rocked and bounced. From his rearview mirror Charlie watched Clubba slide across the backseat, feet in the air and weird noises coming from his mouth. "Ah, nuts!" he muttered under his breath. "Forgot to seatbelt him in."

Walker reached back and opened the window separating the driver compartment from the caged backseat. "Knock it off or I'll have to—"

He stopped midsentence, stunned by a sight that defied everything he had seen thus far in his fifteen years of law enforcement. Dark chunks of disgusting slime dripped from the roof onto Clubba who lay on his back. The slop dribbled onto his hair and upper body. He was covered in it. Eyes bulging, he heaved again launching another mouthful toward Charlie.

"Oh, n—" Walker bolted into action, trying to slam the window between them shut. He was quick but not quick enough. His left shoulder and the front of his uniform dampened with the second round of regurgitation. "You stupid piece of—"

There were bad smells in his line of work, but this was the worst. The vile odor washed over him and cut off his words. His head reeled and he fought his own almost overwhelming urge to cough up his cookies as well. No way; not on the job. Charlie scrambled out of the cruiser trying not to breathe until he got fresh air.

The silence on the radio hadn't gone unnoticed. "2 Adam 22, your disposition; 2 Adam 22, respond!" The dispatcher's tone held a note of agitation.

Officer Turley came running. "Hey Charlie," he said, "are you all—whoa! What the—"

"Just get out of my way," Walker growled.

"What ha-happened?" Turley asked.

From Turley's strained tone, Walker knew his compatriot was struggling not to laugh.

With the area subdued, six officers came over and surrounded cruiser 22. Two of them, Emery Johnson and Tyson Bradley, partners since joining the force together four years ago, glanced inside the cruiser. "Hey," Johnson said, "isn't that the big bad boy, Clubba?"

"Looks like," his buddy Tyson chimed in. "He's so bad that when he gets arrested he pisses and pukes himself." The chorus of cops snickered and whooped in merriment. Everyone except Charlie Walker. He plucked at his shirt in a futile attempt to prevent spreading the contents of Clubba's stomach to any other part of him.

"You're dead," Clubba said lying in the filth on the plastic-covered seat. "And those two old men. You're all dead cuz I'll break every bone in your bodies."

"Not where you're going," said Officer Turley standing just outside.

"Shut up!" Clubba kicked his feet against the back door.

"Temper, temper," Turley said.

"I'll beat the shiiiii—uaggh!" He stopped midthreat. A chunk of vomit had dripped from the ceiling and landed in his mouth.

"Maybe he'll get eighteen months the way things are with the overcrowding in Lincoln," Turley said to Walker.

"I'll take what I can get for this guy," Walker said. He shot a disgusted look at his shirt and plucked it between index finger and thumb, holding it as far away as possible. "Jeeze," he said and swallowed hard.

Dutch Louis, the area sergeant, arrived and immediately issued orders. "You two—" he pointed to Tyson and Turley leaning against Walker's trunk. "Get this goof," he pointed at Clubba, "into biohazard coveralls and transported to Central Headquarters. See if he'll talk to the detectives. If not, book him." He inhaled sharply.

"Ch-Charlie," he said and pointed at Walker in an obviously lousy attempt at not laughing. "Get that cruiser to city maintenance for decontamination; I'll drive you back to the precinct for the bodily fluids contamination report."

Charlie nodded and walked toward his cruiser. "Ah…never mind," Louis said turning his head to pull in a deep lungful of clean air. "Get cleaned up and call it a night. Go home. I'll take care of the reports."

"Thanks," Walker said glumly.

Louis scrunched his nose. "Mother Mary, Charlie. You stink!"

The two old men slowly walked side-by-side away from all the commotion. The larger man, known as "Big Brock," a twenty-five-year beat cop, was also known as the "squad gorilla" by the Sarge. In his day, men cowered when he glared at them. Though the years have bent his spine and softened his countenance, his dominating personality would never age.

He looked down to his much shorter companion and said, "Tiny, how did you know this guy Clubba was so bad? I heard you were on to him before we even formed the Ol' Blue Unit."

Tiny shrugged his shoulders and said, "All my life I've had to quickly pick out the bullies at school, in my neighborhood, wherever I was. Being as small as I was, they always came after me. I guess I got good at it. Once I became a cop, it was easy to see what other cops couldn't. I spent my whole career riding guys like this Clubba, I always like to keep them focused on me. That always distracted them from the schemes they were working, then they would make mistakes and I'd nail 'em. I've been trackin' this Clubba for a couple of months. Now he knows who I am, and I'm going to make him focus on me. This whistling tooth seemed to catch his attention, I think I'll use it to ride this bully, Mr. Clubba."

CHAPTER 3

DOUGLAS COUNTY ATTORNEY BILL KYLE WASN'T IN THE mood for a jury trial. With ten years in the prosecutor's office, he never tired of putting criminals behind bars, but this case was hardly worth wasting his breath on. Te'quan Yates Koak was a neighborhood celebrity as the calls flooding his office indicated, but these charges were minor felonies at best. If the deal was good enough, his defense attorney would plead it out. The question was how good was good enough?

"Hey." Detective John Spears of the Domestic Violence unit popped into Kyle's overstuffed office and settled his lanky frame into a wooden captain's chair. "You ever read those things," he said with a nod at the thick Nebraska penal code books lining his east wall.

"Of course," Kyle said with a slight smile. "But not as often as I used to."

"Know what you mean," Spears said. "So what are you doing with that Clubba character?"

"You're about the tenth person to stop by in the past month asking the same question. Probation probably," Kyle said.

"You know he laid hands on that girl, right? Shanese?"

"Yeah," Kyle said softly. "I know."

"The problem is dealing with the Sudanese community in general. It's next to impossible to get any information from anyone, even if they wanted to talk with us, which they don't. Most are terrified of any government agents, let alone ones that carry guns."

"So I've heard," Kyle said. "You're not the first to explain this to me. I know the cultural differences are striking, and there's a lack of education and fear of being surrounded by so many white folks. I'd probably stay in my little community too."

"It's a problem all the way around. Some in the community smile and wave but never a word to us directly. There's just no conversation with the group, and without that, we're totally ineffective," Spears said.

"I've heard," Kyle said with a bit of good humor, "that they all share the same birthday."

Spears chuckled. "They don't keep track of those things, so when they arrived, no one knew exactly how old they were. The majority took the birthdate of January 1 coupled with the year estimated. New Year's Day is always hopping with everyone celebrating and parties all over the city."

"Seriously though, Bill." Spears met Kyle's gaze directly. "This Clubba reinforces the perception that the American police can't be trusted. Plus, everyone in the community owes him for helping them. I'm not sure if it's intimidation or admiration, but nobody speaks against Clubba. Ever."

"So I've been told."

"These girls coming forward—it never happens," Spears said, plopping his feet on the corner of Kyle's desk. "If we don't put this thug away for as long as possible, we'll lose total credibility in the neighborhood. They're risking their lives."

"How do you figure that?" Kyle asked and grabbed a manila folder off his file cabinet.

"This guy controls every freaking Sudanese in the city," Spears said. "If we don't help the ones who stick their necks out, we've set the precedent that we don't care. Nobody will ever talk to us. If we protect these girls and put Clubba away for as long as possible, we might get a foot in the door up there. We need this, Bill."

"He'll be out in less than two years—and that's all charges together."

"I don't care. We need this, man."

Kyle scanned Te'quan Yates Koak's name on the docket. "Sounds like a regular godfather."

"That about sums him up," Spears said. "We've tried everything in our power to get Clubba—for the last five years. He's had his hands in all kinds of crimes all over the city. No problem working with different gang areas either; he gets along with every one of them. I don't know how he does it."

"Nobody does," Kyle said. "You lucked out this time. If it wasn't for that young girl with the cell phone, we wouldn't have him now."

"Reward that courage, Bill," Detective Spears said. "Please."

Kyle closed his eyes in defeat. It went against his better judgment to waste time on lesser felonies, but it was a felony. And he—and the people of Omaha—owed the two women who risked physical harm to bring them the evidence. Excellent evidence.

"All right," Kyle said with a short nod. "Let's go for it."

"That video shows Clubba clearly battering the victim, threatening her and choking her, in broad daylight. Yet he's way too overconfident that no one will turn him in," Spears said.

"Then Clubba's life is about to do a one-eighty, isn't it?" Kyle asked.

"His mother and every Sudanese in the city has been calling my office daily."

Kyle tossed the file onto the growing pile atop his battered government-issue desk. "Everyone seems to think he's pretty important to them."

"Yeah, he's a regular Sudanese community organizer," Spears said.

"I may get one to five," Kyle said, "and that's if I really push."

"Then push," Spears said. "We'll take what we can get."

Kyle frowned. "He'll only serve a little over a year."

"Then that's a year he's not terrorizing our streets. Maybe we can make some headway with the folks left behind. At least Koak will be in state pen. Not too much trouble he can get into there."

"You hope," the county attorney muttered.

⁓

"Like the prosecutor said, other than this deal, a jury trial is your only other option, but it's your choice," Joseph Ledbetter said.

Clubba glared at his high-powered and highly paid attorney. "I should have smashed that phone," Clubba said.

"There's no getting around the video, that's for sure," Ledbetter said and pulled out his case file. "We can roll the dice, put the prosecution to its proof, and argue to a jury, but most trials end up in convictions. With your *Candid Camera* antics, the judge could give you consecutive sentences."

Two sentences served one after another didn't appeal to Clubba. He had bigger plans that required his presence in his city.

At the hearing, Clubba's attorney saw that the prosecution had the officers and even Shanese show up. The evidence was there to send his client to prison for a very long time. "Take the deal," his attorney said.

"One to five means you'll be out in little more than a year."

"I can do that standing on one leg," Clubba said. The motion to plead was made at the hearing, and Clubba received the agreed-upon sentence.

Ledbetter nodded to the deputy sheriff who came over to shackle Clubba.

∽

Shanese had lucked out; a plea bargain meant she wouldn't have to face him in court and testify to his face. However, if she thought this was over, she was dumber than Clubba thought.

After his hearing, a small crowd gathered in the marble-floored halls outside his assigned courtroom. Clubba's gang members, soldiers as he liked to call them, met his gaze as he shuffled out. He jerked his head toward the elevators where Shanese and Melia stood with their backs to him.

If Shanese had squealed once, she could do it again. Clubba didn't need the police nosing around his business. He nodded to his lieutenant, now in charge while he was in prison. He gave a curt nod toward Shanese. "Don't thug her up," he said in Sudanese, "yet."

Message delivered. Clubba would take personal action on this one.

His proxy gave him a short nod. Message understood.

"A year max." Clubba's attorney pulled his attention back to the issue at hand.

"Yeah, I can handle that," he said.

The deputies each grabbed one of Clubba's arms to guide him back to the holding cell. He turned and lock-stepped down the aisle. A distinctive whistling sound, the one he'd first heard months ago stopped him in his tracks. That odd whistle…his arrest. Clubba jerked around and spotted a short man leaning on an exit door next to the same taller old black man. Their laughing images were seared into Clubba's memory.

Clubba shot them a glare. Renewed rage raced up his spine. In an old brown rumpled suit and yellow tie, the unknown little man met and held Clubba's gaze. Laughing through his dentures, the irritating trill came with each breath reminding Clubba of his greatest defeat and worst humiliation. Had they been anywhere else, Clubba would have taken him down immediately. Here, he was helpless. "You," he sneered through gritted teeth, struggling to control his growing fury.

Scanning around him, seeking his soldiers, Clubba realized he was alone. He glared back at the old men.

With a tilt of his head, the smaller man grinned at him. He waggled his eyebrows and flourished an empty urine bag back and forth through the air.

Clubba sucked in a contemptuous breath. Stupid old idiot seemed to relish antagonizing him. That was his first mistake; Clubba would make sure it was his last. He could wait to settle this score in a year. "Dead," he said flatly.

The deputies tugged Clubba back to reality and pulled him by the arms down the hall. "Whoever he is," he muttered through clenched teeth, "dead."

As the two old men casually shuffled from the cause of their entertainment, the taller, Big Brock, leaned down and said, "Tiny, you've been tailing this Clubba for months, how's it feel to nab him?"

Tiny looked to his partner and said through whistling teeth, "So far, so good. Now I'm gonna tail him all the way through prison. I know he's up to something big." Tiny's words whistled as he spoke, and he and Big Brock shared a laugh as they ambled away from Clubba's greatest humiliation.

CHAPTER 4

THE ONLY PENITENTIARY CORRECTIONAL FACILITY IN THE state is located on the southwestern edge of Lincoln, Nebraska, about sixty miles southwest of Omaha. Every gang member across the state served their sentences there. Any associate arrested in the state had a ready-made network inside; all the bad eggs were in one basket.

Walking into the orientation center, Clubba sensed the interest of the other inmates checking him out. The cry of "fresh meat" echoed through the cinder-block walls behind him and the rest of the shuffling crowd headed to intake. Everyone watched for someone they knew, a fellow affiliate to add to their clique. Clubba knew the drill. They patiently waited for the flash of a discreet sign to identify which "G" was his. For security and protection, gangs were segregated—a lesson learned quickly by wardens all over the country to avoid maximum bloodshed and maintain a shaky peace.

Several bangers from the major gangs immediately straightened when Clubba strode through the buildings en route to his cell. Their slight change in stance said they recognized him. Those he didn't know quickly flashed a generic Blood or Crip sign. Clubba suppressed a smile. He could provide satisfactory responses so each gang could identify him as a trusted associate. Here he'd be one of the few inmates who could freely mingle among rival gangs without fear of being viewed as a threat, someone who could be trusted. The sense of being watched didn't bother him; it was expected.

Clubba went through the orientation drills from inventory to body search. The latter came with the complimentary squat and cough routine. Clubba tried to remove himself from the whole thing, but each time an irritating whistle popped into his head. The old man was going to drive him nuts. Each time he thought about the old man's gap-toothed grin and belly laugh, he hit his thigh with his balled fist in imitation of his bat landing on the chest of an enemy. The little man's day would come. Clubba would make sure of it.

Clubba pushed the thought aside. Right now there were more pressing issues. He needed followers and an organization within these walls surrounding him. Clubba loved the game of chess and played it as often as he could—but only with a skilled opponent. Chess kept a man sharp, thinking ahead, focusing on the next move. Mastering the game let him set up his opponents to believe one thing so he could do another. Through it, Clubba learned to always plan his next move.

Over the next few weeks, Clubba worked with members of the major gangs in his pod or building. It didn't take long to establish himself as an associate to every group there. Eventually he sat in the commons area with any gang cliques he chose, freely socializing with all.

With the ease of a gifted quilter, Clubba wove and stitched himself into the myriad prison groups. Like using a single connecting thread, Clubba accomplished his goal without anyone noticing.

Once again, however, Clubba sensed someone watching…just like the first day he arrived in orientation. He glanced over his shoulder and saw nothing. With a shrug, he shook off the sensation.

⌒

Clubba was definitely being watched. And not merely by other inmates. Earnest Yates, an older man well into his fifties, watched Clubba flit seamlessly from one group to another whether in the chow hall or the yard. The boy was always on the make.

Behind bars for almost twenty years, Earnest Yates's white jumpsuit reminded everyone of his "trustee" status at the prison. Respected by the black and brown inmates and ignored by the white ones, his position gained him access to parts of the prison unknown to regular inmates. It made it possible to observe a lot, hear a lot, and know a lot. Earnest received daily perks from his status like special details and better living conditions. He wore the coveralls like a uniform. Officials thought him a model prisoner, but truth was, once he hit forty-five, he didn't have the time or the patience to cause any problems. He already knew how to play the game.

From the day Clubba had sauntered in with that arrogant look on his face, he broadcast his game to Earnest loud and clear. Flashing a covert sign to then unknown Bloods who eyed him, Clubba would turn around and signal affiliation stealthily to a Crip...and so it went. The kid had shocked him, Earnest recalled, still watching Clubba weave his personal magic to almost every group in their building. A humorless smile tweaked the corners of Yates's mouth. The boy was no run-of-the-mill associate, that was for sure. Whatever his game, Earnest thought he might find a good use for him.

For Clubba, his success in infiltrating the major gangs of the main population was to suit his long-range purposes. Truthfully, he considered them beneath him, stupid and disgusting. They were also simple. Keeping himself in their good graces was a no-brainer...just listen to the bragging and play right into it.

"You guys crazy!" he'd say and then listen to their stories and laugh along with them. No one had ever tumbled onto how much intelligence he'd obtained—exactly the way Clubba wanted it.

They may be criminals and dumber than a box of hammers, but Clubba made sure no one got a hint of his thoughts. On a daily basis, he played cards or checkers—which he particularly considered a game for simple minds—or just made small talk with those who valued his opinions. He fawned over them, made them feel bigger and better when he spoke about his past gang activity. Whichever crime they'd committed became his focus; everyone tried to out-gansta one another. Clubba let them think they were bigger, badder, and better than he'd ever be and pumped up their egos and pride. They never suspected a thing.

Earnest threw a disgusted glance in Clubba's direction. "Listen to that crap," he said to Toni Delmotti, a fellow trustee.

"Best keep yer mind in the game," Delmotti said and took Yates's knight in their afternoon chess game.

"You hearin' that?" Earnest asked. "He plays those fools for idiots every day."

"Who?" Delmotti took Earnest's bishop.

"Te'quan Koak," Yates replied glumly. "Been watching him since he got here a month ago. Dude strolls in like he's some sort of celebrity. Starts playin' the bangers right off. One by one, he's got ev'ry one of them in his stable. Got my twenty-year date coming up, and I never seen anything like that guy. Nobody done that in so short a time. And he's slick. Real slick."

"How long he in for?" Demotti asked.

"Little over a year," Earnest said.

"They wasted a space for a fool to serve that little time? He must've pissed somebody off. What he do?"

"Something about messin' with his girlfriend. They call him Clubba…like in somebody who likes to use a bat for somethin' more than baseball."

"Them young ones all got a claim to fame these days," Delmotti said.

Yates had been in and out of prison since his teen years. Both he and Delmotti were "ol' men in the pen" to the general population. Earnest had to admit he'd seen more than his share of violence both inside and outside the pen. Even if he was paroled tomorrow, he was done for. His body betrayed him physically, and he could never get back in the game even though his mind was still sharp.

But, Earnest thought, if he could play Clubba's game with the man himself, the kid would come in handy once he was paroled.

"And checkmate," his partner said with a grin.

Earnest shrugged the loss off, his gaze pulled to Clubba once again. The boy was smart and talented. Picking up the final pawn of his game, he twirled it between his fingers and focused on Clubba's broad back across the room. Yep, the boy might definitely come in handy.

⌒

The newly completed Ol' Blues retirement center had turned out better than anyone hoped. Television stations repeatedly aired spots of feel-good clips featuring retired officers who had served the community for years moving into their new quarters. Public opinion was squarely behind the first-of-its-kind home. Regional coverage picked up the stories, and it wasn't long before even national news outlets raved about the soon-to-be-opened Omaha experiment. Using the concept of incorporating state offices, state-of-the-art medical and educational services, and incorporating all of this around the design of a huge police precinct captured everyone's imagination.

Local media often sought feature stories of the retired officers who resided there, especially on a slow news day. Adam Jones, the new anchor with the local ABC station, led his photographer up to the doors. "Just a few clips," he said to reception. "We need a human interest story for tonight."

&

In the penitentiary, Earnest Yates watched the news story. Behind Jones and off to his left the camera zoomed in on one group of former officers before zooming out and letting the anchor finish his story. Earnest didn't hear a word; one of those officers, the one a good six inches shorter than everyone else, caught his attention.

"Tiny!" Earnest said and drew in a shaky breath. The cop Earnest owed big-time for too many trips behind bars—including this last one. "Still alive?"

Earnest slumped back into his chair, his mind spinning. He might not get the last twenty years of his life back, but maybe he could find a way to pay Tiny back for all the problems he'd caused Earnest over the years.

Back in the day, Tiny was always two steps ahead of him. Earnest clenched his fist at the memory. Every time Tiny'd arrested Earnest, he'd say the same thing. "You don't stop this, I'm gonna be all over you like a dirty shirt." Then he'd smile or laugh and Earnest wanted to punch his fists through the cop's face. Tiny always acted like he was six feet tall when he barely came up to Earnest's shoulder. Earnest frowned. Just like Napoleon, Tiny would take on anybody any time. The man was fearless; Earnest had never seen him back off as much as a millimeter.

Earnest had even tried to get Tiny jumped back in the day. Knowing what shift the cop worked and his precinct, Earnest pumped up some of his younger, dumber underlings in the neighborhood, getting them drunk and high. Then he released them on the unsuspecting neighborhood. His boys started fights with people just walking by, and Earnest knew it wouldn't be long before Tiny showed up. Sure enough after only five minutes, a cruiser jolted to a stop by the altercation and out hopped Tiny.

When Earnest's boys saw him, they laughed. Even at the cop's call for backup, they still laughed. Earnest stayed in the shadow of a project apartment. A smile of anticipation split his lips. He couldn't wait to see Tiny beaten up—hospitalized even. Earnest's boys circled Tiny, but he seemed to understand the tactic they were going for: inside a circle was an indefensible position.

Tiny didn't wait; he launched an attack by springing on the biggest pawn in the group! Earnest stared in wide-eyed disbelief.

"What the hell is he doing?" Earnest wondered. Like a crazed psycho, Tiny started swinging his nightstick. The speed and ferocity of the attack made the youngsters pause. They each froze at the sight of the little cop slashing, first into the skull of the biggest, mouthiest young man, then directly into the one to his right.

In a heartbeat Earnest's two young gorillas lay on the ground, blood trickling from a gash in each scalp. Moans of pain drifted to Earnest standing in the shadows. Three of Earnest's lunks remained, and they should've been enough to finish anybody off. Once the initial shock wore off, they tackled the little man and swung wildly at him. Sirens wailed in the distance. Earnest willed them to pound Tiny into the pavement and run.

The attackers turned toward the sound of backup and then to Tiny. One brute caught the small cop from behind in a chokehold, and Tiny bit a chunk out of his forearm. The youngster jerked his arm back with a scream and ran into the night. The last two exchanged a panicked look and eyed the cop. Tiny spat a chunk of bloody flesh onto the ground and hurled a string of obscenities at Earnest's last two men. "I will beat the holy living—"

In almost choreographed unity, they'd turned and run into the darkness just as the summoned cruisers turned the corner.

In the next week, word of the attempted beating spread to the streets. Earnest had tried to set Tiny up and not only failed miserably but ended up creating a professional persona that everyone respected and feared—on both sides of the law. "Don't mess with the short cop," Earnest would hear them whisper. "He's crazy!"

Once that reputation was made, Earnest couldn't budge his associates to make a move against Tiny again. The memory of the whole incident gnawed at Earnest through the years. Even now a renewed resentment filled his being. Instead of getting even, Earnest made him a legend!

To make things worse, Tiny had always seemed to know Earnest's game, all his setups. One beautiful fall evening, Earnest stood on the front porch of his pregnant girlfriend's house. Reclining against the railing with his back to the street, Tiny's soft-spoken but stony words floated toward Earnest.

"Thought you'd get me, didn't you?" Tiny taunted Earnest.

Earnest whirled around scanning the yard for his nemesis.

Across the street, Tiny waved from his patrol car, his face slightly above the open window. "Now it's my turn. You'll be in prison or the grave—doesn't matter which to me!"

Smiling at Tiny, Earnest had stuck his hands out from his sides and shrugged in an I-don't-know-what-you're-talking-about move.

"Don't lie to me punk. I-will-have-you!" Tiny bit off each word and punctuated the last one with an index finger pointed directly at Earnest.

Heat crept up the back of Earnest's neck, and he tamped down his growing rage. Somehow, Tiny had known who set him up. All the hustling he'd done, all the secret empire building and money laundering would be no more. He was a sitting duck; the ferocious little cop intended on ruining him. Instead of running across the lawn and putting his fist through Tiny's face, Earnest turned on his heel and walked into the house.

Earnest left the door open and Tiny watched as a female—probably his girlfriend, and pregnant by the looks of things, approached him. With a point toward the door, she said something to Earnest. A quick slap shut her up and she stumbled back, a look of shock on her face. Tiny clenched his teeth, his hand flying to the door handle and intent on a domestic intervention.

At the same time, the girl stepped into the open doorway. Her hand covered her cheek where Tiny knew there'd be a bruise tomorrow. In an oh-so-brief moment, she locked her gaze with Tiny's before closing the front door.

Tiny slumped back in his seat and exhaled. What a gift! The girl was the key to putting Yates away. A smirk pulled at Tiny's lips.

Over the next weeks and months, Tiny secretly contacted Earnest's girlfriend, always making sure to talk to her when he observed a bruise or any evidence of physical abuse. In turn, she'd told Tiny about Earnest's hustling. Tiny always knew where to catch him and took special delight in tossing his keister in jail.

In five short years, Tiny had nabbed Earnest for two major felonies and ten serious misdemeanors. Earnest hadn't spent much time on the outside and little to none with his girlfriend. Evidently that was the way she'd wanted it. With Earnest in prison, she and her child could live a happier life. Tiny was only too happy to help the two of them out.

Earnest slammed his fist on the table in front of him, rattling the chess set and knocking over the pieces. Those last two felonies had gotten him fifteen to twenty-five years to be served consecutively. What Earnest wouldn't give for the chance to even things up with the cop who'd always been in the right place at the right time, always able to catch him, always able to nail him.

Karma just handed him the perfect setup. Earnest now knew where Tiny lived. Twirling his opponent's pawn between thumb and forefinger, Earnest smiled. "And I have the perfect patsy for the job." Lips drawing up in a cold smile, he glanced at the back of Clubba's head. "Just perfect."

The game was on.

"HEY, CHELINI BROTHERS!" THE SARGE CALLED OUT TO two men across the room that buzzed with activity. Equipment and machines hummed between stacks of papers and reports. Telephone conversations droned under it all. "We got a surveillance and security detail I want you two to handle."

Pauli Chelini, son of Italian immigrants born in the 1950s, glanced up. Olive complected with a still thick shock of hair more pepper than salt, he had a widow's peak that Dracula would've envied. "Yeah, Sarge."

Tony, younger by thirteen months, carried the same stocky frame of their younger days. Both brothers shared dark brown eyes and bushy brows, but where Pauli had thick hair slicked straight back, Tony was chrome-dome, shiny bald. "Coming," he called out.

Both men dropped their reports and walked over to their superior. "What is it, Sarge?" Tony asked.

"Looks like that hood Clubba plans on having his ex-girlfriend and her sister whacked because they testified against him. That prick doesn't like any loose ends," the Sarge said.

"Probably juice up his goons with wet and let 'em loose," Pauli said. "No tellin' what kind of ruckus they'll cause."

"Where are the girls staying?" Tony asked.

"One of those three-story jobs at Sixtieth and Etna, right?" The Sarge yelled into the air at nobody in particular.

"Right Sarge." A Blue replied from behind him. "First-floor apartment with Grandma."

"Got it?" Sarge asked.

They nodded.

"Word is he has his bangers looking for them; it's just a matter of time before they find them. His usual MO is to have his gang prowl around so the victim sees 'em before making their move. Terror's the precursor to the violence with these mopes."

"Clubba's the one who loves the terror. Likes people to be scared of him. He'll wait till he's outta prison and finish those girls his own way. That way he keeps the respect of his community and his other pallies," Tony said. "You sure he doesn't have some Italian in him?"

The Sarge cracked a grin. "You may be right; he'll just keep 'em terrified to step outside and avoid any new charges. He'll leave the bashing for himself."

The Sarge clicked his tongue. "I love hating that punk. Well—" he yelled into the air again, "we ain't gonna let that happen will we, boys?"

A chorus of grunts and cheers of agreement filled the squad room.

"Pauli," Sarge called out when things settled down. He slid off his chair and walked to the middle of the tiled room.

"Yo!" he replied.

"Set up an over/under surveillance on this. For the over, get an apartment above the grandmother's—the closer the better. Keep the windows dark; set up the audio and video equipment with a full view of the courtyard surrounding the apartment." The Sarge paced between the desks. "The under will be you two harmless old Italian men playing chess in the courtyard. Can you still speak Italian?" he asked the brothers.

"Grandma Chelini'll haunt us for sure if we don't," Pauli said with a wink at his brother.

"Good," Sarge said. "You can waltz around the grounds with your special hearing aids specifically designed with video recorders and directional microphones that can pick up anything within fifty feet. You'll be transmitting to the audio-visual center in the over. All anyone wearing these things has to do is look in the direction of the subject and everything they say gets recorded."

"Mama mia, I love this stuff!"

Sarge took a deep breath and sighed. "I want everything Clubba's punks do and say recorded when they're in the area. Get it all set up for the gang unit to cuff 'em and stuff 'em."

"Got it, Sarge," the brothers said simultaneously.

"Tiny!" the Sarge barked over his shoulder en route to his office. "Fill out the forms for the equipment we need and get it to supply. The Ol' Blues are gonna be loosed on those punks—finally." He bit the last word off through gritted teeth.

⁊

Surveillance at the apartment on Etna ran as smoothly as the Sarge could ever want. A new crime spree in South Omaha now held his attention—standing in front of a big-screen television where a local news anchor, looking particularly serious, read her teleprompter. In the background over the anchor's left shoulder a picture featured a woman on the ground raising her hand and pointing toward two robbers in dark clothing running away with her purse in tow.

"A rash of these thefts has hit the metro area," the reporter stated. "Police tell us the gang unit has been assigned. As you can see in that security video, the male suspects approach the victim, speak briefly to her before knocking her to the ground and grabbing her purse. This woman and several others have been hospitalized."

The female reporter added, "Unfortunately, there is no concrete description of the assailants. They have been described as white, black, and Latinos. After knocking their victim to the ground and taking her purse, they run to a waiting vehicle for their getaway. Anyone with information about these suspects is asked to please contact the Omaha Police Department."

Sarge watched the two surveillance videos released to the public through narrowed eyes. "Can't see anything from those angles, but there's a different vehicle at each scene. Sometimes a sedan, sometimes an SUV." The Sarge took his cigar from his mouth. "Smitty!" he bellowed into the precinct war room.

"Staff took him; they're doing somethin' with him, Sarge!" A Blue in the precinct office said. "I think the staff is bathing and changing his piss 'n shi—er...I mean—uh, ah," the anonymous voice stuttered. "Poop bag. Sorry, Sarge. I know ya don't like cussin'. He should be finished pretty quick; they took him away about forty-five minutes ago."

"Fine. Have him report to me soon as he gets back," he snapped. Sarge re-ran the surveillance video several times. "If anybody can get anything outta this, it's Smitty."

The Sarge and William Smith had joined the force together in the late sixties. They'd kept in touch through the years but didn't socialize together much. Smitty loved the graveyard shift and worked it for twenty-five years until he was gut-shot chasing two punks who robbed a liquor store. As they fled, one turned and fired. The shot hit the ground three feet in front of Smitty and ricocheted up. The bullet splintered and damaged his colon, and he ended up wearing a colostomy bag and riding the front desk at headquarters for the remainder of his career.

He was the quintessential cop. Married three times, his life was typical of too many police officers. Wives hardly survived their spouse working midnights, drinking too much, missing birthdays, anniversaries, school programs, and recitals let alone living with the hard-nosed cop attitude Smitty wore like a second skin. Everybody lies! Only believe what you can verify and only half of what you see, he'd always said. That worldview worked wonders on the street but not in a marriage.

Out of three marriages, Smitty had two daughters. One hadn't spoken to him in nineteen years and still didn't. The other, Brittany, adored him. At twenty-nine she was a gorgeously stubborn redhead with a fiery temper. Guys stared at her, but she always had other things to do besides date. She was a criminal justice major at the University of Nebraska at Omaha and—in Smitty's mind at least—taking entirely too long to get her degree.

Along the way, she'd become a Mormon. Smitty didn't mind; they didn't drink or smoke, and he actually admired those young guys in suits. Even Smitty admitted they were a cut above. If anyone seemed honest, it was those guys although Smitty never quite admitted it out loud. Five years back, Brittany caught the missionary zeal, quit college against her father's wishes, and served an eighteen-month mission in Africa. Working the refugee camps, she helped refugees from South Sudan who'd escaped their war-ravaged country.

Surprisingly, she picked up the language quickly. She'd become a local celebrity with her red hair and milk-white skin. Sudanese children and women loved to touch her hair and would press her arm and squeeze. Once they let go, capillary filling occurred, and they'd watch in awe as her skin would go from white to pink. They'd never seen anything like it and never tired of the new game.

Brittany was the only person who really understood her father, other than Sarge, and she was also the only one who could talk sense into him. Smitty had the uncanny ability to see little details everyone else missed. Having worked the streets all those years, little details were important to him, and Smitty was the one who could always figure out what any bit of information meant.

Before retirement, the Sarge had made daily mail runs to headquarters that always included a stop by Smitty's desk. If he had a particularly troublesome case, he'd run it by Smitty to get his take on things. Nothing was one hundred percent, but Smitty was a good ninety-nine percenter—exactly why Sarge had chosen him as one of the first in the Ol' Blue Unit.

Within fifteen minutes, Smitty walked up. Tall at over six feet, his flowing white hair still bore a touch of the deep brown on the sides… remnants of a more youthful time. "Hey Sarge. What you got?"

Smitty was still in his classic hospital robe—no back. Sarge suppressed a hearty grin and smart-aleck remark. It was all part of the precinct façade. They all hated it and would rather wear regulation clothes, but that wasn't happening. This was the mother of all undercover work, and they had to dress the part. No more blue uniforms for street officers or shirt and tie for detectives. There'd almost been a full-scale riot over the issue.

Patients, the medical staff explained, wore the medical robes; the cops demanded professional attire. Eventually the Sarge negotiated a compromise. Cops wore the top of their uniforms specially built with snaps in the back for easy opening, but the bottom had to be the robe.

Uniform shirts were worn over the robes, but the bottoms were those awful tush-exposing cotton things. The Blues called them indignity bottoms. Baring an adult diaper or occasional urine bag or two wasn't all; their skinny legs, black shoes, and black straps holding up their black socks also saw the light of day. Uniformed officers kept their hats on with their matching shirts. The arrangement had been going for a couple of months, but it still made the Sarge chuckle to himself at the sight. The precinct was a hub of activity with officers scurrying around, yelling back and forth as if the whole scene was completely normal.

Smitty, too, wore his cop uppers and his indignity bottoms. Sometimes, Sarge thought, you just have to bow to the absurd.

"Good grief, Smitty! What did you do?"

Smitty had several pieces of toilet paper attached to his face, each with a red speck dotting the middle. Obviously, in his haste Smitty tried a quick shave after his bath.

"Oh, this." He touched a spot and grinned. "Trying to stay pretty for Boss Nurse."

Boss Nurse, as she was known to the Ol' Blues, was actually nurse Betsy Carroway. A large woman at millimeters over five foot eleven, she weighed three hundred pounds if she weighed an ounce. Raised in Mississippi, she could speak with the sweetest gentility and in the next breath, if needed, verbally assault an unruly patient. Her pointed Southern drawl, quick instruction, and wide-eyed stare made every cop in the unit jump.

If an officer didn't want to take a shower and tried to argue, her eyes got wide, hands went to her hips, and a barrage of rapid-fire words flew out of her mouth, starting with, "Wha'd you say?" Or "Get your diaper-wearin' self up to that shower right now, you hear? Or I might just join ya'll."

Everyone took his shower.

"I'm sure she'll be duly impressed, Smitty," the Sarge said with a wide grin.

Smitty echoed his good humor. "The last thing I want is her mad at me. I heard she actually picked up a Blue and shoved him in the drink, clothes and all. She'd make a pretty mean cop, don't you think?"

"That she would." Finished with the small talk, Sarge clicked on the DVD. "Here's what we got on those South O snatchers."

Smitty watched intently. "I heard about this. There's been a slew of this stuff recently."

Sarge pointed to the split screen. "This is surveillance on two of them; the department isn't sure if they're related or not. The news makes it sound like they're different groups of guys, possibly different gangs that are randomly hitting victims around town."

"How many?"

"Twelve victims so far. Three are still in the hospital with broken ribs. Four got concussions when they hit the pavement."

Smitty raised an eyebrow. "Not from getting punched?"

The Sarge shook his head. "No, the perps knocked them to the ground so hard, the women got concussions."

Smitty tapped his index finger at the now blank television screen. "Anything else for surveillance?"

Sarge shook his head. "No."

"Only two tapes?"

"For now. More are coming. Our lab guys are—hacking or whatever they call it—at police headquarters. We should have more in a couple of hours."

"Until then," Smitty pulled out a chair and settled in, "I'll rewatch what we have."

"Then I'll leave you be. I know you like to study tape alone. I'll check with the other squads too. You'll let me know if you get anything."

Smitty waved Sarge off without taking his gaze from the screen. "Sure," he said absently. "And don't forget the original reports...and backgrounds of the victims."

"Vic—?" Sarge caught himself short. If Smitty wanted backgrounds on the victims, Smitty would get backgrounds on the victims. "Whatever you need," Sarge said and closed the door behind him.

CHAPTER 6

CLUBBA SIGHED AND CLOSED HIS EYES. HIS COMFORT level with the many prison groups hit its zenith. They talked about girls, other inmates, life in prison, and what they were and did in their individual gangs, and then the talk turned to how they'd gotten caught.

"Urine?" LaTrey, a banger from Sydney, Nebraska, all but retched at Clubba's recitation. "Two old guys threw a bag of urine. At you?"

The entire table roared with laughter. Some made explosive gestures with their hands complete with a splashing sound. The laughing went on for what seemed like eternity to Clubba. Before he had a rational thought, he punched his thigh with his fist. Thud...thud...thud.

Chrisz nudged LaTrey. "What he doin'?"

"Don't know," Trey said, "but he does it whenever he talk about gettin' caught."

"Your new name should be Clubba-Pee," the youngest of the crew, Pypa, said. "Get it?"

The table shook with renewed laughter.

Clubba glared down the row of inmates. If he didn't need these punks, they wouldn't ever see the light of day again. He held his temper and his tongue. Revenge was best served ice cold.

⟆

Two days later, Smitty pushed back from his viewing. "Hah!" he said and jutted his finger at the screen. "Again with the four-door escape vehicle."

The lab boys had successfully hacked copies of all videos from headquarters. The additional five clips could be played repeatedly giving Smitty a bigger picture of the ongoing chaos of the different crime scenes. After an hour of comparison, he pushed the call button and paged Sarge.

The Sarge stalked into the office. "The gang unit can't place any of these goofs. They're trying to isolate footage of each suspect to identify and place them in their various gangs across town. What a pain. Now the media's pressuring the Chief, and he's leaning on the gang unit for answers."

"And how are they doing with the matchups?" Smitty asked.

"Terrible—"

"Because those aren't gangs," Smitty said matter-of-factly.

The Sarge stopped midsentence and slowly turned to Smitty. "What? They're all young, male, use the same MO, and they love to hurt their victims. It's their own gang calling card." He cocked his head as though he knew there must be more. "And the Chief, the media, and the guys in the gang unit all say it's a gang. But you look at the video and say they aren't?"

"You know I hate it when cops jump to conclusions," Smitty said. "Especially the young know-it-alls."

"Like the ones that called you 'just another Old Blue'?" Sarge asked. "Someone who was just playing cop until he can retire?"

"I hate that phrase," Smitty said. "Can't wait to prove the little buggers wrong."

"Okay, you worthless Ol' Blue geezer," the Sarge said with a big smile that grew even bigger. "I knew you could crack this case." The Sarge pulled the chewed cigar out of his mouth. "So why do you say they're all wrong?"

Smitty turned back to the television screen. "Watch this," he said with a smirk. He showed the getaway vehicles of each crime. "Do you see it?"

Sarge glanced between the screens. "A different vehicle each time?"

"Yes." Smitty blew out a breath. "But what's the same about each car?"

Brows knit together, the Sarge shook his head. "Don't know," he answered. "All I see are different cars in each incident."

"You got the first point right, but," Smitty continued, "gangs don't have five or six vehicles...newer vehicles. Drive it around once and trade it off to commit another robbery? Maybe they could steal one every time they pull off a robbery, but their chances of getting caught increase exponentially. Even if they bought or rented cars, there's still a high probability of discovery."

Sarge folded his arms across his chest. "Not to mention expensive too."

"Exactly, and where's the money in that?" Smitty walked to a whiteboard and picked up a marker to pull it all together. "Each time we thought we got a license plate number, it was wrong or we couldn't connect it to any suspects. Nothing fit. The family that owned the vehicle were law-abiding folks, and we chalked it up to a bad lead." Smitty crossed to the video screen and pointed. "Each vehicle was a late model with four doors."

Sarge nodded. "Easier to jump into after robbing the ladies."

"And," Smitty continued, "most gangs here in Omaha are divided on neighborhood boundaries meaning they have the same racial makeup for the most part; each group is nothing but black, white, Hispanic, or Asian."

"And the Sudanese," the Sarge said. "Who don't connect with the 'African' American groups."

"They consider themselves Africans, not Americans I heard," Smitty said.

"So all these robberies had a mix of Hispanic, black, and whites." The Sarge frowned. "Not what we usually see in Omaha."

"No." Smitty paused. "It's not."

"Hmmm," replied the Sarge.

"Our average banger gets angry if the woman puts up a fight and punches her in the face, maybe kicks her for good measure," Smitty said and punched the DVD play button again. "Look at these guys. They work in twos. One grabs the purse while the other lays the woman out by getting a couple of steps ahead and shoulder checking her. Some of them whacked the ground so hard their heads snapped back on the cement. These aren't your average gang thugs. These are athletes."

"And you got all that from watching them knock the ladies on their heads?"

"Look at this, oh, dearest sergeant of mine." Smitty clicked through a video frame by frame. "Here," he pointed at the TV, "they have the purse." He zoomed in closer. "Look how they hold it."

The Sarge leaned in for a closer read. "He tucks it like a football."

"Exactly." Smitty pushed back into his chair. "Excellent observation, Sergeant." Smitty swiveled back around. "Now look how they run toward the escape vehicle, how they approach it."

"What the—" The Sarge jerked back. "These guys are…what do they call it…um…high-stepping. Like when they approach the goal line untouched."

"But wait. There's more," Smitty said. "Can you see in the car?"

He zoomed in closer, but even with the fuzziness of the closeup, the Sarge could see the antics. "They're high five'n!"

With a nod, Smitty relaxed into his chair. "Kind of what you'd see football players do after a touchdown. Yes?" Smitty said with a note of sarcasm. "Never saw bangers do that. My guess is they're local football players. That would explain the different races…playing on the same team but living in different neighborhoods. They're all athletes and work as a team. One's a blocker who knocks the sense out of their victims by hitting her like a linebacker. Then the speedy running back takes the ball—or purse in these cases—and darts for the end zone: the waiting vehicle."

Smitty pointed at the vehicle driving away. "I'll also bet that these vehicles are from the players' girlfriends. If we get a license plate, it comes back to a family that doesn't fit the profile, and the detectives just move on. Another bad lead."

"Okay," the Sarge said slowly. "So they're athletes. Between the metro and surrounding areas, there are lots of schools. How do we figure out which one they all attend?"

"If it were me, I'd run the plates again. Give another look at the families of the owners. I'd bet the mortgage most of them have daughters who attend the same school as our perps."

The Sarge shoved the ragged cigar back into his mouth and stood up with a satisfied sigh. "Don't know if it'll fly, but I'll call it into the crime line and let the investigators follow up."

"One other suggestion?" Smitty added. "I'd focus my attention on schools with a large Latino population."

A long paused passed between them.

"Okay, Smitty, I'll bite. Why should they focus on schools with a large Latino population?"

"The victims," Smitty said and pointed to the reports. "The classic blunder for investigators. They focus on the suspects and forget about victimology."

"That's why you wanted the background on 'em," the Sarge said. "And you can wipe that gloating look off your face. What else ya got?"

"The majority of the victims were Hispanic. Most of the robberies took place during the second and fourth weeks of the month. Paydays for most people. I'm thinking our guys are familiar with that particular population. Mexican women generally carry all their cash in their purses. They don't like banks because of language problems. And—" Smitty stood and stretched, "I'll bet there are a bunch of other victims who haven't reported their robberies because they are illegal. If I were to guess, I'd say that one out of three victims have reported it. They're the perfect victims. They carry cash and won't file a report for fear of being deported. They're sitting ducks in this game."

"You got it all figured out?"

"Pretty much."

"Smitty, you've earned your pay." High praise from the Sarge.

Smitty smiled, then let loose with a flatulent salute.

"Applesauce again?" The Sarge asked with a strangled laugh.

"How'd you know?"

"I'm the boss; I know everything."

"When it's pointed out to you," Smitty called back.

Sarge went straight to the phone to relay the new information to investigators. If Smitty was right—and he almost always was—there were a lot of unreported victims and many more potential ones. He hated men who enjoyed hurting women. They had to be stopped, and this was the unit to do it.

CHAPTER 7

"ANONYMOUS," TIM CURTIS, A SHORT, SQUAT GANG UNIT sergeant said. "An anonymous tipster calls and specifically states that this string of robberies doesn't belong to us?" He shook his head in disbelief and examined the transcript in hand. "It's football players? From a local school and we should check for large Hispanic populations. Talk to owners of vehicles we've already determined were not involved?"

He ran his fingers through his cropped hair and frowned. "We need to find out where their daughters go to school. Good Lord, they even said we can expect the next robbery today or tomorrow!" He crumpled the paper in his fist. "Who does this guy think he is? I've been in this unit five years and never seen anything like this."

"We following through with it?" Jorge Thompson, a GU officer asked.

"No clue," Tim said, striding toward the door. "Let's see what the brass says."

He ended up in front of Lieutenant Jack Anderson, an African-American ex-basketball player. His buzz cut sported clean lines and right angles at the temples. He glanced over the crumbled paper Tim handed him, brows drawing together in question.

"How the devil would someone know stuff this specific?" the lieutenant asked.

"Beats me," Jorge said. "It's like our tipster has inside information or something. This isn't the usual stuff."

"I know," Tim murmured and skimmed the notes from the hotline. "It's usually something like, 'This is the guy who did it or where the stolen items can be found,' but this—this is almost a primer on how to conduct an investigation."

"I know," Jorge said. "Damnedest thing. It even tells us who to interview and that it's not our case."

Tim blew a low whistling breath.

"So what do we do?" Jorge asked. "Redirect the investigation? If the suspects aren't gang bangers, then it's not our case—"

Jack stopped the train of thought with a cold glare. "Is this a joke?"

"No," Jorge said. "At least I don't think so, but I've never seen anything like it."

"Me neither. A school with high Hispanic populations," Tim mused, "football players..."

"So..." Jorge said with a shrug. "Transfer it? Give it to Officer Can?"

"No trash can...yet." Tim twisted his lips in what looked like disgust.

"Reinterview the owners of those vehicles again," Tim said.

"No way!" Jorge said. "Are you kidding me?"

"No, I'm not," Tim said. "True, this isn't a normal tip," he continued. "It's much more than a tip; it's an investigative guide to breaking up this group." He skimmed over the paper again. "The tipster seems to have an insight into investigations. I'd like to see how much."

He caught the detective's gaze and held it. "I'm intrigued—and curious. Talk to the vehicles' owners again and be sure each interview is done right. I want the report tomorrow."

"To—"

"Yeah," Tim said. "There's something to this, something different and I want to know what it is. That's all, detective."

Summarily dismissed, Jorge left, his brows furrowed together.

"Back to the drawing board then," Jack said and turned back to his office. "Let me know how it turns out."

The gang unit followed orders. In their absence, a hotline officer brought in a second tip. "I think it's safe to say this is from the same guy. Note the extra instructions."

Once you get a solid lead on which school the kids go to, bring the football coach in and have him view the videos. All of Omaha has seen them and you can't really tell what the suspects look like. There's got to be other video being held back so investigators have a better idea of the suspects. The football coach will be able to identify most of them—Crime Stopper Tip 1A227.

"Whoever it is sure seems to know what he's talking about, that's for sure." Tim exchanged a quizzical look with the hotline officer.

૭

Smitty, Big Brock, and Bensen were assigned to the parking lot of the Southern Wheel Mall. Each sported a baseball cap with communication earpieces that looked like a common hearing aid. Big Brock and Bensen brandished walking canes that could shoot orange pepper spray twelve to sixteen feet. Smitty had a walker. Not that he needed it, but the little metal basket in the front was sure handy to carry the liquid surprise "piss packs" the crew loved to throw at the perps. A few hid their urine packs for four days, and the smell was nothing short of gut-wrenching. Smitty liked to think of it as twenty-first-century street justice.

A dark four-door sedan turned into the parking lot. Exactly what he was waiting for. Smitty signaled the others. If he was right, they had their men—or boys as the case may be. Smitty watched and counted four males; he also noted that they weren't parking, just tooling around. Reconnoitering from Smitty's view. Looking for something. Or someone.

Of course, he thought. A very special someone.

They stopped the vehicle, faced the exit, and waited like a giant spider in a sci-fi flick for a Latina woman. Smitty turned his head and spoke in a low tone into his modified hearing aid. "These are our guys. The dark blue sedan. I'm going to mosey over and set up."

Big Brock and Bensen had taken point at the bus stop bench and now faced the car. With all but imperceptible nods, they, too, pushed off and did their best little old man shuffle toward the mall. Their route took them right by the sedan. One ducked his head to speak to Smitty. "Don't even see us," he murmured.

"Perfect," Smitty said.

In an instant, one of the boys inside jerked to attention and pointed. His companions followed his lead.

About as subtle as Machiavelli in a romance novel, Smitty thought but he, too, checked out the location indicated. As expected, there she was: a middle-aged Hispanic woman. A massive purse hung off her shoulder. It couldn't be more perfect.

"At your twelve o'clock," he said. "That's their gal."

Indicating the transmission was received, the other Blues continued their shuffle toward the car and the suspects.

The car doors opened and two boys got out. They sported the latest in banger fashion: dark hoodie and sports caps. Completely unoriginal but pulling the hoods up concealed most of their faces while the bill of their cap kept the hood from covering their eyes. They'd done their homework or else a friend had clued them in.

The boys got fifty yards south of the victim who walked in a westerly direction. They vectored to their left and zigzagged through parked vehicles on their approach. The other two occupants laughed in obvious anticipation and watched their buddies zero in on the woman.

Good, Smitty thought. Oblivious mopes missed what was happening under their noses.

Big Brock and Bensen strolled past the vehicle and kicked small triangular stop sticks in front of the tires. With their sharp embedded nails, they rendered a car undriveable after a few blocks.

Smitty smiled. There'd be some pretty pissed off parents tonight.

The two guys in the car didn't seem to care about the two old men as one adjusted his hearing aid and the other talked to himself. In instant dismissal, they went back to watching their buddies.

"Everything's in place and a go."

The announcement came through Smitty's earpiece. "Okay, you two stay in position to spray into the windows when they make their getaway. I'm gonna place myself between the two in the lot and their car with a special piss pack delivery as they run by."

CHRIS LEGROW | 73

"Ten-four," came the reply and Smitty clearly heard the excitement from the other end.

The two boys outside ducked down and waited for the woman to draw closer...closer...closer.

"Señorita!" Smitty jumped out and pointed at the two crouching teens. "Banditos!"

She screamed, turned on her heels, and ran back toward the mall. The boys who seemed rooted in place at their discovery comically glanced at one another. The bigger of the two grabbed his buddy by the shoulder. "Let's get out of here!"

In the car, their friends waved them over and screamed to hurry. The driver started the engine, and the second boy threw open the door. Two steps from their vehicle, something hit the bigger teen in the chest, something wet. He dove in the car followed in quick succession by his co-conspirator. The driver revved the engine; burning orange liquid splashed onto the inside of the windshield, droplets exploding into the cab. With a flourish of smoking tires, they screeched off.

Bensen pulled out a cell phone and dialed 911. Another anonymous tip, Smitty thought. Whatever.

He beckoned his crew, and they quietly got into their own waiting vehicle and slowly followed behind. Three blocks away, the stop sticks did their work. The dark sedan veered off the road and hit a tree. The four occupants had opened their doors, screaming and gasping for air. They planted their faces in the freshly cut grass looking for some relief from what could only be described as having their eyes burned out of their skulls.

Police officers arrived. When they got out of their cruisers, they stopped and momentarily surveyed the scene of gagging, coughing, choking suspects. In moments, the boys were handcuffed on the ground.

One of the officers pulled the biggest one to his feet. "Jeeze!" He turned his head to the side and gagged. "You freakin' reek, punk!"

Smitty slowed his car even more. The boy glanced up and Smitty swore he detected a moment of recognition on the kid's face. Smitty smiled at the teenager, flipped him the bird, and drove off laughing.

↺

The radio call of an attempted robbery at the Southern Wheel Mall had come through loud and clear. Uniformed officers had four suspects and were calling for a medical unit for decontamination.

"Yes!" Tim Curtis said and slammed his fist on his desk. "We caught a couple, and by the sounds of things they put up a fight." He picked up the Crime Stoppers tip again and glanced it over: *....expect the next robbery to occur today or tomorrow.* He reread it a second time and for good measure a third. "Unbelievable!" he said out loud. "Freakin' unbelievable!"

A half hour later the phone rang. "You know those kids from the mall incident today?"

"Yeah, what of 'em?"

"Two of the three families had daughters at South East High School. There's a large Latino population, and the school is pretty integrated," the officer on the other end reported.

"Then go to the school and ask the football coach to come in for an interview."

"Why? We could just go to the school and start asking around."

"Just do what I said," Curtis barked. "Don't talk to anyone else; bring me that coach."

"You got it," the investigator said, evidently knowing when to shut up.

An hour later in the conference room, Curtis, Jorge, and a very confused football coach sat around a small table. "Coach Jenson, thank you for coming down."

"Sure," he said. "But why am I here?"

"You've heard about the purse snatchings? Where those women got pretty badly injured when they were robbed?"

"Sure," responded the coach. "Who hasn't? What's that got to do with me?"

"We have some video clips of the suspects. We think they may be some of your players."

"No," Jenson said and shook his head. "Not possible."

"Humor us," Curtis said and started the video.

The surveillance tape showed several different young men participating in each encounter. The coach stared at the screen. Thirty seconds into the first, he melted into his chair and covered his face with his hand. "Mitch Johnson," he muttered. "He graduated last year and was supposed to help me with football camp this summer."

Curtis nodded and jerked his head toward Jorge who wrote the name down.

"Victor Gonzalez," came the coach's agonized voice. "That one"— he pointed to the screen where the boy in question grabbed a purse. "What were they thinking?"

"Coach," Sergeant Curtis began.

Jenson's gaze fixed on the screen transfixed. "Mitch," he said, "knocked that poor woman to the ground, and Victor," he said in a strained voice, "stole her purse."

A tiny Latina woman, her thick black hair pulled back in a ponytail filled the screen. She wasn't more than a hundred ten pounds. The victim rolled on the ground in pain; the two athletes bolted for a waiting vehicle out of camera range. A deadening silence filled the room.

"Show me," the coach said. "Show me all of them. If my players are responsible for this, they'll take responsibility." The coach's voice was flat and furious. "I've known and worked with these kids a long time. For them to do such a despicable thing…" his voice trailed off. "Whatever I can do to help, I will."

⸭

It didn't take the coach long to identify half of the suspects. The final clip rolled. The picture didn't show the suspects as well as the previous ones, but the vehicle was crystal clear.

"Wait a minute," Jenson said. "That looks like the car my son's girlfriend drives."

"Coach," Curtis said, "we think the boys were getting the cars from girls they knew without telling them the reason why. That way if we identified a vehicle, it would lead us to a young woman who could actually be innocent instead of the young men who committed the crimes—and they were right. It threw us for a while." He watched the coach still centered on the screen in front of them. "So are you certain this vehicle belongs to your son's girlfriend?"

"Yes. I'm positive and I'll have him down here in an hour," the coach said. "I guarantee you he'll tell you whatever you need to know." He sat unflinching with the stern yet resolved face of a determined father.

$\backsim$

True to his word, the coach had his son, Jeb, a lanky seventeen-year-old with a scowling countenance, in the same chair Jenson had occupied an hour before. The coach stared straight ahead, not sparing a glance at his son.

Curtis didn't envy either one of them. He pushed the play button once again.

Jeb squirmed. "What's this got to do with me? I didn't do anything to those women. That's not me."

"We know, Jeb." Curtis ran each video clip making sure to point out the women and their injuries as they lay on the ground. He even had the crime lab photos of their faces complete with gashes, blood, and bruises from their admittance to the hospital. Curtis guessed this dad had taught his son respect for women. He also thought Jeb hadn't actually hurt anyone. He was probably one of the drivers. Maybe showing what they'd actually suffered might prick his sense of right and wrong enough to get him to talk.

He ran the videos again, set the photos in front of the kid. The bloodied, swollen faces of the small women seemed to mesmerize Jeb. "I didn't do any of that," Jeb whimpered. Sweat beaded on his temples. One drop slid down the right side of his face. "Dad," he implored to his father. "I didn't hurt any of these women."

Bingo! Sergeant Curtis almost said aloud. Jeb was making sure his dad knew he wouldn't personally hurt them.

"I didn't say *you* caused these injuries," Curtis emphasized the word *you* and paused the screen. If his hunch was correct Jeb's father had probably drilled into his son's head it was wrong to pick on smaller people, to bully anyone.

Jeb slumped into his chair.

Curtis reached over and hit the play button again. He watched Jeb whose gaze focused on the clear video of his girlfriend's car. "I'm glad to hear you didn't actually hurt any of these women, Jeb." The game was to get the boy thinking he was off the hook and to reassure his father that he'd instilled the proper values in his son. Made everyone more compliant and relaxed.

Curtis decided to shock Jeb. "You drove your buddies there, and they did the dirty work." Jeb opened his mouth to speak.

Curtis cut him off. "Don't even lie to me," he said and pointed his finger directly at the kid's nose.

"No! I-I didn't," came the reply. More sweat glistened on the young face.

"Oh sure, you didn't want to hurt those women," he continued, holding his palms above the photos. "That's something good I can say for you, and I honestly believe if you'd known how badly these women were hurt, you wouldn't have been part of this."

Jeb nodded. "That's right! No way!"

Coach Jenson stood and stepped in front of his son. "Jeb," he said and paused a moment as though gathering his thoughts. He stared directly into his son's eyes. "I want you to make me proud tonight. I want your full cooperation here…with these officers. Complete and total. Do you understand?"

"Dad, I didn't think that—"

The coach didn't take his gaze off his son, didn't miss a beat. He tilted his head and softened his face. "Son."

Jeb's chin fell to his chest. A lone tear dropped onto his cheek. "'Kay, Dad."

⸎

Within the week most of the "snatchers," as they'd named themselves, were in custody. The Chief gave a news conference that filled every local channel and a few national ones. Accolades and praise rolled in from everywhere. The community as a whole breathed a sigh of relief.

The Chief was very pleased.

CHAPTER 8

CHIEF RYAN "RUSTY" WILLIAMS HAD TWENTY-SIX YEARS ON the department. Strands of silver mixed with light brown fringe covered the back and sides of his head. He needed bifocal contacts to read anything, but his sturdy frame of five feet ten showed he could still handle himself in a tough situation. He'd worked his way through the ranks and most recently had headed up Internal Affairs for the past decade. IA meant that he'd investigated numerous officers for excessive force issues, citizen complaints, and legal violations. It all served to make him a hard-nosed supervisor who despised trouble-making officers. They made the department and law enforcement in general look bad.

It also made him a major influence over the conduct of the Omaha Police Department. His dedication to his job also made him a lot of enemies. There were more than a few cops he'd disciplined or even fired; they still had buddies on the department and were always looking for ways to undermine him or, better yet, make him look bad to the uniforms on the street or to the public.

After Internal Affairs, as a lieutenant he led an entire crew for the whole precinct. Whenever something happened in his jurisdiction, the officers who had a gripe with him made sure that they spread it around to everyone else that Lt. Williams was to blame. If something particularly embarrassing hit the news, the media would receive numerous anonymous phone calls from officers who wanted Lt. Williams's name and reputation dragged through the mud. Humiliation was good for the petty soul.

Once Rusty made captain, many of the small-minded officers saw the writing on the wall: Captain Williams was on the short list to make Chief. The knowledge served to spur his enemies on. Try as they did, Williams's work ethic, integrity, and his astute knowledge that numerous officers hated him made him carefully calculate all command decisions. Everything in both his public and private life was conducted in such a way as to maintain the integrity of his office while actively and vigorously enforcing the law in the metropolitan area.

No wonder he eventually became the Chief of Police. Now at the top of the command ladder, he brought with him the reminder that, throughout every point of the chain of command, officers wanted him to fail, were waiting for him to fail. And there was nothing he could do about it. Only one office under his purview was outside any chain: Public Information. All statements regarding press releases on crimes and public services were orchestrated through the Public Information Office (PIO) and the Chief's office.

The Chief placed his trusted friend and lieutenant, Monica Thorp, as the PIO supervisor. A petite brunette with caramel streaks in her bobbed hair, they'd known one another for twenty years, having graduated in the same academy class. They had remained good friends ever since, and she had his back as the new Chief. What he needed now was an officer he could depend on to be the departmental face to the media and the public.

Most officers wanted nothing to do with the media—or the public. The pressures of taking the flak when things went bad—and things would definitely get bad simply due to the nature of police work—made most officers balk at the mere thought of sitting in the PIO hot seat.

The Chief met with Thorp to discuss the opening. "Monica, there is just no way to say this, but I have pissed off almost everybody in this department."

"A decade in IA will do that," she said dryly. "You've disciplined officers on every shift and in every district in the city. Those who didn't get disciplined were the buddies of those who did. Lousy job but somebody had to do it."

The Chief rammed his fingers across his bald head. "I don't know who I can trust to work in this office."

"I agree, you've got quite the fan base, Rusty." Her remark drew a mock glare from the Chief. "And we need someone who hasn't had the pleasure of dealing with you for the past twenty-five years." Another baleful glance flew her way. "We definitely need someone with enough law enforcement experience so the rank and file will respect him as well as the media. They need to see this person as a reliable source."

"That's about it," Rusty said.

"Sounds like we'll have to go outside our department!"

The Chief twisted his lips and shook his head. "Very funny, Monica. You know we can't do that; the officer needs to come from our ranks."

Monica shrugged.

"That's the purpose of this meeting, right? You do know that. We need to actually solve this particular problem and soon."

Monica nodded, her gaze fixed on the floor. Without moving her head, she glanced up at the Chief and smiled.

"You have someone in mind," the Chief said in an accusatory tone and pointed at her for emphasis. "Don't you?"

Monica raised her hands in false surrender. "You got me."

"Great. Who?"

"Jake Mitchell," she answered, her tone filled with certainty.

"Jake Mitchell?" The Chief sat in his desk chair, his brows knit together in silent question. "Which precinct is he in? I'm not familiar with him."

"Exactly!" said Monica. "He's been on the department for two years, and you've never heard of him. It's perfect."

"Two years?" the Chief asked. "He's practically a rookie! Nobody'll take him seriously. The media will laugh him out of a press conference, and the other cops won't respect him." He tossed a manila folder containing the current budget figures across his desk. "Get serious!"

"I am serious!" Monica said. "Dead serious. Mitchell's only worked for *our* department for two years, but he was a detective in Salt Lake City over a decade. He applied for the Lateral Academy we offered two years ago; remember, the one for certified officers in other police departments. Pretty sharp guy."

"Why would anyone leave there for here?" the Chief asked.

"His wife and daughter were killed in a car accident on a mountain pass in a winter storm. Guess he just wanted to get out and start over."

"Makes sense I suppose. Definitely no mountains in these parts, nothing to remind him of the past. Anything else to it?" the Chief said. "Got to be more to the story than mountains."

Monica nodded. "I heard he's got family here. Brother owns a huge corporation. Filthy rich from what I hear."

The Chief shot Monica a pointed glance. "You're not putting him in our office so he'll introduce you to his brother, are you?"

"Well, a girl can hope." She fluttered her eyelids. "But seriously, he's perfect." She held up her index finger. "One, not from our department." Her middle finger joined the index. "Two, he has loads of street experience." Her ring finger went up. "Three, he doesn't hate you...yet."

The Chief tossed his pen on his desk. "Day isn't over."

"Four," she continued as if he hadn't spoken, "he's a lot like you. I was a sergeant in another district, but I knew about him thanks to the sergeants' grapevine. A lot of street officers didn't like him. Didn't go drinking after the shift, didn't talk the cuss'n cop talk. Didn't really fit in, but he's a good cop, does his job, dependable. Tell you the truth, I wouldn't mind having a whole squad of Mitchells."

"Really?" The Chief leaned back in his chair to consider that. Coming from Monica, it was high praise. He waved her toward the door. "Bring him in for an interview."

Monica smiled. "He's in the lobby."

Taken aback, the Chief's eyes widened at her presumption. "He's in the—oh, really?"

"Yeah. Really."

He knew her well enough to realize she'd had this figured out from the very start. Still—he let out a long breath he didn't know he was holding. "Fine, then. Send him in!"

"Yes sir," she responded, her grin just this side of impertinent.

∾

"The Public Information Officer," Mitchell said. "Chief, I thought I'd committed some major screw-up. I've been going out of my mind trying to figure out what I'd done to get me called to your office."

"When I'm finished describing the job, you may wish you were in trouble."

Lt. Monica Thorp snorted a laugh but quickly covered it with a cough.

The Chief didn't take his eyes off Mitchell but pointed in Monica's direction. They knew one another well enough to know he meant zip it!

"I know your story, Jake," the Chief began. "Sorry to hear about your family. How are you getting along?"

"Oh," Jake responded, sounding a little surprised. "As well as can be expected, sir. It was really rough in the beginning, but moving here was a good plan."

"Your performance ratings are excellent," Lt. Thorp said.

"That may be," the Chief continued, "but from what I understand, you don't gel too much with the crews you're on."

"True," Mitchell said. "I don't drink, smoke, or chase women; that's not me, not the kind of man I am or want to be. So I really don't relate to a lot of what the other guys do. Makes them uncomfortable, so some of them don't like me." Jake straightened in his chair. "Chief, let's get this in the open. Do you have a problem with Latter-day Saints?"

The Chief looked confused and glanced at Lt. Thorp. "I thought you were Mormon."

"One and the same," Mitchell said.

Another snort from Monica. Again the Chief pointed a silencing finger her way.

"Do you have problems with Mormons, Chief?"

The question took the Chief aback. "Of course not. I respect the Mormons—and I love Glenn Beck."

Another loud snort, only this one came from Mitchell.

"Okay, Jake," the Chief said, "here's the deal. A lot of officers in this department don't care much for me. Some of them—"

Jake held his hand up and finished the sentence, "Think you're a back-stabbing second guesser who'd throw his own mother under the bus to get a promotion?"

The Chief leaned forward to stare at Mitchell, settling his elbows on his desk. "Yeah," he said wryly. "Something like that."

From the Chief's left side came an unmistakable sound.

"Monica," the Chief yelled, all subtlety gone. "Knock it off!"

"The way I see it, Chief," Mitchell said, "you're not sure who you can trust. I know how important this position is and how much you need to trust the person in that position. I also know the unwritten job description is to protect you from being blindsided and looking like an idiot on television."

The kid was a quick study. The Chief nodded.

"This is the only position where the chain of command has only three links: you, Lt. Thorp, and whoever's in this job. I'd imagine the officer here shouldn't have a lot of history in OPD." Jake raised a brow of inquiry at the Chief.

The Chief nodded his agreement again.

"Someone who doesn't have buddies to confide sensitive information to."

"Uh-huh," the Chief said. "Exactly."

Jake smiled and looked almost angelic. "But has plenty of law enforcement experience so the media will take them seriously, and let's face it, this someone also needs to be just stupid enough to take this job."

"About sums it up, don't you think, Monica?" the Chief steepled his fingers and tapped his chin.

Lt. Thorp crossed her arms as though clearly impressed with herself for recommending Jake. "I'd say so."

"Well, Chief, then I'm your guy. I think this'll be a challenge, and I'd like to be considered for the position," Jake said.

A heavy weight the Chief hadn't realized was sitting on his shoulders lifted. Jake seemed to fit every necessary qualification, and for that the Chief was grateful. "Welcome to the team then. Outside this office, proper titles are a must. Everyone needs to understand that you and Monica are my spokespeople—nobody else. In my office, however, rank is left at the door. I want frank assessments, honest advice, and I want you to feel completely comfortable talking to me or Monica about anything. We can disagree and disagree strongly about how to handle a situation, but once the decision is made, we all support it outside of the office. That's the way it has to be."

"No problem," Jake said.

CHAPTER 9

DURING HIS DECADES OF INCARCERATION, EARNEST YATES gained a keen familiarity with the prison, including its buildings, corridors, and grounds better than almost anyone else. Maybe even the administration. At this point in his residency, it was all second nature to him. His focus had become the human elements surrounding him. These days he sensed who would crack up within the first week and who wouldn't, who'd make it in prison and who'd flame out. Over the years the gangs had changed very little. They differed, but the thuggish personality remained the same.

So predictable, Earnest thought. All of the punks were so predictable. On arrival the first thing they sought was a familiar flash of a sign. That was acknowledged with a head nod or a clandestine sign of their own. Once through orientation, they knew whom to hook up, and the same tired conversations would be hashed and rehashed to the point that Earnest wanted to break their teeth.

They wouldn'ta caught me if I'd done this. Or *I would have gotten away if it wasn't for that*, or his personal favorite, *I don't know how they caught me!* The latter were the complete morons, easy to manipulate, easier to use. Add a touch of drugs or booze, and they moved from moron to total idiocy. They were the stupid pawns who'd shoot up a house or a nightclub just to get what they thought was respect. These guys were ripe for the picking.

Earnest figured it would take him a week and he'd get them to do whatever he wanted, anything he wanted. He smiled at the list he wanted to accomplish. Once they considered him an OG, original gangster, they'd be his. One word would be all it would take to get a hit ordered on another inmate...maybe even a guard.

Through the years, Earnest had ordered hits on hundreds of guys, which included guards who pissed him off or didn't treat him with respect. Had to be careful about guards though, and Earnest saved his ire for the ones who particularly irritated him or for those who were too good at their jobs.

Back when Earnest got and sold contraband, back before surveillance cameras and other electronic security, he constantly worried about guards finding his stashes of drugs, homemade liquor, or weapons. A determined guard could ruin months of work and land him in isolation. So every once in a while, Earnest had to make their lives difficult. Make it so that their lives weren't worth the risk of uncovering his stash. Like cops, guards simply wanted to go home after their shift with the same number of holes in their bodies that they'd left with.

That was ten years ago. Earnest didn't want to work that hard anymore. Now he could sit back and figure out how to get the young ones, his pawns, to do the work for him. One lived longer that way, he told himself. That was why Earnest took particular interest in the new guy they called Clubba and his activity. Already he'd established relationships with every gang in the joint and somehow moved freely between each one.

The more Earnest watched him, the more the kid reminded him of Earnest himself. Only Clubba seemed able to provide something to each gang. That's what allowed him to weave in and out of the long-established and strictly enforced territories within the prison. But exactly what did he provide each one? Earnest could associate with the factions by providing the goods or services to them. He'd always been able to get or make the necessary contraband and have it delivered directly to his consumers. As a result, he, like Clubba, moved freely among the gangs himself. But Clubba didn't provide contraband, didn't provide services, and he sure didn't work as hard as Earnest.

Daily he watched Clubba play chess with his fellow trustees. That was unusual. Younger inmates didn't pay them much attention and could care less if they overheard their schemes or not. Everyone, especially the old guys, knew and kept the time-honored prison code: keep your mouth shut.

After chess, Clubba strolled the grounds and commons like he owned it. He'd talk to the leadership of one faction, seeming to take a keen interest in what they said. Then came the handshakes and thug hugs, a quick embrace around the shoulders typical among gangs. It was like he'd just delivered something to them...but what? It drove Earnest crazy.

But there was more, something else about this Clubba. No matter where he was, whether in the commons, speaking to someone on the stairwells or in the hallways, whenever he was asked how he got caught, he always punched his fist into his thigh. Repeatedly. A distinct thudding sound accompanied the action especially when they called him Clubba-Pee. It was enough to silence everyone within earshot, and no one ever laughed. Some inmates thought he had a mental condition, and no one wanted to push the issue.

Earnest observed Clubba daily as he intricately worked with gangs who hated each other. One day he was with the Bloods, the next day with the Crips. Earnest shook his head at the thought. Nobody—*nobody*—did that! He received similar treatment from each group: thug hugs, smiles, and laughter.

And then he'd leave. Earnest watched him speak over and over to the prison gang leaders—all of them. He couldn't figure it out. He wasn't giving them anything, so he must be doing an errand for them. Maybe he gave some items to the lower bangers before meeting up with the leadership. But no.

Again Earnest came up with nothing. He knew what to look for: a handshake where pills got exchanged, a hug with items dropped into the collar of the person being hugged. But there was none of that with Clubba. Earnest watched as the younger man left the area. Maybe he left something on his seat. No sign of it. Maybe he left it by the window or under the table. Again, zip, nada. Earnest frowned and shook his head. Nobody got access like that for free! Nobody! Not ever!

When other prisoners saw the tall, thin Sudanese guy walk by and they started messing with him, they quickly learned that one word to the gang leadership earned a beating to remember. Not dirty looks, not threats, an immediate and thorough beating. Nobody in the joint, it seemed, messed with Clubba.

෭

After two months of surveillance, Earnest was getting nowhere fast. The usual ways and means of learning about another inmate weren't working for him. Earnest's surveillance needed to be closer, needed more intimate details. One thing was immediately apparent. Clubba was rarely written up for any violations. That slight English accent gained him differential treatment from the guards. For them, it seemed, talking to Clubba was fun. Totally different than conversations with the usual population. Just by sounding different, he became interesting. Guards went out of their way to talk to him. Unbelievable!

By staying out of trouble, Clubba had quickly gained trustee status. It wasn't so much that Clubba stayed out of trouble. He actually had the bangers handle his trouble for him. Clever kid, Earnest thought begrudgingly. If Clubba was providing shanks or any metal tools or equipment to the bangers, he had to be doing it through his work detail in the kitchen. It would be an easy delivery from there. That had to be it.

Through his own behavior and status, Earnest easily attached himself to Clubba's assignments. As he watched from a discreet distance, his trained eye could spot what Clubba might steal whether equipment or other items. Yep, Earnest would know in a heartbeat. After all, he'd been doing it himself for years.

After two weeks, he had the same thing as when he'd started: zero! Clubba put on quite the show as a model prisoner. The guards were duly impressed, and as a result, he gained even more trust. Earnest clenched his teeth in frustration. Clever kid, he silently acknowledged. But Earnest knew how to get good treatment and access to all the details with the guards too. What he couldn't figure out was what Clubba was doing for the bangers.

On kitchen detail one afternoon, Earnest silently watched in wide-eyed fascination. While cleaning the massive, stainless steel prep table, Clubba slowly but with obvious intention worked his way over to a gigantic white man standing by the sinks. He stood six feet eight and weighed around three hundred and fifty pounds. Earnest immediately knew who he was and what he thought of blacks. Everyone knew. The man advertised it in swastikas tattooed on his huge bald head.

"Big Whitey" took no notice of the dark-skinned Sudanese man who drew close enough to be within talking distance. Earnest stood over a pot of chicken noodle soup and pretended to work. Truth was if it had boiled over, Earnest wouldn't have noticed. The strange affair unfolding in the room held him fast, mesmerized by the audacity of the younger man and the sheer brute force simmering from the older one.

"You know," Clubba began in a stronger, more demonstrative English accent, "I simply can't stand these bloody black African-Americans."

Big Whitey stopped rubbing the cleaning solution onto the surface in front of him and slowly raised his head to meet the younger man's gaze, then quickly did a double take and stepped back. "Wha'd you say t' me?" Big Whitey asked in a low, threatening tone.

Either oblivious to the mounting tension in the room or purposely ignoring it, Clubba continued as though it was simply a pause in their ongoing conversation. "I mean their manners. Despicable. They gallivant about in an absurd manner, constantly claiming to be some kind of brotha', trousers pulled down below their bums, and what on earth are they even saying? I mean honestly, what they've done to the Queen's English is positively dreadful."

Big Whitey stared dumbly and stood transfixed. He even managed a nod of agreement.

Clubba inched a few millimeters closer, continuing his one-sided conversation to the massive man. "If we were back where I came from, we would not put up with such shenanigans. I cannot wait to conclude my stay in this ghastly hellhole and," he took a breath before delivering his brilliant finish, "return to Africa where I belong."

Earnest rolled his eyes and stirred the simmering pot. The kid had simply walked up to the biggest, meanest Aryan in the place and started a conversation—a conversation! Not an argument. Not a fight. A conversation. What was more, Big Whitey was talking back to him. Earnest sneaked a quick glance at the two, and he was smiling.

"You…you want to go back? To Africa?" Big Whitey asked. "Where you belong?"

Clubba beamed and nodded his agreement.

"Ain't that somethin'?" he asked with a wide grin. "We been saying that for years!" Big Whitey threw back his head and let out a big laugh.

Earnest had never—not once in a decade and a half—seen Big Whitey laugh. Ever. Earnest shook his head. He couldn't believe his eyes and ears.

"Te'quan Koak, right?" Big Whitey asked. "I'd shake yer hand if mine weren't covered in crap."

"Yes," Clubba agreed. "Quite nasty."

CLANG! Earnest's huge stirring spoon slid from his hand to the floor. The noise snapped him back from his dumbfounded staring.

Big Whitey and Te'quan focused their attention toward the sound and stared at Earnest who was no fool. He wanted in on this, wanted more information on Clubba. "What make you think we want yo' uppity black African self here anyway?" Earnest shouted in his best street attitude.

Big Whitey's gaze narrowed into a warning glower. "Want som'ma me?"

The threat to fight received, Earnest turned his gaze to the floor and shook his head, "No."

Big Whitey pointed toward the door. The game over, Earnest quickened his pace and walked out. He threw Clubba a glance from the corner of his eye signaling *we'll talk later.*

"Shocking insolence," Clubba said to Big Whitey as Earnest passed. "Absolutely preposterous! In my country that behavior would get his tongue cut out or a hundred lashes minimum. People know their place over there and act accordingly, but here? I mean really."

Big Whitey seemed fascinated by everything the African said. "Never agreed on nothin' with a black man."

"I understand the racial nature of American prisons," Clubba said, "and from the reaction of that particular person, I'd have a rough time of it if not for the services I provide each gang."

Big Whitey caught the gaze of a several Aryan brothers. With a jerk of his head, he signaled for them to come over. Three tattoo-laden Aryans surrounded Clubba. Two of them glanced at Big Whitey as though looking for instruction.

He shook his head as in we ain't gonna hurt this guy. Pointing to Clubba, he asked, "What kind of services?"

"Services?" This was Clubba's game, and he played it with gleeful anticipation. "Where should I begin? Oh, my manners, gentlemen." He glanced between two Aryans. "Te'quan Koak, at your service. A pleasure to meet you."

They frowned and exchanged a confused glance before looking at Big Whitey.

Again the almost imperceptible shake of the head to signal no, don't hurt him. "Services."

"My family is from the Sudan. I'm sure you're aware of the war with those horrible Muslims," he said, referring to the most recent minority for American scorn.

Big Whitey nodded

"After we escaped," Clubba continued, "I was educated in England and my family sent me to America for additional education and to see about moving here."

The Aryans set their jaws in steely unison as though they didn't like the idea of yet another immigrant, let alone black, family moving in.

Clubba sensed the brewing agitation. "After being here for a year, I realized, who do we think we are to just move to this country?"

Three shaved heads bobbed in agreement.

"I mean it's a wonderful country, but realistically it's a white man's land, especially after they conquered the aboriginals and all. We have no more right to move here than white men—no offense," he swept his hand in an arc in front of the Aryans "have moving to Africa. Don't you agree?"

The trio of tattooed heads nodded full-fledged assent.

"After getting pissed one night, I got into a spat with a bloke on the street and hit him with a bat. That's why I'm here. After that, they called me Clubba and the nickname stuck." Clubba doubted the white gangs talked to the black ones at all, and that played into his best interests. They didn't need to know he was an actual associate of all the major black gangs in Omaha. Unless and until he wanted it known.

Big Whitey looked directly at Clubba. "What do you provide the blacks?"

The Aryans exchanged a glance as though their patience was being tried. Clubba took the clue. "It seems," he said quietly, "that no one here speaks Sudanese—not the guards or the administration. I have a cousin who visits several times a week. I pass information in Sudanese, and he takes it back to their crews in Omaha. Faster, easier, and more secure than sending coded messages or paper that's going to be seized. Harder to catch as well."

A moment of silence passed while they digested what had been offered. The Aryans glanced from one to another eventually settling on Big Whitey. "And you'd do the same for us?"

Clubba pressed his palm over his heart. "Exactly. Mister?"

The two Aryans snickered because he didn't know that he was talking to the leader of the Aryan Brotherhood. Let 'em laugh, Clubba thought. As long as he got what he wanted, let 'em laugh.

"They call me Big Whitey."

"Apropos," Clubba said. "Let me know what you want sent and when."

Big Whitey grunted and turned back to his cleaning.

His covert work successfully concluded, Clubba went back to scrubbing stainless steel. A self-satisfied smile turned up the corners of his mouth. With the Brotherhood in his pocket, he'd woven his influence everywhere. Life was good. They were all his for the taking.

CHAPTER 10

"BUT WE WERE HERE LAST MONTH!"

"Yes, Chief, we were," Lt. Thorp said, as she drove the Chief and Jake, "but that was for the initial phase of the retired officer program. This is like their grand opening. Everyone who's anyone in local government will be there—including you. These days we need your face in the media for as many positive stories as we can get."

Lt. Thorp drove the car through the main gate.

"It's awesome," Jake said. "They've got like fifty retired officers living there now that it's up and running. When it was first mentioned in the news, I thought it was a great idea. Now it's a great facility. Did they actually rebuild an old precinct?"

Lt. Thorp nodded. "Down to the minute details. It's the coolest thing you'll ever see."

The trio drove up to the imposing brick building, and the Chief surveyed the lawn and outer areas. Beautifully manicured with walking trails on the periphery and benches dotting the well-sculpted lawn, it was a place a golf lover would envy. News crews flitted through the area filming outdoor clips and preparing for the tour inside. Community representatives, neighborhood watch groups, and civic leaders rubbed elbows with state officials and an antigang group.

Approaching the main entrance and parking lot, Lt. Thorp pointed to a group of reporters approximately thirty yards south of the main doors.

"I'll handle it," Jake said. "I've got a brief statement about the Chief recognizing that these retired officers have a great deal of experience to impart through community outreach."

"That ought to play well with the citizen organizations here," she replied.

"Right," Jake said. "I'll also mention the officers' wealth of knowledge about crime and the city in general. Hopefully we'll get a good shot of the Chief and his staff entering the main doors. That should avoid any awkward front door cramming with cameras in our faces and five reporters shouting questions at him simultaneously. You agree?"

"Completely," the Chief said. "And I'll give a brief statement afterward." The Chief liked the way Jake caught onto difficult situations before they happened and always seemed to have a quick solution for them. "We'll let you off here," the Chief said.

Jake opened his door and hopped out. The car moved toward the portico, and the Chief turned around. His PIO hollered to the press who immediately called to their camera crews and sound people who gathered around for his prepared statement. Jake spoke directly to the cameras and pointed toward the doors where the Chief and Lt. Thorp would exit.

"Wow," Lt. Thorp said. "He's handling the media better than I ever thought he would or could. Looks like he's got knack for this stuff."

"That he does," responded the Chief. "I'm glad he's with us. That was a good call."

Lt. Thorp flashed a cheeky grin.

"Don't let it go to your head." In full uniform, the Chief stepped out when the driver stopped. Once Thorp joined him, they walked side-by-side to the main doors. Several facility supervisors met them. True to Jake's prediction, the media didn't crowd the entryway, and they got a nice camera shot of the procession.

Jake finished his statement and joined them.

"This is absolutely the most impressive teaching and medical treatment facility in the region," said Dr. Wicker, director of the physicians, nursing, and medical training unit. "With the State of

Nebraska Health and Human Services in the adjacent wing, we can quickly resolve any medical or social service needs for the, ah…" Dr. Wicker pointed to the closed doors of the Ol' Blues precinct, "patients."

The Chief noted his pause and stifled a chuckle at the particular challenges of having such an unusual population of clientele. If there was anything he knew, it was the cop personality. This collection of hard-nosed ex-officers was like nothing these doctors and nurses had ever seen. "I take it these Ol' Blues aren't the easiest group of people to work with?" the Chief asked with a smile.

"You could say that," Dr. Wicker said. "The hardest part is convincing them that they're actually patients."

The Chief exchanged a glance with Lt. Thorp who raised a brow in obvious agreement.

Before Dr. Wicker could say more, a reporter caught up with them. "Chief, we need a good shot of you entering the precinct."

He plastered on a well-practiced smile and turned to the reporter. "No problem," he said. Catching Jake's gaze, he motioned him forward. "Now that you're here, we can go."

Jake stood behind the Chief, and they turned toward the Ol' Blue Precinct.

"Oh, dear," the doctor said in a low, worried tone.

It hit Jake that there might be a problem with bursting directly into the precinct without knowing exactly what was happening on the other side of the entry doors thirty feet away.

The Chief started forward, and the media readied their cameras. "I understand that you let them wear specially designed uniforms."

"Well…ah…y-yes, Chief," Dr. Wicker said.

Something about the way the doc diverted his gaze and kept glancing out the corner of his eye toward the media cameras didn't sit right with Jake. There was more going on here than any of them knew.

The doctor cleared his throat. "There were…well, there still are some disagreements about how to allow that and still maintain correct medical procedures."

Jake focused on the doctor's face instead of his words. There was definitely a problem here, and whatever it might be, the doctor was stalling. The media, the Chief, and the entire entourage edged closer to the precinct doors. An entire room full of retired cops who didn't like being told what to do by civilians met modern medical protocols. If anyone knew how to make the medical staff sorry, it would be the Ol' Blues. A definite recipe for disaster.

Jake skipped ahead of the group. Twenty feet from the entrance, he grabbed the Chief's elbow. "I think you should start the tour of the state offices first," Jake said in a low tone.

He'd hoped the Chief caught his warning.

He didn't. He eased from Jake's grasp and continued toward the door and continued his conversation with the doctors.

Exasperated, Jake shot Lt. Thorp a look he hoped said *stop him*.

She squinted at him quizzically. Ten feet from the entrance her eyes widened in recognition. "An excellent idea, Jake," Lt. Thorp said. She stepped in front of the Chief, blocking any chance of entering the precinct. "The...ah...staff in the state offices are waiting."

"Nonsense," the Chief said. "I want to see the Ol' Blues and—" he reached for the door handles.

Jake held his breath. He didn't know what waited behind for them, but he doubted it was good. The Chief was two feet away...one foot... and then it was too late.

"—so do the people of Omaha." The Chief smiled and nodded at the eager media.

Jake surveyed the medical staff milling around. They exchanged worried, no, terrified gazes. The Chief swung the doors open wide. The press obtained a great over-the-shoulder shot of the Chief and shifted their focus into the Ol' Blue Precinct.

For a moment, everyone froze. Jake, Lt. Thorp, and the Chief surveyed the surroundings.

"It's like going back in time," the Chief said.

"Way back," Thorp agreed.

Officers perched behind desks in the traditional blue uniforms, complete with hats and patches. Vintage fans hummed from the top of file cabinets. "Like in the days before air conditioning," the Chief murmured.

Several men clacked away on actual typewriters, the sound echoing throughout the cavernous floor. "I've never heard that before," Jake said absently.

"It's like something out of a black-and-white movie," Lt. Thorp said. "Back in the old days when a precinct office was noisy and you had loads of investigations going on at the same time."

None of the officers even looked up.

The Chief smiled and spread his arms out as though he wanted to embrace the entire group. "Will you look at this," he said. "It's fantastic."

The Sarge glanced up. Recognition of the Omaha Police Chief lit his eyes.

Jake noticed Dr. Wicker's face. His gaze locked with the sergeant's, and the doctor seemed to be pleading *whatever you're planning, don't do it—please!*

Cameras readied, the media and medical staff stood behind them. Jake couldn't shake the aura of tension zinging up his spine.

The Sarge yanked a chewed cigar out of his mouth. "The Chief is on the floor," he called out.

Typewriters stopped. All activity halted. Every Ol' Blue shifted his attention to the group at the entrance. Chief Williams smiled and brought his hand up in a salute. In the same moment, the sergeant stiffened. "A-ttention."

Most of the old cops snapped upright; others eventually, slowly, drew up in the same stance. The Chief's eyes widened and his mouth dropped. His hand froze in midair never making it to a full salute. A deafening silence fell over the room adding to the apparently total shock of the visitors.

Dr. Wicker covered his face. A soft, "oh, no" leaked through his lips.

The Chief stayed frozen as though trying to comprehend the scene before him.

It was Jake who immediately understood. He nudged Lt. Thorp who spared him an incredulous glance.

Before the visiting dignitaries, media, staff, and police command, dozens of retired officers stood in their uniformed uppers and their indignity bottoms. They all faced different directions.

Some looked forward, their short medical robes stopping at their knees revealing black shoes, socks, and suspenders. Others stood half-turned away from the entrance; a few adult diapers were in plain view while others sported baggy underwear with catheter tubes running from an insertion point to a urine bag attached by a belt on their leg. A few let it all hang out—no underwear at all.

Cameras rolled and flashed. Not that anyone there would need to review anything. This moment was permanently burned into the memories of every visitor there.

⁂

Ten minutes passed in complete silence on the drive back to Omaha headquarters. From the backseat, the Chief broke the quiet. "You were trying to stop me, weren't you, Jake?" he asked matter-of-factly.

"Yes, sir, I was," came his muted reply.

A hush fell over the interior of the vehicle again.

Lt. Thorp pulled to the side of the road and plunked the vehicle in park.

"What—" Jake began.

"Yeah," said the Chief.

Both palms covered her face and her shoulders shook.

"Monica?" the Chief asked with a worried note in his voice.

Snort. Snort. The sound leaked through her fingers and filled the car.

"Monica!" the Chief said.

Her hands fell away from her face. She collapsed in paroxysms of uncontrolled laughter. "Admit it," she got out through another spasm of mirth. "That was the funniest thing you've ever seen!"

Jake couldn't help it. He snickered and clamped his lips together trying to stifle his urge to join her.

"Dear heaven," she said and dissolved into a renewed fit of giggles. "I have to sit here for a minute or I'm gonna pee my pants!"

Jake couldn't hold it together any longer. He disintegrated into his own chortles of merriment.

The Chief glanced upward. "I'm surrounded by idiots," he said and joined in the levity of the others.

Monica composed herself and settled the car into drive again.

The trio fell silent for another minute or two. "So," the Chief said, "other than that, Mrs. Lincoln, how was the play?"

The car came to a stop once again.

⌒

At home, Jake plopped on his couch and shook his head. The media would run that footage for at least the next week. He figured it would show up as an Omaha Press Club skit. His phone rang. Before he could say hello, hysterical laughter came from the other end.

"Hey, Ben," he said to his brother. "Let me guess. You saw a promotional clip for the six o'clock news with a bunch of pantless old men in police shirts."

"Yeah! You should've seen your face!" his brother said. "Can't wait to see the full report!" A renewed round of guffaws came through the phone. "Oh, man! Jake what have you gotten yourself into?"

Jake sighed and raked a hand through his hair. "I know the Chief stepped in it today, Ben, but he's a good guy. I like him and this work has been good for me. It forces me to think about a million other things besides myself."

His brother was quiet for a moment. "Just say the word and you can work for me any time. You know that, little brother, right?"

"Sure but being the personal bodyguard of my big brother isn't my thing. Not right now anyway."

Ben had moved to Omaha twenty-five years ago and made his fortune developing call centers. In the eighties, the Midwest had been the perfect place for telemarketing startups: good work ethic, no accent. Anyone anywhere could understand the telemarketers. Ben's telemarketing empire laid the groundwork for both inbound and outbound phone sales. Cable was a natural expansion, and Ben expanded to serving inbound infomercial calls. There wasn't a day that went by that Jake didn't see Ben's handiwork on some channel. It had made him millions; he was currently a soft-spoken billionaire. It was Ben who'd talked Jake into moving to Omaha and joining OPD.

"You know, I had no idea I'd see you on national television."

"Ha, ha," Jake said.

"Seriously," Ben said, "that was the funniest, most uncomfortable thing I've ever seen. It was great!"

"Glad I could make your day."

"Actually," Ben said, "I should probably come clean. I'm part of the committee that made the facility a reality."

"What?" Jake gripped the phone a little tighter. "Then this was your fault. I'm tellin' Mom!" he said in his best indignant tone. He chuckled. "Sounds like something you'd get yourself into, though. It really was impressive. There are so many cops who just retire and lose their zest for life. The next thing you know they end up dying soon after retirement. Jeez, listen to me get all sappy. Tell me about your committee."

Ben paused a moment.

"Come on," Jake said, "out with it."

"We call ourselves The Bureau. It's just a group of like-minded individuals with similar resources. We get together once a month and discuss various issues and what we can do to facilitate a solution to the problem."

"Like-minded and with similar resources, Ben?" Jake asked. "More like a billionaire social club. Mighty small club."

"Actually," Ben said, "Omaha has more millionaires and billionaires than most places. We don't show it off like people in other parts of the country. It's not the Midwestern way."

"I'll give you that, Ben. If I wasn't your brother, I wouldn't know you were loaded."

"Thanks. I think. We started this over a year ago, decided to design and fund the facility you saw today."

"It was incredible," Jake said.

"That's what the rest of the world sees too," Ben said. "But there's much more—" Ben stopped talking abruptly. "We're very proud of what we've accomplished there."

Ever the cop, Jake noted the brusque shift in Ben's conversation. It was more than weird, but this wasn't the time for questioning; he was his brother after all. But, still, it bothered him. A lot. Jake decided to stow the information in his mental file and wait until the time was right.

᠆

A plasma TV perched in a corner of the commons area. Twenty-five inmates surrounded it; three guards watched through their security monitors. Chaos erupted.

"Diapers! Some of them cops wearin' diapers!" The inmates fell back into their chairs and hollered with laughter.

"Tonight at six and ten o'clock, watch what made the new Chief of Police freeze—" the news anchor read the teleprompter without cracking a smile as the camera cut to the wide-eyed, open-mouthed stare of Williams and followed his line of sight into the Ol' Blue Precinct, "when he received a bare-all welcome at the new retirement home for police officers."

"Oh," one inmate yelled from the back of the room, "you know I'm watch'in that!"

"Oh yeah!" another chimed in. "Prime time viewing."

The news spread quickly. Nobody would miss this.

CHAPTER 11

DR. WICKER, HIS STAFF, AND SEVERAL STATE WORKERS milled around inside the staff lounge, their attention focused on the television. Slumped in a wooden chair, elbows on the table, and chin resting on the palm of his right hand, Dr. Wicker shook his head. He spoke through his fingers, almost afraid of the upcoming news program.

"This is going to be a disaster," he said. "An unmitigated disaster."

"Nah," Nurse Betsy tossed out. Known as Boss Nurse by most everyone, she shrugged the imminent broadcast off.

"If you're trying to comfort me," Dr. Wicker said, "it's not working."

"It's not that bad. I know these Ol' Blues can be difficult to deal with sometimes."

"Sometimes?" Wicker interrupted. "How many times have they literally run us out of there? And always due to—" he sliced his index and middle fingers through the air, "quote, police business, unquote." He slumped further into his chair. "Betsy, I honestly think they don't realize they aren't cops anymore. They treat us like we're in their way, that somehow we keep them from doing their job. It's absurd."

"It's all they got," Betsy said. "Let 'em have that at least."

"Yesterday," he continued as though she hadn't spoken, "during rounds, one of them actually threatened me with arrest."

Betsy's face ignited into a full smile. "No, they didn't."

"Yes. Obstruction of justice if I didn't get out of his way."

"What the devil?" Betsy asked no one in particular. "Guess it's hard to give up the power. What else could he have been talking about?"

"No clue," Dr. Wicker said.

The new nursing instructor Jaiden Walsh spoke, "We knew going in that this was going to be a facility like nothing we'd ever seen."

"True," Dr. Wicker said, "but what we didn't know was how stubborn these old guys can be. One time I entered the precinct office to visit a patient and was told he was busy. Would it be possible to meet with another officer from the same unit? I tried to explain that I had to see that particular officer who was my patient."

"And?" Betsy asked.

"And was told to take a seat. I'm a doctor. I don't take seats and wait to see a patient!"

"Well, I just started here," nurse Walsh said, "but I'm sure that if we just work with them, they can and will be quite amicable."

Dr. Wicker rolled his gaze to the ceiling. "Give me strength."

"Um," nurse Walsh interjected, "they do take particular interest in humiliating the students. They call them rookies and always insist on getting shots in their buttocks instead of their arms."

"What's the problem?" Dr. Wicker asked.

"Some of the newbies," the instructor said. "One poor CNA student gave me such a pleading look, and before I could say a word, the cop stood up, spun around, and spread his robe—or whatever they're calling them these days."

"Indignity bottoms," Betsy said.

"Anyway, he spread it wide open exposing his bare backside and anything else that happened to be hanging around. 'Okay, rookie,' he said, 'gimme your best shot.'"

Wicker exchanged a glance with Betsy.

The instructor held up her hand. "I'm not done. Each and every other patient," her voice dripped with sarcasm, "started whistling, clapping, or cheering. They fell all over themselves and one another trying to line up for the same thing."

"O…kay," Betsy said. "They can be tough."

"They're wantonly ridiculous," nurse Walsh said. "That student burst into tears and ran out the front door. I haven't seen her since!"

"Bet she won't have to put up with that at the Metro or Clarkson nursing programs," Betsy said. "You'd best warn those kids in the acceptance interview that these guys will try to crack them. They need to be tough nuts."

She stood to leave, stopped as though something had grabbed her thoughts. "And next time they pull that garbage, use a bigger needle. They tried that with me too," she said and held up an index finger. "Once." What could only be called an evil grin on her face, Betsy gave a curt nod. "Humph," she added a satisfied grunt. "Haven't tried it since."

Betsy turned up the television volume. The nightly broadcast brought the two anchors into view. "When we come back," the good-looking young man said into the teleprompter, "we'll show you the video that has all of Omaha in an uproar."

A young woman with piercing blue eyes smiled. "Hail to the Cheeks in a moment," she said coyly.

"H-Hail to the Cheeks," Dr. Wicker muttered and covered his face.

"It won't be that bad," Betsy said. "They can't put bare butt cheeks on television."

A teaser shot of the Ol' Blues, their exposed wrinkled backsides covered by a superimposed yellow happy face to shield delicate viewer eyes, faded to a commercial.

"Uh…" Betsy didn't move her head; she shifted her gaze to Dr. Wicker and started to laugh. "That was their butt cheeks on TV."

Behind a Formica tabletop, Wicker plopped his face into his folded arms. The Boss Nurse's smile widened. "I stand corrected."

"Oh, dear." The words came out as a muffled moan. It was all he could manage.

§

The evening crew of guards checked in and headed to their assignments. In Clubba's wing, the CO's brows knit in confusion at the crowd gathered in front of the television.

"Is there a fight on?" he asked a departing day shifter.

"Glad to get out of here," the second man said. "And no. No fight." He jerked his head toward the commons. "You'd better see that."

In the middle of a large group of inmates, Clubba laughed and joked in preparation of seeing the police look stupid. Earnest liked the back of the group; that way he watched the interaction of everybody there. From that he could gather what was going on with each. This time there was no one flashing a gang sign. No one offered anyone else a dirty look. No one dissed anybody's girl or group or anything else. They all focused intently on what had embarrassed the police chief today.

"Good evening," the news anchor said cheerily. "There have been numerous occasions for the local police chief to attend public gatherings. Some of them include appearances for civic groups. Others are more formal as when new officers are sworn in. Earlier today the Chief was a guest in a very special facility."

"But I doubt it was the reception he's used to," his female companion said with a smirk.

"They callin' it 'Hail to the Cheeks!'" an inmate hooted.

"Our onsite reporter, Rob Carson, was there for all the details. Rob, what happened down there today?"

A young man in his twenties stood outside the new police officers' retirement home. "That's right. The Live-at-Five news team were inside this facility earlier today. As the Chief walked through, he got quite the surprise from some of these "Ol' Blues" as they're calling themselves. According to sources at the facility, these men don't like wearing the hospital gowns—you know, the gowns everyone that's ever been to a hospital knows about. The ones that don't close in the back." Not a wisp of amusement touched the reporter's face. "It seems that the medical staff and caseworkers compromised with the men by allowing them a police uniform shirt. That's just a shirt; the bottom half of the gown had to stay. It appears that the retired officers were very unhappy with the situation as you can see."

The reporter ducked his head and the channel ran footage of the Chief opening the doors to the Ol' Blue Precinct.

"Things started off quite well, as you can see. When the doors opened, it was like a time capsule. They even had typewriters and officers talking on the phones to neighborhood watch groups and other civic organizations. Everything went smoothly...for a few moments. Once the sergeant of the precinct saw the Chief of Police at the door, the Ol' Blues made their protest."

Tape rolled, showing the Sarge calling attention and all officers regardless of which way they were facing standing at attention.

"And I have to add this scene even caught me off guard," the reporter continued. "I doubt it was what the Chief had anticipated in response to his visit."

Whatever the reporter said after that couldn't be heard over the din in Clubba's wing. Every inmate pointed and laughed so loud that the volume could have been on high and they still wouldn't have heard. The sight of the old cops melted them into gales of hysteria. The camera panned back to the Chief in his frozen salute.

"Needless to say," the reporter said, "the Chief was stunned." The tape rolled and caught Chief Williams, eyes wide, mouth frozen in an open *oh*.

The group toppled in renewed laughter. The volume of the TV had no meaning. The camera panned back to the precinct. A very short man faced the camera at full attention.

The revelry stopped abruptly for Clubba. The recognition was immediate. His fingers curled into a fist, and he hit his thigh in reaction. He wanted nothing more than to pound the little man into oblivion.

Two inmates sitting beside Clubba stopped mid-laugh and moved off to the side. Most looked at each other, shrugged, and went back to watching the television as though they were used to Clubba's antics.

Earnest, too, had an instantaneous realization. Clubba's response interested Earnest who turned his attention to the cop, Tiny. His time was coming.

"We'll turn it back to you," the reporter said.

In the newsroom, the anchor tried to maintain his composure. His companion was losing hers. "Thank you..." she finally said. "We'll be—" Her mouth opened but nothing else came out. "We'll—"

High fives reigned in the commons area of Clubba's wing. Other inmates still chuckled, and even the guards got a good laugh at the Chief's expense. Clubba, however, wasn't laughing. It didn't escape Earnest's notice.

There was something in that newscast that really got to Clubba. The kid might be a decent ally once Clubba got out. He needed to know what it was about the group of Ol' Blues that made the man react so strongly. After all, a young man with that much anger could be quite useful.

CHAPTER 12

FOR THE PAST FEW MONTHS, SHANESE AND HER LITTLE sister, Melia, had been staying with their grandmother. She knew it was just a matter of time until Clubba's boys figured out where she was hiding. Shanese had more information on Clubba—stuff that had nothing to do with his threats against her. He'd make good on those just for fun, but there was another side to it as well: business. One way or another, he'd make sure she didn't talk.

She'd been with him long enough to have realized that he loved to watch the look of terror on his enemies' faces once they realized his game: getting them "his way." It was bad news all around. Either he'd beat the person senseless with his bat, and they'd die or wish they had. If he let them live, they got instructions to do exactly what Clubba wanted when he wanted it. Life was easy. Do what you're told or your family was next. Clubba made believers of everyone in the neighborhood. Nobody doubted him and nobody ever crossed him— until Shanese and her sister.

She was as good as dead. So was Melia. Just talking to another guy was insult number one. Two was when her sister recorded his threats, and three was taking the evidence to the authorities. One way or another, Clubba was going to get them. Both of them.

Melia would most likely be first. That way he could immerse himself in the pain all around: Melia's would be physical. Shanese's would be emotional from what happened to her sibling and their grandmother's anguish for them both—Shanese couldn't even think of it. She wasn't sure her grandmother would live through it. Regret washed over her. She should have kept her mouth shut. Then none of this would be on their heads.

From two buildings to the west, Shanese could see her grandmother's ground-floor apartment. Things were quiet and peaceful here on Etna, and she should be grateful—and would be any other time. Deep foreboding filled her.

Shanese picked her way along a windy path. This had seemed like such a good idea in the beginning. It was the first—and safest— place she could think of. Her grandmother was surrounded by plenty of people her age. In fact, lots of older people lived in the subsidized building. The gangs didn't pay much attention to them.

She and her sister had quietly moved in late at night so as not to arouse attention. Lots of other elderly men moved in too. First an old white man and his son came about three weeks after Shanese and Melia. They lived directly above them. They were nice enough, Shanese supposed; they said they ran a small audio-visual equipment rental store, and it must've been true because she'd seen them hauling in different cameras and lots of electronic wires and equipment.

Once they'd settled in, though, neither Shanese nor her grandmother saw them much. They heard them walking around, but the guys pretty much kept to themselves. Four more had moved in after that, and they seemed to be everywhere. Mostly they wandered around, talked to each other a lot and played checkers. Shanese shrugged and watched two of them loudly discussing their current game. No wonder the bangers didn't care about this place; there was nothing to do. Boredom was one way to prevent gang activity, she guessed.

A loud laugh drew her attention across the street. Two Sudanese teens circled around and nodded toward the apartment complex; fear skittered along her spine. Clubba's thugs. It had to be.

Young men didn't just come around and walk through this area. No, they were here for a specific reason. One of them boldly stared directly at Shanese. Her breath caught in her throat. She knew him from the day at the courthouse, the day Clubba got sentenced. The thug pointed directly at Shanese, then turned and said something to his companion. The other thug in turn snapped his head toward Shanese. She stood rooted to the spot, frozen in a dark, anxious spiral. They stood there for what seemed like a decade, but it couldn't have been more than a few minutes. She knew their game. They needed to make sure she saw them. The first, bolder one pulled a cell phone out of his pocket. Speaking fluent Sudanese, he grew more animated, yelling excitedly into his phone and pointing a finger at her.

They stayed where they were and didn't venture across the street. They were the surveillance—observing, waiting, and watching like a couple of vultures with their prey. Her initial fright dissipated; self-preservation took over. Backing up until she came to the corner of a second building, she sidled between them and turned toward the back door of her grandmother's apartment. She didn't run directly to the door, but zigzagged between a couple of buildings so that Clubba's henchmen lost sight of her. Then while still shielded by buildings and some bushes sprinted with all she had toward her objective.

"Please be open," she pleaded to anyone in the universe who might be listening. The sliding glass doors of her grandmother's apartment in sight, she ran full speed toward it and grasped the handle in a firm grip. With a final glance over her shoulder to make sure no one had spotted the exact place where she was staying, she exhaled in relief and yanked to open it. Three inches in, it stopped with a thud. Panic consumed her. She glanced around trying to see Clubba's thugs. She saw no one. Their goal was to pinpoint her exact location. She tugged on the handle again, and once more it jolted to an abrupt stop.

"No," she said out loud and fought back tears. Grandma always kept a small wooden broom handle, a homemade charley bar, in the bottom grooves. The door wouldn't budge. She knocked on the glass and tried to keep it quiet. That was a laugh. A tear slid down her cheek. It was just a matter of time until his thugs would have her cornered. She didn't know where else to run, where else to turn. A shout from some men in a language she didn't understand came from behind her. She couldn't make it out but it sounded angry. It seemed to come from where she'd last seen Clubba's guys.

Then from directly in front of her came a yell, "What you want?" Her grandmother tore back the curtain with her left hand and wielded a large metal serving spoon in the other. She obviously didn't expect to see her granddaughter, Shanese, on the other side. Her dark eyes widened, filled with fear. In a heartbeat, the charley bar was gone and the door opened.

"What is it, baby?"

"Clubba's homies," Shanese breathed out. She couldn't keep the tremor out of her voice. "They saw me...I think they're calling others." The initial panic over, Shanese collapsed onto a couch and buried her head in her hands.

Her grandmother glanced right and left, then closed the back door and jerked the curtains into place. "Did they see you come in here?"

"I don't think so, no, but they were yelling about something. I could hear them, but I couldn't make out the words. I don't think they saw me, but they were definitely trying to find me. It sounded like they were running up and down the street to see which apartment I entered."

Shanese drew in a deep breath in an attempt to calm, if not herself, at least her voice. She willed herself to slow her breathing. Her gaze darted around the small apartment. "Where's Melia?"

"In her bedroom playing a video game."

Shanese relaxed and turned her head to face her grandmother. "What exactly were you going to do with that?"

She nodded at the gigantic serving utensil still clenched in her grandmother's right hand. Grandma let it slide onto a countertop where it landed with a hard metallic clang. "Child, I don't know. Guess I'd slam the knuckles of anyone trying to get into my house."

The mental image brought up a giggle. Shanese had no doubt that, if necessary, Grandma would not only slam their knuckles, but she'd chase Clubba's thugs down the hall, out the door, and through the courtyard of the entire complex.

The smile on her lips evaporated. Shanese wished she could have made out what they were hollering about. They should have been right behind her...should have beaten her right outside her home. Her grandmother and kitchen weapon wouldn't have stood a chance. She shook her head. It didn't add up. Why didn't they find her? As she thought about it in the cool aftermath, it might have been an argument. The shouting had sounded odd, like four or five guys mixing it up. But there had only been two...and she couldn't make out the words. Shanese closed her eyes allowing the relief of being safe and home drift over her. At least, she thought, they don't know which apartment.

&

Shanese wasn't the only one who'd spotted Clubba's boys on the other side of the street. From the vantage point above her grandmother's apartment, another set of eyes watched the varied entryways to the complex on digital monitors. They'd been spotted five minutes before Shanese had even known of their presence.

The over surveillance had been assigned to Tiny who still whistled through his dentures. With all the assignments and cases handed out, he just hadn't had time to get it fixed. As much as he'd enjoyed infuriating Clubba at his arrest and trial, Tiny knew they had to keep up the pressure. He wanted Clubba's focus on him and not the young lady in the apartment below.

The Ol' Blue lab tech, Michael Beckham, masqueraded as his son. Tiny had begrudgingly accepted him after the Sarge insisted. Beckham was handpicked by The Bureau member Steve DeGoff as the lead for all covert operations. Seemed DeGoff persuaded the kid to work for him instead of NSA. Still, in Tiny's book the kid was just another civilian. He threw the younger man a glance and exhaled a long breath. As long as the kid didn't slow him down, Tiny supposed it was fine.

From the apartment window Tiny spotted the two young bangers approaching half a block away. "Got ya," Tiny blurted out. Then an unintelligible combination of sounds. "Ha ja brick!" as his body jerked and fumbled like he was holding a hot potato.

His enthusiasm shot his lower dentures out of his mouth, and they clacked against the window. "Aw, nuts," he half whistled and half hissed. He reached out to catch them with his right hand and succeeded in slamming his binoculars against the window.

"Jeez!" His cohort jumped, spilling his thirty-two-ounce soda on his lap. "You're freakin' me out here. What's up?" Glancing at the ground, he spotted Tiny's dentures. "Oh."

Reaching down, Tiny picked up his choppers, brushed them off, and popped them back in. "Crap," he muttered.

"Dude, you need to get those fixed."

"After this job," Tiny said and with a sidelong glance added, "I wasn't talking about my teeth; I was talking about this." He nodded outside toward the east entrance.

The tech just stared at his monitor, his eyes narrowing as he scanned for whatever Tiny was talking about.

"Get out from behind that desk," the older officer said grabbing him by the shoulder and shoved him toward the window. "Look!"

The tech blinked and scanned the area Tiny was waving toward. "What's the ruckus?"

"Across the street?" Tiny asked. "The two standing there?"

Beckham surveyed the area. "Two of what?"

Exasperated, Tiny grabbed the younger man's chin and pointed him directly at Clubba's boys. "Them…those two guys hanging out. They look Sudanese and they're wearing the super large white T-shirts. I'll bet they work for Clubba."

The tech frowned at Tiny. "How do you look Sudanese?"

Tiny shook his head in disdain. "Tall, slender, and very dark skinned."

"Really?" the tech went back to his monitor and zoomed in on the guys Tiny pointed out. "I had no idea."

"Yeah, Sherlock," Tiny mumbled, "no sh—"

"What'd you say?"

"Nothing. Get me Pauli and Tony on the radio," Tiny said.

"No problem." The younger man grabbed the radio, and in a second Pauli and Tony both responded.

"Hey Tiny, what you got?"

Tiny held the microphone in his right hand and glanced over the tech's shoulder at the monitor. "Looks like Clubba's guys finally found the apartment complex. My guess is they don't know which apartment is Shanese's grandmother's, but they're gonna watch—what…wait a—"

"What?" asked Pauli.

"Wait for what?" Tony asked.

"Shanese is down there," Tiny said, "walking by the buildings toward the south entrance."

"So?"

"So she just looked over and saw them. Nuts! And they spotted her. She's running from them!"

Shanese zigzagged through the courtyard and Tiny smiled. "She's a smart girl," he said, "she isn't running directly back to her grandmother's; she's running between the two buildings."

"We're on our way," Pauli said.

From above, Tiny watched him and Tony work their way over to the location of the Sudanese gangsters. One of them pulled out a cell phone and punched in a phone number. Probably putting the word out that they'd found Shanese.

Beckham followed the drama as it played out on screen. "Tell Tony to watch the guy on the phone."

Tiny shot him a questioning look.

"I can record what he's saying—while he's on the phone! Tell him that. Now!"

Tiny gave a small shrug. "Tony, keep your eyes on the guy with the phone. Super scientist here can record his calls." Tiny gave the tech a sideways glance. "You can do that?"

The tech nodded. "Yep. The glasses record audio and visual."

Actually impressed, Tiny smiled. "I love ya, kid!"

"Can't get that from binoculars," the tech said with a smirk.

"Don't get cocky on me."

"The other guy's running up the sidewalk," the tech said.

Tiny pulled his field glasses up to his eyes again. "Probably trying to keep an eye on Shanese…not really following her."

Michael asked, "Just trying to find out where she's going?"

"Yeah," Tiny said. "That's what it looks like."

"Weird," the tech replied. "Why not chase her into the complex?"

Tiny thought about the odd behavior. Weird indeed. Turning the thought over in his head, he scrunched his lips to the side and rubbed his chin. "I'd bet the mortgage they were instructed not to. If they did, it would be obvious witness tampering. My guess is that Clubba explicitly said to just watch her. Make sure she stays right here."

The under surveillance duo, Pauli and Tony, wound their way toward the two bangers. They couldn't really sprint. Instead they broke into something that could only be called a goosey jog. A floor above, Tiny laughed out loud.

Tony fixed his attention on the one talking into the phone. The kid sounded excited, and he threw his opposite hand around in silent explanation.

The other guy stared at the apartments and followed Shanese's progress.

"Pauli," Tiny barked into the radio. "Throw a piss pack at the one on the horn."

The tech shot him a questioning look.

"Watch and be amazed," Tiny said with a smirk.

Tiny and his "son" watched from above. From his fanny pack, Pauli pulled out a plastic bag about the size of a small water balloon and filled with something that appeared dark yellow. With deadly aim, he tossed it at the kid on the phone. It splattered directly in front of him exploding in a burst of putrid urine.

"Got him," Tiny said with a chortle. "Dead-eye got another one."

The banger stopped and looked down at where the pack had hit and then at his clothes. The hand with the phone dropped to his side. Tiny knew the moment the smell enveloped the thug; he turned away to drag in a lungful of clean air.

Pauli and Tony had made it to the middle of the street when the kid noticed them.

He yelled something in Sudanese.

They yelled back in Italian.

As near as Tiny could tell from the street-level ballet before him, between the shock of being sprayed, the stench of the days' old urine, and the confusion of two animated Italian men, the thug looked totally confused. He bellowed at his companion. The second one stopped watching Shanese and came running. Before he reached his partner, he skidded to a stop about ten feet away. Three angry men, two languages, one dust up. He didn't go any closer to his partner whose overlarge white shirt now held yellowish-brown stains.

"Dumbfounded," Tiny said. "That's what he is."

"Exactly what it looks like to me," the tech replied.

"See," Tiny said, "those piss bags confuse everyone who gets hit with 'em. It stops 'em in their tracks, which is what we wanted. And his buddy stopped looking for Shanese." He jerked his thumb toward the opposite window. "She just ran to the back of the building; probably going the patio door, smart girl."

"I've heard you guys love to toss those things." The tech shook his head as though he'd never seen anything like it. "Do they come in different sizes?"

"Of course they come in different sizes," Tiny said. "Some are small enough to fit in our pockets or fanny packs; bigger ones go in the compartment on a walker."

"Isn't that dangerous?"

"Sometimes—not often—they break."

The tech scrunched his face in disgust.

"At our age the nurses figure we wet ourselves. They clean us up and that's that. Except for the occasion when someone does wet themselves," he said with a frown. "But it's all worth it to see those hoods' faces," Tiny continued with a laugh. "They're completely disoriented."

The tech shared Tiny's laughter.

"In a minute or two, they'll figure out that the cops might show up. My guess is they'll skedaddle. That'll buy us some time," Tiny said.

"How much?"

"Don't really know. They'll be back, and next time with the rest of Clubba's hoods."

A long pause hung in the air before Tiny snapped back to the assignment at hand. "We're going to need more surveillance equipment out here," he said. "We need to watch everything."

"Why?" Beckham asked. "Don't we have enough to collar those two clowns?"

"We will once we get the conversation translated," Tiny said. "They haven't actually done anything yet. Hopefully we can set them up with witness tampering. We might get more than just two thrown into jail."

"Well," the younger man said, "I got everything he said on the phone recorded."

"Let's get it to the lab." Tiny watched the chaos below. As predicted, Clubba's boys turned around, said something to each other, and left. Pauli and Tony continued haranguing them, but they didn't understand a word they said.

Tiny smiled at the brothers. Clubba's hoods scurried away but not before bellowing something back in Sudanese. Probably a threat, not that it mattered. The Chelinis each cracked a smile at the departing bangers and started to laugh.

Pauli waved at the camera location. "How was that, Tiny? You see that idiot's face when his shirt got soaked with piss? I almost laughed right there!"

"You guys were great," Tiny said. "Nolan Ryan couldn't have delivered a better pitch. Now let's get this information back to the Sarge and plan our next move."

"You got it."

⁓

Tiny informed his superior about the afternoon's events.

"Good work," the Sarge replied. "We'll get the boys in the lab to set up additional surveillance."

"We've got good camera coverage here," Tiny said. "I'd suggest we set up a couple cable repair vans on the perimeter. Those goofs seemed really careful not to cross the street. My guess is that they'll stay outside the apartment area itself."

"Afraid to cross the street?"

"Yeah," Tiny said. "Wouldn't even come over to follow the girl."

"You're probably right," the Sarge said. "Get back here and we'll figure out the rest of our plans."

"Will do," Tiny said.

The Sarge hung up his phone. "And now to set the trap..."

CHAPTER 13

THE OL' BLUES ESPECIALLY LOOKED FORWARD TO Tuesdays when Smitty's daughter, Brittany, brought dozens of homemade treats. She'd meander throughout the precinct dispensing small talk and goodies to every Blue but particularly the ones without family or whose family couldn't make it in for a visit. They returned her smiles and laughed at her lighthearted teasing. Invariably she landed five to six marriage proposals per visit—especially after they tasted her cookies.

Try as they may, none of the guys could ever get the best of her. And try they did. Cops were natural pranksters, but Brittany was used to it; she'd grown up listening to her father's stories. Armed with that imparted knowledge, she always seemed to know what to expect. But it was more than that; she simply had a way with people. Add to that over a year of her service as a missionary in the Sudan, and she'd returned a remarkable young woman. Always kind and compassionate by nature, those qualities had grown almost to perfection in her father's eyes. Plus she had the ability to understand and speak fluent Sudanese.

Smitty didn't know which trait he loved most. It didn't matter that she hadn't graduated from college in any of the half dozen majors she'd chosen. He guessed it was a woman's prerogative to change her mind, but this kid's educational record was getting ridiculous. She'd try one major for a semester, then change her mind by the summer. It drove Smitty crazy and filled him with concern for his daughter's future. Marriage wouldn't be a bad thing either in his mind. He wanted a couple of grandchildren to play with before he died. Knowing his daughter well, it would happen in her own good time.

The main doors of the retirement center burst open. Brittany strode through with boxes of home-baked delights. "Hey, there," she said with a chin lift of acknowledgment toward the nurses.

Calls of recognition from the staff filled the hall, and she shifted a box onto the head nurse's desk. "Sweets for the sweet," she said with a grin.

"Thanks, Brit," the nurse said. "Again."

"No problem." As per her usual routine, Brittany started her rounds in the rear wing where the bedridden officers stayed. Two proposals later, she wound her way through the passages dropping off cookies and a hefty dollop of tenderness. An hour later, she headed into the precinct to see her father and the officers he hung with. She entered through the back doors and trekked down to the officers' personal rooms.

As often as she'd been there, there was always someone to greet her or announce her visit to the Sarge. That, she thought, was odd. "If I didn't know better I'd think you guys had an early warning system at my approach." She said it jokingly, but a current of seriousness lay beneath the surface of her words.

Inevitably, the officers shrugged it off with the standard, "It's just procedure."

She wasn't so sure. They always acted as if they had something to hide.

Moseying down the corridor, she noticed a large group of officers in the Sarge's office. The lights were off, and rapt attention from all attendees focused toward the front of the room. Heading for the open door, no one even noticed her. Conversation focused on a security video that the Sarge was lecturing on. Not wanting to interrupt, Brittany slipped into a chair in the back and watched.

"This," the Sarge said, "is the video from the capture of the purse snatchers at the Southern Wheel Mall. Notice how the spike sticks were placed. An excellent job. The punks didn't even notice you. Bensen, you placed yourself right where you could fill the cab of the vehicle with pepper spray, and Smitty," the Sarge said with a hearty laugh, "you just couldn't resist, could you?"

In the back, Brittany perked up. Smitty? Why was he talking about her dad? With a frown, she focused her attention at the ongoing video. Several old men yelled at a woman who turned and ran back into the mall. The apparent robbers ran toward a car—to get away she realized. One elderly gent with a walker, something he obviously didn't need, pulled out what looked like a large water balloon. Brittany strained to make out his face, stunned when the camera showed the man with a walker turn and the face was undeniable. *Dad!*

She watched in horror as he chucked the bag at one of the robbers, hitting him smack in his chest. The room erupted in whoops and hollers like something one hears on Super Bowl Sunday. Some of her father's compatriots pounded him on his back. Brittany shook her head, unwilling to believe what she'd seen. Not possible. Not her father.

"Okay, now for case at hand: surveillance from Sixtieth and Etna. Tiny got some good video of what happened there, but we also got great audio. We've got surveillance cameras throughout the inner part of the apartment complex here." He pointed at the schematic. "And here, but we didn't have a lot outside. That'll change soon. The boys in the lab are setting things up as we speak. We'll have converted the vans into cable repair vehicles with twelve cameras and mikes across the street. By tomorrow the entire place will be surrounded."

He sounded extremely pleased with himself, Brittany thought.

"Tony recorded the punk's phone conversation," the Sarge continued. "Unfortunately, we don't have a clue what he was saying because it was all in Sudanese. We don't speak it, and those who do won't talk to us, but you can bet he let the rest of the gang know he found Shanese and where. We doubt that they figured out which specific apartment. Not that it matters because from their behavior, they've got orders not to go onto the property. It'll be enough of a reminder for Shanese that Clubba knows where she is."

The Sarge turned up the volume and played the audio. Clear baritone words chattered out into the air. The end showed Pauli and Tony throwing yet another liquid-filled balloon at the guy on the phone and yelling their own response.

"So, boys," the Sarge said. "Who wants to try Google translate on this?"

"Tried it before, doesn't work so good," one man said.

"Don't even bother," another chimed in. "It can give you a general idea but other than that—" He shrugged his indifference.

"Okay then, since we can't understand what they're saying, we'll have to figure out their plans another way. Makes it doubly hard to combat what they're doing, but—"

The sound of a female voice from behind them by the front door of his office stopped him cold.

"He said," Brittany offered from her seat in the back, "that Clubba's instructions from prison were that he only wanted Sudanese soldiers, no American gangs. They'll be there tomorrow night, and they're to stay for the next month until Clubba gets out. He said Clubba specifically said not to go near her, only let her see that his soldiers are there...and she better not talk."

The lights flicked on. Every head in the room turned around to see the translator. Brittany pulled her hand from the light switch, crossed her arms, and glared at everyone she saw in the room.

"She gets that from her mother," Smitty said.

She shot her father daggers. "Oh, I haven't finished," she said. "In the last part, he talked about getting hit by yellow slime. Yellow slime?"

She glanced at each officer in the room. At least they all had the decency to look chagrined. "What...are...you...all...doing?"

The Ol' Blues glanced back and forth at each other and almost in unison turned to Smitty in a silent plea. "Um, hi, sweetie," he said sheepishly.

⸎

"Don't you 'sweetie' me."

It didn't take much to set Brittany's ire boiling.

"Oh my goodness...oh my goodness...oh my goodness gracious!" She paced back and forth in front of where her father sat.

"Now, listen, honey. You have to settle down and—"

"Settle down?" she asked through clenched teeth. "Settle down? I just watched my retired father and"—stabbing her index finger at each occupant, she continued her tirade—"every one of you in some sort of vigilante type of…thingie!"

"Actually it's an undercover operation," one of the Blues murmured.

"Under…I don't care what you call it. Have you all lost your minds?"

"No need to freak out," another Blue said calmly. "It's not what you think."

Whirling to face the man, she plopped her hands on her hip like a mother lecturing an errant teen. "It isn't?"

He squirmed in his chair. "W…well actually," he began but withered under her glare. "I guess it pretty much is exactly what it looks like."

Smitty rolled his eyes. "Oh good, Sam. Way to settle her down."

"Settle me down?" Brittany crossed to face her father. "Tell me you're not going out and arresting people! Oh, Daddy, no."

Smitty wouldn't lie to her and she knew it. "Sweetie, absolutely not," he said. "We're not arresting anyone, just getting information to help the police is all."

"Is all?" Brittany asked, incredulous at what she heard. "I just watched you throw a water balloon at a purse snatcher at a mall parking lot!"

"Actually," an anonymous voice from the group said, "it was a piss pack."

"Piss pack?" she echoed and turned in the general direction of the comment. "As in urine-filled water balloons?" Her widened eyes bespoke her disbelief at what she was hearing.

"You guys aren't helping here," Smitty said loud enough for everyone to hear.

"Helping?" She continued. "Help me what, Daddy? Settle down? Calm down? Understand this insanity? How much? Enough that I'll meekly go back to being a good little girl who brings cookies to all you poor little men in desperate need of visitors?" She said through gritted teeth.

A chorus of, "I like your cookies," rebounded through the room.

Brittany glanced up toward the ceiling. A long breath of exasperation flew through her lips along with a hearty, "Arrggh! I can't believe this—you guys," she said as she glared at first one Blue then another and another until she'd eyed them all.

"And you—" She pointed to the man seated by her father. "With the walker. You use that to fight off crooks when they attack you?"

The Blue pulled the walker close to him for fear she may take it away from him. "I—that is," he struggled for an answer. "Well," he finally said, "it does shoot pepper spray."

Spinning around she focused on another Blue. "And you…with the cane. I suppose that's really a…a…gun or rifle or something," she raised both hands in growing frustration. "Right?" she hoped her words sounded as sarcastic as she wanted.

He opened his mouth, closed it, and thought for a moment. "It's a camera and shoots pepper spray." The Blue tried to show her how it worked.

"Brittany!" Smitty called across the room. "Let me explain." He stretched out his hands as though trying to calm her.

"I don't need your explanations," she snapped back. "I heard all I need and I am going to—" She halted, information finally connecting in her brain filtering through her outrage. She turned and looked back at the first Blue she'd yelled at—the one with the walker. "You," she said and pointed directly at his nose. "Did I hear you right? That thing shoots pepper spray?"

Nodding, he pointed to a nozzle out of the handle and smiled. "Yep."

Brittany pulled her hands up to her temples. "Seriously! And you?" She shot a scathing glare back at the Blue with the cane. "Camera and pepper spray?"

A huge grin split his face; his upper dentures started to fall out. With a practiced hand, he grabbed them. "Uh-huh," he said with an affirmative nod and gave her a thumbs-up.

Her mouth dropped open and she closed it again. "I don't believe it," she said and glanced around the room again seeing the walking aids with new eyes. Her anger dissipated as her understanding increased. "This is incredible."

Her gaze lingered at a man with a fanny pack. He reached in and pulled out a triangular black container about six inches long. With a self-satisfied smile, he held it up. "Stop sticks," he said with a toothless grin. "They flatten car tires."

Glancing from one man to the next, a wave of dizziness enveloped Brittany and she weaved to one side.

"She's gonna faint," one of the Blues said.

The Sarge and Smitty grabbed her arms and helped her to a couch.

Brittany blinked and shook her head. Everything started coming back into focus. She watched the ceiling fan circle lazily overhead. Lots of fuzzy, round objects moved around and made noise. Keeping her head still and taking deep, long breaths, she tried to bring the faces around her into view. The Sarge, her father, and five other Blues hovered around the sides of her vision speaking in rapid succession.

"Give her air!"

"Hold her hands above her heart."

"Is she okay?"

"That's her feet elevated, you idiot, not her hands."

"Oh, yeah…put her feet up."

"Get her some water."

"What are you going to do? Pour it on her face?"

She recognized the Sarge's voice.

"I don't know. I've always seen people get water," came the reply.

"Never mind, you knuckleheads." Her father's voice sounded like it came from down a long tunnel. "Just back away," he said. "Back away. Hey, sweetie…look at me. Brittany."

Head still spinning she tried to do what he asked.

"Honey, look at me."

Still trying to get a grasp on what had just transpired, she focused on her father's voice.

"Right here…look at me."

Squinting to help her concentrate, it took a minute before his face came fully into view. "Daddy?" She pulled herself up and ran a shaky hand through her hair. "I'm okay; I'm back now," she said and gave him a half smile for reassurance.

He tossed a satisfied look over his shoulder and relief beamed from his face. "There she is!"

One glance at the Sarge's familiar face, however, brought the upsetting memory back—in spades. "Oh look," he said. "The color's coming back to her cheeks."

Smitty glanced back and forth between the two. "Oh-oh. Round two of angry-redhead mode," he said. "Mt. Brittany's about to blow again."

"Get back," Brittany growled, unable to do much more. "All of you."

The Blues shuffled and did as she asked. Sitting up, she pressed her right palm to her forehead. Benevolence beamed from each and every lined, smiling face. Still irritated at the general principle of old men playing cops and robbers for real perched in the back of her brain, but the initial anger had evaporated.

One Blue leaned on a pair of crutches. She shot him a sidelong glance. "What are those? Bazookas?"

The Blue's face lit up and he opened his mouth to answer.

Smitty silently shook his head in warning.

"Ah," the Blue began, then stopped and exhaled loudly as though he wanted to tell her what his crutches could do but thought better of it. "No," he stated. "Just plain old crutches."

"Thank goodness," she said and plopped against the back of the couch. "Could I have some water please?"

"Hah!" another Blue spouted. "Told ya! They always get water when someone faints."

The Sarge just rolled his eyes. "Just get her some water."

♋

Jake and Monica Thorp gathered in the Chief's office in anticipation of their weekly meeting.

"Morning," the Chief said and walked to his chair. "Jake," he said, settling himself behind his desk, "you don't have enough to do."

"I feel an assignment heading my way," he whispered to Monica.

"Those old cops at the retirement center," he began.

"What about them?" Jake asked.

"They're the current media darlings. Seems everybody loves these guys," he muttered absently. "And their little protest 'Hail to the Cheeks' was of course the high point of my entire week."

Snort!

"Monica, why on earth do you make that noise every time you laugh?"

"I can't help it, Chief," she said. "The sight of those wrinkled butts is burned into my brain."

Fixing her with a withering stare, he continued. "As I was saying, since this story isn't going anywhere soon, I want Jake to visit there a couple times a week. Try to smooth things over for me."

"Okay," Jake said. "To what end?"

"I'd like to visit again—without the protest. I don't know what it was all about, but go over today and get to know them. Start building a rapport with them."

Jake and Monica exchanged a quizzical look. "Today?"

"No time like the present," Chief Williams said, "but give them the courtesy of calling first. Talk to the Sarge and tell him a little bit about yourself. The fact that you lateraled in after ten years from another large department will go a long way." He picked up a memo and glanced at it. "See what you can do for me, Jake."

"No problem, Chief." He stood to leave.

"Have fun." Monica cleared her throat in a dramatic fashion. "I hear they like cookies."

Jake frowned at her. Obviously she knew something he didn't. "I'll bear that in mind. Chief, I'll keep you updated."

Cookies? What the—

CHAPTER 14

"HUH," THE SARGE GRUNTED AND HUNG UP THE PHONE. "How about that?"

"How about what?" his file clerk, another Blue, asked without glancing up from his typewriter.

"A representative from the Chief's office wants to stop by."

The Blue's fingers hovered above the keys, and he gave the Sarge a puzzled look. "Why? Wasn't last time enough?"

"This is different," the Sarge continued. "Jake Mitchell, he sounds like a decent guy. I've heard he's a good cop."

"Never heard of him."

"Me neither," the Sarge said. "Not until he became the Public Information Officer, transferred in from the department in Salt Lake City."

The Blue shrugged a shoulder. "That's a fairly large department," he said.

"Yeah. He was a detective," the Sarge said.

"Why'd he move out here?" the Blue asked. "I wouldn't trade their weather for ours."

"Don't know," the Sarge said, "but I plan to find out." He pushed the intercom button. "We're having a visitor from the Chief's office," he announced, "and there won't be any protests today."

In the foyer, the precinct Blues laughed and hooted.

"Don't worry, Sarge," one called out. "We'll be good!"

"That'll be the day," he muttered. "Smitty and Brittany back yet?" he asked his clerk.

"Should be soon," he said.

Once she'd recovered, and with her father's okay, the Sarge had given the go-ahead for her to get the grand tour of their actual mission and abilities. A person with her language skill was invaluable particularly with the Clubba situation. He was meeting with this cousin on visiting days at the prison. That would explain how he gets the information out and why he was so slippery to law enforcement. Maybe if Brittany paid a visit to the prison to eavesdrop on a conversation or two, they'd be even farther along. "Hmm…" The Sarge leaned back in his chair and stared at the ceiling—an idea kicked around in the back of his head.

"Tiny," he barked.

"Yeah, Sarge," the reply floated in.

"Get with that young lab tech. We need to identify that Sudanese thug—"

"Which one?"

"The one on the phone before he got piss-packed by Pauli. I'm sure the kid got a good video shot of him."

"'Kay."

"Don't they have that facial recognition stuff they use with photos?"

"The whiz kid's got it all, Sarge."

"Good. Once you get him identified, come back to my office. We're gonna schedule an unconventional field trip."

"Got it, Sarge."

"Did I hear we're going on a field trip?" one Blue asked.

"Sure did," another Blue said and flashed a grin. "Hey, who wants to go on a field trip?"

Hands sprang up across the office. "Me!"

"And me!"

"Ooh, ooh…I wanna go, please!"

The Sarge rolled his eyes and slumped in his chair. "It's like having a bunch of freaking third graders."

His phone rang and he snatched it up. "Yeah?"

"Got a guest from the Chief's office to see ya, Sarge," the entrance officer said.

"Send him in."

Jake strode to the door, stopped, and gave two knocks. "Sarge?" he asked.

"Come on in, Officer Mitchell."

"Please," he said walking in, "call me Jake. It's a relief to get out of the madness at headquarters."

The Sarge held his hand out toward a chair. Jake seated himself and jerked his thumb over his shoulder toward the Blues working away in the precinct. "By the way," he began, "I only recognized about half of those guys out there."

The Sarge's brows knit together in a quizzical manner. "What?"

Jake spread his palms and smiled. "Maybe if you had them stand up and turn around, I'd recognize the rest of them."

With a grunt, the Sarge sat back in his chair. "Good one, Jake. I like you already. Sorry about the other day. That little protest was meant for the medical staff. We didn't think it would splat on the Chief the way it did."

"The media's still talking about it," Jake said. "Although I have to admit it was a creative if not revealing expose into the mind of old coppers who aren't ready to die just yet."

"You got it," the Sarge said. "I think some of 'em are too tough to die."

"True story," Jake said, "after we left, we had to pull the car over we were laughing so hard. I thought I busted a rib. The doc was acting so weird that I wondered if something wasn't up before we opened the doors but, honestly, that was the funniest thing I've seen in years." Jake laughed at the memory. "The guys certainly made their point in a very revealing fashion."

The Sarge joined him in another laugh. "Hope the Chief ain't too angry."

"Of course not. He knows nobody can pull jokes like old cops. They're the worst pranksters around. The media, though." Jake exhaled heavily. "They've really hammered him with it."

"Yeah," Sarge said.

"But that's all part of the job," Jake said. "Goes with the territory."

"Make sure the Chief knows we have a lot of respect for him." The Sarge's tone became much more serious.

Jake nodded. "I will."

"So," the Sarge finally said. "Why come all the way out here from Salt Lake City? I hear it's beautiful out there."

"It's an amazing place," Jake said. "Great skiing, professional basketball, symphonies…" His voice trailed off and he seemed to be someplace else. He shook his head and shrugged a shoulder. "To be honest, Sarge, I needed a change—total and complete."

"Okay," the Sarge said.

"I lost my wife and daughter in a car accident and—"

"That's terrible." The news stunned him and he shifted in his chair. "I'm so sorry."

"Yeah, it was tough," Jake responded, "but the move was good for me. I have a brother in town: Ben Mitchell."

"Ben Mitchell?" The Sarge stared at him in amazement. "Mr. Big Bucks? The guy who owns all the call centers and infomercial stuff?"

"Yeah," Jake said a bit surprised. "You know Ben? Of course you do. He said something about like-minded individuals coming up with the funding for this place, right? Called them," he snapped his fingers. "What did he say? Oh, yeah…The Bureau."

The Sarge's eyes widened; his mouth immediately opened to confirm the title. Thinking better of it, he clamped his lips back together.

The splintering crash of broken glass came from the doorway. Smitty and Brittany were back from their rounds. From the look on Smitty's face, he hadn't known there was a visitor.

"Oh, nice one, Dad," Brittany said, her father's hand under her elbow. "Bad enough I almost faint around all these cops. Then when I finally get my water, you drop it." She bent to pick up the biggest piece.

"May I get you another?" Jake asked.

Brittany slowly turned and looked up at the younger man through a veil of red hair. "Oh," she said and swept the errant strands back with her fingers. She straightened and handed the shard of glass to her father. "Yes," she said. "That would be great. Thank you."

The Sarge took advantage of the pregnant pause in the room. It was as good a time as any to get Jake out of the office and fill these two in on him. They needed to keep him—and the Chief—in the dark about what really went on there.

"Turn left and go to the nurses' station toward the back entrance." He waved absently in the general vicinity. "They'll get you fixed up."

Jake glanced at Brittany and smiled. "I'll be right back."

She met his gaze directly. "Thanks," she said softly.

The Sarge closed the door behind Jake and leaned against it. A heavy breath of air burst through his lips. "Holy crap," he said. "Are you kidding? I thought she was going to faint that time for sure!"

Her father nudged her forward and down. Both men stared at her.

"You're joking, right?" Brittany asked.

Both men exchanged a glance. "Well," Smitty said, "you did look a little smitten."

Brittany gave them a sidelong glance and pulled her hair back from her face again. "Not funny," she said. "And not smitten."

"She's fine," her father said.

"I don't know," the Sarge muttered. "I wasn't sure who was going to swoon first: Jake or Brittany."

"Oh, please!" Brittany crossed her arms. "Hardly."

"Seriously," the Sarge said. "Do you know who he is?"

"No and unless this is twenty questions," she shot back, "spit it out."

"Okay. Several things," the Sarge said. "And these are in no particular order: one, he's Officer Jake Mitchell, the Chief's Public Information Officer. Two, he doesn't know anything about what we do here. Three, his brother is on The Bureau."

Brittany frowned. "What's The Bureau?"

The Sarge waved a hand as though he could swat Brittany's question away. "No time to explain," he said. "But please don't say anything about what you've seen today. Do I have your word? Brittany? Not one word."

Brittany shifted to stand up; the Sarge and her father put a hand on each of her shoulders and pushed her back down. Her heels slipped in opposite directions and she plopped back. "This is harassment," she growled, "and after what I've been through, I should report you to the FBI."

"Yep, she's feeling better," her dad said.

She pointed a warning finger at him. "Don't start."

A light knock on the door drew their attention. "Here you go," Jake said and handed Brittany a Styrofoam cup. "In case of future accidents," he said with a quick grin.

Brittany took the liquid from him. "Thanks."

"I'm Jake Mitchell by the way," he said, his gaze lingering on her face.

"Brittany," she said.

Smitty glanced between the two and cleared his throat. "And I'm Brittany's father, Officer Smith," he said with a smile that didn't quite reach his eyes.

"Oh, sorry, Jake Mitchell." He stuck out his hand and Smitty shook it. Jake's eyes widened. "Nice grip," he said. "I'm in the Chief's office."

"I don't recognize you," Smitty said. "How long you been with the department?"

"About two years," Jake responded.

"Two years? And you work for the Chief? In his office?" Smitty's tone rang with suspicion.

"I'm no rookie," Jake said easily. "I was in a lateral recruit class."

"What's that?" Brittany asked.

"A special academy for police officers certified in another department," her father said.

"We don't have to go through the entire academy," Jake said. "Just learn the operating procedures of the new department."

"Where'd you come from?" Smitty asked.

"Salt Lake City," Jake said. "I was a detective there for ten years."

"Yeah," the Sarge interrupted. "Jake's brother lives in Omaha. Ben Mitchell, the telecommunications guy."

Smitty's brows inched up in recognition of the name. "Really? Your brother? Any other family in the area?"

"Nope," Jake replied.

Brittany glanced from her father to Jake; he noticed and her gaze slid off toward the Sarge.

"Nice to meet you," Smitty said. "How you liking Omaha?"

An odd look crossed Smitty's face, something akin to pain. The Sarge glanced down to where Brittany's foot crushed his toes. The Sarge lifted his gaze and with monumental effort kept from smiling.

"You interrogating him, Dad?" Brittany asked. "He just got here."

"Sort of a fact of life with cops," Jake said.

Smitty's face brightened. "Exactly."

"I lost count of how many second dates I've lost due to that practice," she said.

"They pass muster or they don't date my daughter," Smitty said.

"I get it." Jake chuckled. "I'm afraid I have to get back; I just wanted to meet with the Sarge. Maybe next time I could get the grand tour?"

The Sarge shifted, his lips twisting in acceptance. "Jake's gonna meet with us two to three times a week. The Chief wants to make sure everything is going well with the neighborhood watches and the… ah…community service things we do."

Brittany gave him a disgusted look and shook her head.

"You know, Jake," the Sarge said. "Brittany comes here a few times a week as well; she brings cookies for the Ol' Blues. She could show you around."

"Sure," Brittany said. "He can help me with my deliveries. Tomorrow too soon?"

Smitty's eyes narrowed suspiciously.

Jake pulled out his Blackberry. "Sure. How's eleven o'clock?"

"I'll make it work," Brittany said.

Jake tapped the information in with his thumbs. "I need to get going." He glanced from the Sarge to Smitty and nodded. "Nice to meet you—all," he said. "I'll see you tomorrow," he said with a final glance toward Brittany.

"Yes, you will."

The Sarge escorted Jake to the front doors. The younger man turned to him and quietly asked, "Is…ah…Brittany single?"

"Yes, she is. But, Jake," the Sarge began. "Smitty can be a little rough around the edges, but you won't find a better cop anywhere. Every Ol' Blue here loves that girl like she was their own flesh and blood. They don't come any better than that one, if you get my drift."

Jake met the Sarge's direct gaze head on. "I get it," he said. "See you tomorrow."

"Eleven o'clock," the Sarge said. "Might as well take her to lunch afterward."

"Oh, crap," Jake said. "Was it that obvious?"

"No worries, kid. See ya tomorrow."

Jake returned his wave and walked through the front entrance. The Sarge returned his greeting. "I really like that guy."

Turning on his heel, he whistled all the way back to his office.

CHAPTER 15

TINY HOVERED AROUND OUTSIDE THE SARGE'S DOOR, A piece of paper in hand. "His name is Abrahim Koak. On probation with forty hours of community service left." Tiny handed the information over for the Sarge's perusal and followed him into the office. "That tech kid you stuck me with really knows his stuff. He started identifying this guy as soon as we got back." Tiny sighed long and loud. "Turned out the gang unit does have a file on him. He's the cousin of—want to guess who?"

The Sarge smiled blandly. "Don't tell me; let me guess. Clubba."

Tiny grinned and pointed to a paragraph in the report. "Bingo!"

His dentures slipped yet again, but he caught them with his other hand before they popped too far out.

"Jeeze, Tiny. You gotta get those things fixed. They slide out every time you open your mouth too wide." The Sarge snapped the paper up to eye level. "Remind me not to be around you when you sneeze."

Tiny brushed his hand through the air and shook his head. "No time to get new ones right now," he said.

The Sarge shot him a mock glare. "You're driving me nuts with it all—the slipping, the whistling, the—"

"I've had these clackers for years," Tiny said. "I'm used to the whistle and as you well know, there's no pressing need for new ones."

The Sarge dropped his hand to his side and lowered his voice. "Who else knows?"

Tiny shifted his stance, glanced at the ground, then met the Sarge's gaze straight on. "No one and I want it to stay that way."

"I don't agree with you."

"So you've said. Several times."

The Sarge shook his head with heavy acceptance. "Fine, Tiny. Have it your way. I can't believe you've lived this long with all that cancer in your body."

"I choose the way I go out," the smaller man said. "Not the disease."

The Sarge's lips turned up in a slight smile of admiration. There was a lot of toughness in that small package. He gave Tiny a reassuring wink. "Point taken. So, Abrahim Koak has the lead on this assignment, eh? Have the guys down in the lab find out when he's scheduled to visit with his cuz next. Wait—" The Sarge's mind raced. "There might be a better way to get to this guy. Get me his probation officer on the phone. I've got a super idea for community service hours that punk can have. Patch the PO through to my office when you get him."

"Could be a her," Tiny shot back.

"Or her—whoever! Just get me the danged PO." The germ of an idea took root in his brain. The Sarge wanted a couple of Blues to go to the state penitentiary for some interaction with the prisoners: chess, woodworking, tutoring. Anything actually. Abrahim's probation officer could arrange for him to finish his community service hours as a volunteer helping the Ol' Blues on those visits. What the Sarge hoped was that Abrahim would think he could sneak in an extra visit or two with cousin Clubba.

He raised the report and reread it again. The kid at the lab had done some mighty fancy computer snooping. Already Clubba was elevated to trustee status at the prison. He'd have no problem getting onto any service detail he wanted. If all went according to plan, Abrahim would tell Clubba about his community service and upcoming trips. Clubba wouldn't be able to resist.

Of course Brittany was central to the plan. She'd go along and stay within earshot so the hearing aid microphones recorded when they spoke. It was perfect. Who'd suspect the pretty little redhead spoke Sudanese like a native? The Sarge all but salivated over the intelligence and evidence they could turn over to the county attorney against Clubba. Sarge's goal was to bust the lot of those thugs before they ever got a chance to do whatever it was they planned at Sixtieth and Etna. It could work…under exactly the right conditions.

The Sarge plopped into his chair behind his desk; he liked the plan. He hoped they'd take the bait. His phone rang and he snatched it off its cradle.

"Abrahim's probation officer, Sarge," Tiny said from the other end.

"Put him through." Time to put the plan into action, the Sarge thought with a smile. Phase one coming up.

The Sarge exchanged pleasantries with the PO and dangled the community service opportunity. "We thought it would be great for your younger probationers to finish some community service hours. Maybe help you guys clear a few cases off the pile."

"Sure," the probation officer said. "The stack keeps growing faster than we can keep up these days."

"Maybe give them a good role model while we're at it," the Sarge said.

"Now that's a long shot," the PO said with a chuckle, "but you never know."

"Great," the Sarge continued, writing down his thoughts as they popped up. "We'll provide the transportation to and from. Your kids will help the retired officers and older prisoners do crafts, play games— stuff like that. No specialized training required."

"Sounds like you have it all planned out, Sergeant."

"I'm writing as we speak," he confirmed. "How's next Saturday?"

"Should be fine. I think we can have half a dozen kids for this."

"Great." The Sarge straightened up and smiled. "One last thing. There's one young man in particular we were hoping to get. His mother knows some family members of the Ol' Blue Unit, and they asked us to help out," the Sarge lied smoothly. He hadn't spent all those years doing undercover narcotics for nothing.

"Sure," the PO said. "Who'd you have in mind?"

"Abrahim," the Sarge said. "Ah, what was his last name? I've got it written down here somewhere…ah, Koak."

A short pause bled through the line. "Oh yeah," the PO said. "That kid still needs over thirty hours. I'll make sure he's there."

"Great," the Sarge replied. "Have him—them—here at ten o'clock Saturday morning."

"Thanks, Sergeant."

"No, thank you," the Sarge said and hung up the phone. "Phase one complete."

The Sarge leaned back in his chair and called out to Tiny. "The kid's PO is gonna make sure Abrahim is here on Saturday."

"Great!"

"Sarge," Tiny hollered. "We're getting a pool together. Want in?"

"A pool on what?"

"On how long it's gonna take Abrahim to let Clubba know he's coming."

"No," the Sarge said with an eye roll. "Cops!"

⌒

The Sarge picked up the phone and called the lab. "I need the penitentiary visitation schedule."

"Well, hello to you too," Ajay the lab tech from India said. "That'll take a little time."

"By Saturday morning—Friday night would be better," the Sarge growled into the phone.

Ajay went silent. "And you think I can just flip a switch and hack into the pen's records just like that? Doesn't work that way, sir."

"Huh," the Sarge said. "So much for hearing that you young bucks were some sort of wunderkinds down there," he said as sarcastically as possible. "I guess even the best in the business have their limitations. A prison network probably has multiple firewalls and stuff. Might be a bit out of your—"

"What do you need?"

"Access to their visitation schedule," the Sarge said. "I need you to get it, figure out when Abrahim Koak is scheduled to visit Te'quan Koak, which wing the latter one is in and his status. I need the information within twelve hours of the actual—"

"Got it," Ajay said.

Dang! The Sarge said to himself. These guys are good.

"Took us about five minutes," Ajay replied. "Abrahim is scheduled to visit Te'quan tomorrow at eleven o'clock."

"About time," Sarge said. His mental wheels spun in a countdown on the two. His PO will contact him today and inform him of our wonderful service opportunity. "He'll visit on Wednesday. Perfect. Tiny!" he called out.

"Yeah, Sarge?"

"Could you come in here please?"

⟨⟩

Tiny loved the idea. "We've gotta get Smitty on board though," he cautioned. "It's one thing to have his daughter know about our operation, but it's a whole different one to actually involve her in the undercover part of it."

The Sarge pulled out his chewed cigar and pointed it at Tiny. "Let me worry about that…in addition to worrying about you."

"Me?" Tiny asked with a note of offense. "What do you mean?"

"You know how much Clubba hates you. Don't need to remind you about how you set him up with the arrest? Then showed up at the court hearing? That was a dumb stunt—waving and laughing at him. And a mission I didn't approve by the way."

The Sarge crossed to his desk and eased down into his chair. "But I have to admit that was a stroke of genius. Especially the waving and laughing part."

"Thanks. It worked out well."

"Didn't you say he looked like he was going to rush you and if not for the guards he probably would have?"

"In my report, yes." Tiny smiled. "I know this guy's type. He's going to get his revenge come heaven or hell. We've got to make sure he comes after me before he goes after his ex-girlfriend."

The Sarge held up the unlit cigar butt in salute. "Then I say we nail him."

"Something else about this guy, Sarge," Tiny said with a frown. "He's not going to be content as associate to these gangs. I think he wants more."

"How do you know?"

"No hard facts at the moment...I just know."

The Sarge respected Tiny's hunches and he nodded. "What else do you think he's up to?"

"Again, I'm not completely sure, but," Tiny scratched his chin and glanced up at the lights. "This guy is on the move. He wants to do more than just snake through various gang territories."

"To what end?"

"No clue on what his final goal might be." He glanced at the Sarge and smiled.

The gap-toothed grin reminded the Sarge why he wouldn't fix those dentures. He pushed the thought aside to focus on the mission at hand.

"Yet."

The Sarge watched Tiny's back as he exited the office. "Go get 'em, Tiny," he whispered. "Go get 'em."

CHAPTER 16

"EACH ONE OF THESE GANGS WANTS TO USE US," CLUBBA explained to his cousin. "Even the Aryans."

"The white guys?"

"Yeah. We're in high demand," Clubba said. "*Now*," he said in Sudanese, "*repeat it back to me, Abrahim.*"

Abrahim did so—several times.

Once Clubba was satisfied, he relaxed. "*How's the family?*"

"*Which ones?*" Abrahim asked. "*Your family is good.*"

"*What about Shanese? Her sister? And grandmother?*"

"*You mean the walking corpse?*" Abrahim asked and shared a laugh with Clubba.

"*It is very important that only my Sudanese men are there to remind her that I will be back soon.*" Clubba raised his finger in warning. "*Remember. Only my soldiers. I need to know who will follow instructions, and I need you to be my commander.*"

Abrahim nodded as if he liked the sound of that word. "*I will make sure the cockroach woman and her sister see us every day and that nobody will talk to her. She will be a little bird in a cage surrounded by hungry cats.*"

They both laughed again.

"Oh, I almost forgot," Abrahim said switching back to English. "My probation officer is sending me back here Saturday. I'll be able to meet with you more often. They want me to be a—what do they call it?—a volunteer."

Clubba's brows pulled together in a *V*. "Volunteer? For what?"

"To bring a group of old men to the prison for some kind of—ah, I don't know—activity day with the prisoners. It is supposed to be good for the prisoners and probationers to help the old men out. They said trustees were the only inmates who could participate though. No others. Can you do it?"

Clubba mulled the thought over. Keeping a watchful eye on the actions in Omaha would serve his interests best. "Yes," he said. "It will be good to talk more than once a week."

"And no one will be the wiser," Abrahim said. "We can talk freely."

"Time's up," a correctional officer said, indicating the end of the visiting session.

"We'll be here this Saturday at eleven." Abrahim pushed to stand up. *"And I can provide more message services to your friends,"* he said in their native tongue.

"Yes." Clubba responded in kind. *"I like the idea. Make sure you deliver the messages tonight."*

"I will, cousin," Abrahim replied with a curt nod. *"You can count on me."*

෴

As Smitty walked Brittany around the precinct, she said to herself, "How in the world did I get into this twisted mess?" She wished the story her father had spun was just that: a story. "The Bureau?" A group of millionaires and billionaires? In Omaha? They funded the incredible retirement facility? And the Ol' Blues operated under the noses of medical staff, the student nurses, DHHS, and the police? They escaped the facility into the neighborhoods to conduct surveillance operations and thwart the bad guys? Improbable and yet...fascinating. Society just didn't notice old folks. Criminals certainly didn't view them as a threat. That's why the whole thing was so brilliant!

During the tour, her father had attempted to take her to the research lab. They never made it. Two guys guarded the entrance and were having none of it. Without a written authorization from the Sarge, no one got in. After being turned away, she'd looked at her father. "Where on earth did you get those two?"

"The Sarge had made it his personal mission to recruit them and now I see why. That place is the nerve center of the entire facility. Nothing gets by them."

Smitty stopped walking and took her shoulders in a gentle grasp. "Sweetie, what we're doing here is a great service to the police, to Omaha, and to each of us. We've got so many years of experience."

"But you can still get hurt," she'd protested.

"Not really. We just provide anonymous information to the tip line. Help the sworn officers in their ongoing investigations. We guide them by offering suggestions. That's all. And it can literally save an officer's life."

"But."

"It's given all of us a new lease on life. We were just rotting away. Nobody needed us to do what we've done for most of our lives. Brittany, it's just so good to be needed again, to help fellow cops even if they don't know it." He dropped his hands to his side. "To tell you the truth, that's what makes it fun!"

The twinkle in her father's eyes brought tears to Brittany's just at the memory of all those years she'd been so proud of the man she loved and who'd taken such good care of her. Her father relished making a difference in the community, and she adored him for it. She loved being an important part of his life. How could she now be anything but supportive of what he'd accomplished? A smile kicked up the corners of her mouth. And all directly under the noses of all those professionals—even the police themselves.

She chuckled at the thought and turned to her father with a smirk. "Other than bringing cookies," she asked, "is there anything I can do to help?"

"Hm…" Her father had looked as though he was in deep thought and tapped his lips with his index finger. "Yes, you can. Your first assignment is to keep the handsome Jake Mitchell busy and out of our hair—or what's left of it. Can you do that?" Smitty returned her smirk with one of his own.

"I'll give it a go," she'd said and linked her arm around her father's.

"Second," he said in a more serious tone, "the Sarge wants to use you in an undercover operation with those Sudanese kids you saw before."

"Undercover? Me?"

"Yeah," her dad said. "I told him I'd talk to you. I didn't think much of it," he said. "You could get hurt."

"Like you can't?"

"Exactly why I said I'd leave it to you. It's not my call; it's yours."

She mulled that over on the walk back to the precinct office. "Hey," the information officer called out. "The Sarge wants to talk to you two."

Smitty had looked at Brittany and shrugged.

"Hey, Sarge," Smitty said upon entering. "What's up?"

The Sarge looked behind him and leaned to one side. Spotting Brittany, he smiled.

Smitty swept his right hand toward his daughter. "Sarge, meet the newest member of the Ol' Blues."

The Sarge raised an eyebrow at her.

"What's that about?" she asked. "I'm not walking around in diapers you know."

The Sarge blinked and glanced at Smitty who laughed.

The Sarge joined him. "I don't know," he'd managed to choke out. "Young lady, we have a dress code here."

Both men whooped it up again. Brittany crossed her arms and tried not to laugh. "All right, you guys," she said. "You're worse than toddlers. And…I've decided."

"Decided?" the Sarge asked, still grinning. "Decided what?"

"To be your secret agent or undercover whatchamacallit."

"Really? Great. Okay, secret agent whatchamacallit. We'll call you by your code name: Brittany." He collapsed in a fit of laughter again.

"Some code name," she said.

"It's better than you think." The Sarge wiped his eyes. "You're undercover in plain sight. That's our secret and we do it very well," he said and motioned out to the precinct office.

"That you do. I've got to hand it to you guys; you sure fooled me. I don't like being fooled and I don't like being lied to. I believe in being up front and honest with people."

"I know, sweetie," Smitty said. "That's something I've always loved about you. It makes you special."

"Well," the Sarge said, "the nature of our operation makes it so that only a very few of us know everything that's going on. We have too many guys here that talk without realizing what they say sometimes. Can't help it. We're old guys. But I'll tell you what. If I can't tell you about an operation, I'll just say, 'Don't worry about it,' and you'll know there's more to it. Fair enough?"

Brittany frowned but understood. "Okay, fair enough."

"Good. Now I have an assignment for you, actually, two."

Brittany's eyes widened. "Don't I have to be sworn in first?"

The Sarge turned to Smitty and pointed at Brittany. "You heard her say 'fair enough' right?"

"Right." Smitty smiled at his daughter.

"That's sworn enough for me," the Sarge said. "Now if you're finished with the lip service, I still have those assignments for you."

"All right, fine." She threw her arms in the air. "Assign away."

"First, I'm assigning you to provide a pleasant tour for Jake Mitchell."

That was an assignment Brittany didn't mind in the least. "Oh! Well…okay."

"A little something you should know," the Sarge said. "He moved here two years ago from Salt Lake City; he was a detective on that department for ten years."

"Yeah, Dad told me," Brittany said. "He moved here because he has a brother who is on 'The Bureau'—a bunch of very rich people who finance this entire operation."

"Right," the Sarge continued. "There's more. He moved here because his wife and daughter were killed in an awful car crash in one of their mountain passes during a winter storm."

Brittany recoiled at the thought. "How terrible."

"I just thought you should know, but both your dad and I like the guy. He's pretty sharp so make sure you are too. He may get too nosey so try to keep him off the scent. We may have to tell him about our little operation someday, but not yet."

His last word snagged Brittany's attention.

"Wouldn't it be nice to have someone on the inside? Someone in the Chief's office?" Smitty asked.

"Yeah," the Sarge said with a nod. "And he's the guy in charge of the Crime Stoppers tip line. We could use him to make sure the information gets to the right units quickly, and he could get information for us."

Brittany pointed around the precinct. "Does the Chief know about all this?"

The Sarge shook his head. "Absolutely not. And we have to make sure he never finds out. Otherwise he'd be knowingly supporting a group of innocent older citizens to act as agents of the State of Nebraska. That could get him into all sorts of legal trouble."

"But isn't Jake Mitchell's job to tell the Chief everyth—"

"His job," the Sarge interrupted, "is to help the Chief in public affairs and protect the Chief by providing plausible deniability."

"Plausible deniability," she echoed.

The Sarge let that sink in a second. "For us to continue to help the police and the community, the Chief cannot know what we do. Ever."

"Am I supposed to recruit Jake?"

"No," the Sarge and Smitty said at the same time.

Smitty locked gazes with the Sarge and motioned for him to continue.

"We'll handle that," the Sarge said.

Brittany started to leave the office.

"And when you come for the tour tomorrow," the Sarge said, "come hungry." The last words slid out in a much lower tone.

"What?" Brittany asked. "Why?"

"Well. No reason." The Sarge all but squirmed in his chair. "I mean no particular reason, really."

"The day you say something for no particular reason hasn't come yet," she said. "Out with it."

"It's just that it'll be around lunch time and, ah, Jake may want to take you to lunch afterward."

Brittany narrowed her gaze first at her father and then at the Sarge who seemed to be doing anything possible to avoid it. "Are you two meddling in my personal life?"

"No," they both said simultaneously again. At least they had the decency to look sheepish this time.

Brittany's index finger shot up, and she pointed at each man in warning. "I'll come hungry, but you two mind your own business."

They nodded and Brittany fought back a victorious smile. Truth be known she loved the fact that her father and the Sarge, whom she looked up to like an uncle, really liked Jake. She did too. It was a good omen.

The Sarge cleared his throat. "One last thing," he continued. "We're taking some of the Blues on a field trip Saturday."

Smitty turned to his superior, a grin drawing his mouth up. Like a little boy, he perked straight up. "Field trip?"

Brittany slapped a palm against her forehead. "Are you kidding me? My first undercover job is babysitting? Thanks loads. Am I also the bus driver?"

The Sarge drummed his fingers on his desktop as she spoke. Once she came up for air, he pointed at the chair adjacent to him and motioned for her to sit down.

She plunked onto the seat.

"Now then," he said. "If you're finished little Miss-talks-too-much, I'll explain the assignment." He cocked a salt-and-pepper eyebrow at her. "If I have your attention that is."

She tilted her head and crossed her arms. "Continue."

"You are assigned to take a group of the Blues to the state pen—"

"Delightful," she murmured.

"But," he continued as though she hadn't interrupted, "your cover is that you're a civilian volunteer helping these nice little old men. Your real assignment—the undercover part—is to obtain intelligence on this man." The Sarge held up a photo of Te'quan Koak.

Brittany uncrossed her arms and leaned forward to take the picture from the Sarge's hand.

"Also known as Clubba—for reasons I won't go into now," the Sarge said, "but he's a real peach. He's currently an inmate down there. His mother came here as a refugee, but he was born here. He's gotten himself into an interesting situation with the Omaha gangs. Has all the appearances of an associate."

"Associate?" Brittany looked to her father in a questioning way.

"Someone who moves freely between different gangs and establishes alliances with each one usually by providing guns, drugs, or vehicles for gang use in their crimes."

"That alone is an impressive feat to pull off," the Sarge said, "but this Clubba seems to be onto something bigger. We're not sure what he's doing, and the gang unit is pretty concerned about the entire enterprise. They can't figure him out either."

"So?" Brittany asked. "Where do I come in?"

"Glad you asked," the Sarge said. "We've got a handle on his contact on the outside—his cousin, Abrahim Koak." The Sarge handed her a second photo. "He's on probation and we've made arragements for him to serve some community service hours by helping at this little outing. There'll be games, arts and crafts, and junk like that. There'll probably be some prison trustees around too."

"I still don't get it," she said. "What do you need me for other than to ride herd on a wild bunch of Blues?"

"You're central to the plot, my dear." The Sarge took the photographs back and set them on his desk. "When Te'quan sends out his instructions, he goes through his cousin. It's all in Sudanese. So far, it's been like trying to break the Enigma—"

"The what?"

"Never mind. World War II reference," her father said.

"Oh, wait!" A smile of pure delight washed over her face. "You want me to intercept his messages, right?"

"Crack their code, so to speak," the Sarge said. "You got it."

The thought of working alongside her father thrilled Brittany. She'd always admired what he did, and now with the chance to do it too, a growing sense of meaning, one usually limited to those in public service or the military, took root deep inside. "What a rush." she said.

"Welcome to the club," the Sarge said.

"Kind of," Smitty added.

"It must kill these guys not to be of use anymore." She gazed out into the precinct office dotted with bald or graying older officers on the phones. "They don't know anything else that gives them meaning, do they?"

"Pretty much," the Sarge said. "This work keeps the juices flowing, that's for sure."

At that moment, Brittany silently committed herself to being a young Ol' Blue. Whatever she could help them with, she would.

The Sarge loaded her up with proper documentation and what seemed like a ream of other paperwork and sent her to the supply room. "Supply room?" she asked apprehensively. "That didn't go so well before."

"It'll be fine this time." The Sarge yanked the stogie from his mouth and pointed to the door. "You just didn't have the right authorization before."

⟳

Once again her father accompanied her. Inside the supply room, she gave Paps the paperwork.

He glanced through each page with a perpetual frown. "Pretty young to be a retired Blue, aren't you?"

Smitty shoved Paps's shoulder in a playful gesture. "Give her a break; she's a rookie just learning the ropes."

Paps reviewed the papers again then fixed a stern gaze on Brittany. "First," he said, holding up the paperwork in his right hand, "nobody gets in and no supply goes out without the proper paperwork."

Smitty rolled his eyes and leaned toward his daughter's ear. "Here it comes," he said in a stage whisper, "the dreaded supply briefing."

"Jerry and I work hard to make sure this area is the model of efficiency. We make it run and it's our show. All we ask is proper identification, paperwork, returning of investigative property or tools, and," Paps paused and exchanged a knowing look with Jerry who nodded in encouragement, "some of those cookies you bring the guys upstairs would sure be nice."

Unsure she'd heard correctly, Brittany blinked at the two men. Comprehension slowly dawned and she smiled. "One dozen cookies will be on your desk tomorrow."

Paps and Jerry's faces glowed with obvious delight. "Good," said Paps. He glanced at Jerry who nodded his head and rubbed his hands together.

Every one of them, Brittany thought, was a little boy at heart.

Glancing around their domain, she noted that the rooms were organized into an administrative section with office supplies, a janitorial section, and a medical section.

"Come this way," Paps said. "The Sarge wants you equipped with our special audio/visual recording apparatus."

"Awesome," Brittany said. "It sounds pretty Dick Tracy."

Paps chuckled. "Right this way."

Paps turned to leave and Jerry took his place at the surveillance cameras monitoring the outside hallways that led to the supply room. He gave a nod to Paps who lifted a cup filled with pens and pencils on his desk. Only he didn't pick it up, he turned it to the right.

What? Brittany realized the mug was attached to the desk. With his motion came a clicking sound that drew her attention to a closet marked "First Aid."

She tried to follow everything Paps was doing: he walked to the closet and opened it. Inside packages of medical supplies lined the shelves. Nothing out of the ordinary there—certainly nothing requiring a secret entrance. Paps bypassed the obvious items and reached back toward an electrical box complete with *Warning Do Not Touch* in red and a black picture of a lightning bolt in case a person didn't get the previous message.

Paps stuck his hand into the fuse box and with a quick glance her way said, "We like raisin oatmeal the best."

ZZAAPPPP! A spark spit out from where Paps's hand was. He opened his mouth as if in pain. "Jee-aaagh!" he said. He seemed to convulse.

Appalled, Brittany grabbed her father's arm. "Do something," she yelled. "Oh, Paps!"

Her father looked at her with his eyes wide and mouth open, then he gazed back at Paps who jiggled up and down.

"No!" Brittany cried out.

Paps let out a final, "Eee-yaah."

Jerry ran over and grabbed Paps by the arm. "Ahhh-augh," he hollered staring up at the ceiling.

Brittany lurched forward to help the two men. Her father grabbed her forearm.

"Aaaahhh!" the two men yelped. Or did they? After a moment it faded to more of a "Ah…hah, hah. Hah."

Smitty dropped his hand from Brittany's arm and guffawed. He slapped the desk and bent over.

Brittany stood rooted to the spot. Confusion washed through her. "Wh-what's…" The realization that she'd been had by the supply cave dwellers resonated through her.

"Oh!" she said on a low deep breath. "You two! I thought you'd electrocuted your—" She stopped short and crossed her arms glancing between the dynamic duo for a long moment. She let the silence hang in the air. Once their laughter died down, she aimed an accusing finger first at Jerry and then at Paps. "No cookies," she said accusingly. "For either of you."

The laughter dried up instantly. "Oh, come on," Paps said. "Nobody ever brings us treats down here."

"Can't imagine why."

Brittany glanced at her father who tried hard not to meet her gaze. "I'll deal with you later."

She looked back at Paps and Jerry who actually looked worried they'd lost their treats.

"You about gave me a heart attack," she said. "And to think I was worried about you two down here alone. No wonder they don't let you upstairs. They'd have a lawsuit on their hands."

Paps and Jerry shrugged in unison. "Sorry, Brittany," Paps said quietly.

"We didn't mean to scare you so bad," Jerry added.

"No worries," Brittany said. "But never again. Got it? If there's ever a repeat, neither of you will ever see so much as a crumb let alone one of my world-famous brownies."

The men turned to one another. "Brownies?"

Brittany pointed her finger at them and said, "That's right, you two. Best around. If I even get a hint of something like this again, you go to the top of my fecal roster. Nothing for you. Zip, zilch, nada! Got it?"

"Got it," they said in unison. With a glance at Smitty, Paps said, "But did you see her face?"

The laughter boiled over again and everyone, including Brittany, joined in. "Okay," Paps said at last, his laughter quieting down to a chuckle. "Now that the rookie welcome is out of the way, let's get you set up. By the way, those sparks serve to scare anyone snooping around too much. As you can see, they're pretty effective."

"Scared the crap out of me," Brittany said.

Paps hit a fuse and the back of the closet opened up. Jerry smiled and directed Smitty to follow. "I stay out here," he said, "in case a staffer needs supplies."

Brittany trailed Paps; Smitty followed. Once she stepped through the closet, the tiny aperture opened into what looked like a secret government laboratory. "Wow," she whispered.

"Yeah," Paps said with a note of pride in his voice. "We get that a lot."

At least ten men in lab coats were engaged in various projects. One glanced up and saw Paps. "Got the Sarge's order right here."

Paps made it a point to hand Abinya, a Nigerian lab tech, a requisition form before touching the item. He took an item from Abinya and walked over to Brittany.

"These are for you." He held out something that looked like a pair of black glasses?

"Glasses?" she asked. "I don't wear glasses."

"They aren't glasses," Abinya said with a knowing smile. "This is our audio/visual recording apparatus. It'll record everything you see. It also magnifies and records anything you look at within about fifty feet."

"Wow," she said and gingerly held them up.

"The Ol' Blues just call it ball drums," Abinya added.

"Ball what?" Brittany shook her head. "What does that even mean?"

"Eyeballs and ear drums," Paps said.

Abinya frowned in open irritation.

"Whatever you call them," Brittany said, "I think they're totally cool."

"Thanks." Abinya smiled. "We think so too. The Blues don't give many compliments," he said. "They don't want us thinking we're smarter than they are."

"Tell me about it," Brittany said. That was definitely the Ol' Blues she knew.

She slid the glasses on and looked around.

"Just put your finger and thumb on the right lens," Abinya directed. "You should feel a small button."

She slid her thumb and sure enough found it.

"It'll look like you're adjusting your glasses but recording begins immediately. It's digital so you'll have about four or five hours to get everything you need. That should be more than enough for your little trip to the state pen."

Brittany took the glasses off and put them on again. "These are just so cool."

⌒

Jake stared in the mirror and adjusted his tie. This was insane; he hadn't been on a date in, what, almost a decade? He tugged the tail through the back loop and sighed. It wasn't a date. In the two years since his wife and daughter's deaths, he'd really gotten out of sync with the rest of the world. *So if it isn't a date what is it?* an inner voice taunted. He blew out a long breath. It certainly resembled a date. Sort of.

Jake straightened the Windsor knot and tilted his head at his reflection. Since leaving the retirement center, he couldn't get Brittany off his mind. That she was beautiful was an understatement. A flash of her face with that cascade of hair rippling around caught him off guard. He jerked at the tie as if it choked him.

And she had every one of those Blues wrapped around her perfect pinky finger; of that there was no doubt. Obviously she held a special place in the Sarge's heart. Her father, Smitty, guarded her like a centurion. Jake tossed the blue tie on his bed and grabbed a red one from the closet. Although, he thought with a smile, from what he'd seen, she didn't need much protection.

The whole day could turn out to be exactly what it appeared to be: a tour. Show up, be shown around, and that's the end of it. Or, a shiver snaked up his spine. He was as nervous as a sixteen-year-old on a first date. "Jeeze, man," he said with a frown. "Get it together."

He was still trying to accomplish that directive on his drive to the office. Although uneventful, when he arrived, he had the startling feeling that he'd been daydreaming the whole way. He didn't remember a thing. With a shake of his head, he bolted into his office. He needed to sweep the cobwebs out of his head. The job demanded minute attention to detail, and he couldn't be mooning over anybody. All overnight noteworthy police incidents waited in his inbox for his review. Those deemed worthy were sent as news releases for reporters to sift through.

Several officers worked on special reports focusing on categories of Omaha crime such as burglaries or robberies. Those were enough to stir things up for a couple of weeks in the media. The purse-snatching ring was a particular source of pride for the department. The gang unit cleared that series in record time. Only two weeks and they'd brought in ten guys from the same high school. That was some phenomenal police work. He made a mental note to stop by their office and get the lowdown on how they cracked it so fast. There should be some good stories there.

Jake took the stairs to the Chief's office. After a quick knock on the door, he stuck his head inside. The Chief and Lt. Thorp were deep in discussion. "Anything that needs my attention?" Jake asked.

"No," the Chief said and glanced at his watch, "but it's only 9:30 in the morning."

Jake shrugged. "One never knows."

"How'd the visit go with the Ol' Blues yesterday?" the Chief asked.

Thoughts about the retirement center brought Brittany's image to mind. "Beautiful," he said.

The Chief shot a sharp glance at Lt. Thorp.

"Really?" Lt. Thorp asked. "Beautiful?"

Jake snapped back to reality. "Uh, yes…it was a beautiful facility. I only got to talk with the Sarge for a short time though." Firmly grounded in reality, Jake remembered the message he needed to deliver. "Oh… and Chief, the Sarge said to tell you they think very highly of you. That little protest was for the medical staff who force them to wear the robes. He was sorry the media took it to you afterward. He really liked the fact that you sent me out there as a liaison. As a matter of fact, I'll be…ah…going out today for a tour at eleven."

The Chief made a disgusted face. "Wasn't the butt cheek tour enough for you?"

Monica snorted and threw a hand over her mouth and nose in a losing effort to control her laugh.

The Chief glared at her. "Monica I swear, I'm going to get you checked out for a deviated septum or whatever else makes that noise!"

Monica glanced at Jake and then back at the Chief. "Sorry, Chief," she said around a giggle and directed her attention outside as if the Omaha skyline fascinated her.

"Thank you," the Chief said and turned back to Jake. "The tour?"

"Oh, yes. It was a quick look around. The Sarge said I should come back today—see the whole thing."

The Chief leaned back in his chair, his eyebrows lifting. "Oh. The old Sarge is giving you the five-dollar tour, huh?"

Heat crept up Jake's neck. "Yes, well, no…ah not exactly." He struggled to finish his sentence and cursed every cop's ability to ferret out details.

Monica turned from the window to zero in on Jake's evasiveness. "So who's giving you the tour?"

Jake shifted from one foot to the other. "Well, one of the Blues' daughters who goes there regularly. The Sarge asked her to show me around," Jake said and struggled to tamp down his growing nervousness.

Lt. Thorp's eyes lit up and an impish grin grew wider. "Smitty's daughter."

Jake opened his mouth to speak, but the Chief beat him to it. "The redhead?"

Dang nosey cops. Didn't take them long to sniff out the source of Jake's agitation. He shook his head in an effort even he knew was doomed to failure. "It's not like that."

The Chief locked his hands behind his head, leaned back in his chair, and put his feet on his desk. "Oh, really?" he asked with a grin to match Monica's. "And how is it, Jake?"

Lt. Thorp mimicked the Chief's action and leaned back in her chair. Crossing her arms over her chest, she cocked her head and considered Jake. "Yes. Tell us how it is."

"You know, Monica," the Chief continued with a knowing look at his lieutenant, "this gives a whole new meaning to the word *liaison*."

"Oh, definitely," she said emphatically. "Totally agree." She joined the Chief in focusing her attention on Jake with a direct we-know-what-you're-up-to look. At least they were both smiling.

The back of Jake's neck flared red hot and despite his best efforts, his face followed suit. If he were the cussing sort, this would be the time and place to use it.

Snort! That sound could only come from one person.

"Come on, you guys," Jake said, "don't put the horse in front of the cart. I mean, oh, crap! You know what I mean."

Snort!

"Dang it, Monica. I'm with the Chief on this. You've got to get that checked out!"

"You know, Jake," the Chief began in a more instructive tone, "if you really want to make a good impression on her..."

Jake glanced at the Chief awaiting a great piece of advice.

"You may want to pull up your zipper."

The Chief and Lt. Thorp roared with glee.

Jake's eyes widened at the announcement. Turning on his heel, he reached to pull up his zipper and walked out of the office, which made him bump his head on the office door with a thump.

Snort!

Jake continued out the door trying to maintain whatever dignity he had left. Entering the lobby of the Chief's office, he struggled to zip his pants and caught the attention of the Chief's secretary. Fingers hovering over her keyboard, she stared at Jake as if he were a bug under a microscope. Walking and zipping were not only difficult but downright dangerous. He halted in front of her desk.

"Sorry," he muttered and turned his back on her.

A loud *zzziiippp* filled the emptiness. Without so much as a backward glance, he walked through the glass doors and stalked toward the elevator. If there were any justice in the world, it would be a short wait. Seconds passed. Naturally, it was stuck somewhere. A quick peek over his shoulder revealed the secretary still rooted in place and still watching him. The doors opened with a soft ding. Jake strolled in as nonchalantly as possible, smiled, and waved. After pushing the button to garage level, he went to lean back but misjudged the distance. A dull thump on the back of his head reminded him of the mistake.

An exasperated sigh flew through his lips, and he raised his gaze to the ceiling. "This is high school all over again."

CHAPTER 17

BRITTANY'S ALARM BUZZED—REPEATEDLY. REACHING her arm out from under the cover, she slapped the snooze button. She'd had better nights. First she couldn't get to sleep; then she'd tossed and turned all night, her emotions veering from anxiety to pleasure.

The alarm sliced through her thought. She cracked one eye open. 9:00. Paps and Jerry...cookies, the tour...Jake! She sprang out of bed and scampered to the bathroom. The mirror revealed a total mess: hair sticking out—everywhere. She grabbed a couple of ties and doubled them around a quick ponytail and over that came her old reliable baseball cap. Rifling through her closet, she searched for something to wear that didn't look too desperate or carefree; no time for cute or pretty.

She placed one shirt under her chin then tossed it on the bed; she grabbed another, which ended up on top of the first. After the third shirt, she froze, "The cookies."

The third shirt would have to do. Shoving her arms into the holes, Brittany dashed to the kitchen. The whole procedure was routine; she'd done it so many times, she had the recipe memorized. She measured and dumped each ingredient into her mixer and turned it on. A little instant cake mix was her secret ingredient. It never failed to improve the texture and bring out the flavor her cookies were famous for. One bite made every Ol' Blue's face light up.

Cookies in the oven, she shoved her feet into a pair of black flats. While brushing her teeth, the timer on the stove rang. "Coming," she said knowing full well no one could hear her.

Any other day, she would've tasted one cookie. Today wasn't just another day. There simply wasn't any time. She slid them off the pan into a container lined with parchment paper and scurried out the door. They'd just have to cool en route.

Ten minutes before the eleven o'clock tour, Brittany pulled into the parking lot at the Ol' Blue Precinct. "She's here," Smitty said.

The Sarge stopped pacing in his office. The door opened and before she could greet them, Smitty stepped in front of her. "Where have you been? We haven't even showed you what you can show him yet."

"Here." Brittany shoved the cookies at the Sarge. "Get these down to those two crazy guys in the supply room. Tell them any more shenanigans and they'll never see another one."

"What," the Sarge asked, "are you talking about?"

"Just do it; they'll know what you mean," Brittany said.

The Sarge turned to do as requested and Brittany grabbed her father's arm. "Just show me what he can see and what I can tell him."

"You're a lot like your mother," Smitty said. "She could take over a crisis situation really well too."

"Dad!" She snapped her fingers in front of him. "The tour?"

They turned toward the lobby. Brittany stopped at the information desk. "Page me when you see Officer Mitchell, got it?"

The man blinked at her, clearly not used to taking orders from anyone out of uniform. He glanced up at Smitty who shrugged. "Just do it," he said. "Makes life a whole lot easier."

The officer nodded. "Yes, ma'am."

Smitty pulled Brittany aside and turned her to face him. "Just think about what you knew about this place two days ago."

Had it only been two days? "Two days ago I thought this place was a bunch of nice old men doing nice things for Omaha service organizations." She frowned and shook her head. "Now I've been roped in with a bunch of crazy, piddle-pack-throwing, geriatric crime-fighting geezers…some of whom wear diapers."

She ground the last words out through gritted teeth.

Two Ol' Blues heard her. One elbowed the other. "Piddle packs."

They started to laugh and Brittany rolled her eyes. "Don't you two have a poor criminal to zap with your Taser canes?"

One smiled at her, held his cane up, and pressed a button just below the collar of his walking cane. Fifty thousand volts arced between two metal prongs at the tip. A sizzling *ZZZAAAPPP* electrified the air.

Brittany turned to her father and made a face. "See what I mean?"

Smitty shook his head at the two Blues indicating Brittany wasn't as impressed with their toy as they were. They turned and walked in the opposite direction.

"It's not easy to forget what this place really is," she said. "Once you see it, you can't undo it."

As if on cue, the Ol' Blue gave one last jolt to his cane. *ZZZAAAAPP.* "I love this thing!" he said and turned the corner.

Brittany blew an exasperated breath out and looked up at her father. "Seriously? How do you people keep it as secret as you do?"

"They're just showing off for the new girl," Smitty said and patted her shoulder. "You're gonna love this place—and what we do here. I promise." Glancing around he pointed to the opposite wall. "Show him the different station desks. Have the officer at the information table tell Jake what everybody does. They're all trained for exactly these types of tours. Civic leaders are popping in here all the time. We're used to it."

"But I'm not," Brittany said.

"So let the Blues take the ball and run with it. Take the heat off you and put it on them. So," he said, "what are you thinking about the handsome Officer Mitchell?" He paused for effect.

Heat suffused Brittany's cheeks. "I don't think anything."

"Hmm," her father said. "If you say so."

"I say so." She pressed her palms to her face hoping the flush was gone. "Okay," she said in a breathy voice. "I think I can do it."

"Smitty?" The information officer interrupted them.

"Yeah?" he replied.

The intercom speaker announced, "Would the special tour guide come to the main entrance?" he asked. "There's a snappy fella walking into the building."

Brittany scanned the speaker directly above her head. It was like being surrounded by twenty of her favorite uncles.

Jake came through the front doors and into the large entryway that split into the medical wing, the student wing, and the state offices. Impressive, he thought once again, that the facility not only provided a place for retired officers but met a combined medical, social, and educational need not only for the Blues but for students and citizens as well. All nicely packaged under one roof.

At the precinct doors, he paused, took a deep breath and walked through. Like so many others, he was once again taken by the design and authenticity of the interior. It was not only like stepping back in time, but carried an air of legitimacy that swirled around the occupants.

"So you finally got here," Brittany said.

The nostalgia of the past evaporated into the reality of the present. Standing in front of him was a beautiful woman, hands on her hips, pretending to be impatient about a two-minute tardiness.

"Sorry," he said with a quick grin. "The Chief and Lt. Thorp had some last-minute instructions." He spread his hands out in front of him. "What can I say? When the Chief wants to talk, I have to listen." Especially if his zipper was down. Jake made a mental note to thank him for that piece of advice.

"So," Jake said. "About that tour?"

Brittany smiled and Jake realized how incredibly gorgeous she really was up close. The smile lit her eyes and seemed to come straight from her soul. Oh yeah, he was smitten.

"All right, then, Officer Mitchell, follow me."

"Jake," he said. "Call me Jake." He reached out his hand and she shook it. He liked the softness of her fingers.

"Right this way."

Jake figured at this point he'd follow her pretty much anywhere, but she only led him through the offices and corridors of the precinct. Jake spoke to several different officers at several different stations. He knew a canned story when he heard one—he'd gotten those sorts of rehearsals from so many perps he'd lost count. Jake feigned attention but his mind wandered. The stuff coming from the Blues was as dry as the Mojave Desert. Nodding and murmuring approval, he kept stealing glances at Brittany. She'd caught him a couple times, and he would've sworn she smiled when he quickly deflected his gaze.

At the end of the tour, she walked him to the Sarge's office. "Hey," Jake said. He stopped and gazed around. "Hey wait; I remember this place. Isn't this where protective fathers bring their lovely daughters and then unceremoniously dump their drinks on the floor?"

Brittany met his gaze directly. "Oh you remember that, do you?

He chuckled at the memory. "I've got to admit it wasn't one of my more gracious entrances."

She smiled too, though whether at the memory or at him he wasn't sure.

"It was perfect though," he said. "I have to admit I enjoy surprises and seeing you with your hair in your face, trying to maintain your dignity was the most pleasant introduction I've had in a long time."

"Always happy to help out," she said.

"Thanks for the tour."

"Cookie anyone?" The Sarge and Smitty stood behind the Sarge's desk, a large stash of cookies in front of them.

Jake whirled to face them; Brittany followed suit. He'd been so wrapped up in whatever she said, he hadn't noticed the two older men sneak in.

"Paps and Jerry in supply said to tell you, 'Touché.'" The Sarge said to Brittany.

She tilted her head and frowned first at the Sarge and then at her father. "Touché?"

Jake noted a distinctly sour look on both men's faces, but no one gave away anything; Brittany was clearly stumped.

"She must have been in a real hurry this morning," Smitty said to the Sarge.

"These the cookies everybody raves about?" Jake asked and moved toward the pile. "All the Blues seem to love them."

The Sarge and Smitty both smiled. That same feeling he'd gotten on the "Hail to the Cheeks" day filled Jake's chest.

"They are," the Sarge said and pushed the plate of cookies toward him. "Help yourself, Jake."

He reached for one but before his hand touched anything, Smitty stepped forward.

"You must be hungry," he said. "It's about lunchtime, isn't it?"

Jake swiped one of Brittany's sweets and looked at her.

Eyeing her father suspiciously, she said, "I'm pretty hungry too."

Jake bit into the confection as she spoke; it all but stuck in the back of his throat. It was the nastiest thing he'd ever put in his mouth. It was all he could do to keep from spitting it all over her.

The Sarge and Smitty exchanged a bland look and focused on Jake. He returned their attention, still trying not to choke or regurgitate.

"Well," Brittany said cheerfully. "How about that lunch?"

"Lead on," Jake managed to get out around his constricted throat. He pointed toward the door and coughed. "After you."

Brittany breezed out in front of him with a wave to the Sarge and her father. They both returned the salute.

At the Sarge's office door Jake turned back. The two Blues were falling all over one another and trying—unsuccessfully—in an increasingly futile attempt to keep their laughter quiet. Once again, he'd been had. He broke the rest of the cookie in half and threw one piece at the Sarge and the other at Smitty. They both grabbed their chests as if they'd been shot. Jake pointed at each of them signaling that revenge would be his. He didn't know when and he didn't know how, but it was a promise he intended to keep.

Once the couple headed out, Smitty turned to his superior. "I think you're right about that kid, Sarge. I like him too."

The Sarge wiped his eyes and shook off another chuckle. "Any guy who could swallow that awful excuse for a cookie and keep it down and not embarrass Brittany is definitely a guy she needs."

"Yeah," Smitty agreed, "and he's a Mormon too?"

"Salt Lake born and raised," the Sarge said.

"I always respected those young guys who left home and family for two years. It shows commitment. I find that refreshing in a young man."

"Oh, really," the Sarge said.

"Yep. That's why I wasn't against Brittany joining that church."

CHAPTER 18

"THOSE ARE SOME SPECIAL GUYS IN THAT PLACE." JAKE pulled away from the retirement home. "I'd be an idiot if I didn't see how fond they are of you, Brittany."

"Thanks," she said with a fleeting lift of her lips.

He checked his rearview mirror. "In fact," he murmured, "I wouldn't be surprised if they had some sort of tail on us right now."

"They wouldn't dare," Brittany said. Her face grew concerned, and she glanced back as well.

"Hey, I was joking," Jake said.

"I know but—" She shook her head, her ponytail swished from side to side. "I wouldn't put anything past the Ol' Blues, especially Sarge and my father."

Jake laughed and turned his attention to the road ahead.

Lunch was pleasant but over too soon. Small talk usually wasn't his forte, but it was easy this time out. She told him about being a daughter of a cop; he told her about being a cop who'd lost his wife and child. If he read the signals correctly, she enjoyed the time together as much as he had. Jake checked his watch. "Oh man!" he said, "I've got to get going, I've got—I'm so sorry—I have to go."

"Wow," she said. "Where did the time go?"

"I know what you mean," he said. He paid the tab and drove her back to the Ol' Blues Precinct. En route back, Jake noted that she kept glancing at her side mirror.

"I really was just kidding," he said.

She turned a confused face to him.

"I don't think anyone followed us," Jake repeated with a full-fledged smile.

She nodded. "Would you like to have dinner sometime?"

The question startled Jake. "Sure," he said quickly. "That would be great."

He tried to tamp down the excitement that bubbled up at her offer. He didn't want to show too much emotion too soon.

"Great," she said. "This time, I'll make dinner. Do you like pasta?"

He liked her and that would be enough. "I love it."

"Great," she said. "I'll not only cook for you but you can sample one of my famous brownies."

The cookie threatened to come back up. "That'll be something," he said.

Outside a horn sounded, snapping Jake back to reality. In a quick maneuver, he swerved to miss a truck headed the opposite direction. He'd been so wrapped up in the conversation he'd crossed the middle line. "Wow," he said. "That was close."

∩

"Wow," Smitty said to the Sarge from the backseat of a van disguised to look like a cable repair vehicle. "That was close!"

"I know," the Sarge said. "He all but went into oncoming traffic."

"That's one distracted driver," the tech and driver Michael Beckham behind the wheel said.

The two Blues exchanged a knowing glance and smiled.

"By the way," Michael said. "I've got to get surveillance finished back at the apartments at Sixtieth and Edna."

"No worries," the Sarge said. "You can drop us at the precinct—back entrance please."

CHAPTER 19

ABRAHIM KOAK'S CHEST SWELLED WITH PRIDE. IN ONLY one week, he'd discovered the whereabouts of Shanese, Clubba's ex-girlfriend. Not only that, but he'd reported the discovery to Clubba himself. He hadn't bothered to mention the rest of the story and the odd screaming match with a couple of old dudes in a language he didn't know let alone understand. He tried yelling back at them in English and Sudanese but they didn't comprehend his words either. Clubba didn't need to know how quickly things had escalated, how his homies got drawn into it as well. And he especially didn't need to know that the old guys had thrown something at him, something horrible and disgusting.

He still wasn't sure what it had been, but once it hit the concrete in front of him and splattered all over his clothes, the world had collapsed. He couldn't breathe; his eyes watered and his lunch threatened to come up. In one slick move, he peeled his shirt off and threw it in a bush. Luckily the homeboy who'd lost the girl in the complex at least knew which building she lived in.

He didn't know who those crazy men were or why they'd hollered at him, but they certainly appeared to know they were up to something. It was almost as though they were guarding the girl. Abrahim shook his head to toss the stupid thought away. Not possible, he told himself. Old people had enough to take care of with themselves; it made no sense that they would get involved with a stranger.

He checked his watch. Nine o'clock. He needed to be at the retirement home in one hour. A free ride down to the prison was on the day's agenda along with another conversation with his cousin. "This is just too good," he said aloud. If he proved himself a valuable asset to Clubba, it would pay off big-time. Abrahim gave himself a once-over in the mirror and smiled at his reflection. "Once Clubba gets out, I'll be his right hand...one of the chief soldiers."

"Abrahim," his mother called out.

He walked into the living room and hopped onto a couch. "What is it?"

"What are you doing with this probation officer today?" She tossed a handful of herbs into a pot on her stove.

"I'm supposed to take some old retired guys down to the prison where they do arts and crafts or something with older inmates. My PO says that I get community service hours for doing this."

His mother shook her head and stirred her simmering stew. "I don't know this American legal system," she said.

"It's pretty easy," Abrahim said. "If the probation man says I need to do it, then I go."

"And soon you'll be off probation?"

"Once the community hours are done," he replied. "This should about finish it off."

"Good. You've never been so glad about these hours before. If it makes you happy, it makes me happy."

The chance to move up in Clubba's organization thrilled him. A knock at the door announced his probation officer's timely arrival. First stop, the retirement home for police officers. On the drive over, Abrahim tried to tune out the legal lecture about how important it was to successfully complete the terms of probation and finish his community service hours. If that wasn't bad enough, he started in on how important school was and—the most boring part—getting a job.

Abrahim stared out the windshield and let the PO drone on with no response. He was tired of listening to the fool. He had to put up with it though—at least until the court let him go. Too much could go wrong. Like Clubba had instructed: do what he says and don't make problems. If Abrahim wanted to work in the organization his cousin was building, he needed to play the game, at least for a little while.

"Hey," the PO said. "Are you even listening?"

Abrahim jerked his head to the left to face the driver. He wanted nothing more than to hurt the man—and badly—but Clubba's words came floating back to him. Abrahim could keep a lid on things for a bit longer.

"Sorry," he said and hoped his voice reflected the feeling. "I'm just thinking about the afternoon with a bunch of old guys."

"Not only are you going to be with them," the PO launched into another lecture, "you'll help them with whatever they need. That means helping them off the bus, helping them sit or stand. If it means fingerpainting with them, that's what you'll do. Understand? Whatever they need."

"I understand," Abrahim said coolly. And he'd open a new way for Clubba and his friends to contact their soldiers in Omaha. The probation thing was working to his advantage. Little did his PO know but there might be a job in it after all. Just not what the officer of the court thought. It was almost too easy. Abrahim allowed a smile then quickly stifled it.

⌒⌒

The Sarge's intercom buzzed. He pressed the button on the vintage set. "Yeah?"

"Surveillance cameras just picked up Clubba's cousin getting dropped off at the main entrance."

The plot was about to unfold, and the main character had just arrived. The whole thing brought a satisfied lift to the Sarge's lips. "Thanks," he said and directed his attention to the video screen hidden in his desk. He motioned a waiting Brittany to where he sat.

"This is the guy we want you to follow. Clubba's cousin. Name is Abrahim," he said.

She stared at the screen. "Pretty young, isn't he?"

"Welcome to gangbangers 101."

She studied the young man intently. "Okay," she said. "Just to be sure, all I've got to do is let him talk to his cousin, listen in, and record through the glasses, right?"

"Yep," the Sarge said. "That's it—oh, and be sure to give him a bunch of stuff to do with the Blues. Don't make it too easy for him; let him work his way to Clubba. That way they'll both feel that they're exploiting this little get-together. Guys like them want to feel like they're the ones calling the shots, taking advantage of the system."

"From what you said, that Clubba's carving out quite a name for himself with his message services to the Omaha gangs," Brittany said.

"That he is. He'll be guarded," the Sarge said. "If it appears too easy, they'll smell a setup. Your glasses will pick up exactly what you're looking at, so try to sit across from one of the Blues with his back toward Clubba."

"Okay," she said and exhaled deeply.

"This is him." The Sarge brought Clubba's mug shot on screen. "It'll seem like you're looking at the Blue but you'll actually be looking at Clubba and Abrahim and recording every word."

"You remember the day you overheard us with the tape of Abrahim?"

"How could I forget?" she said with a wink. "That's what got me into this crazy club of old guys."

"Blues," the Sarge corrected. "We're Blues." He glanced at her, his face softening. "Brittany, I can't tell you how valuable you'll be on this operation. I'm really glad you're on our squad."

"Me too," Brittany said. "Now let's go get this little cousin, shall we?"

※

A large eighteen-passenger vehicle waited in the driveway. Brittany sensed the excited tension drifting through the Ol' Blue Unit. Never mind that the field trip made them act more like grade schoolers, they understood the real purpose, and it was almost palpable. Standing by the open vehicle door, a large woman affectionately called Boss Nurse rattled off the day's rules.

"Now listen up, y'all," she said. "I want no trouble on this trip. Each and every one of you knows how you're supposed to behave in public. If you got a urine bag, I want to see 'em before we leave. They should be new. I don't want anyone filling a bag before we get back. We'll bring extra just in case, but I don't want to have to change them out until we get back."

The Blues started to check their piss packs and moved on to check one another's.

"Tiny's is almost half full, Boss Nurse," one of the Blues chirped out.

Tiny shot the man a look that labeled him a snitch. "Is not."

"Is too. Look for yourself, Boss Nurse." The Blue pointed at Tiny.

Boss Nurse's eyes widened and her hands flew to her hips. "Tiny, get back an' change that thing out right now."

There was never any arguing with Boss Nurse and Tiny knew it. He turned and shuffled back to the nurses' station.

Boss Nurse shook her head and glanced skyward. "How on earth do these men use so many urine bags?" she asked mostly to herself, but loud enough for all to hear.

The Blues gave each other sly glances and tried not to smile.

Brittany bit her lip attempting the same thing. She watched in fascination. Every one of these men was undercover. By the way they acted, you'd think it was a frat party—for the most part. Needing a nurse or doctor around all the time—or pretending to—was the perfect strategy. They kept the medical personnel busy and right where they wanted them: taking them on tours, changing diapers, giving baths, or doing a myriad of other jobs. A foolproof plan to keep them in the dark and accidentally walking in on a mission briefing or debriefing.

"Absolutely brilliant," she murmured.

One of the Blues caught her attention and winked. In the next breath, he called out, "Shotgun!"

He did a two-step shuffle toward the awaiting van.

"Nobody gets on there until I say so," Boss Nurse said. "Remember who's in charge and who's supposed to do as they're told."

Brittany watched one Blue after another shuffle by and gave her a wink. Once loaded in for all intents and purposes, they really did look like they were going on a field trip.

Tiny brought up the rear. He had a new urine bag hanging below his robe so that Boss Nurse could see it. Brittany hoped she couldn't see the bulge in his jacket pocket that looked suspiciously like a water balloon. Brittany ducked her head and struggled for a stern look for Tiny. She caught his attention and shot him a what-are-you-up-to look and glanced conspicuously at his pocket.

He eyeballed her for a moment, then winked.

Her immediate urge was to turn him in but she kept quiet. She was the rookie; he was the trained officer. The driver started the vehicle. "Okay," she said to herself, "here we go."

With a wave to the van she spotted the young man from the video, the one who'd be the discreet focus of her attention today. He hung back as though taking in the scene before him, trying to make heads or tails of it.

She waved him forward.

He pointed to himself. "Do I go on the van with them?"

Brittany smiled. "Yes, you do—Abrahim, is it?"

He nodded.

"Right this way." She ushered him forward and into the waiting transportation. Already seated, the Blues gazed out the windows. Brittany followed Abrahim. Upon approach she spotted Tiny watching them advance.

Brittany gave a small wave to Tiny and this time she winked.

❦

The driver plunked the van in gear and eased down the drive. Inside broad sighs and low groans filled the air. A middle-aged man, just short of a jog, hurried toward them. The operator stopped and opened the door. Dr. Wicker gave him a nod and hoisted himself onto the bottom step. Wicker took a moment to catch his breath. "Well," he said with a quick smile, "that was close."

The occupants stared at him; no one laughed.

Dr. Wicker cleared his throat and moved on. "Isn't this exciting? I hope you'll all be on your best behavior. This is a special activity for each of you. Remember that each one of you represents all us here."

He glanced around the van. Most of the occupants had directed their "Hail to the Cheeks" offering protest against the doc and weren't too hot about his efforts since then. They just stared at him. "Well..." he trailed off. "Oh, my." He gave Boss Nurse a curt nod. "Nurse Betsy, I'm trusting you to help these patients have a wonderful time."

She arched a brow at him but remained silent.

"Okay then," he said with an uneasy smile, "bye now."

He directed a good-luck glance at Betsy. The Blues continued their stony silence, staring directly at him; Dr. Wicker attempted a nonchalant exit but ended up tangling his feet in the effort. He stumbled, caught himself, and turned to stride back to the facility.

"I'll give it to him," Tiny said. "He does try."

Seated next to him, Brittany leaned toward Tiny. "Does he know about the Ol' Blues?" she asked.

With a sharp laugh, he shook his head. "No way. That poor guy gets so nervous that he would have a heart attack if he knew about the smallest part of our operation."

"What's he like?"

"He's brilliant with the books," Tiny said, "but he doesn't have a clue about dealing with real people. He prefers to be in the background and that makes him perfect for his position. Doesn't ask a lot of questions as long as everything runs smoothly. The trick is making him think everything is running smoothly. He's got a one-of-a-kind operation here without a bunch of bureaucrats giving him directives and red tape. The uniqueness of our operation allows us to individualize our own criteria."

Brittany scanned the faces around her—past their prime but still willing and able police officers acting like infirm old men, cracking cases, and shuffling back to their retirement home. "I still can't get over it," she said. "But it's positively brilliant."

"We think so."

෴

Seated directly behind the bus driver, Abrahim Koak thought the whole thing was dumb, the stupidest thing he'd ever gotten into. The sight of all the weak, helpless old men already made his skin crawl, and he still had the rest of the day to get through. The redheaded woman in the back must be a state welfare worker. He'd have no problem accomplishing his task with her. The dark-skinned nurse, one of the biggest women he'd ever seen, would be no problem, as long as she didn't sit on him. He'd give her a wide berth as well. Along with his cousin Clubba, Abrahim didn't like African Americans. Abrahim didn't know who they were fooling; they weren't African. Not in the least.

He despised everyone traveling today. He'd seen too many innocent Sudanese placed in low-cost housing crawling with gangs, drugs, and other criminals. First victimized by the civil war in their home country, they were victimized a second time by the country that was supposed to be a place of refuge. Abrahim and most other Sudanese witnessed the worst of the African-Americans. Their dislike and disdain for them knew no bounds.

To make matters worse, the Sudanese didn't know how to report crimes; they feared anyone in a uniform. Where they came from, uniforms meant soldiers and soldiers meant death. No wonder a man like Clubba had risen to prominence. Shrewd, quick thinking, and bilingual, he not only spoke but also moved between the American and Sudanese groups with the fluency of a native. His willingness to help desperate refugees now in a strange land meant they not only respected him as a leader, he had their hearts as well. No wonder he'd propelled himself into a fast-growing emperor.

The prospect of being a part of it excited Abrahim. Clubba didn't share all his plans, but if Abrahim was important to Clubba, his future was set. He settled back in his seat and closed his eyes. If it took a few hours of helping these fools to bring it about, Abrahim was more than happy to oblige.

CHAPTER 20

HAVING FINISHED HIS ROUNDS TO EACH GANG LEADER, Clubba sank down on his bunk and checked the list for the retirees' visit. His name was on it; one name stood out. One of the older trustees always seemed to sign up for most of Clubba's details. "Earnest Yates?" Clubba asked under his breath.

Who was he? Better yet, why was he tailing him? He'd seen him during various details, but they'd only spoken once and that had been during the incident with that stupid cracker, Big Whitey.

Yates, an older trustee, had actually helped Clubba manipulate Big Whitey into trusting him and using his services. At the time Clubba thought it a stroke of sheer luck, but on second thought, it might've been more. The ruckus made Big Whitey look at Clubba in a different light. Had the old man been onto his ruse the entire time? Had he spoken up to help him accomplish his goal? Either way, the awareness of being followed didn't please Clubba. He'd missed the tail. White-hot anger shot through him. It shouldn't have taken so long to recognize he had a trailer. He needed to find out more.

∽

Boss Nurse Betsy led the procession of old men with walkers and canes as well as those few capable of walking unassisted from the bus to reception. Single file they went through the metal detector; the walking devices were carried in and handed back once each man emerged on the other side. The correctional guards unwittingly provided an entire arsenal of weaponry. Each Blue took his walking aid, thanked the guard, and winked at his companions.

Nothing would be used unless absolutely necessary, but as former cops they weren't going anywhere unprotected. Brittany stared at the canes she recognized as Tasers, walkers that shot pepper spray, and then there was the Blue with the crutches—the one she'd asked if they were bazookas. Impossible, wasn't it? A bead of sweat gathered at her temple. She caught him retrieving his prop and watched him exchange a mischievous look with Tiny. Dear heaven, it couldn't be!

The tricky old men reminded her of the mission. The glasses! Retrieving them from her pocket, she looked around and spotted Tiny hanging toward the back of the group. Pushing her thumb under the right lens started the recording. A tiny red dot that only she could see indicated the glasses were working. Glancing around the room, she caught Tiny's gaze and winked at him. "Oh great. Now they've got me doing it."

Tiny returned her message in kind.

"Abrahim," she said to the young probationer. "Why don't you go to the second table over there." She indicated two Blues who appeared low functioning. They moved extremely slowly and spoke with a lot of pauses. Brittany arranged the chairs so there was an empty one available by Abrahim and his Blues. She placed herself, Tiny, and two other Blues at an adjacent table that provided her a good line of sight to Abrahim and hopefully this guy, Clubba.

Coloring books, basket-making materials, and small sticks for making flags littered the tabletops. Every Blue acted excited about all the trinkets and activities scheduled for the day, but Brittany knew better. The trustees dressed in their whites entered the room with an assistant warden who gave simple instructions to sit and be nice. They all nodded and headed to different tables.

One headed to Abrahim's. Clubba, about to miss his opportunity, tried to discreetly beat the inmate there. A Hispanic trustee plopped into the only empty chair available. Visibly upset, Abrahim looked between him and Clubba. Clubba lifted a hand in a reassuring way and tapped the inmate on the shoulder. He bent down, whispered something to the other trustee, and pointed toward two Hispanic Blues.

He quickly left and Clubba seated himself in his place; pleasure beamed from his face. *"Kizibwe wange,"* he said in his native tongue.

"Cousin," Brittany thought. His mother's nephew.

"How'd you get rid of him?" Abrahim asked.

"I simply reminded him about the rules in here."

"What rules?"

"Let's just say there are…risks in here if you don't stay with your own race," Clubba said.

Abrahim expelled a long breath. *"Very good cousin; I thought all was lost for a moment."*

"All is fine," Clubba said. Before Abrahim could comment further, Clubba smiled at the Blues. "Hello gentlemen. I think it will be fun to put together these flags, don't you?"

Abrahim blinked in apparent confusion. *"Kizibwe wange,"* he began. *"What are you doing?"*

"Getting them started and busy first. We give the guards nothing to watch and then we can talk."

"Got it," Abrahim said.

"Too much conversation in Sudanese," Clubba said and gently arranged the materials for each Blue, *"would surely be noticed. Getting on with the purpose of the day gives us the cover we need to talk."*

The Blues moved slowly but steadily on creating the flags. Clubba followed suit as did Abrahim.

"Kizibwe wange," Clubba said under his breath. *"What news do you have for me?"*

Abrahim quickly explained his recent activities with Clubba's followers as well as house shootings and three attempted murders that had occurred in Omaha. *"Now with instructions getting out sooner,"* Abrahim said, *"things can be carried out faster. The Aryans are the hardest to deal with,"* he continued. *"They don't like African-Americans. They hate Big Whitey's use of a black messenger, but they're impressed with all the information getting to them. They put their distaste aside.*

Much of it was up-to-date, and they didn't have to wait a week for an encoded letter. That way cost time—"

"*—and time is what they need most.*"

"*Correct,*" Abrahim said.

"*Good,*" Clubba said.

"*The leadership out there finally recognizes that by using the blacks to serve as messengers confuses federal investigators who were undoubtedly watching them. The Aryans like screwing with the FBI and DEA. Using us is not only a source of information but a good laugh as well.*" Abrahim stopped talking and looked expectantly at Clubba.

"*Aryans don't concern me,*" Clubba said. "*We will only be able to influence them when we have one of my soldiers in the prison. Now that we can talk longer, it will work out well.*"

Abrahim's shoulders relaxed and he smiled. "*Indeed. What information do I need to convey?*"

Clubba reclined in his chair, his long arms resting on the table. Like a king, Brittany thought.

"*We only have a month to put my plans in action for the gangs of Omaha. Take twenty of our most devoted soldiers and instruct each to join a different gang. They'll be a liaison to me. I'll have a network of soldiers to influence each one. When I get out, this must be in place.*"

Abrahim nodded somberly. "*It will be as you say, cousin. Each of your soldiers wants to be in your service. Each of their families is indebted to you.*"

That Clubba already knew. Their indebtedness was his currency. What he asked of Abrahim was the next step in developing gang dependence on him and his network.

"*One thing,*" Abrahim said, breaking his concentration. "*How will having a soldier in each gang give you great power? Why not increase our own group? Wouldn't we be a force respected and feared?*"

Clubba steepled his fingers and smiled at Abrahim. "So thought the original gangs. They'd start with many members only to have to watch after them." Clubba shrugged. "*And what did it get them? Individual gangs are limited to their Omaha neighborhood. If found outside their hood, they get attacked or killed. Believe it or not, I learned something in school about history and the war against the Japanese. The Americans employed Native Americans for communication—the Wind Talkers. Because the Japanese could not understand their language, the American army gained a great advantage. They coordinated their efforts throughout the Pacific using those men but protected them from the Japanese. If I control gang communication, I control the gangs. The police, much like the Japanese, don't understand our language—"*

Brittany bit the inside of her cheek to keep from responding.

"Eventually they'll get a Sudanese police officer who speaks the language. Until then, I've got my network set up throughout the city."

Clubba sounded pretty proud of himself to Brittany.

"Think what it will be, cousin. I will control all the communications from prisons to the streets. They will all depend on me—and that makes me very valuable. Then, like the Americans with the Wind Talkers, they will protect me. I won't need my own gang; I will be part of all the gangs. Like the powerful men in Sudan: Warlord!"

Abrahim's eyes widened with realization. *"Genius,"* he said. *"Rule them and profit from them all. There's much money to be made; it's brilliant."* The last words came out loud enough to draw attention to their table.

"Enough talk for this visit. Let's help these old cows make their flags." Clubba turned to help a Blue with his glue. *"No suspicions. Ever."*

Brittany breathed a sigh of relief. She'd gotten their entire conversation recorded. Tiny raised his eyebrows at her in question. Leaning closer she dropped her voice to a low whisper. "I understood most of it, but there were a few words I didn't."

"No worries," Tiny murmured and fiddled with a paintbrush. "We'll review it at the precinct. Until then, I need to keep Clubba off-balance."

"What?" Brittany asked a little confused. "Why? He sounds like he's going to be the top boss of Omaha. You can't disrupt his plans yet. Can you?"

Tiny smiled his gap-toothed grin. When he spoke in hushed tones, she didn't notice that whistle.

"I've been building a special relationship with Clubba," Tiny said. "I want his hatred so focused on me that it disrupts his thinking." He gave one Blue at the farthest table a wink and a nod. The Blue returned the gestures and levered himself up to his walker. One foot went out and the Blue dropped to the floor.

If she hadn't known it was all an act, Brittany would've been taken in by the performance. With masterful grace his left leg jerked and the lower prosthesis spun off the upper stump. The fake limb complete with an attached blue tennis shoe skipped across the floor ramming the foot of a female guard. She screamed and jumped. The Blue hollered on his way to the floor and made sure the walker clattered with a loud crash. Everyone's attention riveted to the ruckus in the room. As though on cue, the Ol' Blues at Clubba's table rushed toward their fallen friend. One grabbed Brittany by the arm and hauled her along with them.

Mesmerized Brittany watched Tiny. He pulled the piss pack out of his pocket and tossed it at Clubba's feet. It hit with a wet *splat*. With all the commotion of the downed man and detached leg, no one noticed.

Except for Clubba and Abrahim. The spray hit them and they froze. From the looks on their faces, they didn't fully comprehend what happened…until a distinctive odor oozed skyward.

Abrahim doubled over. "I know that smell."

Clubba's gag reflex immediately responded to that stench. Bile rose from his stomach to his throat. Rage enveloped him and he threw himself to a standing position.

Guards descended into the confusion but Clubba couldn't hear anything. Somewhere in this room was the source of his wrath. Almost absently, Clubba punched his thigh with his fist. Glaring at each person, an odd sound penetrated the fog of fury surrounding him. A shrill whistle penetrated the commotion in the multipurpose room. Hard on its heels came a soft laugh. It couldn't be!

Earnest Yates had been in prison long enough to recognize a diversion when he saw one. Immediately, he turned away from the pandemonium. He had to admit, though, it was a good one. A leg skidding across the floor and hitting a guard—nobody'd ever thought of that before.

Earnest quickly surveyed the opposite side of the room. Clubba and a smaller, younger man stood with arms in the air, plucking their clothing away from their skin. A yellowish-brown liquid dripped from their shirts to their pants. Earnest was seated close to the entrance with his back to the door in case he had to make a quick escape. When fights broke out, it was always best to know the quickest exits. A person lived longer that way.

Clubba's face, usually calm and controlled in every situation, contorted into a mask of rage; he pointed to a small man. "You."

Earnest followed Clubba's line of sight. The object of Clubba's ire stood about five feet four inches—every bit of him convulsed in laughter. Earnest's heart skipped a beat, and he examined the man closer, homing in on him with laser precision.

"It can't be," Earnest said out loud. He blinked and hoped it would clear his vision. It didn't. The same person, small stature, cocky attitude, fearless in the face of potential danger stared at the convicted felon. The description fit only one person in Earnest's mind, only one who'd dare a banger to come after him. "Tiny!"

The one who'd put Earnest in this hellhole more times than he cared to count. Right here. He could kill him right now, Earnest thought. "Right freaking now," he said through gritted teeth.

The view unfolding in front of him held him still. Clubba looked at Tiny with cold malice. The boy was all but vibrating with enmity. His longing to attack Tiny was written all over his face.

"Well, well," Earnest said and relaxed into a smile. "Looks like the perfect pawn to do the job for me." Earnest chuckled to himself. "How perfect. Clubba gets out in about a month. He can do the killing for me."

Clubba didn't take his eyes off Tiny. *"Kizibwe wange,"* he said, *"keep working with this group. Find out everything you can about this man."*

"Are you all right?" Abrahim asked. "I've never seen you so angry. *"Who is he? Kizibwe wange?"* he asked.

"Just do it!" Clubba responded.

"As you wish."

Brittany tamped down her initial shock. It was like being in a war zone but things were calming down. A guard carried the leg from the other side of the room and handed it to the Blue lying on the ground. He should take a bow after that performance. She spotted Tiny staring down Clubba and laughing. It appeared to enrage the younger man. He turned to Abrahim and spoke in Sudanese. She wasn't as close as before and only heard a few words, but it sounded like he was telling Abrahim to watch Tiny.

From what she saw, Tiny thoroughly enjoyed every minute of the excitement. This Clubba person was frightening on paper; in person, he was absolutely terrifying. Bats were his weapons of choice against his enemies, and he wasn't afraid to let people know he was the one who'd hurt them. None of it appeared to bother Tiny in the least. His antics only goaded Clubba. The more Tiny laughed, the more rage filled Clubba's face.

Brittany cocked her head and listened intently. Was that a whistle? Tiny was whistling? It made no sense, but he seemed to know exactly what he was doing. She only prayed he did.

Once calm returned to the prison room, it was time for the group to leave. At the exit, the Blues turned and waved to the inmates in thanks. The inmates stared after them, confusion etched in every face.

Helpless little old men indeed. Brittany readied the group for the return trip up the interstate. "Let's have an uneventful trek back home," she said.

Tiny kept his gaze focused on the scenery outside. "Don't know what you mean."

A glance into the mirror showed Abrahim glaring at the back of Tiny's head. Brittany leaned over and informed him.

"Good," Tiny whispered. "The bait's set for these mutts."

CHAPTER 21

EARNEST WATCHED CLUBBA STALK BACK TO HIS CELL, THE younger man's massive fists clenching and unclenching. Brows drawn together in unambiguous ire, he muttered all the way down the hall in a language unknown to Earnest. One thing he was certain of. This was prime time to talk with the kid. Particularly now that they had something in common.

♋

Freshly showered and cleaned up, Clubba emerged through the steel bars of his cell a short while later. He didn't stink anymore and his jumpsuit was clean. He assumed an air of self-control and stopped punching his thigh. It was all so unbelievable.

He slumped down into a sofa in the commons area. "He came—" Clubba sliced his hand through the air, "here! That crazy old man came all the way down here…to mock me."

Several inmates threw sidelong glances his way as if he'd lost his mind and skittered away.

"And he doused me with urine—again." Clubba trailed off and stared into space.

"Looks to me," said an older, calmer voice from behind, "as though you've got a man that doesn't like you much—at all." Earnest's low tone validated everything Clubba felt, thought, and lived through.

Surprised, Clubba didn't bother looking behind him. "I wondered when you'd talk to me, Earnest Yates."

Earnest jerked back.

"Surprised?" Clubba asked.

"You know me?"

Clubba chuckled. "How could I not? You been on the same volunteer unit with me for the last three weeks. Never talk to me but you stay close enough to hear what you think's going on and then from a distance. I'm not stupid."

"Then I won't waste your time denying it," Earnest said. He drew his lips into a smile. "You're observant."

Clubba turned around and leaned his back against the cushions, crossing his ankle on his knee. "And you're smarter than you let on."

Earnest acknowledged the compliment by a curt head tilt.

"You've watched me," Clubba continued, "quietly but consistently. And you helped me out with the Aryans."

Earnest's brows drew together in a frown.

"Dropped the metal spoon on the ground and then talked to me and Big Whitey like a street punk. Told me to go back to Africa or something like that. I owe you. If you hadn't acted like a street thug hating on me because of the way I talked, I might not have been able to pull it off."

Earnest's brows furrowed deeper. "Pull what off?" he asked. "And why gain the Aryans' trust? I'm black, too, and we both know they aren't our friends."

"I don't want their friendship," Clubba growled. "I want their trust. It's one thing I need right now."

Earnest glanced around as though making sure they couldn't be overheard. Grabbing a chair, he turned it around and sank into it with his elbows on the back and facing Clubba. "First day you walked into this block, you immediately flashed the different gangs," he said.

Clubba opened his mouth to correct him.

Earnest raised a hand and shook his head. "It was discreet, I'll give you that, but yes, you did. You did it to all members, all gangs, everyone. Groups who are enemies on the outside as well as here on the inside."

Clubba shrugged a broad shoulder. "So?"

"So," Earnest continued. "They let you waltz into and out of their meetings, their living areas, their eating areas. It's unheard of. The first couple of months, you earned the protection of each group in the joint. In twenty-seven years, I've never seen that happen." He leaned in close to make his point. "Not ever. You're the only true associate I've ever seen. Many have tried, some have come close, but nobody—" he stabbed a finger toward Clubba, "and I mean nobody has done what I've watched you accomplish in a few months."

Pride swelled in Clubba, and he beamed his approval of Earnest's accolades. A brief bow of his head at the compliment and he glanced at Earnest. "You say I'm observant? That you've watched me from day one and you've seen what nobody else could? I'd say you're the observant one."

Earnest glanced around the cinder-block walls and sighed deeply. "Twenty years here will do that to a person. You need to watch and learn quickly what's going on around you. I can get everything I need to know about a man in just a week or two. Very little impresses me, but you do. I've watched you for five months, and I'm impressed with everything about you."

Clubba crossed his arms over his chest and eyed Earnest. "Everything? How much have you seen?"

Earnest held up an index finger. "One, you freely walk into and out of each of the main gangs. Two," his middle finger joined the first, "for reasons I don't know, each leader not only talks to you, they protect you. Three, every group trusts you—even the god-awful Aryans! From what I've seen, only Big Whitey talks to you, which means he's telling you things he doesn't want others to hear. Even the other Aryans! And finally, the guards gave you trustee status—more than I've ever seen or gotten and I've been here decades."

Earnest pulled each digit down and clenched them all together in a fist. "Combine all those things," he said and stuck his fist out toward Clubba's cheek, "and you're the most powerful man in the joint."

Much like the fox guarding the proverbial hen house, Clubba thought. His lips parted in an acknowledging smile. Earnest seemed to know everything; Clubba could use a man like him on the inside. "Impressive deductions, Earnest—if I can call you Earnest?"

He tilted his head and agreed. "Manners," he said. "A rare attribute in prisoners."

"My mother insisted on them," Clubba said.

"My compliments to her, and, yes, please call me Earnest."

"If you're thinking about teaming up, forget it," Clubba said. "I'll only be here another month or so."

"Then you need me," Earnest said soberly.

"Perhaps," Clubba said. "Once I leave, there will be other Sudanese, others of my associates sent to continue the connections I've made. I could use someone of your experience, someone who knows prison inside out, someone who can act as a contact inside." Clubba let the conversation drift off.

"And?" Earnest asked.

"You interested?"

The question sent Earnest's mind reeling at the unanticipated opportunity! His plan was to recruit Clubba and settle an old debt with Tiny, but this…Clubba obviously had something else in mind. The boy thought deeply, a characteristic Earnest thoroughly appreciated. He rested his hand on his chin and hoped to appear in deep thought. In reality his mind had been honed by years of quick thinking; there had to be a way to use the offer to his advantage. "I'd be honored."

"Don't be," Clubba said. "You're clever, know the system and the players involved. In exchange for your service, I can get you protection."

"Service?" Earnest asked. "What service exactly?"

"To me," Clubba said, "and my soldie—ah, Sudanese associates."

Earnest noticed the verbal stutter-step but didn't know what it meant. He'd find out soon enough what the kid was up to and what his real game would be. "Protection is always a prize possession here," he said blandly and glanced across the room. No need to tip his hand too soon.

"We'll work out the details as my parole nears," Clubba said. "Too much talking draws attention."

"Mm," Earnest said in agreement. "We'll pick this up later."

"Later," Clubba said.

Earnest strolled back to his house—his current cell. It wasn't much but it was home. So Clubba planned to send others behind bars. Incredible. What kind of power did the kid have outside prison? If he could send his accomplices here, it followed that he could direct them to commit crimes, get caught, and go to prison. It was mind-boggling that anyone would follow orders like that. No one intended to go to prison; when your luck ran out, it just happened.

Thinking back to their recent conversation when Clubba caught himself, Earnest finally understood what he almost let slip. More than compatriots or colleagues, the young men Clubba would send would be his soldiers. But how? How did one have his own army, get others to do his complete bidding? The scope and size of Clubba's plan took Earnest's breath away.

"This guy's a lot more than I ever gave him credit for," Earnest whispered aloud. He continued down the tier to his house. This new wrinkle would take some thinking and planning. His new Sudanese associate would keep Earnest on his toes. "A helluva lot more."

CHAPTER 22

THE SARGE'S OFFICE BUZZED WITH CHATTERING BLUES. From his desk overflowing with surveillance monitors and streaming video, the Sarge worked on the finishing touches of his upcoming presentation. The desk had one-way glass on the top. The Sarge activated the screen by tapping it and turning a built-in lever on a desk leg. Glancing down he could watch in the same way as an evening news anchor from both the cue screens and others built directly into their desks.

The Sarge knocked on the desk leg and gently moved the lever. The glasses were hooked up to a cable that allowed them to be played back. The back of the Sarge's office held a hidden projector. From there, images could be displayed on the white wall to the right of the Sarge's desk. Surveillance and footage from Brittany's intelligence mission played, and Brittany translated for the Blues.

Her father walked up behind the Sarge. "She doing a good job for you?"

"I think she was born for it."

"From what Clubba is saying," Brittany said, "it looks like he wants a hand in all the major Omaha gangs. Here he's saying that he wants a Sudanese...soldier? I think...soldier in each gang as a messenger. He's also talking to his cousin about the gangs protecting him when he gets out."

There were murmurs and nods among her audience members. "This confused me a bit. He used a term I've never heard before.

Something about an 'air speaker' as near as I can figure out, but it doesn't make a lot of sense to me. What about you?"

The audience exchanged puzzled looks and murmured among themselves. "He said it would be like the war against the Japanese," she continued, "where Native Americans communicated for the American military. He told his cousin the gangs would protect him outside the prison just like the Americans protected these 'air speakers.'"

"That's Wind Talkers," a voice from the back of the room said. "Navajos that saved our butts in the Pacific. Japs could never understand them on radio, and it made it easier to communicate throughout the war campaign."

"That Clubba is right," another man said. "If he gets Wind Talker status, the gangs would definitely protect him. Just like the Marines did for the Navajos."

"Clever plan," the Sarge said. "He'll be ruling each gang through his soldiers—one apiece. Then he can dictate their instructions and get internal intelligence."

"What a position of power," Smitty said. "Leader of all the major gangs and he doesn't belong to any of them."

"Reminds me of Tolkien," the Sarge said. "One ring to rule them all...only it's a king, not a ring."

"Clubba did say something about making himself a, uh...I'm not sure how to translate it exactly but we heard it a lot in the safe zone refugee camps around Sudan," Brittany said. "The term means something like a fighting god or war god."

"Warlord maybe?" Smitty shot Brittany a startled glance.

"Yeah," Brittany said. "That could be it."

"That means," Smitty said, "that he's taking a page from the Sudanese fighters who ruled significant portions of his lawless country. They were called warlords."

The Blues in the room fell silent as though chewing on that piece of information.

"This guy thinks he's gonna set up his own little army in Omaha and nobody's gonna stop him?" The Sarge asked and glanced from Blue to Blue in the front rows. "Well, we'll see about that, right, boys?"

Affirmative grunts and silent nods of agreement met his question. The video of Tiny started; the Sarge pointed at the wall. "And this is how we're going to get this little warlord to screw up. We're gonna keep him off-balance, get him so focused on Tiny that he won't be able to dedicate his time to establishing an army or go after his ex-girlfriend."

The video showed Tiny's partner wink at him. As the artificial leg skittered across the floor, the Blues in the audience bellowed with laughter. Once the female CO jumped into the air and screamed, the room howled their approval. Brittany joined in right along with them.

Once Tiny chucked his piss pack at Clubba and his cousin, the Blues exploded with renewed merriment. "Ooooh!" The audience chorus erupted the moment the explosive liquid burst onto Clubba and Abrahim.

"Look at his eyes," one Blue shouted. "He's a comin' for you for sure, Tiny."

"Which is exactly what we want," Smitty said. "And when he does, we'll be waiting for him. Warlord prick!"

Brittany sat down, the Blues' remarks swirling around her. She watched her father and the Sarge make their comments. It showed a side of these men she'd never seen before when delivering cookies and coaxing a smile out. These men were undercover the entire time she visited, acting weak and old. She smiled and glanced at her father again. Talking strategy with the Sarge, he caught her eye and winked.

The Blues in the room convulsed with laughter again, many pointing at the screen. Dragging her attention from her dad to the screen image on the wall, one of the Ol' Blues yelled, "Women?"

"Uh-oh," a smart aleck in the front row called out. "Potty break."

Brittany watched her own hand push the door open; there were three stalls to choose from and Brittany picked the first. Rule one of covert surveillance: shut off the video glasses during private time.

"Yikes." She sprang from her chair and dashed to the front of the room to stand directly in front of the broadcast.

"Down in front," came a comment from her left.

"Get out of the way," said another on her right. A few unmentionable comments drifted up from the middle of the audience.

She silenced each one by pointing that vicious finger of hers moving it from left to right to make sure every Blue, including the Sarge, got her full meaning.

While thoroughly enjoying the terror that flashed on Brittany's face and her unflinching stance in front of two dozen former cops, the Sarge wasn't about to let Brittany lose her dignity. He stopped the video and froze.

A litany of boos started at the back and rippled forward. Every Blue in the precinct had wanted to see the undercover assignment and congratulate Brittany on her first mission, so much so that everyone had left their posts unattended. The Sarge blinked.

The Blues in the room continued their phony displeasure of missing Brittany on the porcelain throne. Person by person they caught the look on the Sarge's face and quieted instantly.

The Sarge reached down and hit what looked like a slightly warped piece of wood on the floor under his desk. The emergency shut-off button. Everything and everyone went quiet; all attention flew to the Sarge.

The unmistakable image of three-hundred-pound Boss Nurse Betsy entering the precinct office burned in his brain. And she made a straight line for the Sarge's office; every Blue heard the unmistakable sound of her overstretched polyester pants rubbing together.

At the front of the room Brittany smiled. "Wow," she said to no one in particular, "I really scared those old poops."

She turned to the Sarge and followed his line of sight. Through the smoked windows of his office, the silhouette of someone on the opposite side showed through. Whoever it was certainly had every Blue's attention including Sarge's. The huge silhouette moved along the windows toward the Sarge's door. At fifteen feet out, a strange whooshing sound reached her ears, but Brittany couldn't identify what it was.

Smitty sprang to his feet with an agility that surprised Brittany. He grabbed her forearm and pulled her toward the audience. Boss Nurse drew closer; everyone stood and faced the door.

Smitty tugged Brittany and stuck her behind a Blue. "That's Big Brock," he whispered. "Sit on the floor, stay still, and for Pete's sake be quiet."

She knew that tone of voice brooked no argument. Brittany pulled her legs up and slumped on the floor trying to make herself as small as she could. Although she hadn't realized it at first, Big Brock had his indignity bottoms on—and she was directly under him. A glance skyward confirmed that analysis. Thankfully he stood more than six feet tall and wore crinkled boxers that stuck out below the leg holes. A quick glance up showed her she was directly below... the coconuts. Squeezing her eyes shut, she rested her forehead on her knees. "Oh great," she muttered.

The words no more than left her mouth and Big Brock demonstrated the art of being old and male. He loudly broke wind, jumped slightly and turned his head down toward Brittany. "Sorry."

Brittany highly doubted it, but before she could follow the thought up, she cupped her hands over her mouth and nose. Dang! She had to stay still to keep from being discovered, but this was above and beyond anything she'd imagined. This secret agent stuff was nothing like James Bond. Nothing!

The Sarge called out, "Green light."

All the Blues moved a step forward—except for Big Brock. Brittany gritted her teeth in frustration.

"Red Light!" The Sarge called out.

Several guys froze; others laughed and moved anyway.

"Got ya, Smitty." The Sarge said with a whoop.

"Did not." Smitty responded. The room of Blues broke into renewed laughter like they'd done earlier during the video.

"What're y'all doin' in here?" bellowed Betsy.

The entire group froze and stared at her. She returned them with one of her own and lapsed into an uncomfortably awkward ten seconds. His back to her, the Sarge pointed at a nearby Blue. "You moved!"

A line of others against the wall joined in. "Yep I saw him; he moved all right."

"He's out," called another. The Blue shrugged and took his place against the wall.

The Sarge turned to look at the head nurse. "Oh, hi, Nurse Betsy," he said.

The Blues against the wall waved and smiled, but those still in the game stood like statues.

"What's going on here?" she demanded.

"Just a friendly game of red light/green light," Tiny said.

"Green light," the Sarge called out.

Britany opened one eye and looked through the legs of those standing. Several sets started to make odd-looking shuffles forward.

A muffled laugh came from Nurse Betsy. "Look pretty funny trying to sneaky walk, guys."

"Red light!" the Sarge called again. "Got you…and you."

"No you didn't!" a voice piped up.

"Oh, yes I did," the Sarge said. "Right, Nurse Betsy?"

"You bicker like a buncha little kids on a playground."

One Blue shifted from foot to foot. "I've gotta tinkle."

"Oh, all right," Boss Nurse said. "Come on…and make sure you hold it. I don't want you wettin' the floor." As they walked away, she said, "Ol' Blues, humph, more like a Senile Squad."

Two other Blues—on the opposite side of the room, a fact Brittany was completely thankful for—let loose with a flatulent encore. Boss Nurse made a disgusted sound, then walked away with the Ol' Blue holding himself as if trying to keep from having an accident on the floor.

Brittany shook her head. Seems like these guys could fart on demand.

"That'll make sure Boss Nurse doesn't come back," Big Brock said.

Brittany kept her eyes on the ground and nodded. "Good."

The Blues left behind started to chuckle.

"Okay, Brittany," the Sarge said. "Come out, come out wherever you are."

She pushed to her feet and stepped out from behind Big Brock.

A sheepish look crossed his face. "I'm really sorry 'bout that."

She pointed at him and slowly turned her attention to the Sarge. She let the indicting finger linger at Big Brock. His countenance grew more ashamed with each second that passed.

"I wish I knew how she did that," her father said.

"Officer Brittany," Sarge said, still smiling from the recent incident. "You did pretty good today. The intelligence you provided will help develop a strategy to deal with this self-appointed warlord—and I use the term loosely. You certainly earned your pay." With a quick glance around, he said, "Call it a day, folks."

"Sarge's compliment is about all low-paid cops get," her father said from behind her.

"Sure feels good, though," Brittany said.

"It's what keeps us coming back," Smitty said and slung an arm around his daughter's shoulders.

"You know," she said, "I was happy to help."

"I know."

"And I want to do it again," she said.

Her father breathed out a long breath. "Why doesn't that surprise me?"

A TUG OF WAR RAGED INSIDE JAKE: HIS ATTRACTION TO Brittany versus what? He wasn't exactly sure. For years since his wife's death, anytime he so much as looked at a beautiful woman, guilt would consume him. Forget about asking her on a date. They weren't really Jake's type anyway so it never mattered. Loads of men went after the hotties. Not Jake. Those women were too into themselves and viewed men as an appendage not a companion.

With Brittany, things were different. She didn't seem to know how pretty she actually was. How could she not know what a knockout she was? And she was kind. She took care of all those old cops as though they were all related, like an adopted grandchild or niece. She visited regularly bringing cheer as well as treats. She gave of herself as well as of her kitchen. No wonder those Ol' Blues adored her.

Jake stared out his office window and rubbed the back of his neck. So why the confusion now? His relationship with his wife had been beautiful. At the last anniversary dinner, almost in premonition, Sarah had turned the conversation to a path he'd never imagined and didn't like. *If I die tomorrow, Jake, promise me that you'll marry again.*

Never, he'd protested vehemently.

Seriously. I want you to. It's important to have someone in your life. And Abigail…she'll need a mother—trust me. I've seen your efforts to dress her. They'd shared a laugh at that. *Really, though, she's going to need a woman's influence to become the kind of person we want her to be.*

Losing them both at the same time, he'd never imagined how empty life could be, so meaningless. Nobody needed him; he was completely and totally alone. It had taken awhile—too hard to leave the graves behind—but his brother had finally coaxed him to move to Omaha. The change helped, got him outside himself again. Working for the Omaha PD made him focus on what it meant to be needed again—if not by his family, by people of the community.

And now this. Brittany awakened a new need—something he'd buried over three years ago: the need to belong to someone and have someone belong to him.

Just the kind of woman you need, Jake, Sarah's voice whispered as though speaking in his ear. He sat rod-straight in his chair and looked around. Seeing nobody, he slumped into his seat again and scrubbed his hand across his eyes. *I know, babe, but she could have any guy she wanted. Why would she...*

Jake, my love, she's the kind of woman you need. I want you to be happy. Abigail and I will always be in your heart. It hurts us that you're lonely; Brittany is who you need...and she needs you. It's all right; it would bring us joy to know you have love in your life again.

Jake wasn't sure he was really in his office or had simply lost his mind. *A mom is important, Dad; you need to have a mom with a dad,* the voice of his little girl said. *Right now you're just a dad. You won't be happy without a mom.*

Tears prickled at the edges of his eyes. One slipped out to trickle down his cheek. "Thanks, babe."

⌒

Jake sat at his desk a long time processing the incident that had just occurred. Finally he shook his head to clear things and bring himself back to reality. He grabbed the stack of morning press releases. "I am at work," he muttered.

Reports typed and completed. That only left his departmental rounds before he could give Brittany a call. Excitement shivered up his spine.

His question was the same at each unit. Any notable persons or crimes they wanted released to the public? Robbery, homicide, special victims. One by one each got the same query. If anyone had a name or case, they could get a tip through Crime Stoppers. Anonymous or not the tip line was worth its weight in gold.

Jake accumulated the necessary information and headed to the gang unit. He'd been meaning to contact the sergeant there since they'd busted the purse-snatching ring.

Photos littered the unit's office. Each snap was categorized according to gang affiliation, area of town, and the information of the various gang members. Jake was always impressed with the sheer volume of information the unit amassed on any single individual. It took a special kind of cop to do what they did.

Most uniformed officers couldn't stand the sight of gangbangers. They'd rather cuff 'em and stuff 'em than speak to them. Common knowledge on the streets was if you caught a banger for one crime, they'd committed a host of others they'd gotten away with. Detectives in the unit would talk to the criminal associates even though they despised them. The easiest part of their job was to get the hoodlums bragging about themselves, their gang, and their activities and then compile the findings into an intelligence gold mine.

That gold mine blazed at everyone who walked into the unit. Jake was no exception. He smiled at the incessant activity. "Always gathering intelligence."

The unit sergeant perched behind his desk.

"Hey, Sergeant Scott," Jake called out.

"Oh, hey, Jake, You startled me for a second."

Jake reached over the desk and shook his hand.

"What can I do for you?"

"Well," Jake began, "accept my compliments on the work with that purse snatcher bunch."

Scott smiled broadly. "Yeah, that one felt good. They hurt a lot of women."

Jake motioned toward all the photos. "Which gang was it?"

Scott stretched and pushed back in his chair. Pointing from one wall to another and another, he blew out a breath and shook his head. "Funny thing...none of those."

Jake frowned and snapped his attention back to the sergeant. "None of them? Was this a new gang?"

The sergeant shook his head. "Nope, just a bunch of nit-wit football players who got their kicks from taking money from Hispanic women at the first of the month. Most of those idiots didn't even need any money; they came from families with decent incomes. They just wanted the thrill of stealing and getting away with it, stupid pricks!"

"So," Jake began and pointed his finger around the room. "You found all that out without any of this intelligence?"

"Actually," Sergeant Scott said and looked directly at Jake, "your office is the one that figured out who the suspects were."

"What?" Jake turned back to the sergeant in puzzlement. "My office?"

"Yeah. A tipster off the anonymous line gave us awesome information. Not the usual, *Hey police, I know who is stealing those purses.* It was someone with intimate knowledge of that neighborhood. The guy knew everybody on the block including the troublemakers."

"Really?" Jake asked.

"Yeah," Scott said, "he pieced together victim similarities that went beyond race, sex. He talked about how many times the women had been victimized in the past." He shook his head. "It was uncanny— stuff we usually look at. Obviously no one knows who it was, but the guy literally told us how to solve the case. Gave us the time frame for the next robbery, the type of school the suspects attended, and get this—he's the one who told us that they were football players."

"Sounds like he told you guys how to conduct the investigation," Jake said. "Pretty wild."

"I know." Scott threw his hands into the air. "I've never seen anything like it—ever." He glanced up at Jake. "Any way you could find out who he was?"

Jake laughed and shook his head. "Nope," he said flatly. "No caller ID on the Crime Stoppers phone. It's one way we keep anonymity and that's the key to our success. I couldn't find out if I wanted to."

"No way at all? I'd sure like to shake his hand."

"The only way I could find the identity of a tipster would be to ask if he wanted to be identified and get him to talk to the Crime Unit he provided the tip for. Sometimes we get people that will do it, but most of the time they don't want their name involved."

"Yeah, I suppose." Sergeant Scott nodded. "I'd give my right arm for a cop with those instincts. It takes decades of experience to hone investigative skills like that."

Jake smiled in agreement.

"See you tomorrow." Jake turned to leave; the sergeant sent him off with a nonchalant wave. Jake walked out of the gang unit office and turned the corner. *It takes decades of experience for investigative skills like that.* Like those of a retired cop?

Nah! All he'd ever heard from older cops was how badly they wanted to retire and get out of their crazy job. The image of the collection of Ol' Blues came to mind. Jake shook it off. Those guys were so old, they didn't care about Omaha crimes. Jake shook his head and chuckled.

The Sarge, Smitty, Tiny, and others he'd met were still sharp, even though they were pranksters—evident from the devious grins on the Sarge's and Smitty's faces when he bit into Brittany's cookie and about barfed. Was there something more than met the eye there? The place was filled with walkers, canes, diapers, and medical personnel. No way anybody there would be involved. He paused outside his office door and reconsidered. Shaking his head, he returned to his desk. Nope. No way those codgers were involved. No way at all.

At their stage of life, they wanted to play cops and do some good in their community, not do street surveillance and undercover investigation. The memory of an oatmeal-raisin cookie stuck in his throat brought him back to Brittany. "I've got to give her a call," he murmured, a familiar shiver curling in his belly.

Looking right and left, Jake went to his phone. Monica wasn't around so it was the perfect time. He pulled Brittany's number out of his pocket and stared at the dial pad. This was going to be harder than he thought. He sucked in a steadying breath and punched in the digits. Hard but not impossible.

Standing in the middle of her kitchen, Brittany noted the disaster she'd left behind in her haste. Mixing bowls, utensils, and crumb-coated cookie sheets lay in disarray. Flour still dusted her laminate counter… and the floor. "Wow, I was in some kind of a rush."

Running a sink full of hot water, she added a hefty dollop of dishwashing liquid. It still amazed her that she'd so readily bought into the fantasy that the Ol' Blues were helpless and old. Well, they were old, but hardly helpless. They played their parts well and functioned among the criminal element so smoothly it defied logical thought. At the pen they'd gone from weak and disabled to agile and vigorous. It still seemed almost unreal, but her respect for them—and the job they did—had grown exponentially. They were cops through and through. Gathering intelligence one minute, laughing at her forgetting to turn off her video recording, then switching back to brainless kids playing red light, green light. They were simply amazing.

Brittany picked up the plastic container of cookies. That was odd. The container usually came back empty. This was almost full. On closer examination, the texture didn't look quite right, so she took a bite. Inside her mouth, her taste buds revolted and she spit it into the empty side of the sink. Coughing and gagging, she rinsed her mouth out. "What?"

The ingredients still littered the counter: butter wrapper, cinnamon, pudding box, salt, soda, flour, oatmeal and raisin containers. Wait a minute…where was the sugar? Realization dawned. Sugarless cookies! She must've measured salt instead of sugar. No wonder it tasted so horrid; no wonder her mouth had puckered in mutiny!

Paps and Jerry said, "Touché."

She covered her face with her hands. Oh, no…they obviously thought she'd done it on purpose, and they'd been so looking forward to their favorite. She picked up the partially eaten cookie and her eyes widened. Jake! He'd eaten one! Well not the whole thing, but he hadn't said a word. He just swallowed and took her to lunch. Her heart softened and she pressed her hand on her chest. What a nice guy; he'd rather put himself out than hurt her feelings. He was definitely a rare bird.

Although, how he managed to keep a straight face was beyond her. "Oh my, I've got to call him and apologize."

The last word came out in a strangled chuckle. The image of Jake downing his bite of salt-laden dessert, while mortifying, was too funny for words. She reached for her phone, and it rang in her hand. She put the phone to her ear unsure if someone was on the other end or it was an electronic screw-up.

"Brittany?" Jake asked.

She smiled and laughed. "Jake, you sweetheart."

"Wow, I was only expecting something like, 'Hi, how are you?' Definitely not sweetheart!"

"I just tasted a cookie from this afternoon," she said. "They're horrid. I'm so sorry. I must've mixed up the salt with sugar. I all but puked."

Jake's deep chuckle vibrated through the air. "I know the feeling but I didn't want to embarrass you. When you walked out of the office, the Sarge and your dad just smiled at me. I knew they'd already tasted the stuff and were watching for my reaction."

"Sounds typical," she said.

Jake swiveled his chair and looked out his office window. "And in the interest of full disclosure, I didn't eat the rest of it. After you walked out, I broke it into two pieces and threw them at those jokers."

"Good." Brittany laughed along with Jake. "Those two troublemakers deserved it."

Jake set another dinner date with Brittany; she'd take care of the menu and he'd go to her apartment. Maybe dating was like riding a bike. Satisfaction filled Jake from head to toe. He hung up his phone and settled back in his chair. "Yes!" he said and lifted both his fists in the air.

Snort!

The all too familiar sound snapped him back to reality. Jake gritted his teeth and rolled his eyes. His lieutenant must've sneaked into the office while he was on the phone.

Snort!

Jake jerked upright in his chair. "Dang it, Monica!"

"Welcome back from Brittanyland," she said.

"Dang it," he muttered under his breath.

24

A HERD OF NURSING STUDENTS FOLLOWED THE resident who followed the lab-coated doctor on morning rounds. Nicki Jensen hung at the very back of the pack and caught one of her compatriots, Sharon, a second-year nursing student, staring a little too long at her. Nicki tugged a hank of hair forward in an attempt to cover the left side of her face.

"You okay?" a much younger Sharon asked.

Nicki nodded. In truth things were anything but okay. Some days she wasn't sure she'd last until spring graduation—and a full-time job. Some men were cut out to be house-husbands. Hers wasn't one of them. The stress of recently losing his job grated on Jeff. It didn't help their relationship either. Steeped in self-pity and simmering anger, no amount of compassion or understanding could soothe him. With full-time school and two little girls to tend and raise, Nicki needed a babysitter; the role naturally fell to him.

In actuality, the girls took care of each other. Ages four and five, they did a pretty good job of it. They played in their rooms and could obtain the food they wanted. They also played just outside the apartment in the courtyard grounds. Jeff left the door open and called it "watching the girls." Nicki shook her head. Life was like a snowball rolling downhill threatening her with disaster as it gained steam.

"Mrs. Jensen," the resident's voice pulled her back to reality.

"I'm sorry," she said. "What?"

"Your patients are waiting," he said with a nod at the west end of the wing.

Nicki blinked and looked around. Everyone else had gone on to their assigned duties. "Yes, sir."

She liked the geriatric rotation, enjoyed talking with the retired officers who seemed to appreciate that she took her time with them. Some of the younger kids dashed from one bed to another without ever seeing the person these patients used to be. Nicki loved their war stories the most, but she didn't want any in-depth discussions today. She tugged her collar higher.

"Hey, Nicki! What's up?" Fred Kinney, one of her favorites, called to her.

She hung just outside the door and forced a smile. "Not much, Fred. How's it going for you?"

"Old and tired," he said. "Not necessarily in that order." He gave her a sly wink.

She chuckled. Same routine but he never thought it got old, and she had to admit, it was a great line.

"Why are you standing around out there?" Fred's roommate, George Johnson, asked. He was bedridden but his eagle eye never missed a thing.

Nicki straightened and shook her head. "I need to head over to the lab," she lied.

"Sure you're not avoiding us?"

"Avoiding you?" she echoed. "Why would I do that?"

"Don't know," George said, "but you are."

"No—"

"Then come in and sit a spell," George said.

"Do you need something?" she asked. If she went into that room, they'd ferret out what had happened and she wanted no trouble—especially from the police.

"No, but—"

"Then I have to go," she said already easing into the hall. "I'll stop by later."

"Well that was odd," George said to Fred.

"No kidding," Fred said. "Something's definitely going on."

Each doctor, nurse, phlebotomist, or aide who entered the room got peppered with the same question: "What's wrong with Nicki today?"

Each query brought the same response: "I don't know."

Nicki managed to stay busy and away from most of the rooms during her shift. Keeping her distance from her classmates was easy; anything that needed to be done outside patient rooms, she volunteered for. And the doctors? She wasn't sure if it was her that they never actually noticed or nurses in general. Steering clear of them was no problem. She checked her watch—almost supper time. Maybe the residents would be too busy eating to be bothered with her.

Hovering at the first door, she asked, "Anybody need anything?"

As though on cue, each waved her on and shook his head. The second door went the same way. Nicki almost believed she was home free.

She finished her rounds, then passed George's door en route to the nurses' station, his soft voice drifted toward her. "Come in here, child."

His voice sounded so much like a caring grandfather, Nicki blinked back tears. She shook her head. No time for breakdown.

"Nicki," he said and motioned her forward.

How she ever thought she could keep anything away from these trained investigators, she had no idea. True to their roots, they could spot evasiveness in a heartbeat. Investigation was in their blood. She took a few steps into the room.

"Look at me, Nicki."

She complied, still blinking away the emotion that threatened to spill over.

"You know I was a detective for almost nineteen years, right?" George asked.

Nicki didn't trust her voice. She nodded.

"In domestic violence," he said.

Nicki took a deep breath.

"I'm used to people keeping things from me after an incident," he said conversationally. "Back in my day it was called wife beating, but it's still the same old game with different titles."

George motioned her forward and she complied but hovered back several steps from his bed.

"Dang," he said. "That looks about three days old; did he hit you over the weekend?"

Nicki pulled her hair over her left ear and neck. Even through the makeup, the bruise had spread from the front of her ear, along the jaw; finger lines reached back toward her neck where Jeff had slapped her on the side of the head.

"Not unusual for a victim not to want anyone to know," George continued. "He slapped you with his right hand, didn't he?" Without waiting for confirmation, he kept talking. "My guess is that you have a couple bruises on your back or your back side where he either punched you or kicked you as you ran away."

Despite her best efforts, a lone tear trickled down Nicki's right cheek. She waved her hand and shook her head. "You don't understand," she said. "Things are just really difficult right now." Nicki reined herself in and once again tamped down the twin feelings of shame and disgust simmering just below the surface.

"Please don't say anything," she said fixing a direct gaze on George. "My husband hasn't worked in over six months. I've never seen him like this. He just doesn't want to do anything—not even watching our daughters. We got into an argument about him needing to do a better job of that and he just snapped."

"How many children?" George asked softly.

"Two girls," she said slumped in a chair beside his bed. "He seems more interested in drinking beer, watching cable, and playing video games than in them."

"Tough to lose a job," George said. "Sorta punctures the male ego."

Nicki smiled at him. "Yeah, but it doesn't excuse his behavior with his daughters."

"How old?"

"Four and five," she said. "They kind of watch one another. I leave food they can open and easily eat just in case…"

George eyed the bruise with a growing frown.

Instinctively she put her hand to the side of her neck. "He's never hit me before. Ever! I don't know what got into him: drinking or depression or—I don't know. Everything's going wrong for him. I graduate at the end of the semester. I'll be working and that'll help." She laced her fingers in front of her to keep them still.

"Help with what?" George pressed.

"With the stress," she said. "I'm sure things will get better then."

"Perhaps," George said and took her hand in his.

"Don't say anything," Nicki whispered. "If my instructors find out, they'll have to report it and I can't deal with a police investigation or Child Protective Services swarming all over us to see if my girls need to be removed. Please," she said again searching the Ol' Blue's countenance for a shred of empathy or compassion. "It would be more than I could bear."

George nodded and released her hand. "Why don't you freshen up," he said indicating the bathroom.

When she returned, he gave her his "cop stare." "I'll let it go this time," he said. "But anything else...all bets are off."

Nicki nodded. "I understand." She took in a steadying breath and headed to the door. "Thanks, George," she said. "I always feel better talking to you."

Tugging her collar and hair over the bruise so no prying eyes would discover her secret, she headed out the door.

"Come back anytime," George called after her. He waited until he heard her one door down. He picked up his phone and punched in a number. "Hey, Sarge, this is George; I have a little operation that needs my attention. I'll need two additional Blues to accompany me. One to push my wheelchair and the other will need a walker for my backup."

"Okay," the Sarge said. "Anything else?"

"Probably a doctor's visit as my cover and transportation, of course." George ticked off his mental list. "I think we can take care of it in an afternoon and be back within a couple of hours."

"What's the assignment?" the Sarge asked.

"A husband who thinks it's all right to slap his wife around...one of the students here."

"Awesome," the Sarge said. "Delivering a little tuneup?"

"Yeah," George said. "Sort of furthering his education. Shouldn't take more than three hours."

"Consider it done."

"Thanks, Sarge."

Sarge hung up the phone and yelled to nobody specific. "Hey, I need a pusher for George in C Wing and one backup."

With no hesitation from anyone in the precinct, one hulking Blue, a Samoan named Big Al Afasa, six feet four and two hundred forty pounds nicknamed Tinkerbell or "Tink" waved his hand in the air. "I'm in. I'll be the pusher."

"I'll be backup," Harry called out. "I've been waiting to use that new walker."

"Done and done!" The Sarge barked. "Get to supply for the clothes and any special equipment for that walker. I hear they have some new Taser darts; no wires!"

The Blues exchanged a glance and pretended to punch each other in the chest. "Let's go!"

"Oh yeah. I'm all over that." Both men headed out of the precinct.

"Wait!" the Sarge barked. "Almost forgot." He shoved two sheets of paper in the air. "Requisitions for the equipment and clothes."

Tink grabbed the paper. "How could you forget?" he asked. "You recruited those two sticklers."

"Don't I know it," the Sarge said with a chuckle.

❧

In the supply room, Paps and Jerry checked over the papers and the two Blues. "Who gets the wheelchair?" Paps asked. "I see you're both walking just fine."

"George in C wing," Henry said. "Looks like a student nurse who got smacked around by her husband. George wants to have a little chat with him."

"Great," Jerry said with a smile.

"This walker is equipped with the wireless Tasers," Paps said. "Why do you need it?"

"I'm backup," Harry responded.

"You're Taser happy from what I hear," Paps said. "One of these days you're going to hit somebody and fry their pacemaker."

"Look, Paps," Harry said, "can't we just get our clothes and gear and get outta here?"

Paps threw Jerry a you-want-to-take-this-one look.

Jerry glanced over his reading glasses at the two Blues and picked up the phone. "Need confirmation on the walker."

Everyone could hear the Sarge's bark through the phone. "I filled out both forms, yeah, clothes, wheelchair, and specially equipped walker. Yeah wireless Tasers—and don't forget transportation. Oh, and have the boys in the lab put a doctor's visit in the nurse's computer schedule."

"Clear," Jerry said and hung up the phone. "Rig 'em up, Paps."

Harry and Tink exchanged an are-these-guys-for-real look and got dressed. The best part of the job was through the special exit, past the phony electrical box and into the lab where the techs outfitted them with the latest equipment.

"Now where, Tink?" Harry asked.

"Down here," he said and motioned his partner forward. "It's a special tunnel that'll take us to a specially outfitted van. You've never done this before?"

"Nope; I usually go out the front."

"Then you've got a treat in store," Tink said with a nod to the driver and aide. "They'll take us out a special underground route that opens into a fake garage. We and the equipment will stay in the back here." He knocked on a false wall that concealed them from any probing eyes. "Between that and the tinted windows, no one will ever notice us."

"That's one way to keep Boss Nurse out of our hair," Harry said in obvious admiration. "Pretty cool."

"Exactly the point."

The driver and aide, brothers Chris and Andy, both trusted employees, had worked for Ben Mitchell since they were sixteen and seventeen years old. They looked outside the maintenance building and determined the coast was clear, opened the garage door, and drove out. Even if someone had seen them, their rig looked like every other vehicle stored on the premises. They pulled up to the front of the retirement home to pick up George.

The aide hopped out and ran the paperwork to the nurse's station. Betsy's eyebrows shot up in surprise. "What do you mean a doctor's appointment? This is the first I heard of it."

"Check it out," Andy said. "Should be on the schedule."

She turned to her computer and clicked a number of keys.

"There it is," Andy said from behind her shoulder. He pointed at the screen.

"Hmmmph!" she said, "I didn't see that this morning."

"Guess if you're around these old guys long enough," Andy said, "you start forgetting things like they do."

Betsy glanced at the computer again and shook her head. "He's in C wing."

"Yeah, we know; we've gotten him before."

"Need someone to take you to his room?" she asked.

"Nope, we'll take it from here, thanks," came the reply.

George was dressed and ready to go. Once he was secured in the van, they hit the open road, the third row seats electronically retracted. Tink and Harry gave him a smile and thumbs-up.

George smiled and eyeballed his partners. "In this operation," he said after a few minutes, "we have a young couple going through tough times. Husband lost his job and is starting to hit the booze pretty hard. He stays at home with their two girls but seems to be drowning in self-pity. Over the weekend, he slapped his wife during an argument. She's one of our nursing students—Nicki."

"I know Nicki," both said in unison.

"Exactly," George said. "She's got the human touch—something a lot of the others haven't learned yet. She works harder than anyone else and she takes the time to actually talk with us."

"Maybe because she's older," Tink said.

"She carries a big burden if she's expected to be the breadwinner," Harry said. "We gonna slap the hubby back?"

George smiled. "It pisses me off too," he said, "but Nicki says he's a good man, and I believe her. We're just gonna have a little talk and see if we can bring him back around to being a decent husband and father. You follow?"

Harry and Tink nodded their agreement. "Does this mean I don't get to use the new Tasers?" Harry asked.

"We'll see," George said with a half smile. "Pull over by that apartment," he said to the driver and pointed across the street a block down. "At the playground."

The driver pulled to the curb and parked; the aide helped George out and into his wheelchair.

"We'll call you when we're ready to go back," George said. "Harry, set up a checkerboard at that table over to the right."

Harry moved to lay the game out but kept his head down. "Looks like he's spotted us."

"At least he's watching where his kids are," George said. "Hopefully today's little preventive measure will help him and Nicki both."

&

Jeff Jensen lay on the couch and stared at the ceiling. He'd hoped when Nicki started nursing school their lives would get better. They'd worked out a plan. Jeff worked nights and during the day, he could watch the children while Nicki attended school.

Jeff opened another beer and wiped his hand across his face. It seemed as if he was always tired. It didn't help that his company cleaned offices. It was hard work but it was at night. In the beginning he was proud of Nicki who loved school; nursing was an excellent profession. The plan was once she graduated and got a job, they could refocus and build a nice life for their children.

Everything had gone well for the past eighteen months until his company got into legal trouble for employing illegal aliens. The fines hit, the company closed up, and Jeff was out of a job. Just like that.

In a heartbeat he'd become worthless to his wife and children. With no money coming in, Nicki was forced to take out student loans. They only prayed they could pay it all off in a lifetime. Over the months, the pressures of no money and mounting bills weighed heavily on them both. When they weren't arguing, they didn't talk at all. Nicki just got up and went to school. The kids needed to be taken care of, but all he wanted to do was drink. Besides, the girls could take care of themselves. They watched out for one another. Once again he wondered what his place in the world really was. He took a long pull off his beer.

Speaking of the girls—Jeff stuck his head out of the apartment door and spotted them playing; three other women were out with their kids as well. "Good," he said to himself. "They'll help keep an eye on them too."

Jeff left the door halfway open, just to be a good parent, and downed the last of his brew. Pulling the bottle from his lips, he noticed new people on the playground: three old men. They were talking, nothing unusual there, but Jeff had never seen them before. One pulled out a checkerboard, and they seemed to settle in at a picnic table for a friendly game. Jeff observed them a few more minutes then turned back into his apartment. The sharp spritz of a bottle opening signaled the start of another afternoon for Jeff.

"This guy seems to be content to just let the kids run around while he watches television," Tink said.

"Good," said George. "We'll give him about fifteen minutes then go pay him a visit."

Jeff set his empty bottle on the coffee table and stared from the television to the ceiling and contemplated the mess his life had become. "For crying out loud, I'm almost thirty years old! I've only held stupid jobs, never actually had a career. My wife has to go to school so that we can have a better life. Nice job, Jeff."

The shadows in the living room shifted and darkened. Three men blocked the sunlight streaming through the front door.

"You sound pretty pathetic, son," George said from the entryway.

"What the—" Startled, Jeff jumped up from the couch. The checker-playing old men from the courtyard stood at his open front door. One man walked into his living room and toward the coffee table. The man in the wheelchair appeared to be in charge. Unsure of their intention,

Jeff turned the bottle upside down and grabbed the neck brandishing it like a weapon.

Phet! Phet! The two sounds flew from the walker.

The darts hit Jeff, and his arms convulsed across his body in a crisscross manner. The glass bottle skittered across the room and shattered against the wall. A strange high-pitched shriek escaped Jeff's lips. "Jiijee…ahhah…youghtt!"

Jeff fell face first onto the television table with an audible thud that made the three older men wince.

"Wow," Harry said. "That's one feathery trigger."

"What the devil is wrong with you?" George asked. "We're in his living room, scare the wits out of the guy, then—oh, jeeze."

"That's gonna leave a nasty mark," Tink said.

They stared at Jeff's stiff body. "Good," said George. "It'll match what he did to Nicki."

"Those darts really worked good!" Harry said with giddy enthusiasm. "Did you see? Dropped him like a sack of potatoes!"

Tink chuckled. "It sure did but we gotta tell the research guys about that trigger."

George peered from Harry to Tink. "Help the man up, will you?"

Even Tink, well known as the squad gorilla and even better known to glare down most hoodlums in his career, couldn't lift the younger man. "This getting old is for the birds," he said.

They tried to pick Jeff up but neither had the strength to budge him. "Grab his feet, Buddy," Tink said. "We'll drag him by his feet and put 'em on the couch."

"I think his feet should be higher than his head, that's what we did when Brittany fainted," Harry said. "Hey, get some water. We did that too."

"He didn't faint," George said, "he just clonked his head on the table. Big difference, you know."

Harry returned with a plastic cup of water and dumped it on Jeff's face and chest. He sprang up, sputtering and gagging.

"Hey, it worked," Harry said in obvious surprise. "Wait'll I tell Sarge."

George rested his elbow on the armrest, chin in the palm of his hand. He glanced at Harry and then Tink who were completely focused on Jeff regaining consciousness. "Can one of you push me over there? I'd like to talk to the lad."

Tink and Harry sprang into action. "Sorry, George."

He pushed George toward the couch so that his knees were level with Jeff's forehead. "Harry, go down and watch the girls, will you?" George asked.

"Sure," he said and was out.

"No need for another go-round with the hair-trigger Taser," George said.

Tink nodded. "That's for sure."

They waited patiently for Jeff to come to.

His world spun. He blinked at the increasing light. Slowly but surely his surroundings came into focus. Jeff shook his head. A sharp, stabbing pain shot through his forehead. "Ah," he managed to get out and raised a hand to scrub at the pain

"Atta boy," Jeff heard. "He's coming out of it."

Through a narrowed gaze, Jeff once again saw the men who'd entered his home. Their outlines were fuzzy, and they spoke to each other directly above him. "Hey. He's looking at us."

George reached down and lightly tapped Jeff's cheek. "Helloooo. You with us, Jeff?"

Jeff pushed up onto an elbow. "What's going on?"

"You fell," the man in the wheelchair said. "Smacked your head really good."

Jeff struggled to sit up; two massive arms pushed him back down. The big man bared his teeth in the semblance of a smile.

"Just lay there a little longer, Jeff," the man in the wheelchair said.

Jeff's head cleared, the two elderly men stared down at him. "Who…who are you?"

"You can call me George," the man in the wheelchair said. "We're here because we understand things have been kind of stressful here since you lost your job with the office cleaning business."

Jeff shot George an angry look. "How do you know about that?"

Jeff tried to get up again.

"Jeff," George said. "You still have the Taser darts attached. You looking for another jolt?"

Jeff froze, glancing from one man to the other. "No," he said with a shake of his head. "I'm not."

"Good," George said in a softer voice. "You're a smart boy. I'll get straight to the point, Jeff. You're letting the stress get to you and we don't like what we're seeing."

"We?" Jeff asked. "You mean you old men—you thugs and henchmen who broke into my house and assaulted me? What do you know about my stress?"

"Settle down," George said. "We didn't break in. The door was open."

Jeff warmed to his topic. "Who do you think you are?"

"That's enough," George said pointing a shaky finger directly at Jeff's nose. "You're gonna start making some changes around here or you're going to be the recipient of a lot more visits from me and my associates."

Jeff stared hard at the men. There was no fear, concern, or weakness in their faces. They gave off a vibe of intimidation. Not like any old men he'd ever known.

"Can I sit up?"

The big man looked at George. He nodded and Jeff slowly sat up.

"Uh," Jeff said, "are you guys robbing us? We don't have anything."

The big man started to chuckle. "Hey, George, he thinks we're crooks."

George laughed too.

"Then what do you want?" Jeff snapped a little too loudly.

George put his finger up as if to silence him. "I'm glad you asked. We're here to keep you from destroying yourself and your family."

Confusion flashed through Jeff again. His brows knit together and he shook his head. "What?"

"Let me make this real simple. You," George jabbed his index finger at Jeff's chest, "are going to stop drinking. You're also going to start taking better care of your children or I'll have Child

Protective Services in this house quicker than you can ever imagine. I understand your wife is almost finished with nursing school?"

The amount of information the man knew about him took Jeff aback. Where in the world had he come up with all this? Jeff nodded yes.

"Good! You're going to be more supportive of her and you'll start by helping run the house while she's studying and at school. That'll take a lot of pressure off and allow her to become a nurse. Yes?"

Jeff could only nod yet again.

"Of course it will!" George barked. "When she starts her job, the two of you can work out how you're going to get some training in a field that interests you."

"O—" Jeff said slowly, trying to gather in everything George was saying, "kay." He strove to keep his tone as nonthreatening as possible. "But how do you know all this? About me and my wife?"

"Jeffey-boy," George said, "We're just some old men who overhear things in the park. Your daughters, Chelsea and Joy, are adorable by the way."

"Ah," Jeff slowly responded. "Thanks, but h—"

"We're tired of seeing families break apart," George continued, "so we decided to do an intervention this time. Hope you don't find us too intrusive?"

Jeff spotted the walker with its little red button. "Not if you don't come back."

"Smart guy," George said.

George gazed around the apartment. "You could definitely do more cleaning so everything doesn't fall on Nicki."

"How do you know—" Jeff stopped himself from asking how he knew his wife's name, but decided to sit quietly and hope they left soon.

"Look at us, young man," George said. "We've all been where you are: young, trying to provide for your family and all the pain and frustration that goes with it. You'll pull through this but you've got to let your wife help. She's very gifted at what she does and eventually you two will have a wonderful life together. But you've got to pull it together, man. You understand?"

Jeff's head throbbed and he looked at the darts still hanging on him. "Yes, I do."

George nodded and the big man gathered up the walker. "We're leaving now but we'll be back if things don't change," he pointed at Jeff to emphasize his point, "for the better."

The big man walked up to Jeff. He flinched and turned his head. "Don't worry," he said, "this will only sting a little."

He grabbed the darts and plucked each one out of Jeff's upper chest and stomach. The first one hurt. "Ow! That's more than a little."

"Sorry kid," he said and took a step back.

The big man pocketed the darts and turned the man in the wheelchair toward the front door. George put his hand up. "Wait."

The man pushing turned him around to face Jeff. "If I ever hear so much as a peep about you touching Nicki in anything but a loving manner—you ever hurt her in anyway, we'll be back and those electrical darts? That'll be nothing compared to what we'll do."

Jeff swallowed hard. He didn't know who they were, but they came off like a white-haired SWAT team. They actually scared the crap out of him!

The door swung open and two little girls clambered through followed by Harry who looked more than a little frazzled. "Chelsea and Joy wanted to come up for a snack," he said.

"Hi," Chelsea said with a bright-eyed smile.

Jeff watched the men who'd terrified and threatened him moments earlier melt into a puddle of grandfatherly love.

"Well, hello there," George said. "Aren't you two the cutest I've ever seen?"

"Wow," Joy said and bounded up to George. "Three kid's grandpas!" Smiles lit each man's face.

"What are you doing here?" Chelsea asked.

George's smile widened. "Oh I'm just an old grandpa and I got confused. I thought this was where a friend lives but it's not. When you get older, sometimes you forget; I'm sorry."

The girls beamed at the visitors. "That's okay," Joy said. "Right, Daddy?"

The men all turned a threatening look at Jeff. Message received loud and clear. "That's right, baby. Daddy was just showing them out."

George waved at the children. "But we did give your daddy a little direction of our own."

George glanced up at Jeff. "Maybe we'll see each other again."

"Not if I have anything to say about it," Jeff answered.

"Good."

The three men left the apartment without another word.

Jeff watched them from the living room window. He lost sight of them once they left the park. His mind whirled trying to make sense of what had just occurred.

"I'm hungry, Daddy," little Chelsea said.

"I'll get the cereal," Joy said.

Jeff watched his small children moving around the kitchen and a wave of shame hit him. What had he been thinking, let alone doing? The old men were right—on all counts.

"Wait a minute," he said to his daughters. "How about Daddy makes some pancakes?"

The girl's eyes widened and they smiled at one another. "Yeah!" each one said with a giggle and bounced up and down.

Jeff had forgotten how good it felt to do what was right. He twirled his fingers in Chelsea's silky hair. "Who wants theirs in a heart shape?"

Still bouncing around the kitchen, each girl raised her hand. "Me!" "Me!"

Giggles trilled through the apartment.

Jeff gathered the ingredients and put each one on the counter.

"I didn't know Daddy could make pancakes," Chelsea said to her older sister.

"Daddy hasn't made pancakes in a long time."

CHAPTER 25

ABRAHIM'S PROBATION OFFICER SHOT THE YOUNG MAN A sharp look over the reading glasses perched at the end of his nose. "Why are you so interested in volunteering at the police officers' retirement home?"

"I enjoyed our last outing," Abrahim lied smoothly. "Those old men are cooler than you think."

The PO's stare intensified. "Seriously? Since when are police officers cool?"

"Since I spent time with 'em." Abrahim met the PO's direct gaze with one he'd perfected a long time ago. One that until recently had gotten him out of more scrapes than he had fingers and toes.

The PO shifted in his seat behind a desk piled with too many files. "Not saying I believe you," he said, "but it's a great way to work off your community service. If you mind your manners, it could get you off probation a little sooner."

The PO directed what Abrahim thought was supposed to be a stern look. Didn't make it; it only made the PO seem like a jerk.

"Kind of odd that this struck you so suddenly when you hardly did anything for the four months before."

Abrahim shrugged off the suggestion, "My mom wants me off probation, she's always nagging me about it." He pasted on a wide smile that he definitely didn't feel. "'Sides," he said, "I kinda liked taking 'em out and working with them. I thought if I could do it some more, it would help us both." The fabrication slid off his tongue smooth as hot butter. He hoped it was enough to satisfy the officer.

The PO's face still didn't look convinced, but he shoved a set of paperwork at him. "Give the top one to your driver and have the nurse sign the other one."

This time the smile that split Abrahim's face was genuine. His cousin would love how this whole thing went down. After all, he was the one who'd taught Abrahim all he knew about manipulating people. It was the only way to get along in the justice system.

&

Three days later, Abrahim's driver pulled to a stop outside the home. "Okay, Abrahim, we're on from noon to four o'clock every day. I'll pick you up at four. Make sure the nurse signs the community service sheet or it'll be like you never completed the hours."

"Yes, sir," Abrahim said. He hopped out of the car and waved as his driver pulled away. "Fools!" he said to himself. "I'll know everything I need to about these guys in one week; Clubba will know too."

The Sarge glanced at the security monitor and smiled. "Well, well," he said. "Look who decided to give some community service. Hey, Tiny," he called across the lobby, "you gotta see this."

"What?"

The Sarge pulled the unlit stogie from his mouth and pointed. "Know who that is?"

Tiny took one glance and made a disgusted sound. "Sure do. What's he doing here?"

"Best guess is killing two birds with one stone," the Sarge said and shoved the cigar butt back in his mouth. "Spying on us—you in particular—and being his cousin Clubba's eyes and ears on the ground."

"No coincidence here," Tiny said.

"There's no coincidence period," the Sarge said. "We'll have to make sure he gets educated correctly so when Clubba gets out—"

"—we'll have a little surprise for him," Tiny said with a harsh laugh.

"He's getting signed in with his paperwork so I'll make this quick," the Sarge said. "Make sure he knows you have a nightly walk around the grounds every evening. That should interest Clubba. My guess is that he'll come calling as soon as he gets out of prison."

"I'm sure he will," Tiny said and struggled to draw breath. He pressed a hand over his heart and wheezed.

"Sit," the Sarge directed and indicated a chair in front of him.

Tiny did as indicated, a move that said everything about his health. Tiny at one hundred percent would've told his superior where he could stick that order.

This wasn't good. The Sarge bent down in front of him. "You don't have much longer, Tiny."

Tiny raised his gaze and shook his head. "Doesn't matter. I've already lasted three times longer than the doctor said I would."

"Between your heart and the cancer—"

"I could go at any time. Tell you the truth, Sarge; it'll be a relief. I had a good life but I'm so blasted weak and tired." His shoulders lifted and fell in a deep sigh. "And I'm so sick of pissing myself."

The Sarge settled his hand on Tiny's shoulder. "You're one of the best cops I've ever known, Tiny. Bar none. Without you this whole operation would never have worked. Clubba's furious and he's sent his cousin after you. Yet here you sit, calm and cool, ready to act as bait." The Sarge shook his head and looked out the window. "When it's my time to go, I hope I can call my shots like you have."

"Don't get all sappy on me," Tiny said. "I'm not dead yet."

"No, you aren't," the Sarge said. "Maybe we'll name a toilet after you."

A slight smile lifted Tiny's lips. "I want a nice silver plaque right on the floor between the feet of every Blue that uses it. They can think of me each time they drop a load."

The two shared a quick laugh. Tiny's ended with a coughing spasm...and blood. The Sarge reached for the handkerchief in his pocket and dabbed the blood from the corner of Tiny's mouth. "Good as new."

"You're a lousy liar." Tiny peered at the monitor. "Abrahim's headed toward the precinct."

"Time to move."

Tiny reached for the Sarge's arm and held it a moment. "In the end, all us Blues take care of each other. I'm proud to have known you all these years, Sarge."

The Sarge managed a weak smile for his friend. The knowledge that Tiny wouldn't be around much longer pierced him to the core.

"Like I said, you're a lousy liar so don't say anything." Tiny shook his finger at him. "Nobody is to know about what I'm doing, Sarge. Not until this assignment is finished, understand?" Tiny pushed out of the chair and turned toward the door. "It's not the end of my tour yet. Not today." He turned back and jerked his head toward the incoming boy. "Let's go meet the little spy Clubba sent us."

⌒

Earnest Yates lay in his top bunk and stared at the ceiling. What he'd learned about Clubba had impressed him. Protected by every major gang, he controlled all the information going out. The plan was to keep his Sudanese soldiers in the prison system to extend that sphere of influence to both sides of the walls. Earnest jackknifed into a sitting position.

"Lay still," his bunkmate growled.

"Shut up," Earnest said. He turned the thought over in his mind. *Both sides of the wall*—that was it! Once Clubba left the pen, he'd extend his influence outside as well. That meant he'd get special protection from each of the gangs in Omaha and maybe farther. He wasn't aiming to be just an associate; he was gunning to be the kingpin.

Clubba's biggest problem was an over-inflated ego. He thought he couldn't be touched, that he could get away with whatever he wanted. Earnest laid back on his mattress and smiled into the darkness. How often had he seen that same hubris trip guys up? Once they thought they could get away with anything—or everything—they got overconfident. A quick way to die in the joint.

On the outside, cops would take a special interest in him. He'd get caught and be back here within a year or two. Earnest had seen it happen repeatedly. Hell, it happened to him. Until he walked out of the place, Earnest planned to work on the overconfident kingpin. Maybe he could get the kid to do him a little favor.

8~

Late that afternoon Earnest approached Clubba in the common area. "Know that little freak who threw that bag of piss at you?"

Clubba met Earnest's gaze blandly. "Not yet but I will. You can bet on it."

Earnest plopped down across the table from Clubba without being invited and broke an inmate taboo. Inmates don't sit when no invitation was extended. It was a great way to get the beating of your life. Clubba stiffened and straightened in his seat.

"I already know," Earnest said quietly.

Clubba's dark stare zeroed in on Earnest. "Tell me," he demanded in a whisper.

Earnest eased forward at the table. Clubba's tone and underlying ultimatum let him know everything he needed. He didn't want to be overheard and he had a weak spot: a lack of knowledge. Earnest had something of real value to Clubba. "Why?" Earnest asked. "Why is he so important to you?"

Clubba clenched his left fist into a tight ball. "Never mind," he growled. "Who is he?"

Earnest gazed around the room and whispered back. "He stays at the retired police officers home in Omaha."

Clubba drew back and frowned. "What is his name?"

"Yeah, man," Earnest said with a chuckle. "He came with that group of retirees."

"I didn't pay any attention to them," Clubba mused. "My cousin was with them; he had all my attention."

"Well that group of men," Earnest responded, "was from the police retirement home. That means the little guy, who by the way seems to have it in for you, is a retired cop."

Clubba glared at the Formica top, both hands in white-knuckled fists. "Most cops hate me. Nothing new there," he said sarcastically. "Does this ex-cop have a name?"

"You don't get it," Earnest whispered with a smile. "That little creep harassed me too when I was on the outside. He was a lot younger then, and a little more agile, not the cranky old buzzard you see now."

Clubba glared at Earnest. "You saying I was schooled by an old man?"

"Nah," Earnest said quickly. "*Yeah.*"

Clubba slammed his fists into the sides of the table. "His name!"

"Called Tiny," Earnest said. "Fitting don't you think? Always loved going after people he thinks are crooks…and not normal crooks. He likes the ones who seem to have a following, those who have associates or who're building some sort of business. Once you get on Tiny's list, he won't stop. The guy's like a pit bull."

"Tiny," Clubba repeated. "Tiny man; tiny cop. Who lives at this retirement home." He rested his elbows on the smooth surface and tapped his knuckles on the table. "I'll show this Tiny what happens to people who mess with me."

"How's that?" Earnest asked.

"For him…my special way."

Earnest noticed Clubba's distant smile and spaced out look as though the younger man was in deep thought. It was a good time to start grooming his pawn so Earnest could have something to do about the "special" that was going to happen to Tiny.

"Tiny." Clubba stared into space, past Earnest. His whisper sent a chill through Earnest. "He was in the park, he was there when I was first arrested, there at my court hearing, and here at the prison just to insult me one last time. Such dedication."

"I think Tiny's had his eye on you for a while. Being retired, he probably didn't know how to get you like he did when he was a cop," Earnest said.

Clubba thought a long moment. "I remember when I was arrested, I couldn't figure out who'd told the cops where I was. Now I get it. There were always some old men playing checkers in the park across from my crib. None of us ever paid any attention to them."

"'Cause nobody cares about old men," Earnest said.

"Exactly. You think those old dudes were tailing me?"

Before Earnest could answer, Clubba shook his head. "No," he said. "No bunch of feeble old white guys could ever catch me. No way."

"You positive?" Earnest asked, fighting a mocking smile. Tiny was exactly the one stalking Clubba and his boys.

"You think?"

"Possible," Earnest said.

"Improbable."

"You getting out of here in a little over a week, right?"

Clubba eyed Earnest, intently holding his gaze. "Yeah, so?"

Time to set things in motion, Earnest thought and purposely shrugged his shoulders. "Nothing really…I mean if I found out who'd stuck me in this," he gestured at the ceiling, "hellhole, I'd make sure he got my personal attention when I was released."

Clubba didn't respond. Good, Earnest thought. Let the kid chew on that thought over the next few days. The seed had been planted, watered, and mulched, the harvest would be Tiny's death. With any luck at all.

CHAPTER 26

ABRAHIM WAITED HAND AND FOOT ON TINY OVER THE next three days. He read him boring stories from books bigger than anything Abrahim had ever seen. He fawned over the old cop, always asking for an anecdote about crimes and criminals, and wondered how Tiny liked it in the retirement home.

The fool even showed Abrahim where he walked every evening at seven o'clock. Abrahim knew the schedule, where Tiny walked each and every night and how important it was to the man to maintain that routine. Stupid old cop had no idea what he was giving away. Abrahim had everything he needed to give Clubba. Everything he'd need to take the old man down. Easy, easy, easy. Clubba would take care of this one personally. Abrahim smiled at how simple his assignment was. By the time Clubba finished with this old codger, he'd be a bloody body on the sidewalk. And all because Abrahim had set him up. Clubba would love it and he'd be rewarded accordingly. Abrahim couldn't help but smile.

Tiny walked into the Sarge's office and closed the door behind him. "That didn't take long."

"What didn't?" The Sarge growled around the cigar stub in his mouth.

"Clubba should have everything he'll need to come after me." Tiny spread his palms in front of him. "Like taking candy from a baby," he said with a smile.

The Sarge returned Tiny's smile. They'd worked enough years—decades actually—together to know one another exceptionally well. "How long?"

Tiny lifted his right shoulder in a noncommittal shrug. "Dunno. Sometime within the next ten days, I'd think. He gets out next week; I should be at the top of his list."

"Tiny."

Tiny held up his palm to the Sarge. "Don't even try to talk me out of it. With any luck Clubba will come calling and I'll be dead. It's what I want…the way I want to go out."

The Sarge nodded solemnly. "I understand—believe me, I do." He stood and moved an oversized three-ring binder to the side.

"What's that?" Tiny asked.

"Standard Operating Procedures Manual," the Sarge replied.

"Good cover," Tiny said. "Nobody in their right mind would ever pick up that thing to read."

"Exactly. That's what makes it the perfect place for my special intercom button. Only this broadcast goes straight to the hearing aids for Clubba's special unit." He jabbed the small black knob. "Staff meeting for Clubba's soldiers dragnet task force at zero one hundred hours," he said. "All members report to the main supply conference room."

Tiny sucked in a deep breath. "Here we go."

"You can change your mind," the Sarge said.

"Never."

⚬

Meeting in this conference room took special planning. First, surveillance was set up so no nurses or staff would notice the Ol' Blues sneaking through the complex. Their intricate setup involved video, motion sensors, and specially trained Blues who arranged a backup security ring protecting the rooms of those out of their beds.

They'd create a diversion if a nurse headed toward the room of anyone attending the briefing. If all went according to plan, the nurse would change course and attend to the Blue who'd thrown his false teeth at her or had run naked through hallways. They'd come up with the most outrageous means to keep the nurses busy and allow the task force meeting to continue uninterrupted.

If a nurse or other staff member noticed a missing patient, an alarm would sound and the entire facility would go on lockdown until they located the missing patient. They all knew it would be disastrous if it happened during the task force conference. They brooked no interference.

The Sarge called Smitty. "We're gonna need Brittany at the meeting."

"Shouldn't be a problem. I'll give her a call."

&

"Tonight? Are you out of your mind?" Brittany all but yelled into the phone.

"Look, I'm sorry, honey," Smitty said in a soothing tone he hoped would settle her down. "And it's not really tonight; it'll be tomorrow morning at one a.m. Don't come in the main entrance; go to the northside parking lot. You'll see the vehicle maintenance building straight ahead. Just park and ring the bell. Somebody will take you to the conference room via the tunnels."

"Vehicle maintena…what?"

"You remember the maze of tunnels behind Paps and Jerry's area," Smitty said.

"Pap and Zap? Yeah," she said. "How could I forget?"

A long pause filled the air. "You know you can't just spring stuff like this on me," Brittany said.

"Why? You got a hot date?"

"No," she said a little too quickly. "I mean yes."

"With?"

"Jake if you must know. He's coming over for dinner and maybe a movie."

"Really?" Smitty asked.

"Yes, Mr. Meddler, really. Look, I know you love me and it used to be cute when you always wanted to know the name and birthday of any guy I ever dated. I didn't realize you were using it to run criminal records, but that wasn't half as bad as grilling every date I ever had. I should've just sneaked out of the house instead."

"Yeah," Smitty said with a chuckle. "Those were good times. At least I never cleaned my weapon in front of them."

"I'm grateful for small favors, Dad, but no date ever lasted too long if you found something you didn't like. That stops now. I'm an adult and I can make my own decisions."

"As long as he's out of the apartment by eleven thirty, you should be good to go," Smitty said.

The deep, long-suffering sigh on the other end told Smitty he'd won.

"Yeah, Dad. He'll be out by then. I have to go; I have a dinner to prepare."

It was Smitty's turn to pause and he couldn't help his next question. "What are you wearing tonight?"

"Clothes," she said. "If you're lucky. Don't worry about it. I'm an adult; I can handle myself."

"Sorry, Sweetie," Smitty said. It was tough to just give up all the old cop-dad habits he developed during her growing-up years. The urge to keep her safe just never went away…probably never would. "See you sometime after midnight."

"Okay, Daddy," she said softly. "Bye."

Brittany hung up the phone and turned to her kitchen. "All righty then," she said, the memory of the awful tasting cookies still fresh in her memory. "Let's make something Jake will like this time."

⁊

"Man," Jake said. "That was delicious! You certainly know your way around the kitchen."

"Thanks," Brittany said, flashing him a quick smile.

"Big improvement on those oatmeal raisins, too."

She tossed her napkin across the table and hit him directly in the face. He caught it with a laugh. Something inside Brittany relaxed into a feeling of comfort and happiness. The evening kicked off on a high note, and she hoped it continued. Conversation turned to one another's family. Brittany's father was still alive; Jake's little family had been torn away in that terrible accident. He had one brother who lived in Omaha and actually had something to do with the Ol' Blues retirement home. Looked like fate had brought them together in time and space.

After dinner they sat on her couch to watch a movie Brittany couldn't remember. She'd caught Jake staring at her a few times. Nothing unusual there; she was used to men staring at her. This time, however, she really wanted him to look at her. Whenever she caught him observing her, she'd smiled; Jake just blinked and tore his gaze away to the television screen.

Never one to tiptoe around an issue, she decided to lay everything out in the open. "Jake," she began, "we've only known each other a short time. You seem like a great guy but it's probably hard to get back into the dating scene again."

"You have no idea," he said with a smile. "I was terrified to ask you out," he said with more than a hint of exasperation.

"Me? Why?"

"You're a very intimidating redhead, Brittany. I've been a cop for almost thirteen years, and I've faced street thugs who scared me less."

She tossed a small pillow at him. "Hardly."

They shared a quiet laugh and she grew serious. "The reason I mention it is that I want you to know that what you have in your heart for your wife, Sarah, and your daughter, Abigail, is something you should always cherish. I'd never be jealous of those memories."

Jake nodded. "Thanks," he said quietly. "I appreciate it…more than you know."

Brittany watched Jake struggle with his emotions. Maybe she shouldn't have said anything. Then again, best to get everything out in the open and deal with whatever came. She reached over and grabbed his hands. "I always heard that tears are the key that unlock the memories of the ones we loved. Those memories are part of you, Jake. They always will be."

Jake was silent a long while. Finally, he nodded and turned to her. "Thanks. That's just what I needed."

Brittany's hand rested on the back of Jake's. His thumb held her hand in place and he lifted her hand to his lips for a gentle kiss that made her heart flutter in her chest. His sincerity and tenderness took her breath away. Drawn by a force she had no control over, she tilted her head and moved closer to her hand…and Jake's lips. With a small smile she gently pulled her hand away so she could kiss him. Her heart thudded in her chest with every beat. Time stood still; everything moved in slow motion.

Jake slowly responded; he laced his fingers with hers. Her breath caught in her throat. Before her eyes closed, she caught a glance at their intertwined hands and his wristwatch. Fifteen minutes until midnight. Her hooded eyes flew open and she slid out of his reach and off the couch.

Jake recoiled.

"The time," she blurted out. "Look at the time."

"I don't believe this," Jake said and blinked at her. "What?"

She grabbed his wrist to make sure she hadn't misread the watch from upside down. She hadn't. *The task force meeting. Dad will have my head if I miss it.*

"Brittany what the devil's wrong? I'm sorry if I scared you," he said. "I didn't mean to make you feel uncomfortable; I—"

"It isn't you," Brittany said and glanced up. "It's me—trust me on this."

A perplexed look came over Jake's face.

"Look," she said in an effort to reassure him and yet prevent him from finding out about the plans. "Trust me—the last thing I want to do is rush off, but…I have to go."

"G-go?" Jake stammered.

Please don't make this more difficult. "Yes," she said, "actually you're so sweet, I could kiss you."

Jake blinked as though trying to figure out what rabbit hole he'd fallen down. "My feeling exactly. What's going on?"

She had to get out of there! Brittany's mind raced. "Uh…it's my dad…ah…I've…got… to…oh…get him his medication by twelve thirty. Oh Jake, I'm so so sorry. It's been a wonderful evening and I totally enjoy time with you, but I completely lost track of the time… and my father. I have to go."

She put her palms on either side of her head and said, "I've ruined the evening. I'm just so sorry!"

Jake's shoulder slumped and he let out a long sigh. "You sure it's not me? This is about your dad? I mean," he gestured at her hand, the one he'd kissed.

Still standing in front of the couch, she glanced down at her hand, realizing that Jake was referring to the hand he kissed.

She chuckled. "I promise it's not about you," she said. She lifted her palms to each side of Jake's face and pulled him close. Her lips brushed his; he lowered his head to deepen the kiss. Brittany tore herself away from his delicious touch and backed up toward the front door. "I've gotta go. I'm—"

"—sorry," he said. "So I heard."

Grabbing her keys and her purse, she continued to apologize all the way out.

Jake slumped onto the sofa, a mixture of shock and excitement. The first from her waltzing out the door like Cinderella; the second from her tantalizing kiss. "Wait a minute," he said. "She left me in her living room."

His phone rang. "Mitchell," he answered.

"Jake, tomorrow can we please start where we left off?"

What was it about this extraordinarily frustrating, funny, personable, aggravating woman that kept him coming back? "Sure," he said. "Whatever you want; whenever you want, but let's make it earlier in the evening."

Brittany's sigh of relief was audible. "Yeah…awesome. Thanks. I'll talk to you later."

Jake shook his head and peered around him. A mountain of dishes filled the sink and her countertops. He shook his head and smiled at his predicament. "One cooks," he said. "The other cleans. Sounds fair to me."

CHAPTER 27

HANDPICKED BLUES STOOD IN DOORWAYS AND corridors. Ever-present cameras documented the movements of the nursing staff or anyone else who might venture into the wing or walk toward the supply room.

One by one, silently and stealthily, members of the task force made their way toward the appointed area. Each Blue paused every ten to fifteen steps and leaned against the wall as though he was tired and taking a quick break. Once assured the coast was clear, they'd scan up and down the hall and do it all over again. It accomplished slow but steady progress. Along the way, the watchmen Blues providing security would give the movers a thumbs-up as they passed. If they didn't acknowledge, however, it meant there was someone following or checking out the Ol' Blue in the hallway.

An immediate alarm—a pretended scream from a nightmare or a sleepwalker acting like he was in a foot pursuit down the hallway—let everyone know when to stop and feign coincidence that several Ol' Blues were milling around at one o'clock in the morning. Best part of old age was they didn't have to explain a thing. Just acting confused would do it. Nursing aides would simply escort them back to their beds only to have them try again.

Paps and Jerry ticked off each person as they passed by. "Missing one," Paps said.

"Yeah," Jerry agreed with a nod. "Brittany."

Paps checked his watch. "Almost time," he said. "Wonder what the holdup is?"

"Dunno," Jerry said. "Her escort's waiting in maintenance. Once she arrives and he'll verify there's no threats, bring her here.

Brittany pulled in with five minutes to spare, completely disgusted with the way her evening had ended. Instead of being wrapped in Jake's arms, she'd be wrapped up in an investigation. "Ugh." Slamming her car door shut, she tried to get a handle on the temper that matched her hair. It wasn't working. "Never," she muttered, "have I ever had an evening with a guy like that. First time it happens, the old bladder-bomb throwers decide to have a meeting. Just flipping perfect."

She stalked up to the maintenance building. Hands on her hips, she gazed around for the promised guide. "Come out, come out wherever you are," she said to the night air. "Let's get this super-secret meeting started."

"Right this way, Miss Brittany." The voice floated from a dark corner.

She almost laughed. Honestly…could it be any more clandestine? In the middle of Omaha? Recognizing the Blue from her previous sessions, Brittany followed his lead and almost bumped into his back. He'd stopped abruptly and peered around in an overly dramatic gesture. "Seriously?" she whispered.

He glanced at her with a small smile and reached up to grab an old oil can. It didn't move; it shifted as the Blue pulled it forward. A hoist spit out the same hissing sound as when mechanics lifted her car into the air and she got her tires rotated or oil changed. This time, though, the hoist wasn't lifting a car. This thing moved up in a similar manner, but here the entire floor under it was taken directly up into the air. Brittany's arms flew out to sustain her balance.

"Quite the lift," she said and watched as an elevator rose from the floor. "Wow, now that's cool."

"Yes, ma'am." The doors opened and her attendant held a hand out indicating she should get in. "Ladies first."

Brittany entered the elevator and it along with the car hoist went down into the floor. The elevator went down about twenty-five feet. The hoist perfectly covered the floor, and it was back to a mechanic shop again.

"Your chariot," the Blue said.

Brittany chuckled and slid into a waiting golf cart. "What?" she asked. "No seat belt?"

"Nah," the Blue said. "Not going that far or that fast."

"I thought most fatal accidents happened within twenty-five miles of home," she said. "That's what my dad always preached to me when I was growing up."

"That's true," he said, "but we're professionals."

Brittany smiled as they made their way to the conference room. Once inside, she spotted the Sarge who acknowledged her with a one-fingered wave and slight dip of his head. Seated in the front beside him were the Chelini brothers, her father, Tiny, and ten others Blues.

Silence thickened in the room and Brittany followed everyone's line of sight. One monitor showed the unmistakable shadow of a person walking the halls. The outline was well known to them all.

"Oh-oh," the Sarge said. "Boss Nurse Betsy's working the night shift."

Brittany blew air through her lips. Just great. Their odds of detection just increased ten-fold. One thing she didn't want was a repeat of red light, green light. No way!

"Who's running foot pursuit tonight?" the Sarge asked.

"Speedy Benjamin" came the reply from the back of the room.

"Good," the Sarge said with a smile. "This'll be fun to watch."

The entire room shifted attention to the scene unfolding on the monitor. Boss Nurse Betsy had a routine too. On Friday nights, her rounds were perfunctory, getting her back to the nurses' station quickly. The swish of her polyester-clad legs rubbing together echoed through the hushed hallways. She could hear an occasional yell, or even the sounds of "*bang, bang* watch out he's got a big gun" from bedrooms as she walked by.

The Ol' Blues' code for Nurse Betsy was Big Gun. Once that phrase hit the air, everybody knew who was around. She waddled past several doors and glanced in making sure all was well.

A male voice split the silence sounding like an imitation of a siren. "Stop right there, punk; don't move! He's running! He's running!"

"Here we go," she said, obviously familiar with the odd behavior. "Sleep runners on four."

Down the hall and directly opposite of the supply room, Speedy Benjamin bolted away. In his day, he had been a track star and could still run surprisingly fast.

Nurse Betsy spotted him and cursed under her breath. She stopped by an intercom. "Speedy's on the run again."

The alarm spread to the entire night staff instantaneously.

The Sarge watched Speedy smile when he heard it. He tore off like a shot…in the opposite direction of the supply room entrance that led to the area where the conference room was located.

Inside, bets were placed and the Blues watched the surveillance screens. "I'll take five," one said.

"On who?"

"Benny of course."

"Nah," another said. "Betsy'll get him…eventually."

The Blues watched as Boss Nurse gained her stride, which took a while because Officer "Speedy" Benjamin scooted down the hallway at an amazing speed. He could out-shuffle anyone at the precinct. That included nurses. He purposely didn't wear any diapers when he ran. It made the nurses uncomfortable while grabbing him, and it usually got him a few more hallways before they would finally catch him.

"There goes Speedy," one Blue yelled and laughed.

It took several minutes for Boss Nurse to get to full speed. Great on the straightaway, but she couldn't corner worth crap.

Speedy Benjamin slowed as he approached a T-intersection. Boss Nurse gained speed, stethoscope dangling back and forth from her pocket, arms pumping beside her wide girth. She got within five yards of her prey; he bolted to the left at the intersection. Boss Nurse flailed her arms as though it could help control the upcoming turn. It didn't.

Taking the turn, her rather large butt cheek banged against the wall. The overhead emergency exit sign crashed to the ground.

Attendees inside the conference room convulsed with laughter.

"Is this a party?" Brittany asked her companion.

The Blue shook his head. "Just monitoring the security system; keeping the nursing staff away."

"Are they gambling?" she asked.

"Never bet against Boss Nurse," the Ol' Blue said with a smile.

Her gaze flew to the screen that held everyone's attention including the Sarge's and her father's. A cheer went up.

Brittany watched in fascination as an Ol' Blue did the funniest quick step ever. Hot on his tail galloped the large head nurse. Much like the gingerbread man from the fable, more and more people fell in behind the head nurse. Younger student nurses took up the chase. Nametags fell off; clipboards clattered to the floor. The scenario played out like a real-life Keystone Cop episode. Brittany chuckled and shook her head, then froze.

The runner was completely—and totally—butt naked in the back! Not like any *COPS* episode she'd ever seen!

The race held every Ol' Blue enraptured. They'd lean to the left each time the speedster turned left almost like they were on a roller coaster. Hands flew in the air. "Whoa," rippled through the men.

Even Brittany had to laugh when the students easily caught up with Boss Nurse Betsy but couldn't get around her because the hallway was too narrow and she was too wide. The runner obviously knew he was on camera. His gestures and mugging showed his knowledge of every camera hidden throughout the facility. Every Blue knew where they were; the staff didn't. Finally, the speedy Blue slowed. He'd taken them all as far away from the meeting as he could.

Glancing directly up at a camera, he gave a wide grin and headed straight for the staff bathroom.

"Oh no," a Blue yelled out. "He isn't going to—"

Sure enough, Speedy Benjamin ran right into the bathroom/locker room of the female staffers. Boss Nurse Betsy, only three yards behind, called to the five other nurses over her shoulder. "He's going for the locker room!"

Benjamin charged through the door. "On the ground, punk, or I'll split your skull like a melon."

One lone female student, fresh from the shower and wrapped in a towel, spotted him. "Wait," she shrieked and tried to maintain her dignity by squeezing the towel that was wrapped around her with her arms to her side bent at the elbows. Her hands tried to stop the human foot pursuit freight train that was about to run her over. The Blues couldn't see inside the locker room, but they could see that Boss Nurse Betsy had somehow stopped her mammoth frame.

Then Officer Benjamin had come to an abrupt stop inside the door and yelled, "I caught the punk," then pointed at the student nurse. "Don't even think about moving or I'll—"

Five student nurses thumped into the back side of Boss Nurse who had only been able to stop by grabbing onto the large door handle. Then like an accordion the students scrunched into her large derriere, all five student nurses, with dangling stethoscopes, rubber gloves, and whatever else they were carrying when the alarm was sounded, bounced off the boss's large fanny, and flew back out the door and onto the hallway floor.

Boss Nurse herself had rather miraculously stopped just inches from Speedy. Boss Nurse glared at Speedy Benjamin. "It's a miracle I didn't run you over."

It was a scene that would live forever in the secret recorded video of the Ol' Blue Unit. The terrified student wrapped in a towel, Boss Nurse gasping for breath with her hands on her hips, and five student nurses tangled on the floor, like a twister game gone very bad.

The Blues doubled over with laughter; several leaned on a friend to remain standing. The howling laughter got to Brittany too. She laughed so hard her eyes watered and her sides ached.

"All right, all right," the Sarge managed to get out between pangs of amusement. "Now that Speedy has cleared the way for this meeting, let's get started."

Every Blue took a chair, the laughter died out, and the Sarge held everyone's attention. Except one person.

An unmistakably feminine chortle continued without hesitation. The room full of Blues gazed past the Sarge to the source of the merriment. Sarge's gaze followed. Brittany stood, legs crossed, leaning against the wall. "S-sorry," she managed to get out. "That was the funniest," she gasped, "thing I ever saw."

The Sarge smiled at her. "And now I'd like to start the meeting."

Brittany stayed in her peculiar stance and waved at the Sarge with her free hand. "I can't move; I'm gonna pee!"

Her comment brought on another gale of laughter from the Blues. The howls grew louder when she shuffled her feet along the floor and scuttled over to the bathroom across the hall.

"These videos definitely need to be at this year's Christmas party," one Blue hollered out.

෧

Brittany reentered the room to the obvious delight of everyone in the room, especially her father, Smitty. She pulled up a chair next to him.

"You're a great addition," he whispered to her. "Maybe they'll make you an honorary Ol' Blue."

She smiled her thanks and turned her attention to the issue at hand.

The Sarge looked around the room, waiting until he had everyone's attention. "Okay, boys—er," he paused and glanced at Brittany. "And you too."

She rolled her eyes at him but appreciated the inclusion.

"We're focusing on the surveillance at the apartment complex of Shanese, Clubba's girlfriend. Everything's been going really well there. The boys in the lab got us some terrific video and audio of those Sudanese soldiers of his. Turns out all the guys walking around are Clubba's gang. Looks like he only trusts his very own soldiers for this particular operation."

The Sarge turned to Brittany. "We're gonna need you to translate what these guys say and let us know what's going on immediately. The boys in the lab have something for you but it won't be ready until tomorrow. After this meeting I want you to go home and get some sleep. You're gonna need it because we need you translating as soon as possible. According to our sources, Clubba gets out on Friday."

"Another sick day coming up." Brittany said.

&⌒

Clubba leaned closer to Abrahim. *"You're sure about this, cousin?"*

Anxious to impress his relative—and hopefully soon his boss—Abrahim nodded. *"Every night seven o'clock this Tiny walks around the perimeter of the grounds. A path leads around the back of the building and into a garden area. There's nothing there. It would be a perfect place to—"*

"Silence, fool." Clubba's eyes widened and he held up his hand. *"Keep your mouth shut."*

Abrahim watched Clubba digest the information. Clubba's fist punched his upper thigh and it alarmed Abrahim. This was to have been good news, not bad. *"Cousin?"* he asked quietly, hoping to redirect his attention to the matter at hand.

"What?" he asked and blinked. *"Oh, yes. Tell me about my soldiers who watch my woman at those apartments,"* Clubba said with a smile.

Abrahim breathed a sigh of relief and returned his relative's casual smile. *"You mean the walking corpse. As you instructed only our soldiers are around the apartments. Her younger sister is with her and they both stay with an old woman. Possibly her grandmother. Every time she comes out of the apartment, one of the soldiers makes his presence known from across the street. She takes one look and runs back inside."*

"Excellent! I love it when they know I'm coming and there's nothing they can do about it."

Abrahim nodded. *"I provided those small radios for the soldiers as they watch. That way if she is spotted, they can instantly let the others know where she is."*

Clubba turned his full attention on Abrahim. *"Good idea,"* he said with an appreciative smile. *"Instant communication is helpful for this operation. Now listen, cousin."* Clubba pointed at Abrahim. *"I will be out on Friday—two days from now. I don't want that stupid cockroach getting away. I want at least five soldiers around the apartment twenty-four hours a day."*

"What's your plan?" Abrahim asked. *"Her first—or the cop?"*

"First I will visit Tiny," he said and paused. *"Then,"* he said through gritted teeth, *"I will finish my unfinished business with Shanese. The thought of bashing both of their faces in has made my time in here tolerable,"* he said with a smile that didn't reach his eyes. *"Most tolerable."*

Abrahim made a mental note to never—ever—cross Clubba. He didn't want a second of that cold fury directed at him.

↬

From a distance down a blind hallway, Earnest Yates watched Clubba talk with his young visitor. The only word he understood was *Tiny*. Earnest couldn't help but smile. "A perfect pawn," he whispered. "That stupid fool will go after Tiny as soon as he's out of the joint."

More than pleased with himself, Earnest turned and headed to his cell. Clubba's thirst for vengeance would serve him well.

CHAPTER 28

BRITTANY'S FINGERS FLEW OVER HER NOTEPAD, translating tape after tape of the Clubba-Abrahim conversations. Only occasionally did she need to go back and listen a second time and never a third. The language came back as though she'd just left Sudan and the people she'd grown to love. These two knuckleheads would've been taken to task in a village so fast they wouldn't know what happened. As it was, they were free to choose however rotten they wanted to be.

It became apparent to Brittany both men were posturing for each other, one currying favor, the other making his presence known and throwing his weight around. They reminded her of a couple of cats sitting outside a canary cage. She fidgeted in her chair and ran her fingers through her hair in frustration. These two so enjoyed terrorizing the girl, her sister, and grandmother, it disgusted Brittany. No human being should have to put up with that. No one.

"Hey, Brit," Abinya called from behind her.

"Yeah?"

He proffered several communication devices in his hands and held up one. "At first we thought they'd use cell phones for communication like this." He held one up. "Now they're using a small handheld CB anybody can buy at an outfitter store." He held another device up. "They're much faster. But—" he put it back in his opposite hand, "once we saw them using those simple little CBs, it was easy to listen in and record their conversations," he said, pride lacing his words. "How'd it turn out?"

Brittany glanced up from her work and paused the recording. "It's like being right there when they're talking. You guys outdid yourselves. I can hear them clear as church bells."

"Awesome," he said with a quick wink. "Glad we could help."

She watched him trek out of her work area and leaned back in her chair for a quick breather. In a heartbeat, Abinya was back, standing next to her video screen with a geeky smile. Two more techs, Karew and Thane, hovered at the doorway. "Do they let you guys out much?" she asked the trio.

The three exchanged a confused look. "Let us out where?"

Obviously, sarcasm wasn't on the technologically brilliant guys' agenda. "You guys must be the cream of the crop from the *Fortune* 500 companies around here. The way the Blues brag you up, I thought maybe you could walk on water."

Brittany was right, the huge corporations that had originally hired these scientists picked them from the likes of MIT and other scientific organizations throughout the world.

Karew, the short but brilliant audio/visual engineer from India. Abinya, a Nigerian computer/robotics specialist, came to Omaha to work for Ben Mitchell's company and built all their special weapons. Thane, a freckle-faced, redheaded computer geek, did incredible things with the computer. He never graduated from college. After the first two years he was showing the professors how to use the computers in ways that they never dreamed.

Each had been quickly snatched up by one of The Bureau's companies and put on this special assignment.

"Us?"

"They're all very impressed with your work here."

The compliment brought beaming smiles from the three men. "They brag about us?" Thane asked. "Really?"

"I can't count the times I've heard the Sarge say, 'Those boys in the lab did it again.' Trust me on this," Brittany said. "Being a daughter of a cop, it's high praise indeed."

The techs glanced at each other again. "I didn't think they liked us," said Karew.

"Yeah, they look over a job that took us hours and all I get is," Abinya launched into his best impersonation of the Sarge, "Is that all you got? Honestly, I don't know why we keep you guys around."

The techs chuckled and Brittany couldn't suppress a conspiratorial smile. "That's just how cops talk. They don't get syrupy or fawn all over people. You'll never hear 'Oh that was wonderful work' or 'We're so lucky to have you.' A cop will understate every time or try to make you think it was barely acceptable when the work was exceptionally well done."

"Brilliant," Karew said as though they'd made a brilliant scientific discovery. "They like us."

"They really like you," Brittany said.

"Then why," Karew said, "do they call us dweebs?"

Oh, man, had the Blues been giving these guys the business, Brittany thought. "They probably do think you're dweebs, but," she raised a finger for emphasis, "you're their dweebs and they'll do anything to protect you."

The men chewed on that piece of information and nodded at one another. "We'd really better get back to work."

"Me too," Brittany said. The men left and she could only shake her head. None of the techs could contain their excitement at having been accepted by the real cops upstairs; they all but fell over one another getting into the hall. Her advice had obviously made their day...or week...maybe even their year! "Where would we be without the dweebs of the world?" she asked aloud. "Losing the battle for the streets probably."

She arched her back and stretched before picking up the earphones for round two. She worked another three hours and took her translation to the lab. Once they worked their magic, the video was completed with her audio translation. Brittany and the techs carried the DVD to the Sarge and Smitty for review.

Once the recording ended, the Sarge studied Smitty a moment without saying a word. His eyebrows climbed his forehead as if to say *Wow!* The Sarge peered at the techs and then Brittany, still saying nothing. Finally he shook his head and turned to Smitty. "I don't know," he drawled, "you think this stuff is worth the money we pay these guys?"

The look on the techs' faces went from anticipatory smiles to lower than the floor. Brittany shook her head and bit her lip.

Smitty threw his hands into the air. "I don't know; I've seen junior high kids on YouTube post better videos."

The techs turned their worried looks to Brittany; she winked at the group. "What these two worthless excuses of old crime fighters are saying is you guys did a great job, right?"

The techs focused on the Sarge and Smitty. "Really?" Thane asked.

"That's what I said, didn't I?" The Sarge all but yelled at them. "Go make yourselves useful and see if you can fix that hair trigger on those wireless Taser darts. I don't want one ending up in our keisters."

"Thanks, Sarge," Abinya said with a smile. "Next project," he said and turned toward the door. His compatriots followed like ducklings in the spring.

The Sarge turned his glower on Brittany. "You translate for everybody?"

"Everybody who needs it," she said in her sweetest tone.

"Humph. I need a copy of that DVD. Gang Unit gets one too as soon as possible, so they can nail them before they realize they've been had."

His grin reminded Brittany of a crocodile.

"They should swoop down on these punks just in time for Clubba to see his little empire start to crumble on tomorrow's news."

"From your lips to God's ear," Smitty said.

⚬⚬

Jake Mitchell hadn't had such an excellent evening in, well, he couldn't remember when. Certainly not within the past two years. He tried to keep his walk steady and simple so his lieutenant didn't notice anything new. A large envelope marked *URGENT* in red letters waited on his desk. He picked it up for closer inspection. *For immediate delivery to the gang unit* blazed on the front label. Jake turned it over several times. It wasn't the usual way for a tip to come into his office.

Who was he to judge though? He'd drop it to the GU's sergeant. Let them decide what to do with it; he had better things to contemplate.

He grabbed the package and headed out on his usual rounds. At the gang unit, he spotted Sergeant Scott. "Hey, Sarge," Jake called to the other man. "Got an unusual package for you."

"Oh yeah?" The sergeant took the large manila envelope, turned it over carefully, and peered up at Jake. "What is it?"

"Not a clue," Jake said. "But I'm dying to know."

Scott took out a letter opener and slid it across the seal to access the contents. Gingerly, he slid the packet onto his desk. "A DVD?" the sergeant asked.

"There's a piece of paper too," Jake said.

More information that may help you with Te'quan Koak. From your friend who helped you with the purse snatcher case.

The sergeant turned deadly serious.

"What's wrong?" Jake asked.

The gang sergeant looked up from the note. "This is the same guy that helped us with the purse snatchers."

"Great," Jake said. "So what's the problem?"

Sergeant Scott slid the DVD into his computer and pointed to a picture on his wall. "Te'quan Koak aka, 'Clubba,'" he said.

"Okay," Jake said. "I'll bite. What's his deal?"

"He's been building some sort of gang infrastructure. We really haven't seen anything like it. He acts like—and is treated like—a leader of his gang, but the whole thing doesn't mesh with what we see in the gangs here in town."

Jake studied Clubba's photo and turned his attention back to the sergeant. "I thought these punks were pretty straightforward. Spray paint their territory, sell drugs, rob, steal, and shoot at people."

"This guy is different," the sergeant said. "Looks like the whole Sudanese population in Omaha looks to him as some sort of godfather. He also has a bunch of Sudanese guys who seem to take orders from him, but again not like anything we've ever dealt with. Clubba appears to be an associate with other gangs but somehow he has his own too. Really weird. I mean some gangs are cool with others, but Clubba seems to be down with all the major gangs—and I mean all. He must deal in guns or something they all want but only he can get. No clue what that is."

Sergeant Scott started the video.

Jake stood behind his shoulder and watched too.

"Busted him on a domestic violence charge; strangulation and terroristic threats, he got eighteen months in prison. At his court hearing, his thugs kept giving the woman—girl really—threatening looks."

"Which means 'stay quiet,'" Jake said. "I remember a few cases like that back in Utah. Where is she? Anything happen?"

"Not that we know of, but this dude is called Clubba because he likes to use a bat on whoever causes him any trouble."

Jake winced at the thought. "Ouch. Guess that's enough to keep people in line, especially if they aren't familiar with the language and don't know how to get help in the community."

"Exactly!" Sergeant Scott said. "Just like the Italians when they migrated here. The mafia kept people in line by whatever means necessary, but this guy is a little different than those thugs were. Clubba likes to personally deliver the beatings; that way everybody fears him. From what little intelligence we've gathered, that's how he likes it, wants it, and it works for him. Very well. Nobody talks about him to anyone—especially us."

"That bites," Jake said. "You can't do anything without decent intelligence."

"Tell me about it. Only reason we got him was because his girlfriend's little sister videoed him threatening her big sister for seeing another man. He lost his cool, threatened and strangled her, in the middle of the street, didn't care who saw him. Between that and the bat in his hand, we got him on all three charges."

"Nice work," Jake said. He admired anyone who could take a violent jerk like this Clubba off the street.

"It wasn't nearly enough," Scott said. "Let's see what's on this." He clicked the play button. An apartment complex unfolded. "Looks like that one up on Sixtieth Street," Scott said and leaned in closer to his screen.

Jake pulled up a chair beside him. "Explain what you're seeing."

The sergeant pointed. "Look across the street—they look to be Sudanese."

Jake frowned. "What do you mean?"

"Sudanese are pretty tall generally, very dark complexioned with the rounded foreheads you see there. Sometimes they have tribal markings scarred across their foreheads. They're each wearing large white shirts too. That's pretty typical of Clubba's thugs as well." Sergeant Scott pulled back and tilted his head. "In fact, I'd say they have the whole complex surrounded."

"Surrounded?" Jake echoed. "Why would they surround that?"

A long moment passed. The sergeant turned to Jake the same moment Jake turned to him. "The girlfriend."

"Of course," Jake said.

"They're making sure she stays put."

"Not to mention intimidating her," Jake said.

"Look at 'em." The sergeant pointed to the group milling around outside. "They're not even crossing the street; they're just standing around. They're not even trying to hide."

"Suppose they want her to see them?" Jake asked.

The sergeant nodded. "Yep. They're also letting her know that they know where she is. And warning her to keep her mouth shut."

Jake watched the monitor and nodded solemnly. "Makes her stay put, that's for sure, but why not just go get her? It's like a game of cat and mouse and they're just—" The conclusion washed over him like a bucket of ice. Jake met the sergeant's gaze. "Didn't you say Clubba likes to take a bat to his enemies himself?"

"Yea." Sergeant Scott's eyes widened. "Oh, holy, crap!" He pulled up the Nebraska Penitentiary page and scanned over the inmate population and their release dates. "Oh man," Scott said. "He gets out tomorrow. Those mopes are holding her there for him. As soon as he gets out, he's going to bash her head in!"

"Let's get 'em," Jake said.

Sergeant Scott grabbed his phone and called the gang unit secretary. "Get ahold of the entire unit; I want everyone in the conference room in two hours." Turning back to his monitor, he smiled. "This is gold, Jake. Gold. We can grab every one of them for felony witness tampering."

"Awesome," Jake said. "I love it when things come together like that."

"No kidding; stuff like this doesn't fall in our lap every day. I'll set up a sweep. That way we can nab a good chunk of his gang and put it with the other evidence we'll get."

"Should be more than enough to nail Clubba," Jake said.

Scott smiled and turned his attention back to his monitor. "Let's send this thug back where he belongs."

CHAPTER 29

"SMITTY." THE SARGE STALKED TO HIS DOORWAY AND called for his righthand man.

"Yeah, Sarge."

"C'mere," he said with a jerk of his head toward a chair inside.

Smitty hurried in and took a seat. "What's going on?"

"I need you to set up a quick response team. The gang unit should be about to hit those punks and hit 'em hard."

"Right," Smitty said. "What'd you have in mind?"

"The GU should have their whole unit there, not to mention the assistance of the black-and-whites."

Smitty nodded his agreement. "And?"

The Sarge reached up to the frame surrounding a photo of the President of the United States and pulled down a hidden map of the Sixtieth and Etna apartment complex. "You can bet once these punks realize what's coming down on them, they'll scatter throughout the whole area. Our goal is to nab 'em all—every single one." He switched his gaze from the graphic and back to Smitty. "How many Blues do we have there right now?"

"Ten," Smitty said. He stood and walked over to the apartment diagram. "The Chelinis have Blues posted here." He circled between the buildings. "Here." He circled the walkways on the main entrance. "And here, at this maintenance path. Looks like the entire outer perimeter will be covered. What about the inner perimeters? There are so many buildings in this complex, we could have Clubba's thugs running all over the place."

Nodding, the Sarge pored over the layout. "Good," he said. "Very good. I want another ten at the choke points around the parking lot in the middle. There's a donut shape to the entire area on the map with a playground and parking lot in the middle. Here." He pointed at a walkway that led to the swings. "And here." He pointed at another choke point between buildings that also led to the inner courtyard. "These are the obvious escape routes they could run through if they do and will run through this complex."

The Sarge rubbed his chin. "If I were that gang sergeant, I'd put some coppers right in the middle of the complex for the thugs that escape the chase."

"You're figuring on a chase?" Smitty asked.

"Wouldn't you?"

"Yeah," Smitty said with a smile. "And if I was thirty years younger, I'd look forward to it."

"I want every single Blue with a weapon."

"Weapon?" Smitty asked.

"Our weapons," the Sarge said. "Walkers, canes, and crutches."

"Sorry," Smitty said. "I must've stepped back in time."

"I know the feeling," the Sarge said. "Let the boys at Sixtieth and Etna know."

"You got it, Sarge." Smitty seated himself at his desk and pulled out his radio for the call. "Tony, you there?"

"Yeah, Smitty," the friendly elder Chelini brother asked. "What's up?"

"Sarge wants a secondary security detail set up."

"What?" Tony asked. "Why?"

"He thinks the gang unit is gonna pounce on these punks any time now. And he wants everybody with walking assistance."

"Ah," Tony said. "Everybody gets weapons."

"Yep," Smitty replied.

"Fun stuff."

"I'll be out with the supplies as soon as I can. Once I get there, we'll get your people set up and get the escape prevention units organized."

"Okay, no problem, Smitty. We're ready to rock and roll."

True to his word, Smitty and the Somewhat Quick Response Unit, a term the Blues had for a bunch of old coppers who couldn't respond very quickly, had arrived. Tony and Smitty posted extra men at all potential escape routes. The complex all but looked like a retirement center itself. Old men milled around throughout the apartment complex.

To the casual observer there would seem to be some sort of activity planned for the senior residents of the complex. They were standing around buildings, talking to each other as if it was just a normal day. However, if one were to look closely, it would be clear that these weren't just a bunch of old men talking about the weather. Years of experience had taught them how to carry on what looked like a normal conversation while setting up ambush positions. They may have been talking, and slowly walking, but they were taking in everything, and they were making mental notes of how to bushwhack Clubba's thugs.

Smitty jutted his chin across the street. "Seems to be more of his soldiers around than usual," Smitty looked again, "Whoa! There's way more. There's gotta be twenty guys out there!"

"Yeah," Tony said with a frown. "Sure does. That doesn't bode well."

Smitty was in deep thought trying to figure out how the estimates of the actual number of Clubba's people could have been so wrong. "Definitely doesn't. They may be changing the guard or calling out their members to make sure she doesn't go anywhere before Clubba gets out."

"Good," Tony said. "If more of them hang around and talk, maybe the gang unit will arrest 'em all. We might get a load of those hoods off the street."

"Sounds like a plan," Smitty muttered. He got on his radio with an announcement to the Blues in the complex. "Boys, this may be a bigger job than we thought, we got three times as many gang members than usual. This place will be a hornet's nest any minute."

In response to Smitty's announcement there were anonymous hoots and hollers from Ol' Blues excited for an old-fashioned raid. "Don't worry Smitty, we'll get 'em!" and "They ain't going anywhere!"

Smitty smiled and said for all the Blues to hear, "Let's round 'em up like the old days, boys."

⌒

Sergeant Scott's briefing was quick and to the point. His team's attention focused on the aerial photo of the Etna housing units on the front viewing screen. "We're going to disembark in the neighborhood behind the gang members because they're watching the apartment complex, not the neighborhood behind them. Then come up from their rear by going between the houses, as quickly and quietly as possible." Scott directed. "I want to surprise the thugs by popping out behind them and nabbing them before they have time to react."

Sergeant Scott looked at the officers for understanding; heads nodded showing collective understanding. "If we do this right, we just might catch at least seven to ten of them. I want quick takedowns, and I want them secured and stuffed in a cruiser even quicker. The faster we clear the area, the less chance of any disturbances by their friends. I want them outta there and booked for witness tampering."

Sergeant Scott perused the maze of escape routes any of them could take. He pointed to a table where some of his undercover officers sat. "For good measure I want two cars with you, eight officers here." He indicated directly in the parking lot in the middle of the housing units. "And nab anybody who tries to run through; it's a huge complex so we'll try to grab as many as we can during the initial contact."

"There's bound to be a couple who run inside and away from the initial officers," Officer Turley said.

"Yep," Scott said. "Monitor the radio and converge on the route they're using to escape and cut them off. Got it?"

"Absolutely."

Scott scanned the room filled with officers and detectives. More nods and murmurs of understanding and agreement met his analysis. It was a good plan. "I'll monitor our frequency. Stay tactical; stay safe."

One glance told him all he needed to know. Everyone was definitely ready. The possibility of arresting an entire gang in one operation psyched up everybody involved. "Let's hit it."

∿

Shanese plucked at the curtain covering the living room window and peeked out across the street where a couple of dozen of Clubba's hoods still hung around. Over the past month, she'd performed the same useless routine watching the young men under her ex's control deliver their silent message. *He's comin', woman.* She didn't know whether to cry or vomit. They scared her. A lot. But not as much as the thought of Clubba's bat cracking against her skull. She rubbed the thin material between her index finger and thumb absently.

The waiting was the worst—not knowing when or where the attack would come. Clubba fed on the terror, and she prayed she didn't let fear get the best of her, that she could face him straight on and take what came. She prayed but doubted she'd have the strength.

"They still there," her grandmother said from the kitchen. "Just like yesterday and the day before that and the day before that. They ain't goin' anywhere, girl."

"I know…but I think there's more today. A lot more."

"Uh-uh-uh," her grandmother clucked behind her. "That Clubba nothing but trouble from day one. Didn't I tell you?"

"Yes," Shanese admitted reluctantly. "But I was in so deep and so quickly, I—" She broke off that line of thinking. It didn't do anyone any good. What was done was done and pretty soon she'd have to deal with the consequences. Fear coiled inside her and she drew in a deep breath to brace herself. She almost wanted it over and done with now.

Before Shanese let the drape slide closed, several groups of older men outside caught her eye. Dozens of them. Tons more than ever before. Puzzled, she turned to her grandmother. "Grandma, is there some senior activity today?"

Her grandmother wiped her hands on a blue kitchen towel and slung it over her shoulder. "Not that I know of. Why?"

Shanese dashed to the kitchen window and peered as far as she could see to the right and then to the left. There were always a group of old men—she recognized several—who hung out or were observed walking around or playing checkers. Today, though, there were loads more. Not only did they line the benches, some stood between the buildings. She tilted her head and frowned. Almost like they were waiting.

"Grandma, did you see all those old men outside? You sure nothing's going on? A party maybe?"

"Party? With who?" She threw her towel on the countertop and padded into the living room. "What you talking about?"

Shanese pulled the curtain back; her grandmother took a step forward, surprise flitting across her face. "That's a lot of men. Any of them cute?"

Shanese shot her grandmother a shocked look. "I didn't look."

"Doesn't matter. What's cute to me is different than what's cute to you. Lemme see." She drew back the window covering and scanned the older gents at leisure.

"Grandma." Shock turned to scandal; Shanese couldn't believe her grandmother's actions.

"I'm old; I'm not dead, girl."

Shanese shot her grandmother a glare.

"Don't give me that," she said with a tsk of disgust. She pointed across the street. "Them Clubba's boys?"

"Yes," Shanese whispered.

"They ain't nothing but trouble."

"I know that now."

"Look at all those men milling around out there. I don't recognize any of 'em. Do you?"

"I've seen some of them around. I think they live here. They're usually playing checkers when the weather's nice."

Her grandmother's attention stayed with the newcomers. "Maybe I'll go introduce myself."

"Grandma!"

"Just to see what's up," the older woman said not taking her focus off one particular gentleman, between buildings.

"Hardly," Shanese said, unable to keep the smile from her face.

"Well, a girl can look, can't she?" Glancing left and right and then left again, her grandmother shook her head. "That's really odd though, child."

"What is?"

"I've never seen that many older men in the neighborhood before. The odds have definitely improved."

Shanese couldn't help it. In spite of Clubba's men hovering around like vultures, in spite of his reign of terror, in spite of the upcoming and promised beating, she laughed, and for a moment, her burden was lightened.

CHAPTER 30

SMITTY, SUPERVISING THE INNER ESCAPE ROUTES FROM the apartment the Blues had used for surveillance, looked like a television producer with ten screens showing the entire complex. He immediately spotted the cops in the undercover cars. Reaching up, he nonchalantly tapped his hearing aid that doubled as a radio and broadcast to all the Blues. "Gang unit evidently put some undercovers in the parking lot—middle of the complex."

"Smart move," Smitty said to himself with a smile. Always good to see a well-planned operation. "Make sure everybody stays put. Let the gang unit deploy and close in on Clubba's thugs. My guess is that they'll come in from behind using the houses and bushes as cover. Then for good measure from inside the complex. They'll run directly toward the undercover officers," Smitty said, "We'll slow 'em down for the uniforms to catch up and collar the punks."

Smitty wondered how he could warn the gang unit that there were way more bangers on the scene than ever before. Nice thought but too late. Smitty lifted his head, and checked again. A gang officer sprang behind a bush and grabbed one of Clubba's soldiers from behind. The ambush was on!

Smitty tapped the earpiece radio. "Be alert, guys; gang unit's gonna jump 'em."

As predicted, ten officers bolted from behind Clubba's men.

"*Police!*" The cry went out in Sudanese.

"On the ground. On the ground."

Sudanese soldiers scattered. With the officers coming from behind, Clubba's soldiers ran right toward the apartment complex. Officers were hopelessly outnumbered. Those with a suspect proceeded to handcuff them. Others sprang into the chase.

One officer, Steve Turley, a ten-year veteran, stopped, quickly trying to comprehend the pandemonium exploding in front of him. He grabbed his portable radio, knowing Sergeant Scott was monitoring, and yelled, "We're way outnumbered. There's gotta be over twenty suspects running exactly where you said."

A terrified Sudanese soldier not paying attention thumped straight into Turley's chest sending his radio flying, Turley wrestled the kid to the ground and cuffed him. Turley hoped his message got out.

Smitty smiled—a familiar adrenaline rush shot through him. "It's on, boys. They're heading right for us." From his position in the upstairs apartment, Smitty observed the undercover officers scrambling out of their cars heading toward the mayhem. "Looks like the undercovers got the message. They're piling out of their cars and heading straight for you guys."

Memories of hitting the pavement and running down criminals like they'd done in days gone by flooded every Blue on the detail. Each one had stationed himself at a choke point with the same assignment: pepper spray them when they run by, break off once they pass, and work your way to the vans. Head back to the precinct.

⚮

"Grandma," Shanese yelled. "The bangers are coming. All of 'em. They're coming!"

"Get out the back door, child, and take your sister. Run! Run now!"

"What about you?"

"Got a plan. You two go now."

With a nod, Shanese grabbed her sister by the hand and obeyed her grandmother's directive. She had no clue what the plan was, but she prayed her grandmother would be safe. Guilt for bringing this into her home washed through Shanese but she shook it off. No time for that now. She and her sister ran out the back door.

"Fire!" her grandmother shouted, hoping a neighbor would call 911. Nobody would do anything in this neighborhood if she yelled help. "Fire!" she screamed again.

Shanese glanced over her shoulder and frowned. What was going on? Her sister tugged her forward.

"Come on,"

"But—"

"No buts. Grandma said run."

Her grandmother grabbed the thick, oversized metal spoon from its drawer. Wrapping both hands around the handle, she backed into the far corner of her kitchen. Sounds from outside floated through the open door where her granddaughters had fled. Screams and yelling and commotion filtered in. Maybe somebody had actually gotten involved and called the cops…if she was lucky. If she wasn't…her grip tightened around the thick metal, and she took a deep breath. If those Sudanese weasels came looking for trouble, they'd find it.

Smitty watched the scene unfold in amazement. Pepper spray permeated the air; he held a handkerchief to cover his nose. Curses in English, Italian, and Sudanese floated up through the din surrounding the apartments. One gang officer caught a banger and the fight was on. Five of Clubba's boys ran straight for the Chelini brothers who sprang into action, yelling in Italian. Before the thugs got to the Chelinis, they ran directly into a cloud of pepper spray. A piss pack hit a straggling soldier and exploded all over the younger man in all its five-day glory.

The targeted teen screamed in Sudanese, grabbed his eyes, and sank to his knees in utter defeat. Two ran toward the trees on the north side of the street; one ran straight into the brick wall of an apartment and fell to the ground knocked out cold. Two officers, Peterson and Gonzales, both of the gang unit, rounded the corner and stopped cold. Officer Peterson grabbed one banger, threw him to the ground, cuffing him as he recoiled from the disgusting stench of urine.

Gonzales approached the second banger who was out cold and followed suit. Clubba's men rubbed their faces into the cool grass and gave no resistance to the handcuffs. Peterson and Gonzales exchanged an *I've-never-seen-anything-like-this-before* look, shrugged their shoulders, and jumped on the next banger they could reach. Once they cuffed one, they moved to the next. Gonzales keyed his microphone. "Need two transporting officers at Sixtieth and Etna."

Peterson glanced up to catch his breath. Two older men smiled and waved at him. Peterson noticed several others strolling by. One of them winked, "Nice work, kid."

They sauntered past the noise and commotion as though they'd done it a hundred times...just fading away. Mesmerized, Officer Peterson watched in fascination. The banger under his control kicked him in the leg. He slammed the pepper spray–blinded kid with a bad attitude into the ground face down. "Stop resisting."

Screams and shouts both foreign and native flew through the police radios. Undercovers in the parking lot didn't need an invitation. They poured out of their vehicles as fast as they could manage and bolted toward the sound of commotion.

"Where they at?" yelled Kerry Cunningham, a seventeen-year veteran. Nobody knew. Kerry's partner, the lead officer Tye Mason, himself a twenty-year veteran, yelled to the other officers. "Run to the noise. Stay with a partner. Don't get isolated. Go! Go! Go!"

The officers ran to the fray; more white-haired men than anyone had seen in one place were hanging around various buildings watching the officers run by.

"Get back inside!" Kerry yelled to one particular gent. The reply caused a brief pause. "Yeah right, sonny; I was doing this before you were born," the old man with a shiny cane hollered back.

Kerry and Tye ran as fast as they could. Rounding a corner, Kerry met a large piece of metal. *Clang!* Pain, sharp and thick, shot through his head. He fell face first onto the ground and laid there a long moment trying to fathom what had hit him. He turned onto his back. "What the—?"

An elderly woman wielded a very large, oversized, thick metal spoon. "I'm so sorry, officer," the woman said and tried to help him up. "I thought you was bringing trouble to my door, and I didn't see the word *police* until you tumbled to the ground cuz it's on your back."

"It's okay, ma'am. Just...put that thing away."

Tye stopped at the sound of his partner hitting the ground. "You all right?" He drew up beside him and pulled him to his feet, steadying the older lady at the same time. "Holy crap, you've got a knot the size of an Easter egg on your forehead."

Kerry's fingers flew to the spot. Sure enough it was swelling like a helium balloon; it was going to be a doozy.

"I thought you was one of those no good thugs," the woman said. "I'm so sorry, officer. Can I get you a glass of water?"

Kerry watched the look of recognition cross his partner's face as he realized what had happened. He grinned from ear to ear.

"Ma'am," Tye said, "why don't you go back inside before you kill one of us?"

"Yes, sir," came the courteous reply. "I'm really sorry about that."

Kerry looked over at the woman. "No problem," he said. "I'm fine and we've got to go."

All tenderness fled the older woman's face; fiery indignation flared in her eyes. She pointed the metal spoon toward the sounds of the fighting. "Go get those no good thugs right now."

"Yes, ma'am." Kerry and Tye spoke simultaneously, turned on their heels, and dashed toward the tumult.

"That gramma-lady decked you." Tye laughed out loud.

"Shut up. There are old folks everywhere around here. Watch out."

‿

The gang unit and uniformed officers zigzagged through the maze of twenty buildings. Each held four apartments. The insanity of chasing one suspect let alone twenty was a lose-lose proposition, and every cop knew it. The bangers had a month to scout everything out; they knew where to run and where to hide.

"It can never be easy, can it?" Sergeant Scott muttered. Monitoring the radio traffic in a unmarked police van at the original dropoff point, he was pleasantly surprised to hear of the initial successes that his officers were having catching three to five bangers at a time.

As the officers secured the bangers, Scott noted that six of his officers were on the radio calling for medical attention for pepper spray exposure. There were so many he said, "Everyone's pepper spray cans must be empty."

Scott said. "There's twice the number of bangers we anticipated; it's stretching our ability to nab any more." The sergeant told a uniformed officer in the van with him, "Call for more cruisers."

The officer keyed his microphone and contacted the dispatch center. "We need every available cruiser in the precinct."

The radio dispatcher replied, "That's clear, 2 Adam 10, 15, and 16 report to Sixtieth and Etna to assist the gang unit." All three cruisers advised that they were clear on the call and en route.

"More police cruisers on the way, Sergeant." The officer said.

"Good," Sergeant Scott replied. "I just hope they get here in time."

From a small mound, Abrahim and one of his soldiers were able to get a brief look at the pandemonium of running soldiers and police officers. Abrahim was initially shocked that the police were able to sneak up behind his entire group of soldiers. The panic of the police pouncing on his soldiers sent them all running into the large apartment complex. Now, however, the initial shock had been overcome, and it looked like his soldiers were taking advantage of the many escape routes the maze of apartment buildings provided. They were running in every direction with all this confusion, so he knew the police would not be able to have an organized response.

"Many will escape," Abrahim said to himself with a smile before he resumed his own attempt to flee.

What Abrahim and his soldiers didn't know was that there were undercover officers sprinting from the middle of the complex. They heard the radio chatter and could tell that there were numerous fights going on. This fueled their desire to get into the fray—even though they had to sprint one hundred yards through the apartment complex—they dispersed two by two between the buildings.

The frustrating thing for the officers was that nobody could give a good location over the radio as to their location in the huge complex. Unlike on TV cop shows, it was extremely difficult to find an address or an exact location when an officer is running after a suspect and screaming at the top his lungs for the suspect to stop. The undercover officers could only run toward the screaming and hope to find and assist the officer in the arrest.

Another problem was that there was screaming everywhere. It echoed off buildings, and since the commotion was so loud, there were residents coming out to see what was going on. The officers were yelling to one another, at the bangers, and to the residents to get back inside for their safety—at the same time attempting to provide some coherent information on their radios.

Sergeant Scott who could hear the problems the officers were having finally said, "We're losing control." Then Sergeant Scott heard the voices of his undercover officers starting to enter the fray. "There's some good news," he uttered as he listened to the radio.

&

Smitty was also monitoring the progress of the undercovers sprinting to the aid of their fellow officers. Smitty smiled. That was good planning to put those undercover boys in the parking lot, but they are still going to need some help. Smitty tapped his hearing aid/microphone and broadcast to the Blues, "Looks like the undercovers from the parking lot are finally joining in, stay sharp boys."

There were acknowledgments from the Blues who were still waiting to ambush the escaping gang members. Smitty smiled and said to himself, "Those punks should be approaching our Blues any minute now."

Officer Steven Turley was back in the chase. He had recovered from being plowed into during the initial part of the operation. As he approached the apartment complex, he could see that there were various officers cuffing the suspects on the ground. There were officers still in hot foot pursuit in various directions toward the inner parts of the complex. Even with the number of bangers that had been caught, Officer Turley said to himself, "There's still too many of them."

Just then he saw the undercover officers rounding corners and trying to tackle the bangers as they ran straight toward them. This obviously surprised many of the bangers who thought they were getting away by running through the complex. They tried to stop in their tracks and change direction. Some fell and were caught, but there were still those able to break free.

Turley got on his radio and said, "Sergeant Scott, this operation has turned to a catch-whoever-you-can pursuit!"

Sergeant Scott replied, "I know, but do the best you can, more cruisers are on the way, but I don't know if they'll get here in time."

Turley acknowledged and started after the two bangers who were about thirty yards in front of him. He looked and couldn't believe what one of them was doing. The banger was talking into a small radio, and it looked like he was yelling instructions.

❧

Abrahim bellowed instructions in Sudanese to his soldiers over their CB radios. A few had been captured, but with a little luck most of them might slip away. Scanning the familiar area, he turned in the direction his men were headed. From his vantage point he saw why the cops were catching some of his soldiers. Rounding the buildings were cops wearing black vests filing in from the middle of the complex. White block lettering proclaimed *POLICE* on their vests moved exactly where the soldiers were heading.

Abrahim yelled into his CB radio, *"It's a trap,"* he screamed. *"More cops coming from the parking lot."* Abrahim could see that more cops meant more of his soldiers were going to get caught. The only way more of his soldiers would escape would be to keep the cops tied up by fighting with them if they got caught. If they are fighting, they can't be chasing us. Some of his soldiers had to be sacrificed so that the rest could escape.

American cops were used to regular gang members giving up when caught. They didn't want an assaulting-an-officer charge added to whatever else they were arrested for. Not the Sudanese. Unfamiliar with the criminal justice system, they loved to fight and would punch, kick, and bite—anything to get away.

Abrahim was no exception. *"Fight them."* He yelled into his radio, *"If they catch you, fight them; this will help the rest of our soldiers escape."*

Over his radio, each soldier repeated it to one another. Abrahim smiled and watched. His directive to battle proved effective. One, then two, then three of his men broke away and ran between the buildings. Abrahim couldn't help but chuckle. "Fools," he muttered. "You didn't bring enough cops!"

The soldier he had with him pointed at an officer who was starting to run toward them. They quickly sprinted away leaving the sound of the chaos behind them. Abrahim knew that officer could not catch them with the lead they had.

ᘒ

A pair of Blues, Kim and Paul, milled around between buildings. "Hey look," Kim said and glanced down at a long, gray garden hose coiled on the ground beside his feet. Glancing over at Paul, he picked up one end. "Grab the other end and stretch it tight," he said with a chuckle. "We'll trip the punks after we spray them?"

Paul nodded and shot Kim a conspiratorial wink.

Smitty pressed the hearing aid-radio in his ear. "Kim and Paul, three of them headed your way."

Once the bad guys were in sight, Kim pushed the button on his walker and shot a cloud of pepper spray twenty feet ahead of them. Three tall young men raced around the brick corner, glancing back over their shoulders. The Blues saw too. The officers giving chase were a good thirty yards behind the boys. Escape looked within reach. Paul and Kim stepped out. The mocking bangers didn't see the old men as threats to them and focused on getting away. The boys ran straight into the orange plume.

Eyes and mouths wide open in the melee, they drew in the caustic spray. In a heartbeat, their eyes involuntarily slammed shut, their noses, mouths, and throats seared. The burning chemical pain of two million Scoville Heat Units, a measurement of hot spices, overcame them. Their hands flew to their eyelids to no avail. Still intent on escape they continued running—straight toward the outstretched hose of two grinning Ol' Blues, Kim and Paul.

Their plan couldn't have fallen into place better if they'd scripted it. Kim and Paul exchanged an evil grin. Clubba's punks hit the hose and ran right past them, pulling the rubber from their two sets of hands. "Nuts," Kim said. "I thought that would work."

Ten feet later, the bangers could move no more. Pepper spray had worked its debilitating mission. They screamed in their native tongue but no relief was in sight. Kim and Paul smiled again at each other. Maybe their plan didn't work the way they wanted, but it still succeeded.

Kerry and Tye responded to the cries. Three young males gagged and pressed their palms into their eyes. One dragged a hose along behind him. Pepper spray still hung in the air but nothing as intense as seconds earlier.

Two senior citizens stood by and watched the altercation like it was a Friday night fight; they grimaced and cheered, scowled and smirked as the young men squirmed.

"Watch it," Tye muttered so only his partner could hear. "You know what happened the last time we came across one of these old folks."

"Oh shut up," said Kerry with the darkening contusion. "On the ground now," he roared at the three men. Two started to lie down. The third shrieked something in Sudanese at the officers. Instantly the young man met the ground hard. "We ain't playing," Tye said.

The three were cuffed in minutes, then picked up and ushered toward the designated pickup spot for arrestees. Walking by the same two old men brought renewed smiles and then laughs directed at Clubba's men.

"You boys enjoy the full effect of that pepper spray," one gentleman called out.

"Yeah," the other chimed in, "all the way through your nose, your sinuses, and into your lungs."

Kerry peered at the three thugs. Mucus flowed in gobs out their noses.

"Oh, hey, that's the walrus effect," Tye said. "Look, Kerry, those long strings of mucus hang from their nose."

"Yep, looks like tusks," Kerry said.

"Not so tough now are ya, punk?" Kim said.

"Okay, guys," Tye said. "Get back in your apartments. Show's over."

The two older men turned slowly. "Hmph. You'd think they'd be thanking us for delivering those creeps to 'em."

"Yeah," Paul said. "You'd think."

Kerry and Tye exchanged a questioning look. "You hear that?" Kerry asked.

"Yeah."

Both officers peered at the old men moseying away. "You don't think—"

"Nah." Tye shook his head. "One of our guys pepper sprayed them. It just took a little time for it to take effect."

"Dude," his partner said with a nod. "That lady with the spoon really laid one on you."

"Tell me about it; my head's still throbbing." He pushed his perpetrator forward. "Let's go."

☙

Abrahim and his soldier hit their stride, putting distance between them, the ruckus, and a very tired Officer Turley still trying to recover from having the wind knocked out of him. Escaping was the only good thing about this mess. There were too many unknowns: how many of his soldiers had been caught and arrested, how many had been injured, what were they charged with? Mostly he didn't know how he'd explain it all to his cousin.

Then as if in answer to his fear, he saw them. Shanese and her sister, holding hands and running for their lives. If I kill her myself, Clubba will still be pleased with me, Abrahim said to himself.

Shanese knew that if she could get out of this hornet's nest filled with Clubba's thugs she and her sister would be able to find another place to hide and hopefully survive. Shanese told her sister, "Just run! Don't look back." Shanese didn't know that Abrahim and one of Clubba's soldiers were bearing down on them from behind. Abrahim pulled a knife from his waistband, and smiled in anticipation of killing for Clubba.

Shanese yelled to her sister, "Just past that old man, and we're..." Shanese had looked back at her sister when she trailed off mid-sentence by the sight of two of Clubba's thugs chasing them. One she recognized as Abrahim, quickly gaining on them. Shanese's eyes widened in terror as she saw Abrahim smiling and clenching a knife in his hand. "Don't look back!" She yelled to her sister, "Don't look—" She was cut off by a loud, determined yell from in front of her. "Keep running, darl'en. I'll take care of these hoods." Shanese looked forward to see an old man, waving them past with one of his crutches. Shanese didn't have time to think, she just ran past the man towards the urban neighborhood and hopefully safety.

Thirty yards in front of them, Abrahim spotted an elderly man on crutches. By the way the aged one walked, it appeared as if he wanted to intercept Abrahim. "Stupid old goat, out of the way, old man," Abrahim shouted. Pulling closer, Abrahim realized that he recognized him, but from where?

As he approached to pass, Abrahim watched the geezer lift the bottom part of his left crutch and point it at him like a gun. He met Abrahim's gaze and smiled.

Boom! Whatever was inside that crutch hit Abrahim in his right shoulder and spun him around. He'd been hit with a police bean bag round, a lead pellet cloth container shot from a 12-gauge cartridge at 300 to 400 feet per second. Though officially deemed nonlethal, anyone hit would well wish they were dead. It's brought full-grown men to the ground in agonizing pain.

Boom! Boom! Abrahim's companion toppled to the ground, beside him.

Boom! Something knocked the air out of him; Abrahim grabbed his abdomen and sank to the ground beside his soldier.

Bean Bag Charlie, one of only a few of the retired officers who could still shoot a shotgun and not land flat on his back, stood over Abrahim and smiled. "Nothing stops a moving mass like two of those babies straight to the gut."

Abrahim and his companion lay on the ground moaning and struggling to breathe. Abrahim gazed up at him. "I...I know you," he said through gasps of air. "At—" he struggled to gulp a breath, "at the police home."

Bean Bag shrugged his shoulders. "You sure, son?" he asked. "Cuz all us old guys look alike."

Bending over, he plucked up the bean bags and left the scene. Passing Officer Turley who'd just caught up to them, Bean Bag Charlie turned and pointed back at the two young men writhing on the ground. "Make sure your sergeant knows," he jerked a thumb over his shoulder. "The tallest one," He indicated Abrahim, "that's Clubba's cousin."

CHAPTER 31

CLUBBA KICKED BACK IN FRONT OF THE COMMON ROOM television set. Tomorrow…tomorrow," he sang happily.

"Don't rub it in," Earnest said with a sidelong glare at his partner. Honestly, the fact that Clubba was so ready and willing to work with Earnest still amazed him. Clubba would network his accomplices on the outside; Earnest would handle them on the inside. "News is on," he said with a lift of his chin toward the screen.

"Yeah," Clubba said with a knowing grin. "My last day watching from this place." Clubba said loud enough for all to hear and envy him.

Earnest eyed the younger man. Without realizing it, Clubba had given all his hot-button issues to Earnest who made it a point to fan the flames of anger in Clubba. The mere mention of the old man with the whistling teeth sent the youngster into tornadic wrath. Earnest took the opportunity to goad the boy at every opportunity. Earnest wanted Tiny dead; Clubba wanted to kill him. The way Earnest figured, if his plan worked out the way he wanted, Clubba would be the pawn that helped him get the last laugh. Earnest wanted nothing more than to dance on Tiny's grave—literally.

"We have breaking news on a major police operation in the area of Sixtieth and Etna Streets," the anchor said to the prompter. "We go there live when we return."

Clubba turned away from a conversation with a handful of other prisoners in his vicinity. "Sixtieth and Etna," he said with a sudden serious tone. "That's where my soldiers are."

"Something going on up there?" Earnest asked.

A prisoner at the table behind him tossed a wad of paper into the wastebasket. "Heard something's goin' down in North O. Sounds like somethin' big to me."

"You have no idea," Clubba whispered.

Earnest watched him closely; the television held his rapt attention. "What's up?"

Clubba shushed him.

The anchor's handsome face grew somber. "We go now to the scene."

"Shut up!" Clubba growled at the chatting prisoners surrounding him. Nobody disputed him although he drew frowns, questioning looks, and shoulder shrugs in return.

"I'm at this group of apartments at Sixtieth and Etna Street," said the young female reporter. "As you can see behind me, there are numerous police cars. Officers are still swarming the area collecting stragglers."

The camera panned the area zeroing in on both uniformed officers and vested undercover detectives. "About fifteen minutes ago, a call went out for more officers, and as you can see," she said swallowing a chuckle, "respond they did."

The reporter stepped to her right; the camera obligingly zoomed in on the dwindling action. Ten marked cruisers filled the street; officers escorted handcuffed perpetrators to waiting police vehicles. About fifteen to twenty young men cursed and shrieked at police. "We still don't know what brought about the initial altercation," the reporter said, "but—"

A uniformed officer put his hand on the head of one young man to ease him into the back of a patrol car. The boy jerked away and raised his mouth to the sky. *"Sudanese soldiers!"*

Clubba sat rooted in place; he couldn't believe his eyes. The entire police department swarmed through Shanese's neighborhood. Caught up in the dragnet, he recognized his own men handcuffed and under arrest. "No," he whispered. "Nooooo."

Every prisoner within earshot turned toward Clubba.

"What's wrong?" Earnest asked.

᠁

"When we first arrived on scene we noticed a lot of senior citizens," the reporter said, once again facing the camera, "but this entire complex of apartment buildings are single-family dwellings. Still, it appears that a great many older residents live here. Most have headed inside now but there were a great many outside. This," she said, indicating the ongoing cleanup, "would send me back to the safety of my home too— even on this otherwise gorgeous day. Back to you guys in the studio," she said with a bright smile.

Before the camera stopped rolling, it caught four elderly men in the background moving toward a nondescript van. Another, obviously younger man, brought up the rear as though shepherding them along. As though sensing the media, he turned and spotted the broadcasting duo. Immediately ushering the older men into the vehicle, he slammed the door closed, hopped into the driver's seat, and sped off.

"Totally weird day," the camera operator said to his companion.

"You're telling me," she said. "Looks like the showdown at the O.K. Corral—without bullets."

᠁

Clubba stalked back to his cell; he punched his white-knuckled fist against his thigh with every step. "This can't be," he muttered. "Fifteen to twenty of my soldiers…they've got almost all of them." The realization of all his networking, all of his planning, all of his currying favor with people he thought below him—gone in minutes. His warlord empire collapsed on the grass at Sixtieth and Etna.

Clubba fell onto his bunk and stared at the ceiling with unseeing eyes. Stunned, he struggled to make sense of his crumbling world. Bewildered and disbelieving at what he'd just witnessed, he sucked in a deep breath of air. Never had he considered his plan wouldn't be successful. Everything he'd ever attempted had succeeded. There was no reason to think his latest venture would be anything less. Now it was gone—all of it—in an insignificant corner of North Omaha. What now? He only had a handful of soldiers left—if that. Everything he'd built or hoped to build rested on his Sudanese soldiers. With them behind bars, he had nothing. "Nothing!" he screamed to the solid walls.

Clubba lay quietly for a long time, willing away the panic that threatened to consume him; deep, steady breaths steadied him and calmed his rage. Nothing good ever came from an angry decision. He continued his rhythmic breathing until a long while later, a slow but ever widening smile crept across his face. There was one thing worth reaping: revenge. "First the old man, then that stupid woman and her sister."

Yes, revenge would be oh, so very sweet. Hearing the sound of his bat against each head would bring him stature again. He wouldn't be down for long.

Outside Clubba's cell, Earnest leaned against the cool cinder-block wall. Ah, Clubba, he thought, you're such a perfect little pawn. Tiny's days were numbered.

♊

"Everybody okay?" the tech asked the occupants of the van.

"Get us back to the precinct—and fast!" Smitty ordered. The Chelini brothers, Kim and Paul, sucked in gulps of air through wide smiles. Each man nodded. "We're good," Paul said.

"That dang camera caught us for sure; somebody's bound to have seen us." Smitty said. "Floor it!"

The driver followed the order. Three blocks away Smitty turned to the rest of the Blues. "Once we get back to our rooms, you can't be puffing and panting. We all need to act like we've been there the entire time."

The van screeched into the special maintenance garage, and the Ol' Blues piled out and into the entrance under the hydraulic hoist. Specially made golf carts awaited them. The shuttles zipped through the tunnels and the supply room. Each Blue entered his individual quarters.

The doors to the precinct burst open. Boss Nurse Betsy followed by three apprehensive student nurses marched straight in and headed toward the back doors, gateway to the Blues' private living quarters.

"Are you sure about this, ma'am?" the student behind her asked timidly.

"Sure? Oh yeah, I'm sure." She huffed and scuttled around a corner. "I saw that Smitty bold as polished brass. On television no less. I've always known something funny was going on around here. I can feel it in my gut," Betsy said. "Got 'em dead to rights now."

In his room, Smitty closed his eyes and willed his galloping heart to slow to a calmer beat. Luckily he'd prepared for this type of scenario and had worn his indignity robe under his street clothes; moments earlier he'd stuffed his outer garments in the bottom of his closet.

From the hall, sounds of a small commotion made its presence known. With every passing second the sounds grew nearer and louder…and headed straight for his room. Breathe, he told himself, just breathe. In…out…in…out. The clamor outside drew closer and Smitty hopped up, a brilliant idea blossoming in his head.

His door thudded open. "Smitty!" Boss Nurse Betsy exclaimed, her eyebrows hiking higher on her forehead. "What the—"

Smitty, holding the colostomy bag he'd just detached, jumped like he'd been shocked. "Oh—" he whirled around in phony surprise and flung the bag in question toward the door.

Nurse Betsy's arms flew out to her side as though she could protect her students from the inevitable. "Noooo!" The plea hit the air just as the bag landed directly in front of her, the contents splattering onto her legs and several of the students in her wake.

Nurse Betsy squeezed her eyes closed, her hands still splayed out at her side; the students shrieked and groaned.

"What'd you do that for?" Smitty asked. "I was just—" In his doorway, the contents of his colostomy bag dripped down Boss Nurse's legs. Her eyes still closed, it looked a lot like she was praying for strength not to kill him.

"Nurse Betsy thought you were on television," one of the student nurses said with more than a touch of sarcasm. "She actually thought you'd sneaked out of the facility."

"Sneak out?" he asked as innocently as he could muster. "Why? Better yet, how?"

Nurse Betsy glared at him and shook her head. "Get a mop," she directed. "Get this place cleaned and disinfected ASAP."

Moving as one, the students turned to leave. They showed their displeasure in long audible sighs, muttered remarks, and grimaces but they did as instructed.

"I don't know what's going on," Boss Nurse said, piercing Smitty with a withering stare, "but when I find out…"

She stalked out of Smitty's room, her threat resounding in his ears. Smitty sank into a chair and covered his face with his hand. He never wanted a repeat of this afternoon's race home. Boss Nurse was the last person they needed meddling in their affairs. It had been a close call—way, way, way too close. One good thing had come out of it though, Smitty thought. He'd finally found a use for that stupid crap bag.

CHAPTER 32

JAKE, THE CHIEF, AND MONICA HOVERED AROUND THE
radio channel, monitoring the melee in North Omaha.

"Holy smokes," the Chief said, "it sounds like the gang unit nabbed
a mob of that Clubba's thugs. We got a count yet, Jake?"

Shaking his head, Jake looked up from his notepad. "Nothing
complete, Chief, but by my count, we got about twenty bangers. What a
hornet's nest that place is. From what I've gathered, Sergeant Scott's group
thought there'd be maybe five or ten of them hanging around the housing
units. Once they flushed them out, there was almost a couple dozen."

"Outstanding," the Chief said and leaned back in his chair with a
wide smile. "Absolutely fantastic. We'll need a press release as soon as
we get all the facts sorted out. The media's already there, but they're
wrapping things up now that the gang unit and the uniformed cruisers
are leaving."

Jake nodded and stood up. "I'll let Sergeant Scott brief me once I
get over there. Should have an initial statement put together in about
an hour. A more complete release can come out after everybody's
booked. They'll be busy with that for a while."

"Good. Get on it, Jake. I'll wait for your call," the Chief said,
redirecting his attention to the action on the radio.

Jake stopped back at his office to review the news video from the
scene. "That was one crazy ambush," he said, jotting more notes on his
yellow pad. Toward the end of the coverage Jake glanced up. As the
camera panned the area, Jake did a double take.

"What the—" He shook his head and pressed the back button. Jake stared at the television screen with a frown. "That's Smitty getting into that van." Jake reviewed the scene three more times to make sure he'd seen it correctly. It was definitely Smitty. Jake plopped down into his seat and stared out the window at the cloudless sky.

What the devil was Smitty doing in the middle of a police action? His mind whirred and brought him back to the oh-so-familiar female voice who'd translated the anonymous DVD sent to the gang unit. "Of course!" Jake said to himself. "The voice belonged to Brittany. Who better to translate the surveillance video than a former missionary to the Sudanese people." It was perfect, but it still didn't explain Smitty... or the other Blues in the van.

"Oh, man," he said and propped his elbows on his desk. Brittany translating, Smitty at the scene, and the other Blues accompanying Smitty. There's only one explanation.

"The geezers have gone rogue."

෬ඌ

In all, twenty-three Sudanese soldiers had been captured and charged with a list of offenses ranging from felony witness tampering, felony assault on an officer, and flight to avoid arrest, to obstruction of justice—and that was just for starters. The task of positively identifying each one, determining the juveniles and the adults in the group, and processing the resulting paperwork would tie up the officers for the next few hours.

Eighteen suspects went to the hospital for exposure to pepper spray. Each still howled in pain, mucus still dripping from their noses and down their faces too.

The officers in charge watched in mild amusement. Fair payback for dragging them through the wildest mass apprehensions of their careers. Not much sympathy for the mouthy, whimpering, mucus-dripping bangers could be mustered from anyone in blue.

A few of Clubba's boys were clearly slow learners and made the big mistake of assaulting the nurses trying to help them; even more charges were added to their already looming prison time.

Street cops have a special place in their hearts for the emergency room staff. Many a cop had been bandaged up after a fight by an already exhausted nurse who gave them a smile and a good-natured scolding for getting hurt. Tonight was no exception.

Kerry Cunningham's nurse gave the oddly-shaped, swelled goose egg over his right eyebrow a confused frown. "I could swear this thing looks just like one of my metal serving spoons—even has the same drainage holes."

Cunningham stayed quiet, but his partner Tye couldn't resist. "One of those punks must have really got the drop on him," he said barely suppressing a chuckle. "I mean, to be able to thump his melon like that—must have been the biggest dude in the group!"

Each time the nurse touched the lump, the wincing officer shot his partner a dirty look. Tye broke out in renewed laughter.

Having had enough, Kerry gave his partner the finger. An older ER nurse slapped his hand away. "None of that," she spat.

"Sorry," Kerry said and dropped his hand.

Tye snickered. "Got checked by two old ladies in one night!"

Kerry shot him another dirty look. "I'll get you later," he said.

The officers appreciated what the nurses did for them. Among cops, anyone who hit nurses was going down and down hard. The floor of the ER isn't soft dirt. Many a thug ended up leaving his front teeth on the floors of ERs after punching a nurse.

◦──

It wasn't until well into the morning hours of Friday that all the interviews were completed, charges for each of the identified bangers were decided upon, and the booking had begun.

The gang unit had its hands full. Officer Steven Turley sat back and looked around the holding area in the gang unit offices. There were many other officers working to get all the necessary charges to the proper suspect. All the officers were combing through records, fingerprinting for positive identification, and then booking the subjects once they were identified. Officer Turley loved police work, but the paperwork required to identify, charge, and book for charges was a nightmare.

"Oh well," Turley said as he tossed his hands into the air, "this is why the city pays us the big bucks."

⌒

Clubba had gathered all of his cell belongings and had gone through the bureaucratic release routine that every inmate has to endure to leave the state penitentiary. Clubba knew that the police would not take long to connect him to the Sudanese soldiers who had surrounded the apartments where Shanese was staying. Clubba had arranged for a ride back to Omaha, and one of his remaining Sudanese soldiers was waiting for him in the parking lot.

"Well Te'quan, I hope we don't see you again." The guard said. Clubba barely acknowledged the remark with a "humph" and walked away.

⌒

The gang unit conference room was packed with exhausted, red-eyed officers who could barely stay awake. They had gone all night without sleeping to get all the suspects processed. The sun had risen two hours prior to the meeting.

Sergeant Scott gave a short statement and told the officers what a great job they had done. Jake Mitchell was in the room and added, "The Chief was very impressed with the job you guys did last night and will talk to you after you've had some shut-eye."

Sergeant Scott announced, "Twenty-three witness tampering charges, and a host of other charges pending. Good work."

He scratched his head as he added, "I just don't understand how only two of you used up all of your pepper spray, and we had eighteen exposure victims. Don't worry about it now, it's what, oh-nine-thirty hours and we can pick this up later."

Turley, who was fighting the urge to lay his head on his desk and just go to sleep, suddenly got a jolt from remembering what an old man said to him while they were arresting some of the bangers. Turley raised his hand and said, "Don't know what this means, but

I caught two of the thugs who were hurt. They said something that didn't make sense about an old man and exploding crutches. There was an old man there, and he said to tell you that one of the thugs was the cousin of Clubba."

Suddenly Sergeant Scott's bloodshot eyes got wide, and he looked at Jake, "Clubba! What time is he supposed to be released?"

Jake realized that with all that had happened, they had forgotten about the head of the snake. "All I know is he is scheduled to be released today."

The sergeant yelled, "Get me the number to the state pen. We've got to nab him before he's released!"

CHAPTER 33

CLUBBA GOT INTO THE CAR AND TOLD HIS SOLDIER named Mok, a seventeen-year-old who had been a soldier for Clubba since he was thirteen, "*Drive. Get me back to Omaha, but don't take the interstate. That will be monitored, and I'm sure they'll be able to link me to my arrested soldiers last night. Take the longest route by the country roads, we'll take our time.*" Then he looked at Mok and asked, "*Is there anyone else we can pick up once we get to Omaha? I want at least two of my soldiers with me.*"

Mok told Clubba, "*Yes, my cousin Ka.*" Another soldier. "*He didn't get arrested last night, we can pick him up when we get to town.*"

Clubba looked over at Mok and could not believe that he had lost so many of his soldiers. It was good to know some escaped the police. Clubba looked back toward the road and simply responded, "*Good, call him and tell him to be ready.*"

Clubba sat back and smiled, looked forward and said, "*I have a little appointment to keep at precisely seven o'clock tonight.*"

&

Sergeant Scott returned from his call with the penitentiary. Jake saw the news wasn't good. "Thirty minutes," he sergeant yelled. "Missed him by thirty minutes. He left in a tan sedan."

Scott pointed at an officer directly in front of him "You. Call the state troopers. Give them the information we have and tell 'em to be on the lookout for this vehicle. They'll be pissed that all we got is a brown sedan occupied by two Sudanese men but do it anyway."

He pointed to a second officer. "And you, write an affidavit and get it over to the county attorney's office. I want a warrant for Clubba." The sergeant then pointed to three remaining officers. "You, you, and you—find out where Shanese and her sister are hiding. That's where he's headed. I know they're on the run, but find out where her relatives live and track her down, otherwise she's dead."

The officers jolted out of their previous exhaustion with a renewed burst of adrenaline and bolted for phones, exits, and their unmarked cars. The race was on to save Shanese and her sister.

Throughout the day, the state police, the Omaha Police, and the fugitive task force in Douglas and surrounding counties scouted for Clubba. It was like he'd evaporated with no trace. What should have been an hour commute for him stretched to hours.

Clubba and Mok meandered through gravel roads and two-lane highways through the picturesque back roads so plentiful in Nebraska and miles away from the interstate. Five hours later he spotted the familiar green and white sign that announced his destination. They picked up Ka who carried a large gym bag. Mok's call and cryptic message about Clubba needing help in a special matter was received. Justice would be dispensed in Clubba's own special way.

"Where is she?" Mok asked.

"And her videotaping sister?" Ka asked.

"You fools, that's exactly what the police expect us to do." Clubba turned to Ka in the backseat. "I have to pay a visit to the man who was involved in my arrest."

Ka and Mok looked at each other and smiled in acknowledgment of what he meant. Ka reached into the gym bag. "Then," he said, "You'll need this?"

Clubba smiled. "You read my mind."

In his hand Ka held a wooden bat.

In the Sarge's office the Somewhat Rapid Deployment Unit stood in anticipation. The Sarge made sure that an officer was placed at the entrance to the Ol' Blue Precinct. No more surprises from Boss Nurse Betsy.

The video cued up with surveillance of last night's events playing out. The Sarge debriefed each officer on his role in the situation.

Brittany arrived late; the reception officer waved her through and buzzed the Sarge to alert him to her arrival. Everybody had their backs to her, but the Sarge pointed out her father and she scooted in next to him.

"This was amazing; we got lucky, boys," the Sarge said. "We caught 'em as they were changing the guards. Seeing as it was the night before Clubba was sprung, they had what looked like the whole gang there. They wanted to make sure Shanese and her sister didn't get away."

Pointing out the strategy of the gang unit, the Sarge smiled. "I like the way their sergeant thinks. He had an outer perimeter and, for good measure, he had unmarked cars and undercover officers in the middle of the complex. That made the difference in the whole operation." The Sarge pointed at the still photo of the Sudanese soldiers.

"That unit was outnumbered and had no way of knowing there were going to be that many hoods. Even with our help there would have been a lot more of 'em escaping. The undercovers jumped into it right as they started zigzagging through the buildings, which is what we figured they'd do."

"There were a few surprises though," The Sarge plopped down and watched the film with a huge grin. Big Al pointed at the screen. "What's that lady doing with that metal sp—?"

Just as two undercovers ran around the corner, he had his answer.

"Wooah," every Blue said at once as the officer went face first into the grass. "That woman is Ol' Blue material," someone in the back called out. Everyone cheered in agreement, including Brittany.

"This is one of my favorites." The Sarge nodded at the screen where Kim and Paul stretched a hose across an escape route. All the Blues watched, clapped, oohed, and ahhed as Sudanese soldiers ran through clouds of pepper spray. The hose was yanked from the hands of both of the Blues. At their dumbfounded looks, everybody howled.

Brittany laughed and crossed her legs, just in case.

"We did save one special clip for Brittany." The Sarge froze the film and pointed to Abrahim. "Know this guy?"

Brittany peered closer at the screen. "That's Abrahim. I didn't know he was—"

Spotting the single Blue on crutches, her eyes widened. He pointed the bottom of each crutch at Abrahim and his pal. The recoil of the 12-gauge bean bags pummeled each in quick succession, and they dropped in a heap on ground completely debilitated.

Brittany stood and stabbed an accusing finger at the screen. "I knew they were bazookas!"

Every Blues in the room howled and slapped each other's back.

Smitty looked at her with a loving gaze. "She gets that from me," he said to the Sarge.

Brittany smiled and glanced at her father. She'd always known how much he loved her but now that she was one of the guys—a young Ol' Blue—it raised her even higher in his eyes. She loved it.

Her phone rang. Jake. She walked out of the room to take the call.

"Now watch what Smitty did to Boss Nurse Betsy," the Sarge said behind her.

"Jake, I'm so glad you called."

There was an uncomfortable pause. "Brittany," Jake said. "We need to talk. Can I come over?"

Concerned, Brittany frowned. "Of course but I'm at the precinct."

"Yeah," Jake interrupted her. "Ahh…that's what I need to talk to you about."

Brittany checked her watch. "It's five forty-five."

"I know. This can't wait; I'll be there in twenty minutes, okay?"

"Sure," Brittany said and paused. How odd. "I'll be waiting for you."

Smitty walked out of the Sarge's office. One glance at Brittany's face said she was concerned about something. "What's up?"

"That was Jake. He sounds concerned about something. He said he needs to talk to me. He'll be here in twenty minutes."

Smitty frowned. He didn't like the sound of that. "I'll let the Sarge know."

The Blues filed out of the Sarge's office, the great mood spread to everyone.

Brittany walked out into the late spring evening to see Jake. The sun was setting. Long pink fingers of dusk raked across a quickly darkening sky. Standing in front of the retirement home, she spotted Jake arriving and waved.

His returning acknowledgment was less than enthusiastic, and he especially looked at a loss for words. Brittany frowned. This couldn't be good.

The moment Jake saw Brittany, he was ripped from within. Torn between his growing love for her and the realization that she may be involved in some sort of vigilante group was the worst feeling he'd had since arriving in Omaha. His mind raced and he tried to piece together exactly what he wanted and needed to say.

As though sensing his apprehension, Brittany reached for his arm. "Let's walk the pathway; it's quiet."

They strolled through the flower lined path in silence. As dusk grew deeper, warm lights illuminated the lane. Short greenery, red tulips, and purple iris nodded in the evening breeze. "I love it here," Brittany said. "It's so peaceful."

She stopped by a black iron bench. "So," she said. "What's so important that you want to talk tonight?"

Tiny shuffled by.

"Hey," Brittany said. "How are you, Tiny?"

Tiny stopped as though she'd awoken him from deep thoughts. Jake squinted at the older man, his internal radar alerting him to something weird about the situation but giving him no clue as to what.

"Hey, you two," Tiny said. "Beautiful evening."

"Yes," Jake said, not quite able to put his finger on what was wrong here.

"You two take care of each other." Tiny smiled and shuffled away, heading away and going farther down the path.

Jake watched the older man leave and exchanged a confused glance with Brittany. "That was weird."

"Yes," she said. "It certainly was."

She turned to Jake who took a deep breath. "I heard your voice," he said. "On an audio tape…"

CHAPTER 34

"TINY HAS A PLAN," THE SARGE TOLD THE BLUES IN THE conference room. "He's gonna put an end to Clubba's little empire. Tiny recognized what was going on before anybody else."

"He's always had a way of fingering troublemakers," Smitty said.

"And knowing what they're up to," Harry said.

"One last thing," the Sarge said. "Tiny wants to go out of this world by setting Clubba up for a crime that'll put him in prison for the rest of his life—maybe even one that'll fire up Old Sparky and the death penalty."

The Sarge swallowed hard and took a deep breath. "Tonight at precisely seven p.m. Clubba will come for him."

"I thought he was coming for the girls," Smitty said.

"Yeah—isn't that what we've been thinking all along?" Big Al asked.

"Tiny knew if he kept tightening the screws, Clubba would come gunning for him." The Sarge blinked several times in a row as though something was in his eyes. "Clubba got out of prison this morning."

"Wait," Smitty said. "You mean the guy is on his way to kill Tiny right now?"

"Tiny thinks so. Him first, then the girlfriend, then the sister." He pulled in a shaky breath. "I trust Tiny's intuition." He checked his watch. "Almost seven now; Tiny's already started, on his way through the grounds. Our job is to work our way to the places where Clubba can ambush him. Get your gear and work your way toward the westernmost area of the trail where the shrubs are thickest. My guess is that Clubba won't be alone. He likes witnesses to see how he deals with his enemies. Let's go; get your gear and head out."

"Darkness," Clubba whispered to the two companions flanking him, "is our friend. Look there." Clubba pointed out the shadowy figure of a short man drawing closer from about twenty yards away. "Just as Abrahim said." Clubba stood silently, bat in hand, itching with anticipation. "That's him," he growled. "That's the one I want."

Clubba tightened his fingers around the handle and swung the weapon through the air as a test. A soft *whoosh* sliced through the cool evening air. Clubba grinned with excitement. Oh, yes, this would be perfect. The familiar sound of the wood meeting a human skull echoed in the recesses of his mind. Finally, revenge was his. Once he bashed the head of the cop who'd mocked him for over a year, they'd see who'd laugh last.

Brittany realized she could keep nothing from Jake. Beginning slowly, she explained the real purpose of the Ol' Blue Unit and what they'd done over the last year.

"I knew about the purse snatchers," Jake said, "but the others?" He shook his head in confusion and admiration for what the Blues had accomplished. "Wow...just...really?"

"Fraid so," Brittany said.

Her nod scattered her mane of fiery hair in the breeze. Jake clenched his fingers to keep from brushing it away and slumped back. "This had to be expensive," he said at last. "Where's the funding coming from? Not the state."

"No," Brittany said. "There's this group—The Bureau they call themselves—very rich people who provided the money for everything."

"Ben," Jake said out loud.

Brittany shot him a questioning glance.

"Ben's my brother; he's on this Bureau thing." Jake leaned forward and rested his elbows on his knees. Head down, he tried to grasp the reality of what went on inside this place, trying to make sense of it. "Oh, man."

"I was shocked when I first found out, the day we first met in Sarge's office."

She smiled at the memory. "These guys are still cops, Jake. They're helping the active duty officers with needed information. It saves lives."

Still staring at the ground, Jake remained unconvinced, and yet somehow it made sense on a warped level.

Smitty and six other Blues walked toward the couple on the western part of the trail. "Dad, what's going on?"

Smitty smiled and glanced from Brittany to Jake. Brittany put her hand on Jake's knee, "He figured it out, Dad; he knows."

Smitty glanced toward him. "I need to go. We'll talk later. Jake, we can use your help. Clubba's coming after Tiny."

Immediately Jake straightened and stood, meeting Smitty's gaze directly. "How's that possible? We've got protection assigned to his ex-girlfriend."

"Don't you think he knows that?" Smitty asked with a lift of an eyebrow. "Tiny's been working the guy over for months, and Clubba's wanted to kill Tiny since the day he was arrested. This way he goes for Tiny and leaves the girlfriend and her sister alone." Smitty smiled. "Quite a guy, our Tiny. You in or not?"

"Tiny walked by here not fifteen minutes ago, heading that way." Jake pointed toward the shrubs down the pathway.

A distinct yelp erupted from the shadows forty yards away.

⌒

"But...Clubba," his driver Mok said hesitantly. "Even if it is him, look—" He pointed toward a small group of people farther away. "They'll see us."

"Them?" Clubba asked with a sneer. "That bunch of old men? Fool, I need you both to act like the soldiers I trained you to be. Got it?"

Mok and Ka hesitated, glanced at the bat in their boss's hand, and nodded.

"First," Clubba said and pointed at the small figure drawing nearer to their position, "I kill that one. Then you two take care of anybody else who tries to interfere. Understand?" he asked with a distinct glare at each young man.

The two nodded again and Clubba smirked at how easy it all was. To lead people all he had to do was show them who was stronger, and it was always him. The bat made sure of that.

The targeted man walked straight down the path, never glancing to the right or the left. Heart galloping in his chest, Clubba willed himself calm. He'd need every sense he had to accomplish his goal. Two more steps, he thought, watching the little cop approach. One more. Eyes widened with expectation of the coming blow and the excitement of watching terror flood the man's lined face, he stepped out from behind the bushes. "Now!"

Tiny stopped and gave Clubba a disgusted look. "What's the matter, *Warlord?*" The term dripped with disdain and sarcasm. "Lose your little army?"

"Wha—" The element of surprise evaporated and Clubba froze in place. "How did you know?"

"Simple," Tiny whistled through his broken dentures and started to laugh. "You're stupid."

Rage enveloped Clubba. His arms, chiseled and sculpted from the prison gym, drew back. His swing caught Tiny across the chest. Air flew out of the older man's lungs. The cracking of ribs delighted Clubba. He hoped he'd broken at least three; if he got lucky he'd punctured the lung.

The old man yelled in pain; the sound never failed to thrill Clubba. "Laugh at me, old man? Laugh at this!" Clubba raised the wooden cudgel overhead and put all his strength behind the second blow. It landed in the middle of the man's back, bringing with it another well-earned howl of pain from his enemy and a shiver of delight up his spine. "Who's laughin' now, you old goat?"

Caught up in the delivered thrashing, Clubba didn't notice Mok and Ka slink off in the night, never heard the stampeding footfalls of a herd of old men headed his way, never saw one lone man outpacing everyone else. Wrapped up in the glory of battle, reveling in the pain of his enemy, suffused with the metallic scent of fresh blood, Clubba was in another world. The soft give of human flesh beneath the solid wood traveled through his limbs and coiled in his gut. The snap of bones breaking brought on orgasmic waves of delight.

"Go on…laugh at me." He turned the body over with his foot and stared at the smaller man on the ground. "Not so funny now, is it?" Clubba taunted. "C'mon. I dare you."

Weapon in hand, Clubba slowly raised it over his head, readying himself for the final, glorious death blow, but he wanted his nemesis to see it, anticipate it…fear it. "What's the matter, you little—"

Boom! Boom! Two shots in quick succession flew from Jake's nine-millimeter sidearm. Clubba stumbled back, bat still raised overhead. Bewildered, he glanced down; two large holes in the center of his chest spread crimson blood and soaked his shirt. "Just a bunch…of stupid…old…men."

Boom! The third shot hit Clubba's throat, stopping his words and severing his spinal cord. He collapsed, falling to the earth. As darkness slowly started to cover his vision, he heard the distinct sound of his weapon of choice making the same cracking sound that he loved to hear from his victim's skulls, only this time, it came directly from his own.

Jake's ears reverberated from the shots.

"Jake!" An alarmed voice he'd know anywhere—Brittany—came from behind him. Swiveling around, he instinctively aimed his weapon that direction.

Clubba's well-armed soldiers held very large, very sharp knives against her neck.

"Drop the gun or I'll slit her throat," Mok said.

Jake hesitated. Dropping his weapon was a bad idea and went against everything learned in training.

As though to emphasize their point, Ka sliced through her cotton shirt and into her shoulder. Brittany screamed in response. Blood mottled the fabric, trekked down her bicep, and dripped off her elbow.

Every inch of Jake's skin heated with rage. Every nerve in his body screamed to do whatever it took to help Brittany, but years of training kicked in. Despite what his heart demanded, Jake remained calm and controlled his voice.

Holding his arms out, to indicate he wasn't targeting them, he pointed the muzzle at the ground and tried to change their focus, "How old are you? Sixteen? No more than seventeen, right?" Jake braced himself against the image of Brittany between the two and strove for a fatherly approach. "You're too young for this. Believe me you don't want to—"

"Shut up!" Mok cut off Jake's attempt to stall. "We are Sudanese soldiers!" Mok said the words like a threat. He threw a knowing glance at his partner as though committing them both to the current course of action.

"Drop it," Mok said. "Or we slice her up in pieces."

The fatherly routine evaporated, Jake gritted his teeth and forced himself to breathe. "Leave now and you might get away."

The companion poked his knife tip deeper into Brittany's already wounded shoulder.

An anguished cry flew through her lips. Surrounded by the two thugs holding her upright, Brittany's head dropped. One blade still at her throat and the other in her lacerated limb, she wobbled; her knees buckled.

Mok smiled at Jake, the type of smile that all bullies possessed, when they have their victims where they want them. Evidently he thought he was in control of the situation. Jake wanted to rip the punk's head straight off, to rush in and pull Brittany to safety, but there was no way to reach her two assailants before they'd do what they'd threatened. Edged weapons at close range were too lethal. He'd never make it in time.

"Okay." Jake bent down and placed the gun on the ground with the grip toward him waiting for the right moment when he would grab it and shoot. "It's on the ground," he said. "Right here…"

Mok lifted a long lock of Brittany's red hair with the blade's tip. Spearing Jake with a direct gaze, he smiled again. "You were walking with her because you have strong feelings for her, no?"

Once again Jake pushed down his internal fire. Only a clear head would keep Brittany safe.

"If you want her to live, you'll give us the gun and let us leave. If you follow, we slice her open and the next time you see her will be on a slab. Understand?"

Five Blues and the Sarge slowly approached from behind closing in on them. Relief washed through him, and Jake put his hands up in the universal sign of surrender. Having no clue what the Blues were up to, his only hope was to play along. "Fine." The only way out of this, he figured, was to keep talking until the Blues played their hand. "Have it your way. Leave her and go."

"Leave her?" Mok said and laughed.

"He thinks we're stupid," his companion said. "She comes with us, as insurance." He motioned to Jake's gun.

They weren't taking Brittany and they weren't taking his weapon. That much Jake knew for certain.

Ka released his hold on Brittany's right arm. Striding toward Jake, a victorious smile lit his face.

Phitt! Phitt! The oh-so-soft sound filtered through the night like twin zephyrs. Mok slid to the ground in an animated convulsion. "Yeee-aaahhh!"

Smitty wrapped his arm around Brittany's shoulders, catching her as her captor fell away. Halfway to Jake's weapon, Ka turned to his partner who writhed on the ground surrounded by a group of white-haired men—and the girl.

Jake seized the moment and grabbed his gun off the ground. "Drop it," he bellowed. "Now."

The knife hit the cement path with a loud *clank*.

Jake glanced at the Blues. The officers they once were shined in their faces. Jaws clenched, eyes steely, anger radiated from each one. Ka glanced at the convulsing Mok and snatched up the knife his accomplice had dropped, brandishing it threateningly once again.

No one had kicked it away; Jake cursed the oversight.

Ka laughed and brandished the stiletto toward Jake.

Jake's finger tightened on the trigger.

"Jake, no!" Smitty hollered.

Phitt! Phitt! Ka dropped in his own painful spasms.

Relief flooded through Jake. He sucked in a lungful of clean air; adrenaline drained from his body. His finger slid off the trigger and he holstered his weapon. "You guys get their knives?"

"Yep," the Sarge said.

A semicircle of the Blues surrounded the bangers still writhing on the ground. Each Blue shook his head. Taser darts still jolted Clubba's men.

"I thought they were supposed to stop after five seconds," Big Al said.

"We really gotta get those things fixed. Those guys are flapping around like fried bacon," Benjamin said.

"Tiny…" the Sarge asked. "Who's with Tiny?"

The group hurried over to their friend and colleague.

"Jeeze, Tiny," the Sarge said. "I—I'm sorry…we—"

Tiny lay on the ground, his limbs pointing at odd angles. He struggled for every breath, a terrible grinding noise sounded with every inhalation.

Jake knelt beside the Sarge who seemed to struggle with comforting his friend and containing his emotions.

"You did it, Tiny," the Sarge said. "You were right all along."

Tiny lifted a world-weary gaze to his superior. Blood trickled from the corner of his mouth. "End of tour, Sarge," he said with a wan smile. "End…of…tour."

He fell silent, his eyes staring into the star-filled sky.

"Tiny." The Sarge swiped at his eyes. "You were a good cop, Tiny. A good cop."

The doors of the retirement home burst open and light spilled out from the juncture where Boss Nurse Betsy stood, arms akimbo. "Ya'll better not be playing with fire crackers out here," she called.

In the background, screams from Clubba's boys morphed into low moans. The occasional zzz-aa-pp of the darts floated over.

"We really got to get those things fixed," Smitty muttered to the Sarge.

Boss Nurse stalked over to the commotion, taking note of the scene. Sliding a strong arm around Brittany's back, Betsy herded her toward the infirmary. "Lidocaine and stitches for you, girl," she said. "We'll have you back in business in no time."

Smitty exchanged a pointed look at Jake. "We need to talk," he said with a nod at the Sarge.

Approaching sirens wailed in the distance.

"No kidding," Jake said. "No freaking kidding."

CHAPTER 35

TAKING A SHORT BREAK FROM HIS BRAINLESS TRUSTEE duties, Earnest detoured to the common area and pounced on the remote. Something ought to be coming out of Omaha by now. He punched the power button; his hopes soared. Revenge was definitely sweet…or at least it would be when he got confirmation. He'd make a point to thank Clubba when he came back—and come back he would. Almost every parolee did. Earnest figured the cops would have the kid arrested before the weekend ended. Tiny would be six feet under by then.

Earnest settled into his favorite chair and smiled as though he hadn't a care in the world. The local news channel interrupted regularly scheduled programming with breaking news. Earnest's smile widened. Good, good, good stuff, man. "Recently paroled…Te'quan…aka Clubba…killed…death of a former police officer…retirement home."

Key words registered with Earnest, but he only listened with one ear. His spirits soared; he couldn't remember being happier than right now. Tiny was dead by Clubba's hand! Man, could he pick a pawn or what?

Life was sweet! After all the years in the joint, the score was finally even. *I finally did it*—his grin widened in self-satisfied triumph—*and from prison no less. I'd like to see somebody beat that.*

Earnest flicked off the TV and headed back to his job. The evening news would fill him in on all the juicy—and he hoped—gory details. Earnest headed to the cafeteria for a lunch that, no matter what they served, would taste like heaven.

He pushed his mop and swiped his broom along the corridors with a smile he couldn't suppress. The hours flew by and Earnest's anticipation grew with each tick of the clock. At five o'clock on the nose, he joined his fellow inmates in the common room, but the news wasn't on.

"Channel twelve," Earnest growled. "Now."

"Who you think you are, old man?" Manny, a tall, extremely fit twenty-year-old from Scottsbluff straightened up and towered over Earnest.

"Clubba killed an ex-cop in Omaha," he said. "Don'cha wanna know more?"

The message swept through the room. Murmurs and whispers undulated along each row. The young man with the remote switched to the requested channel. "Clubba?" he exclaimed. "Man, he gonna be cock o' the walk once he gets back here."

"—with more specifics on the double homicide at the old veteran's home," the well-dressed, handsome young anchor said. "One was a retired police officer; the other was his assailant. Sally Quinn is at the scene with the story."

"Don," the blond reporter began, "Te'quan Yates Koak was the son of a Sudanese immigrant mother and a local African-American father who he never knew."

Earnest straightened in his chair. "What did they say his middle name was?"

"Yates," Luther, a young man hoarding the remote, said. "Like yours."

"I spoke with his mother earlier today," Sally said.

Previously recorded tape rolled and presented Clubba's heartbroken mother, Zarifa Koak. "He was turning his life around," she said with tears flooding her dark eyes. "Getting back on the straight and narrow."

The interviewer nodded somberly.

"Th-they didn't have to shoot him three times," Clubba's mother said around a sob. "They shot my b-baby th-three times."

All the air in Earnest's lungs rushed out; a deafening silence roared in his ears. He'd met Zarifa shortly after she arrived in Omaha. Quickly becoming a couple, they'd lived together until Tiny sent him to the pen this last time. Time stood still. His mind raced. It couldn't be! Te'quan Yates Koak…how could he have missed it? "He was my son," he whispered behind his hand. "My only boy."

"Clubba's dead?" Manny asked.

Murmurs of disbelief ran through the room

The words echoed in Earnest's mind. A double homicide: Tiny and Clubba. The person he'd whipped into a lethal frenzy to take out his nemesis was his flesh and blood. The mission had been accomplished but at what cost? The euphoria of Tiny's death melted into soul-searing grief.

Earnest stood in silence and headed to his room. For the next week he spoke to no one, barely eating a full meal. Eight days after learning that he'd gotten his own son killed, Earnest Yates cleaned his cell and stripped his bed. That night correctional officers found him dead in his cell dangling by his neck, a perfectly knotted, homemade noose wrapped around his throat.

෫

Jake knew what came following a police shooting: paperwork, administrative leave, and a grand jury investigation. Two weeks later he was back on the job, cleared of all wrongdoing; three weeks later he received an official commendation for meritorious service.

Brittany's stitches had been removed, and she was healing well physically. Jake made it a point to spend as much time with her as possible. The more he knew about her, the harder he fell for her.

Jake pulled up to the precinct and turned his car off. His dilemma weighed on him heavily: What to do about the Ol' Blues. The cloudless sky overhead met the deep green grass and foliage in quiet perfection. A gentle breeze sifted through the flowers along the pathway. Hard to believe it was the same place of carnage from two weeks ago. He shook off the memory and stepped out onto the gravel drive.

Making his way inside, he nodded at each officer—ex-officer— who stood sentinel protecting the secrets of the place. The Sarge and Smitty were in the Sarge's office.

"Hey," Jake said in greeting.

"Jake," the Sarge said around the unlit cigar in his mouth. "We were just talking about you."

"Good stuff I hope," he said with a smile he didn't feel.

"Always," the Sarge said. "Your job—among other things—is to protect the Chief, right?"

Jake didn't trust or like the line of questioning. He narrowed his gaze at the Sarge. "Yeah...so?"

"So," the Sarge said, "if word of what we do here got out, he'd lose his job—"

"—for sure," Smitty said.

"The media, the mayor, the community would all say he had something to do with...with what happened this month."

Jake wasn't buying it and shook his head.

"Wait a minute," Smitty said. "Hear us out. After all, it was the Chief who specifically asked us to work with community organizations."

"Not like this!" Jake raked a hand through his hair and shook his head. "You guys are out of your minds."

"Wrong," the Sarge responded. "What we are is full of experience—the likes of which you don't begin to have in your department anymore."

"Jacob."

His brother's voice came from behind him. He turned toward the door and spotted Ben. "You too?"

"Surely you see the capabilities of this organization. The surveillance and planning that the regular police officers can't always do? The technology only we can provide? With you on board, our ability to disseminate that wealth of knowledge will save a lot of lives: cops and civilians."

Jake sank down onto the same couch where he'd first seen Brittany. "I don't know, Ben. How can we possibly keep," he motioned around the office, "all of this secret? How do we keep it all from leaking out?"

"Smitty," the Sarge said. A smile turned up the corners of his mouth. "Take him for the complete tour."

"I'm your liaison," Jake said. "I've already taken the tour, remember?"

"Oh, no," Smitty said. "You took *a* tour; you haven't taken *this* tour."

"Start down at supply," the Sarge said. "Let him see what we're really capable of."

"Got your ID?" Smitty asked.

"Yeah, why?"

"Just go with him, Jake," the Sarge said with a smile.

"And be amazed," Ben said.

⌒

"I can't believe this," Jake breathed, still stunned at everything he'd seen and heard. "I have to deceive my boss."

"Yep," Smitty said. "You can be like Brittany—a young Ol' Blue."

"I don't like it," Jake said, "at all, but I don't see another way."

"None at all," Smitty said.

"And Smitty," Jake added. "I'm going to marry Brittany."

"When did you decide that?"

"After eating those awful cookies." Jake laughed. "Those really awful cookies."

"You Mormons move fast," Smitty said. Smitty's gaze softened. He slapped Jake on the back and caught the younger man in what passed for a burly hug.

⌒

The monthly board meeting of The Bureau gathered in the lavish conference room of Ben Mitchell's corporate headquarters. He sat at the head of the table. At his side sat the Sarge, his usual unlit cigar perched in the corner of his mouth. Gazing out the floor-to-ceiling windows and running his hand over the polished mahogany table, he shot Ben a pointed look. "Nice digs."

"Thanks," Ben said. All members of his ad hoc group turned their attention to him.

Ben distributed a report detailing the Ol' Blues, their true capabilities, and what they'd accomplished in a year. Eyebrows lifted; soft whistles flew through pursed lips. Everyone was clearly impressed.

"I've got one more," Ben said, breaking the silence with a second report on the two homicides at the retirement home for police officers. "You can read this at your leisure," he said, "but I want to point out that these men not only assisted local law enforcement with community relations, but they solved several major crime sprees. A lot of criminals are behind bars—or on their way—because of the efforts of these Ol' Blues. They also prevented Omaha's first warlord from establishing a criminal enterprise. Almost every member of Clubba's organization is behind bars and facing decades in the penitentiary. Not to mention the death of their leader."

"Koak, wasn't it?" Steve DeGoff asked.

"Right," Steve said and turned back to the reports.

"What about the ex-officer who was beaten to death?" Dan asked. "Is that something we're willing to chalk up to business as usual?"

Ben drew in a deep breath. He'd liked Tiny—a lot—and mourned his loss along with everyone else in the room.

"You want to take this?" Ben asked and turned to the Sarge.

He took the cigar from his mouth and cleared his throat. "Tiny set himself up as bait with full knowledge of the outcome. He wanted to go out like that, not in a hospice with machines and tubes hooked to his body. It was his choice and he made it. He was one of the finest cops I've ever known."

Silence settled on the group once more as they considered the Sarge's words. Ben exchanged a concerned look with the older man realizing they'd reached a critical juncture and today's meeting would decide the Ol' Blues' future.

Bud Williams, at the far end of the table, slapped his newspaper on the table. "There's a serial rapist on the loose."

Ben smiled and looked at the Sarge who looked about The Bureau and said, "We'll just have to send a little justice his way." The Sarge smiled and chewed on his cigar. Bonnie Platt clicked her gold-plated lighter and leaned toward him. "No thanks," he said with a wide smile. "Don't smoke."

Settling back into the butter-soft chair, the Sarge smiled.

SO DEAR FRIEND, IF YOU'RE EVER IN A PARK OR ON A CITY street and feel confronted with a dangerous situation, just look for a couple of harmless, nameless old men playing checkers, cards, or simply strolling around with particularly shiny walkers or canes. Make it a point to stay close to them.

They won't mind, you see, because all their lives protecting you has been their only duty. It's all they've ever known and all they'll ever be. Every one of them knows that one day they'll be called for their final "End of Tour." Each wants only to be remembered as a good cop—one who has lived with honor and true to the code of Ol' Blue.

DETECTIVE CHRIS LEGROW, badge number 1557, is a member of the Omaha Police Department's Special Victims Unit. He investigates domestic violence cases that include everything from destruction of property to sexual assault and crimes against vulnerable adults. Formerly he worked for nine years as a Family Teacher at Boys Town. He and his wife, Kara, have nine children.

Made in the USA
Coppell, TX
13 September 2020